Georgia

A Trilogy

Part Two

Michael Boylan

PWI Books
Bethesda, Maryland

Copy edited by Joanna Jensen

Proof read by Lydia Johnson

The Archē Novels

Naked Reverse

Georgia (A Trilogy)

T-Rx: The History of a Radical Leader

The Long Fall of the Ball from the Wall

Epitome of Part One

Jefferson John Brown leaves the share-cropping farm of Marcel Beauchay after Jefferson's father dies. Marcel was a brutal man who beat Jefferson and stole Jefferson's inheritance (from his father, who ran Marcel's farm). Jefferson went north, trying to find less discrimination against people of African descent. He went to Boston, but got the same, though more subtle, treatment.

Jefferson then travelled south to New York City and ended up getting a job with a crusading printer on the Lower East Side of Manhattan. This man, Mr. Peabody, who only lived with his cats (Matthew, Mark, Luke, and John), took a liking to Jefferson. He taught his charge reading, writing, and arithmetic. Jefferson was so talented that after some time Peabody got him admitted to an Ivy League college in Ithaca, New York. Peabody paid all the fees, but Jefferson worked for his room and board. After four years, Jefferson (the only student of African descent at the college) became the first black man to earn a degree in philosophy at that college.

Jefferson returned to Peabody, who was on a campaign to clean-up Tammany Hall. It was a failed mission and Peabody was murdered. Jefferson moved further south to Baltimore and labored in the shipyards among other workers of African descent. These workers had lower wages than their counterparts of European descent.

Jefferson joined the NAACP and began working for union rights for African descent individuals. It became contentious. There was a riot, and a squad of anti-black-unionists raided Jefferson's apartment and killed his wife and child.

Jefferson decided to move back to his old home and resided again in Bella County at the Beauchay farm. This time the owner was Samuel Beauchay, with whom he had grown up. Jefferson was made steward of the farm, which had transitioned from share-cropping to hired farm labor.

One day, Samuel became the surprised recipient of a foundling. People said the mother was Myra Dow, a mixed race manager of the shared farm store (between the Beauchays and Vanderkamps).

After some discussion, Beauchay decided to raise the child but discharge Myra from Bella County. The boy, John Dow, did not know whether he was white or mixed race (defaulting as black in the social climate at the time). He was raised alongside Samuel Beauchay's only child, Jason, who was born very soon after, with Samuel's wife dying in childbirth.

Samuel was convinced by his sister, Dorthay, to take a trip to Texas to try to re-coup and heal from his wife's death. Dorthay found and married a man, George Dodson, who was too coarse for Samuel's taste. In fact, Samuel Beauchay hates his brother-in-law, and wants to find a way to stop George in his attempt to take over and change county life. To that end he creates a trap.

John Dow and Jason had a private tutor growing up. Jason resented John and so tried to make his life unpleasant with a series of "practical jokes" that were borderline harassment. John knew his position and tried to carry on.

Both boys especially like Julia Vanderkamp from the neighboring farm. As children, Julia's brother, Rodney, played with John and occasionally with Jason. When they reached puberty Julia's admirers grew to be just about every boy around that age— especially Victor Stuart. Victor was a confirmed racist who tormented John Dow. The two boys were the most athletically talented in the county in their age bracket. John endured much abuse from Victor.

Julia Vanderkamp favored John because of his natural gentleness. Rodney, Julia's brother, loved sports and dreamed of going to college so he might become a professional athlete. There was some natural tension between these adolescents as they were growing up on their own. How far might some antagonisms go? This question was yet to be answered.

Behind it all is Jefferson who watches over John and everything else.

We begin our second part of the journey with Book Five.

Book Five

The Historical Situation of the Author

Traditionally, authors of tragedies and serious comedies have fallen into two classes: those whose work is done with respect to a Particular Period, and those whose plays seem to *transcend* an historical framework so that they can be performed in modern dress. Now, it is beyond my purpose to fully discuss the merits or demerits of this system of classification. I only wish to assert its existence. When I talk to directors of such plays, I wish to know their feelings about the productions so that I might design appropriate costumes for the spectacle. The types of reactions I generally get concerning the poets (playwrights) of the first variety usually consist of a collection of adjectives that connote a soul of extreme sensitivity that could touch the human feeling so precisely that the sensory aspects of the beautiful are immediately excited. Surely Shakespeare comes to mind as belonging to this class.

The other class consists of those who wish to become such consummate craftsmen that they will disengage themselves from a temporal framework and speak of truths and questions of a more universal nature. Milton would fall into this second class.

As good as these traditional frameworks might be (and who is a little tailor to doubt such traditional wisdom) there seem to be other types of writers that would better fit into different modes. For ultimately a writer can never escape from an historical setting as the proponents of the "transcendent" class would have one believe. One's very creative act is determined by the use of certain conventional choices that happen to be at the writer's disposal: a language that has developed to a particular point, and genres available into which the piece is to be made. The entire form of the work is conditioned by factors that enter into the construction of a work before it is begun.

As soon as this point is conceded, one must absolutely accept the pre-constructional data as historically limiting. The different intentions of writers have had various ends ranging between the Pious, the Good, the True, and the Beautiful.

Piety has to do with religious instruction, or the inclination toward actions that might be regarded as in accord with a particular religious cannon. The Good refers to ethical or moral action: what is right and wrong for a man to do with respect to teleological or deontological ends. The True is that realm which conforms to or represents reality. This is done by a correspondence formula by which the poet's work is a "mirror of nature," or by a coherence formula through which the internal structure of the play aspires to be *itself* a reality by being free of contradiction. Or it may concern a pragmatic formula by which the experience of the drama makes a positive, practical difference in the lives of those who witnessed it. The Beautiful is that which is pleasing to the senses; what is delightful.

Now in my line of work, I am usually concerned with the last category, though not exclusively, for it has been my experience that the first three of these categories form a group that applies to somber reflection, while the last category is immediately felt. If something is only immediately lovely, then it will be forgotten as soon as it appears. The categories of mediate knowledge seem to have a permanence that the beautiful lacks, though without the beautiful, who would bother to be interested in the first place? I strive, therefore, when designing costumes, to be concerned with all of the categories to some extent, though I concentrate primarily upon the beautiful. But there is an importance to each.

This importance arises from their mutual dependence. For if what I do is to be remembered, it must impart something beyond its beauty. And if it is to impart, someone must be inclined by beauty to offer his attention. Having established this as my mode of operation, let us return to the categories of authors. Surely what has been traditionally recognized as the author of feeling is really one who has emphasized the Beautiful, while the craftsman who sought to express eternal verities employed the mediate devices of instruction. All authors stand within an historical perspective and cannot escape it. Some authors, though, are aware of the significance of their particular situation in history and compare their work with what has gone on before them. They hypothesize what "age" they are in, and act with respect to what has gone on before (concerning traditional questions and forms). At the same time, they try to incorporate this historical awareness to what they are facing in their own epochs.

Some writers understand differing historical perspectives (on a single problem) while others could care less about such things. What is important to realize is that while intense study may produce a sensitivity to the vague nature of one's own historical prejudice, there can never be any escape from it. To know about it is to know about a brute fact. Because of this fact there is a formal caution which must be exercised over any and all truth claims one might be tempted to make with his art—especially true of historical fiction. This is due to the distorting influence which certain historical eras may have upon the artistic devices at the disposal of the author. As much as one may wish to convey another time and place, one is incapable of fully leaving his own historical situation behind.

It is impossible to know completely one's historical situation and place within a literary tradition. Since it cannot be known, it cannot be reproduced. So when I create "period" costumes, I never try to reconstruct them exactly (as I might have tried to do in my earlier days when I lived in London, and I pored over the sample boxes at the Victoria and Albert). Instead, I combine some suggestion of the past era with realities of the place and time that I know. In this way, I have honestly tried to imitate the process of a modern person studying, through the distorting lenses of an historical bias, some artifact of the past which, in the process, becomes transformed into a hybrid of the intervening epochs.

Exhibits:

Her lips suck forth my soul; see where it flies!—
Come Helen, come give me my soul again.
Here will I dwell, for heaven be in these lips,
And all is dross that is not Helena.

"Dr. Faustus." Christopher Marlow. II, 1260-3.

I on my horse, and Love on me, doth try
Our horsemanships, while by strange work I prove
A horseman to my horse, a horse to Love,
And now man's wrongs in me, poor beast, descry.
The reins wherewith my rider doth me tie
Are humbled thoughts, which bit of reverence move,
Curbed in with fear, but with gilt boss above
Of hope, which makes it seem fair to the eye.
The wand is will; thou, fancy, saddle art,
Girt fast by memory; and while I spur
My horse, he spurs with sharp desire to my heart;
He sits me fast, however I do stir;
And now hath made me to his hand so right
That in the manage myself takes delight.

Astrophel and Stella. Sir Philip Sidney, 49.

They sadly traveild thus, until they came Nigh to a castle builded strong and hie: Then cryde the Dwarfe, lo younder is the same, In which my Lord my liege doth lucklesse lie, Thrall to that Gyants hatefull tyrannie: Therefore, Beare Sir, your nightie powres assay. The noble knight alighted by and by From loftie steede, and bad the Ladle stay, To see what end of fight should him befall that day.

The Faerie Queene. Edmund Spenser, I viii, stanza 2.

When, in disgrace with Fortune and men's eyes,
I all alone beweep my outcast state,
And trouble deaf heaven with my bootless cries,
And look upon myself and curse my fate,
Wishing me like to one more rich in hope,
Featured like him, like him with friends possessed,
Desiring this man's art and that man's scope,
With what I most enjoy contented least;
Yet in these thoughts myself almost despising
Haply I think on thee, and then my state,
Like to the lark at break of day arising
From sullen earth, sings hymns at heaven's gate:
For thy sweet love remembered such wealth brings
That then I scorn to change my state with kings.

"Sonnet 29," William Shakespeare.

In approaching the gambler's unconscious, the first salient fact we discover is his fanatical belief in infantile megalomania . . . When a gambler Places his stake on a card or a color or a number, he is not acting like a person who has adapted himself to reality; he is "ordering" the next card to win for him, in the complete illusion that he is omnipotent. . . It must always be remembered that the gambler acts irrationally. He allows himself to be pushed into an unequal fight against superior forces, forces he cannot control, and which make him into an *object*. The gambler's preference for being the object, and not the *subject* in the gambling setup, demonstrates his deep rooted passive tendencies.

Edmund Bergler, *The Psychology of Gambling* (N.Y., 1957): 23, 237

Callimachus: I grant Destruction may be slower pac'd. A rich Man, like a strong Town, may hold out for some Years; but, I must tell you, when a Sharper sits down before an Estate, 'tis as good as besieg'd in form; and notwithstanding the Defense, 'tis Odds the Place will be carry'd at last.

"An Essay upon Gaming" by Jeremy Collier.
(Edinburgh, 1885): 20.

Michael Boylan   9

The wrong of gambling lies, therefore, not at all in the excessive indulgence in an intrinsically innocent practice, but in the surrender to chance of acts which ought to be controlled by reason alone and decided by the will in accordance with the moral law of justice or of benevolence. That is, gambling is an attempt to act outside the moral law without appearing to act contrarily to it.

> Douglass MacKenzie. *The Ethics of Gambling* (Philadelphia, 1896): 64.

The methods of cheating at poker are very numerous. Frequently, while playing four-handed, many very large betting hands are dealt out and the players will bet freely on them; but in such cases, the dealer or someone else at the table, who is a secret partner of his, will have a better hand and win. These hands are put out by stacking in various ways some few of which I will explain. One, when it comes to be his deal, will purposely disarrange the cards, so that he may have pretense for turning the cards face up. He will then place four aces at the bottom and four kings at the top. He will then turn the backs up and shuffle them by drawing the top and bottom cards together from the pack, and throwing them in a heap on the table. . . . The man opposite the dealer will get a great betting hand, that is, four kings, while the dealer will get four aces, and win all that is bet on the game. . . . There lived near Huntsville, Alabama, a man of considerable walk of society . . . This man had an only son, a youth of remarkable sprightliness and promise; and had he taken that interest in the improvement of his mind and the preservation of his morals that he should and might have done, doubt whether he would have been surpassed by any for eminence and usefulness. But unfortunately for him, as it had been for many of similar promise, he formed an attachment for the vice of gambling.

> Jonathan H. Green, reformed gambler, Gambling Exposed (Philadelphia, 1857): 73, 90

At a profounder level, as Friedrich Durenmatt the Swiss dramatist has said, all of us today abuse the idea of luck when it comes to the question of assuming responsibility for the predicament in which the world finds itself. No one wants war, no one, and least of all the responsible and high-minded statesmen who make the decisions, want the murderous thermonuclear weapons, no one wants to witness semi-starvation over half the globe, yet in spite of lofty sentiments on all sides, the state of the world is vastly different from what we all wish it to be. We divest ourselves of responsibility and guilt by putting it all down to bad luck. We may be collectively at fault, but not individually, because nobody feels blameworthy. We are fit only for comedy.

> John Cohen, *Behaviour in Uncertainty* (London, 1964): 147-8.

Now what shall I say of this fourteen years' experience as a public advocate of the cause of my enslaved brothers and sisters? The time is but as a speck, yet large enough to justify a pause for retrospection—and a pause it must only be.

Young, ardent, and hopeful, I entered upon this new life in the full gush of unsuspecting enthusiasm. The cause was good; the men engaged in it were good; the means to attain its triumph, good; Heaven's blessing must attend all, and freedom must soon be given to the pining millions under a ruthless bondage.

> Frederick Douglass, *My Bondage and My Freedom* (1845): chapter 23.

My journey was done, and behind me lay hill and dale, and Life and Death. How shall man measure Progress there where the dark-faced Josie lies? How many heartfuls of sorrow shall balance a bushel of wheat? How hard a thing it is to the lowly, and yet how human and real! And all this life and love and strife and failure—is it the twilight of nightfall or the flush of some faint-dawning day?

Thus sadly musing. I rode to Nashville in the Jim Crow car.

> W.E.B. Du Bois, *The Souls of Black Folk* (1903): chapter 4.

Leo

Digestion

Chapter 1

"A Panorama of County Entertainment"

The annual County Fair and Cross-country Horse Race was always the biggest event of the year in Bella County. Not only were all the women in Bella and its surrounding counties busy with assorted entries in the various competitions for home-made jams, pies, pickles, and the like, but the men were also involved in displaying various specimens of livestock for prizes.

Most of all this time of the year was special because there was a kind of electricity in the air. It was a feeling that even a stranger could perceive if he walked into Varner's Junction in late August.

The excitement this year was especially high for two reasons: First, Bill Marsh, who always added extra staff at Fair Time and offered a variety of games (some at very low stakes), was sponsoring a show of exotic dancers. It was said that they came all the way from Jamaica. Many of the townsfolk weren't exactly sure what an exotic dancer was. Some thought that the women performed a secret rite of a forgotten culture that was instigated by and for the purpose of pleasing men. There was some debate on this point. However, it was generally acknowledged that whatever the "exotic" in the title meant, the end result was that the dancers must perform without very much clothing on. This had the town buzzing on what kind of restrictions would be placed upon admission. The younger people in town showed particular interest in broadening their cultural horizons (a fact, by the way, that did not go unnoticed). The local women's group in town, W.A.C.K.O. (Women's Auxiliary for

Christian Kindness and Outreach), were outraged not only for their sons and daughters, but also for their husbands, who, despite various oaths to the contrary, they were sure would sneak a peek while the wives were otherwise engaged during the fair. This unacceptable possibility could be forestalled by posting a sentry at the entrance and exit of the booth or tent so that W.A.C.K.O. could compile a list of which local people went in and out of the forbidden spectacle. But this scheme was vetoed by the mayor after some prodding by Bill Marsh and, perhaps, a little pecuniary persuasion. The best that the women could get would be a post fifty feet from the entrance of the saloon. But this would be next to worthless because there would be no way of telling if someone entering the saloon was going for a drink or continuing out back to the exotic dancers. Since no women were allowed into the saloon/gambling house, known as The Marsh, there would be no accurate tally that could be taken.

The second cause for excitement was that this year's horse race would be one of the best in a long time, drawing riders from a hundred and fifty miles to compete against the favorite, Victor Stuart. Victor Stuart had earned himself quite a reputation for horsemanship in the area for two reasons. First, his father raised horses. His father was so good at his trade that some had attributed the changing of the Stuart financial situation to the fine deals that Victor Sr. was able to obtain from his good stock. Second, Victor had won many smaller and informal races over the last few years and had built himself a reputation for being a hard man to beat. It had been over a year, in fact, since Victor had lost a race. Most people seemed to think he was a cinch to nick-up the first place ribbon.

Victor was a reckless horseman who was experienced enough to know when to take tactical advantage of the various idiosyncrasies of each course to his best advantage. A cross-country race, for those unaccustomed to this strange sport, is a race on paths and through fields of the most rugged terrain, and not at all like the variety of horse racing that many are accustomed to seeing around an oval track. The cross-country racer must be able to negotiate jumps of all sorts as well as rivers and uneven ground. The inexperienced rider may inadvertently ride his horse into a small chuckhole and thereby break the horse's leg and possibly do great damage to himself—both from the fall and from the very real possibility of being trampled by the horses behind him. Such crushing potential gave the race an excitement and intensity beyond the natural splendor of watching well trained animals fly through space.

There were many cross-country courses in Georgia where young men would race, but perhaps few were as challenging as the course in Bella County. It started at the town's square. The best positions for the start were drawn by lot. Then they would head up Robert E. Lee to Magnolia, out Old Number One by the cemetery, and then continue on for several miles past the Jackson's and Macklin's places. At this point there was a very tight turn that had to be negotiated.

After passing across the Stuarts's low field, there was a ford that had to be made through the River Maria. Then it was on to the county stake (marking the end of Bella County proper, at the foot of the Forest Hills where they turned around and came back, essentially through the lower portion of the Lee estate, fording the branches of the two rivers), and then a crossing at Sawyer's Bridge (a very narrow bridge that could not support two horses side-by-side). Finally, back to the town square, where the race ended.

The race was demanding. It had riders traveling through grassland, forest, rivers, and all types of road surfaces. At certain strategic places, there would be officials who would insure that there was no unfair behavior (though between these check points, literally anything could happen). With two days left until the deadline for entrance, only two local boys had entered the race: Rodney Vanderkamp and Victor Stuart. There were about thirteen other entries for this most important race, which sported a winner's purse of three hundred dollars and a second-place prize of fifty dollars (though one could be sure that the winner's purse would be enhanced by a few side bets here and there).

Elsewhere the excitement was building as people seemed to be making a special effort to make this particular fair the best and most enjoyable in the town's history. For example, in the park there were some men working on a Saturday, constructing a pavilion for the bakery competition. This year they were building a small wooden frame instead of the usual four poles and canvas used in years previous. The argument for the permanent structure was that it could also be used to house the town band for Sunday afternoon concerts. The town donated the lumber for the edifice and the leading citizens provided the labor. It was going to be beautiful, everyone agreed.

The workmen carefully measured each board and sawed judiciously, as if they had in mind the possibly significant historical role in which they engaged.

"Where's Mitch?" asked one of the men.

"Didn't you hear?" said another. "He's gone off looking for his daughter."

"Did she finally run away?"

"Yep. And with a blackie, too!"

"No! Jeeze, that's a shame."

Then the workmen were visited by another prominent gentleman of the town, George Dodson. "Hello friends," greeted the growing entrepreneur.

"Hi George," they mumbled discordantly.

"Why so glum? Remember what you're working on, boys," said George Dodson with fully rounded tones as he addressed the town's leading citizens. "This is going to be pretty important someday."

"We were just talking about poor Mitch," said Joe Thomas, who owned the feed store in town.

"Yes, it's a shame, isn't it? I just heard myself," replied George in a pious tone. "It just seems that some of the best people are saddled with the worst luck sometimes. It just don't seem right, does it?"

The rest of the men mumbled their accord with George's sentiments.

All of them had admired Mitchell Evans in their own way. He was a man who usually kept to himself and never caused any problems for anyone else. He had inspired respect from almost every corner of the community. His farm (which he always referred to as a farm and never as an estate) had some of the best land in the county, or at least he seemed to get the most plentiful harvests. He lived alone with his daughter since his wife had died ten years before of tuberculosis. He worked his place principally by himself (though he employed some extra help at harvest).

The workmen, as they continued in their historic labors, thought to themselves that it seemed strange that a wretched fate should befall a man nobody disliked, who was a devout Baptist and who was always doing things quietly to help keep the town running and the less fortunate's lot more bearable.

As the men sawed, George walked around the pavilion and whistled a tune to himself. It was a hot day, but George, for some reason, wasn't sweating at all.

"Well, see you later, boys," said George after a few revolutions about the project.

There was little response.

"Maybe I'll see you fellas later at The Marsh."

***

On his farm, young Victor Stuart was putting his horse through its paces. Victor's father watched his son with paternal admiration.

"You're getting to be quite some rider," said the father to Victor after the latter had finished the workout.

"Can't win races unless you have a good horse," said Victor in reply, to compliment his father's equestrian choices.

"Well, we've been doing so well lately with our horses. A good horse is really an investment. Why, when he's done racing and winning money for us, then we'll put him into a jolly retirement that'll earn us even more money."

"Things are certainly improved over a few years ago, eh?" said the son. His father didn't reply, but put his arm around the boy and walked with him into the house.

***

—well are you going to dazzle us all again this year, Meg, with that apple and black current pie of yours?—oh you girls, you talk so; why you know as well as I do that those prizes are mostly luck anyway; why the prize could have gone to any number of women—just the same you were the one who came away with it last year--I was fortunate, but what about you, Maybel, I've heard that you have a few things up your sleeve like that new pickle recipe from your great aunt—my how word does spread! I only got that recipe two weeks ago and I didn't tell a soul, except my eldest daughter, and now everybody knows; well I have to admit it, it's true, but I'm not sure how it will turn out, after all, I've never made it before and heaven knows that entering a recipe that you've never made before is really a very foolhardy thing to do, I don't know why I'm trying it--oh now, Maybel, you know that you're

one of the best cooks in this town and that you can work a recipe from sight better than most of us can from those that our mothers gave us when we were married—Ruthie, you can certainly turn a woman's head; why I'd feel ashamed to listen to you if I didn't know you were the best seamstress in town—now you know that I'm not, but that does remind me about . . . .

Chapter 2

"A Disturbing Incident in Which the Character of
Certain Parties is Revealed"

"I'm going to have a baby."
 "What?!?" exclaimed John as he felt a type of panic grip him
that he had never experienced before in his life. What was she trying
to say? How could she say this, when all the time she had said that
everything would be all right? He had put this possibility out of his
head. Could there be some mistake? This just couldn't be so—it's the
type of thing that happens to storybook characters, but not to real
people—not to John Dow. How could he fulfill his ambitions,
whatever they were? He didn't have anything particular in mind,
but they certainly didn't include getting married at eighteen! The
thought of married life seemed to crush him like a heavy weight—
not that he didn't want to get married *someday*; after all, everybody
got married someday. But why did *someday* have to be *today*? This
couldn't be right. *All I have to do is to rethink this, like a dream,
and it will come out differently. Now where should I start?* But the
answer distressed John, so he started a different tact.
 Maybe I misunderstood her. It's possible that she was
talking about something else, and he mistook her for saying. . . . But
no. He had heard her and he knew it. *But why me? Why was I
chosen?* Then his mind came back to the familiar theme: he was not
being singled out, but merely reaping the responsibility for his
actions. *But why does an eighteen year old boy have to . . . .* There
was no question that he must marry her (though of late he had

grown rather less fond of her than he had been initially). *Would I have ever considered marrying her on my own if this complication had not occurred?* But John already knew the answer to this.

Somehow it seemed that he was being unwarrantedly buffeted by events over which he had no control. All of a sudden things seemed changed; the world was different today than it had been yesterday.

"What did you say?" asked Dow.

"I'm going to have a baby." Cindy smiled broadly so that the cleft in her chin seemed to budge out at John. "*Our* baby."

"How do you know? I mean, are you sure?"

"A woman knows these things."

"You're sure there's no mistake?"

"No mistake."

"Well, you know I'll do the right thing by you."

"Oh John, I don't know what to do!" Cindy put her arms about John's neck and squeezed tightly. Almost as if on cue, hot tears poured forth from her eyes.

"Don't cry now. It will be all right. You'll see. Things will work out. I'll do right by you. Don't worry."

Then in a moment, Cindy was up again. The tears were gone and she looked as if she had other business to attend to. "I've got to go home now. But you will see me tomorrow, won't you, John? I mean, you're not ashamed to be with me, are you? After all, you put me into this condition."

"Now why do you say such things? Of course I want to be seen with you. There's no question of what to do. I'm an honest man. Things will work out. You'll see."

"Oh John, you're so wonderful." Cindy planted a kiss on John's cheek and with a deft turn was quickly gone.

John's neck was still a little stiff from where Cindy had grabbed him. When she had embraced him he felt like gagging, but restrained himself. Only the slightest cough had emerged. Cindy had taken this heaving of the breast as a token of John's deep affection for her. Once she had left, John still felt like coughing. He had to clear his windpipe, just as one does when he swallows something foreign.

John's first instinct was to take a horse and return to the hills for an extended sojourn as he had just a few months before. He was an accomplished wilderness camper now and had lived off the land for well over a month. He longed to return, but he knew that he had promised to see Cindy the next day, so that was an impossibility. When he got back to the estate, he saw Jefferson and called to him in their friendly manner.

"Can you take a ride with me?" asked John.

"A ride? It's the middle of the afternoon. I've got a lot of things to do; is it important?" inquired Jefferson as he was lifting a heavy box that was to go into the barn.

"I guess it's not that important. It can wait until later," replied John.

But Jefferson sensed something else. There wasn't that ring in John's voice that meant that he was telling all that was in his heart. Jefferson knew that he was holding something back, and that it was probably important.

John was walking back to the house when Jefferson called to him, "Hey Johnny, tell Jessy that I'll unload the wagon later. Have her keep supper warm. I have to go for a ride with my good little friend."

John's face lit with excitement when he heard these words. Jefferson had not called him his 'good little friend' since he had been a small boy. Somehow the name instilled some kind of hope within him that there might be some way that he could accept the role that he would have to assume—a way that he could, with courage, do what he knew to be right.

Dow ran in and said to Jessy, "Jefferson and I are going out for a ride. I don't know when we'll be back. Bye bye." And with that, John grabbed a heal of bread and stuffed it into his pocket and ran out the screen door.

"Well," said Jessy sternly, "I be fixed to know who is worse, the little 'un or the big 'un?" She opened the screen door and watched the two mount their horses. She kept a steady gaze as the two disappeared into the horizon.

John and Jefferson rode for some time in silence. John concentrated upon the animal between his legs. The horse's muscles rippled rhythmically as it bore its master far from the centers of domestic responsibility. When the two riders had reached a ridge, John pulled up and opened his eyes wide. He wanted to take in every detail of his older friend and protector. It was Jefferson who first broke the silence. "Something happened today."

The words were delivered as in a declarative sentence. The factual manner of delivery prompted John's immediate reply, "The girl I've been seeing is pregnant."

"Pregnant, eh," replied Jefferson in exactly the same tones.

"I don't know why it happened," continued John, almost as if Jefferson hadn't spoken. Jefferson shifted his weight back in the saddle and laid his reins gently into the open palm of his left hand. "I guess I was just careless; that's all." John stopped. He was midway between trying to formulate just what he wanted to say and just talking—even if all the words came out wrong. There was no choice. If he thought about it, he wouldn't be able to say a thing. "It's just kind of a shock, that's all. You know, I never really expected anything like this would happen. Though when you get down to it, I should have. I mean A implies B. I don't know. The two had always seemed to me totally unrelated."

John looked over to Jefferson. His friend was gently stroking the sweaty neck of the horse he was riding. John desperately wanted to get some kind of reaction from Jefferson. He wanted Jefferson to tell him what a worthless thing he was and that he of all people should have been attentive enough not to bring an unwanted soul into the world. He wanted to hear some quotation from the Bible telling him how he had broken some sort of sacred law and that now he was paying for it. But Jefferson just sat there stroking his mount while staring at the animal deliberately chewing its bit.

"Well?" asked John defiantly.

Jefferson looked up and shrugged his shoulders slightly, "Well you're not the first person to be in this situation, and you won't be the last." Jefferson straightened up in his saddle. His deep brown skin glistened with perspiration. "What are you going to do about it?"

It was the question, or perhaps the way that Jefferson said it, that bothered John. The young man started his horse trotting and wished to ride away, but he couldn't bring himself to break into a gallop and leave Jefferson behind. The question seemed to say to him: it's *now* that's important. What *has been* has been. You know for yourself whether or not it was worth it, or right, or whatever . . . but all I want to talk about is what you are going to do now. But this was precisely the question that John did not want to raise. *Why was it necessary,* he asked himself? Simultaneously, though, he answered himself, as he slowed his horse's trot and waited for Jefferson to pull alongside him.

"Of course I'll marry her, if she wants me to."

"Is that what you want?" asked Jefferson.

"I don't know."

"What are the alternatives? What will be the consequences of each?"

"No, no, I don't want to—but I know I have to," but why— ALTERNATIVES? What did he mean? How could there be alternatives? Wasn't there only one thing to do in a situation like that? Wasn't there only one just and honorable thing to do? What did he mean by alternatives?

But even as John was asking himself these questions, he felt that perhaps Jefferson was right. Of course there were different things he could do. He owed it to himself—he owed it to Cindy—to think carefully about what would be the best thing for him to do in these circumstances. What kind of marriage would it be if he really didn't love Cindy? Might not that be harder on the child than no home at all? No, nothing could be worse than being brought up all alone.

But he was being melodramatic again. Mr. Russel always said that he was a melodramatic young man. It was usually said with such a tone that left little doubt that having this particular trait was not particularly enviable. However, the more John thought about it, the more he felt that there might not be a single correct course of action. Or if there were one single correct course, he would have to discover it among a fairly long list of possibly correct ones. How different the thought of fathering a child was from what he had always hoped it would be; passing out cigars and slapping everyone on the back. Having a baby was to be intoxicated with the glory of new life.

"Where do you want to go?" asked Jefferson.

John didn't know whether Jefferson meant where he, John, wanted to go in his decision (in other words, what alternatives he wanted to choose), or whether the other was simply inquiring where to steer his horse. John decided to interpret the latter as the intended meaning. This was not because he thought it was the correct one, but because it was the only one he wanted to (or felt he could) deal with at present. "I don't know; back home, I guess."

"Well, if you want to go back home, I know a very interesting way. It's a little longer, but well worth the extra effort."

"Fine with me. Lead on."

"Are you sure you can keep up with me? There's some pretty rugged ground ahead," chided Jefferson as he started to gallop his horse towards the river and a very steep hill that was on the other side. John felt a sudden elation over the fact that Jefferson would still tease him. It was an acknowledged fact that John was the better rider between the two. John loved the feeling of the wind blowing against his skin. It tingled his wearied body through many shades of blue. He became stimulated to the point at which he became aware of the smells that were particular to this section of forest. He knew the forest so well, he could hide there forever and never be seen.

Now all was quiet, save for the noise of the horses: their hooves against the dirt and the patterns of their breathing. Horse and rider moved with an easiness which gracefully attuned itself to the slower pace of sylvan environs. *He was so excited about being allowed to walk alone all the way to the large forest. Jessy had said that he was too young, but Jefferson had persuaded Mr. Beauchay that John could handle himself and that if a boy had a yearning to be in the woods, that's where he should be.*

"Careful, there's some rough ground ahead," said Jefferson as he slowed down his horse from a fast trot to a slow one. But John didn't heed his warning and made it through without mishap.

Then John wheeled his horse around and flung his own head back triumphantly.

"Why if I were only forty years younger," began Jefferson, unable to control his laughter. Watching John often made the older man dream. Involuntarily, he reached up and touched a chain around his neck. As he watched John glory in his achievement, the older man pressed the amulet to his breast.

He was alone at last in the woods. Alone in a world that was so different than the estate. Time was not the same here. Dow felt acutely, though he could not have put it into words, that his heart was actually changing speeds. That internal clock that measures the motions of the universe was now keeping a different rhythm as he entered the still sanctuary.

"Remember this?" said Dow, pulling a leaf from a tree.

"I certainly do. You came home with an armload of them one day. You were quite a collector in those days." *—but why did you take* all *of them—I wanted to—but they're* all *green; you pulled them from live trees—yes, the ones on the ground were all old. They weren't pretty----Look, Johnny, he said taking one of the leaves. This is a vine maple. You can tell that by the largeness of the leaf and the long vein feeding the leaf. Look how many little veins there are, and each one brings food to the tiny cells in the leaf--what are cells--look, see those tiny little squares that make up the leaf; they're like little building blocks. Now you see how special*

*just one leaf is; so amazingly intricate. You wouldn't want to take
so many live leaves when you could spend all of your time on just
one, single leaf and never uncover all its secrets--where are you
going asked Jefferson after a pause—to put them back—but they're
dead now. It won't do any good.—I know but at least I can tell
them that I'm sorry—*

"This is lovely country," said Jefferson, leaning back and
wiping his brow with the back of his arm.

"A person could spend his entire life right here and be
happy," said John, but Jefferson was strangely quiet. They rode on.

"I know this area," said John suddenly, as he started his
horse skillfully through a maze of trees and down a small hill that
guarded a small meandering stream. It was a very ordinary stream
in all respects, one that barely had any water, at present, because of
the season of the year. It might dry up completely before
September, but come spring, it would be full. Then the rocks that
were now covered with leaves and twigs would play host to the
trickling waters that would tumble over and about them in their
frenzied dancing to that mysterious orange-red of the season.

"There's a pool here when the water's high," said Dow to
Jefferson when his friend had caught up with him. *And he looked at
himself in the pool and saw that his appearance was different from
Jason's, just as he had said. Somehow Dow felt that his skin was
slightly discolored and his hair too curly. Curly hair was ugly.
Jason always said so. John dipped his head into the water. The
water penetrated his scalp and his fingers agitated his hair. Water
always made his hair straighter so he drew his head from the pool
and pushed it back with his fingers. It would be a little straighter
now: straight and beautiful. But when he looked down again at the
pool, his image was fractured into a thousand parts, each
reflecting a different part so that he thought that his image was
filling the pool with its fragments.*

"I used to love this place," said John.

"You're getting to sound like an old man there, Johnny boy,"
said Jefferson, imitating the accent of an old man as he turned his
horse and began ascending the knoll.

"Pretty soon I'll have to help you home, gramps," taunted
Jefferson as he broke into a gallop.

"I'll show you who's an old man," laughed Dow as he started
again in chase. When John caught Jefferson the former was gasping

with laughter. They were both feeling tired; Jefferson from the ride and Dow mostly from the difficulty of the day.

"You've something in your hair," said John as he reached toward the other to brush it away. The feeling of Jefferson's hair, which had not turned gray, brought a sentimental remembrance of when he used to rub that hair when he was a toddler. It had such an unusual texture. It was so different from other people's.

"I think it's about time to be turning back," suggested the older man, studying John's face as it was lighted by the gold slanting through the trees.

"You're right. Jessy will be fit to be tied if she has to re-heat supper for us."

"You mean *if* she'll re-heat supper for us," corrected Jefferson. The air was thick with heat and the scents of living things. John suddenly felt a rush of emotion to his face. It was hard to breathe.

It was Jefferson who finally gave his horse a squeeze with his knees that sent the beast forward and on the way home. John reluctantly began to follow. This was his world. These woods spoke to him. No one understood that really—except Jefferson.

Chapter 3

"A Chapter about Jason and his Method of Action
and the Travails of Mr. Beauchay"

Jason was sitting at the table in his room, making a list of the accoutrements that he would need at Yale. *I don't want to go there too burdened with things. Then everyone might think that I'm some kind of stupid rube from the South. On the other hand, I want to bring enough so that I won't be lacking. I think that, all things considered, it would be better to be on the short side than on the other, because I can always buy what I don't have when I get there.* At the top of the page of clean, white paper Jason wrote his name in large, distinctive letters with his German fountain pen. The ink flowed smoothly and the new quick drying ink never needed blotting. Next to the rather baroque signature he wrote "Business." Business was to be Jason's concentration at college. He was going north because the north comprised the established power structure in the country. He was going to meet the Yankees on their own ground and get all that he could from them. He would be friendly and make all the necessary contacts he could. Then when he had acquired the secrets of the northern industrialists, he could return and implement them. Jason imagined that he might have a roommate who was the son of some wealthy oil magnate or railroad tycoon, who, upon becoming good friends with Jason, would invite the latter over to his house to meet the family. Jason would then impress all the gilded people and make his humble felicitations.

The thought of his possible success, and at such an early age, brought thrills of excitement in his mind. It made it hard to do anything else. It seemed so clear to him that he was destined to succeed. He would be leaving in a month and a half, but he would send a trunk off the following week with the things he wanted so that he could travel without any encumbrance. It was thus necessary to list exactly what he must take and to execute its operation. Despite this mandate for efficiency, Jason managed to stop and let his thoughts drift to his neighbor, Julia Vanderkamp. He would miss making his regular visits to the Vanderkamp plantation. Somehow he had set the lovely visage of Julia firmly within his vision of the future. "If only she can hold Victor off until I am back from college and have the kinds of prospects before me which I know I will have," he said to himself. "No woman could refuse the successful image which I will then be able to project."

But for the moment, he had to admit, he would be gone, and Victor would be there. Jason gritted his teeth momentarily, but then relaxed. It was almost as if he suddenly remembered something concerning his rival—something which he, Jason, had planned for young Victor: a sort of bon voyage surprise? In good time, he told himself with a smile. In good time the master plan would reveal itself.

***

As John rode back with Jefferson, he suddenly thought of something that confused him. Earlier in the summer—a little over a month ago—John had taken a five week trip into the hills. It had been a time (just over a month) when his presence was not needed at the farm and he could have an opportunity to do some solitary camping. John wondered about Cindy's revelation to him that she had *just* found out about her condition. This could not be the case. He had not been in town at the right time. These facts pointed to one conclusion; Cindy had known about her condition for some time and had not spoken to him about it. This disturbed John.

It indicated to him that she did not trust John's response. She must have feared that John would not do the honorable thing by her. John resolved to go and see Cindy that night, after dinner, in order to straighten things out. The resolve seemed the right course of action for the present. Strangely, his own resolution produced an acute appetite within him. So, with his mind firmly upon his task, John single-mindedly went about relieving his hunger as a prelude to his other engagement.

***

In the midst of all the preparations for the County Fair, the presence of two rather nondescript men from the U.S. Department of the Interior, Bureau of Mining, was somewhat overlooked by many but not all of the citizens of Varner's Junction. They had come at the request of the state to inspect the golf course that Samuel Beauchay had bought. They didn't make any fuss concerning what they were doing, but the evening that they checked in at the hotel found at least one person wary of their business.

The next day the government workers made their way to the Beauchay Estate.

"How do you do, gentlemen," greeted Samuel Beauchay.

"We want to see the land," responded the smaller of the two from behind his thick wire rimmed glasses. His voice had a quiver like the vibrato of a trained singer.

"But of course," replied Beauchay, speaking to the taller man, who was immensely obese and had the more appealing disposition (if one can judge a disposition from looking at a man's face, which is how Samuel Beauchay made this judgment, an exceedingly difficult task for even MacKenzie's Man of Feeling, passionate soul that he was, much less for a Southern gentleman, who never made frequent pilgrimages to sundry places in order to keep his emotions near the surface). The other just smiled and took off his hat when Beauchay invited the two of them into the house, while Beauchay put on his own hat and traveling equipage.

"Did you have a smooth trip?" ventured Samuel when they were in the modest surrey, rolling down the Beauchay's private road toward Highway Three and the smooth gravel roadway.

"It was as best as could be reasonably expected," modulated the little thin man with the glasses. "But you know that the rails in the South are not what they are in the rest of the country. Most of the trip was even more unpleasant than this old buckboard here."

Samuel Beauchay was silent. He could not decide whether he was more upset over the slander against the South or over the disparaging remark about his surrey. Certainly it wasn't the finest vehicle ever constructed, but then again it was not an ordinary hauling cart with no suspension whatever: a common buckboard.

"No," began the little man again, "I don't think that the railroads will ever improve until something drastic is done about their ownership."

At this remark, Beauchay saw the big man nudge the little man. Presumably it was the role of the big man to keep the little man's lack of manners in check. Perhaps men in the North did not learn manners. How could he ever send his boy to school there? Would he come back a barbarian? Jason aspired to become an efficient technocrat, but that could still be a barbarian all the same.

And what did the little man mean about different ownership? Was this another crack about the South's inability to run its own affairs? Was he suggesting the migration of more carpetbaggers to bully southerners into submission? Or perhaps this man was a socialist and meant that the people should take over the railroads (as many of the radical northerners were discussing most earnestly). The topic, however, was one that was very volatile. Samuel Beauchay decided to concentrate on his own horse's reins and hold his peace.

"You gentlemen don't seem to have any, ah, equipment," began Beauchay after an interval. "Did you leave it at the hotel?"

The little man smirked, "We have all we need in that." He pointed to a small case that the large man had been holding. In point of fact, Samuel Beauchay hadn't even noticed the small black case which almost seemed to blend in with the somber suits of the government workers. Because of their peculiar dispositions, and in order not to seem overly coarse, Beauchay had not studied these men beyond their faces. He made a mental note to do so at the earliest discrete opportunity.

Soon they arrived at the site. "Well here we are, gentlemen."

"This is it?" asked the little man in seeming scorn at having been dragged all the way from Washington to see this puny, overgrown golf course that still had its sand traps. "Tis a pity we didn't bring some clubs," added the little man, perhaps, Beauchay thought, trying to make a joke (though the line was delivered with a completely straight face).

"Yes sir, this is the place," responded Beauchay, trying to be as cheerful as possible.

"C'mon Red," said the big man in a tone that suggested that the little man (who looked as if he were satisfied to sit back in his seat and merely make his inspection from there) get out and go through the motions. After all, it was important to retain their air of professionalism. The face of the big man, as he spoke, further reminded Beauchay of someone who didn't want to hurt Beauchay by cruelly suggesting that this effort was to be largely perfunctory.

And so the two men descended and walked very carefully about the field. As they walked, the little man would occasionally shout something out which the larger man would immediately write down on a tablet that he had taken from the black bag that he kept at his side. The two were a comical pair walking about, thought Beauchay. The thin man scurried while the fat man moved deliberately with his side-to-side waddling.

Soon the pair was finished and began walking back. As they approached, Samuel noticed that they were arguing about something. Though it was too far away to detect the subject of the dispute, it was clear that whatever the topic, it had indeed animated their interests. When the two had gotten into range, the big man motioned and both were quiet. The two changed the manner of their gait and assumed an official air as the little man lifted his long legs and the large man directed his stubby legs as formally as possible.

"I think we've seen all we need to see right now. I assume that we will have your permission to return to make any further observations today or tomorrow?" The little man talked in controlled staccato.

"Of course," said Beauchay, who would have thought such a request rather odd under most circumstances. But upon considering the peculiar nature of these Northerners, he had to assume that it was a part of their twisted code of customs.

"Very good. Now, would you be so kind as to take us into town? I think we're in the mood for a little lunch." As the little man mentioned the word 'lunch,' he glanced over at the big man and flashed a toothy smile.

***

"That sure is somethin'. Ain't it?" said Ike.

"Wat you suppose they up to?" asked Ed.

"I bet they been to the golf course ta tell wither thar's some mineral 'n it or sometin," answered Ike as he took a chaw of tobacco and began mashing it down.

"Deya think thar's gold there?" suggested Ed, as he put on a mock avaricious expression.

"Not likely," replied Jake. "If this thin' is on the level, and I mean if thar ain't no tricks bein' played by nobody, then it might be coal or somethin'. Mind you, I don't think thar is. But if ya made m'guess what mineral thar could be, I'd say coal."

"Well whatever it is, it will sure mean a lot of new jobs, and money in this town," said Ike.

"Yeah Ike," joked Ed, "you'll probably get rich since you're the only general store in town."

"You'll a have ta start expandin' ta meet all that business, Ike," added Jake in the same jocular mood.

But Ike responded, almost distantly, in full seriousness, "Thar other stores sides mine. And if that coal mine come and bring lots of people, it'll bring lots of stores with 'em—maybe some of them northern 'chain stores' like Sears and Roebuck. Sides, a man would be a fool to expand his shop jist on the rumor of somethin' a big comin'."

The other two men sat down in their usual places as if they were embarrassed that Ike didn't get their little joke. "You want me to git out them checkers, Jake?" asked Ed.

"Nope, don't feel like checkers. How 'bout a game of crazy eights?"

***

Going out from behind the hotel was a dark rider who left town the long way: around the cemetery. He would have appeared to have been in a hurry to anyone who might have seen him, except that his destination would have seemed singularly opaque; he wasn't traveling any well-known route. The rider followed a circuitous path of his own device. When he had gotten to where he was headed, the rider dismounted and went up to a shanty and knocked on the simple wood door that was treated with a single coat of stain.

"Come in," said George Dodson with a smile.

"Those men are from the Department of the Interior. Bureau of Mining."

"What else do you know?" inquired Dodson as he went over and sat down in one of the old chairs that stood next to a simple table in the center of the cabin.

"That's all," replied Miles, a little chagrined that his "information" did not appear to be worth anything to his boss.

"You haven't told me anything. That much was evident from the hotel registration. What I want to know is why those two came over to that land today."

"But how can I do that? They're two of da strangest folk I'se ever seen."

"Listen. I'm not your father who's going to teach you to wipe the snot off your face. You figure it out. I deal in results, not excuses. Understand?"

"Yes boss," replied the black man as he crumpled up the hat that was in his hand and turned to go.

"Now git," prompted Dodson with a motion of his hand as he took out a cigar and bit off the end and lit up his smoke. The shack in which he sat had been vacant for eight months or more. The family who had lived there had owed Dodson some money. They didn't make their payment schedule and so—well, now they were no longer in Bella County. Dodson liked the cabin. He enjoyed bringing his subordinates there for a clandestine rendezvous. There was an atmosphere about it that made him relax.

George leaned back in his chair with his cigar and tried to close his eyes. But a certain foreign restlessness crept in and prevented him from enjoying his repose. He almost heard a voice calling him. Quickly his head darted back and forth. Then he was up to the single window covered with tar paper. There was no one. Again he sat down. The light of day was slowly dying. But somehow George Dodson could not rest. He did not like Beauchay's attitude. That stupid Southern cracker was the only one who would not allow himself to fall under his control. This town didn't need any Northerners from the Bureau of Mining.

George Dodson leaned back in his chair again. His cigar had gone out.

His eyes remained wide open.

Chapter 4

"The Fair"

"Step right up here and test your strength, c'mon everybody, nothin' to it, ails you have to do is take this mallet and strike this wooden fulcrum sending a little weight, not much more than a paper weight, up the pole and ring the bell at the top, easy as pie, your grandmother could do it. Step right up and win one of these fabulous prizes, c'mon everybody and try your hand only a dime for three tries.

"C'mon, who'll be first, how about you young man, do you want to try and win that girl of yours one of these fine prizes?"

"Ah, well..."

"How about it, give it a try, no harm done, what have you got to lose?"

"Ah, well. . ."

"The little lady wants you to, how about it?"

"Ah, well. . ."

"Go ahead," urges the girl.

"Do you think I should?"

"Sure, it's only a dime."

"Three tries, for only a dime," adds the barker.

"Do you think I should?"

"Why don't you, it looks kind of fun."

"Well, ah. . ."

"I'll try," says a voice in back of the small crowd that's formed around.

"I'll try too," says another.

"Go on Fredie, tell him you want to try as well."

"Ah, mister?" says Fredie.

"Here you go, sir," says the barker to the first comer as he hands him the mallet.

"Ah, mister?" starts Fredie again.

But the barker is busy showing the first comer what to do. Fredie gets out his dime so that the barker can see that he's willing to give it a try, but after the barker is finished with the first comer, he starts talking to the second.

"I'll do it," says a third as the first makes his second unsuccessful try at ringing the bell.

"Go on, Fredie and tell him."

"Ah, mister?" calls out Fredie, but he knows that the barker will not hear him, and by this time, he half hopes that the barker won't hear him.

"Step right up sir," says the barker to the third man who pushes Fredie aside so that he can get near the bell.

"I think we'd better try later," says Fredie. "Let's go."

"All right," she says as Fredie starts walking, but she lingers behind.

"Are you coming?" asks Fredie.

"Oh, I'll be there in a minute, I just want to see somebody ring the bell. Why don't you walk o'er to the ice cream stand; I'll be there in just a sec."

***

Bang! The rifle shot Bang! And again Bang! Bang! Bang! and still Rodney hadn't hit the can that was sitting on the post.

"Damnation!" yelled Rodney. "This gun just won't shoot straight"

Rodney's father, Mr. Vanderkamp, was walking out of the house, and heard his son's exclamation.

"What seems to be the trouble?" asked Charles Vanderkamp as he started in his son's direction.

"This dang gun that you gave me doesn't shoot straight."

"Oh, really, is the sight out of adjustment?"

"I don't know, but I keep shooting at that tin can and I can't knock it off the post."

"Have you tried sighting it in?"

"I've tried everything," declared the son as he leaned against a tree and set the gun butt down on the ground.

"Well, that's a shame if there's really something wrong with the gun," said Mr. Vanderkamp. "I paid eight dollars for that gun when I was about your age, and it's worked fine for a good many years."

"Well, it don't seem to work now."

"You practicing up so that you can enter the shooting competition at the fair?"

"They've got some good prizes," said Rodney.

"Yes, I know. I always wanted to win that prize, but you know old Beauchay used to beat me every time. First and second we always were; first and second."

"It would be nice to go away on—" put Rodney rather wistfully, as he had entered the junior competition several years before and placed fourth, at first glance a notable achievement until one considers that there were only five contestants and the fifth, Billy Thompson, was found to have had bad eyes and needed glasses the following autumn; though this in no way diminished the stature of achievement in Mr. Vanderkamp's eyes, and in time, to Rodney's either.

"Yes, I always think of the shooting competition as the most skillful of all the events. It requires very steady hands and a real feel for a gun. Marcel Beauchay, they say, used to be the best shot in the state of Georgia. Maybe that's why Samuel became such a good shot. I think it takes more finesse to win the rifle shoot than the cross-country horse race. The race takes more endurance and strength, I'll grant you, and I suppose there's a certain skill in making those jumps and all, and that's probably why everyone makes such a big deal out of it. Oh, I'm not downgrading it, mind you, but if I made my choice, it'd be the rifle shoot; that I think is the most important."

"No one's ever won both of them, have they?" asked Rodney. Though he knew the answer, he liked to hear his father talk.

"No, it's never been done—at least not in the same year. There have been people who have won in different years, like Samuel Beauchay, but he never did it in tine same year. No, in those days, the rifle shoot was a bigger thing than it is today. You see, we had horse races almost every month at the big picnics that used to be held on one of the farms. Truly, it was a grand sight to have everybody in town together for a Sunday afternoon, and at the end of everything, the softball game and other games we used to play as children, oh we used to have some pretty wild games, believe me. . . and you imagine playing teams of hide and seek, in one of the big fields with fifty boys or so when the cotton was high—oh, it was grand, all right, some of those games would last several hours, but at the end of it all, there was always a race, and there were bets, but not the kind of betting that goes on today, because nobody had any money, you know. So instead of money, brothers would bet sisters certain chores, and women would wager a favorite dish for their husbands. Things like that. There was never any judging, we just kind of lined up and someone shot a pistol and that was that.

"But the rifle shoot that was only held once a year at the county fair. . . which didn't used to be much really, except kind of a picnic in town, if you could call it that. It only lasted one day, instead of the full weekend. I don't know, we were a scruffy lot, I suppose," said Vanderkamp as his voice trailed off at the end of the sentence as if, Rodney thought, he were re-living those times for a moment.

Then Vanderkamp walked over to his son and took the rifle from him and looked over the stock and barrel very carefully.

"Mind if I give it a try?" asked the father.

"Be my guest," said Rodney, anxious to see his father shoot (something his father didn't often do anymore).

Charles Vanderkamp assumed a rigid off-hand position and braced the butt well into his shoulder as he pushed his right elbow into his ribs and his left into his sternum. Then he aimed very quickly, and slowly exhaled, held his breath, and fired. The can popped into the air and flew to the left as Mr. Vanderkamp smiled at his success.

Then Vanderkamp turned to his son and handed him the rifle. "The sight may be off for your eyes, son, but as you can see there is nothing wrong with the gun."

Rodney loved to see his father firing the rifle. Rodney never had any doubt of his father's skill, even if the can had been a hundred yards away. His father was very good with weapons. He had spent a great deal of time when he was young teaching Rodney to care for and respect firearms. Rodney remembered how he used to clean his father's gun several times a year while his father spun stories of hunting and competitions. Rodney only wished he could duplicate his father's success. His father's life seemed so interesting that Rodney only wished that his father's life could be his own.

There were many things that Rodney was quite proficient in, namely wrestling and various feats of strength, which is why his father had suggested that perhaps football might be the best sport for him. There was no one that he knew who could whip him wrestling, though he never fought for passion but only for the sport of it, as his even disposition never allowed him to get extremely mad at anyone. How Rodney wished that he could shoot as well as his father and so win the target contest, which would probably be won by Billy Samuelson, a waiter at Mr. Whren's hotel, or perhaps by Billy Thompson. But Rodney had entered himself in both the shooting competition and the horse race; something, to his knowledge, no one else had done this year. *I must have a better chance of winning at something*, he thought to himself, *since I have two chances of proving myself.* But somehow, Rodney felt it unfair that they didn't have any contests measuring the things that he was proficient in: a wrestling contest perhaps, or lifting heavy crates, or bales of hay—which he felt certain that he could excel in. It always seemed that he had to fit himself into what others considered to be measures of some manly skill (which was not at all his specialty). He had to compete against people who often times only shot rifles for entertainment, or only rode horses in their leisure hours, or like Victor Stuart, rode in so many races, that his experience alone gave him a few hundred yards advantage. Somehow the system seemed slightly unfair. It should be established so that everyone could compete at least once in a field in which he alone excelled and so would be able to win the prize.

Rodney took the gun from his father and said a few admiring words to him before he left. How interesting it would have been to have grown up with his father. They probably would have been best friends and done all the things that young boys do together. In all the areas in which he lacked, his father would have excelled, and vice versa. It would have been an unbeatable team. Listening to his father talk often made him wish that he had been born in the days when everything wasn't so large and impersonal as it was now. Now a days, people actually locked their doors regularly every night to prevent anyone from coming in and taking something. Things seemed to be in a very sorry situation. But soon he would be off to college and playing football and baseball for the University of Alabama (his father thought it best that he stay in a southern school, and Alabama would not only let him go to school for free, but would give him a little extra spending money for playing those sports).

How Rodney wished that he could win or at least place high in one of the two events that he had entered at the fair. If he could do well, how his father would beam, not that his father needed anything special to be proud of his son, but still, Rodney knew how happy it would make his father feel if he (Rodney) could come through in the same way that his father had when he was young.

***

It was nearing the end of the day and Fredie broke free from his girl for a moment and crept back to the place where the bell stood atop that large wooden track. The stand seemed to stretch miles into the air, though it only stood four yards from the ground. There weren't many people around now as it was almost time for things to close up for the day. In fact, the man at the booth looked as if he were shutting down.

"Here's my dime," said Fredie as he walked up to the man. "Sorry, closed," said the man.

"But I want to try."

"I've got to close sometime, son."

"Please let me try," insisted Fredie, who hardly knew what he was saying, but was determined to try his luck.

"I've already put away most of the prizes," said the man.

"That's all right, I don't want a prize. I just want to try it."

"Don't want a prize," remarked the barker in surprise. Then he turned and looked at Fredie. Fredie thought that he might have recognized him, but the barker didn't.

"You're a queer one," said the barker, scratching his sideburn. "Well go ahead and give it a few tries, I don't mind."

Fredie handed the coin to the man, but the man didn't notice. "Here's your dime, Mister," said Fredie, holding the coin near to the man's hand.

"Keep the dime, son, and go and give it a few whacks if you want."

Slightly confused, Fredie put the dime into his pocket and searched the ground for the mallet, which, when he lifted it, seemed inordinately heavy, but not too heavy that he couldn't wield it.

**

Then Rodney took aim and fired: a miss. And again; another miss; and again and again and again.

Chapter 5

"A Wager"

Do you think it's wise betting so much?" asked Jason.

"I said three hundred on number four to win, six hundred on number three to win, and two hundred apiece on one and six to place."

"All right," said Jason, writing some numbers onto a piece of paper and then reading them back to Victor.

"That's what l said, now go place the bets," said Victor, who was somewhat upset at Jason's questioning of his ability to make bets. Why, it had only been six months before when this neophyte had convinced Victor to take him along to various races to make his bets for him, as Victor was a registered rider by the state and was prohibited from making bets on racetracks, a fact that Victor had not known, but Jason had told him (not that it really made much difference to Victor at all). The pair had been successful in a way that obviated such pedestrian considerations. But when Jason questioned him, Victor regretted his benevolence at bringing Jason into the picture.

"The bets are on," said Jason, returning to Victor.

"Good, are the odds still the same?" returned the other.

"Approximately, yes."

"What do you mean approximately?"

"Well they slipped a little on one, but were better on four."

"I don't know why I—" but then Victor stopped as he leaned forward to see the horses going down the back stretch. Victor never liked to cheer his horses on. He just sat back. When he felt excited about a race, he looked away so that the emotion might pass. This tactic sometimes worked, but somehow, perhaps owing to his last outing, this wasn't enough as even sitting back he found himself becoming increasingly excited in an anxious kind of way he couldn't control. This made Victor very uncomfortable.

Maybe he should go behind the grandstand and smoke a cigar slowly and relax, not caring how the results come or when they come. But though he could not bear to look, he also had to watch. He was involved in the race in a way that he hadn't been since he first started betting on the horses.

It had been Miles Bon, a worker at the Marsh, who had first approached Victor a few years before, when Victor was just one of many young men who loitered around the old saloon—partly to see what was happening, and also because it had the aura of a slightly forbidden place, which always seemed to attract males in their teens.

Victor had always been fascinated by the roulette wheel, and wished to play, except for the fact that his family didn't have enough money to meet operating expenses, much less afford to give Victor money to play roulette. So Victor contented himself with watching. He would make imaginary bets in his mind and then see how they turned out. After a while, he developed a progressive system of cross betting on two-to-one odds so that he could almost always come out ahead on the wheel in his imaginary calculations.

Perhaps this is what Miles Bon saw, or possibly it was something else that even he wasn't aware of at the time that drew Bon to approach Victor one evening (Victor was one of the few boys who dared to habit the old saloon in the dusk hours, as usually only the daytime hours found young men inside the forbidden walls) and ask him, "Would you like to play?"

"What, the roulette?" responded Victor, slightly surprised that an older man had approached him (a circumstance in the saloon rare enough in itself) or that this man happened to be black—not the kind of black that is someone's fall guy, but the kind of black who inspires fear among young teens (this fear, as a few would discover when they became older, had nothing to do with Miles, or any other person being black, but because of certain character traits that made him mysterious and instantly inscrutable). The real cause of his surprise was that anyone would be foolish enough to approach someone and ask them if they *wanted* to play. Victor felt like retorting, *If I wanted to play, wouldn't I be playing? Now, if I'm not playing might it be because of a reason, namely that either I don't have the money, or I simply don't care to?* But instead Victor was curious, and decided to make a neutral move and see what Miles would do, and so he replied, "Of course."

"Would you like a little stake?"

"A loan?" asked Victor in a voice that betrayed his aversion to loans, an institution in which he had little faith. His second-hand experience watching his father's failures had made him intellectually cautious.

"No, not a loan. It's a bet."

"A bet?"

"Yes, a bet that I'm making on you. You see, I've watched you come in and study that wheel, and I told myself, I bet that fellow must be figuring out how to win at roulette, because why else would he just stand and keep watching, unless he were testing out some theory or other—devising a system."

Victor thought that Bon was a really queer sort to come to the conclusions that he was making from the supposed information that he had. There could be a hundred reasons why someone would just stand and watch a roulette wheel night after night. Perhaps he was observing the fate of one of his friends, or simply a stranger who he happened to find interesting? Or maybe he was escaping something, and the turning of the roulette wheel and that little metal ball relaxed him or helped him forget. Or just possibly he might have liked the atmosphere of the place with its thick aromas of cigarette and cigar smoke mixed with an occasional drifting of illegal alcohol. To state categorically that there was any connection between his standing near the table and the creation of some sort of wild system just didn't stand under even the weakest scrutiny. For this reason, partly, Miles' statement bothered Victor, and also, but by no means consciously admitted or felt by Victor, it was unsettling that Bon was right.

"Go on," said Victor, trying to sound as non-committal as possible.

"Well, I said to myself, I'll bet that if I give that lad twenty dollars, that he'll make me at least ten before the night's out. So that's the proposition; I'll stake you twenty dollars and I get to keep the first ten that you make , and anything you win over that we split 50-50."

"And what if I lose?" asked Victor in a calm and inquisitive voice.

"Then I lose the bet I made with myself."

"I don't owe you a thing."

"Not a thing."

"And if I win—"

"I get back ten dollars, and if you're good enough I'll get back my other ten and some more profit, besides!"

What he's essentially letting me do, Victor thought, *is to try the wheel. He knows that I probably won't make more than ten dollars on a twenty dollar stake, so really I'm playing the wheel free for a night.* Victor might have asked himself why Miles would want to make such a proposition to him, and what if any motivation might have been behind it, but these questions were never considered by young Stuart.

"What'll you say?" asked Bon.

"Sure, I'll try it," said Victor.

"Here's your money," said Bon, handing Victor a twenty-dollar bill.

The bill was crisp as if it had just been printed. There was something about the feel of new money that made it seem more valuable than ordinary money (the kind that Victor had been accustomed to having). He walked over to the cashier and got his chips and returned to the table. The thought of actually having twenty dollars' worth of gambling chips made Victor somewhat cautious. He saw a perfect chance to bet it all on the very first roll and probably win, or so his system went, but he chose not to. He couldn't forget that if he lost, that would be it, the entire night in just one spin. So he played it cautiously and bet only four dollars on eight fifty-cent bets. The wheel spun and he lost every one.

I should have played it the way that I wanted to, thought Victor, *but what if I had lost? But as it turned out I wouldn't have lost. This place is not for the faint hearted.* On the next bet he put down the entire sixteen and came out even as a side bet came through.

So for hours Victor bet, and at the end he had thirty-one dollars: the first ten went to Miles, the next twenty they split 50-50 (so that Miles got $10 more) and the last dollar was also split. Miles got back his twenty plus 50 cents profit. Victor got $10.50 profit. Not a bad haul for a first-timer.

"Here's your big profit," said Victor, walking over to Miles when he was through.

"You can keep it; if you come back tomorrow night I'll play the same game with you. Maybe you can make me more money," said Bon.

Victor considered this proposition carefully. He felt that he had had rather bad luck that evening and yet he still managed to come out $11.00 ahead: $10.50 plus the $.50 Miles let him keep. There was no sense just playing with someone else's money unless you made some more profit from it. But with a good run of luck, Victor was sure that he could do much better than he had, an opinion that had changed since the beginning of the evening.

"All right. I'll be back tomorrow night," said Victor as he walked outside and got on his horse to ride home. The wheel hadn't been as thrilling as he had anticipated. It was just a device that could be scientifically mastered; a piece of machinery that behaved within certain probability limits. All one had to do was estimate the best bets and cover their risks with more conservative bets, a method that would not bring in an overwhelming win, as the conservative bets would offset the larger bets when they came in, but then one wouldn't lose a tremendous amount either. It seemed like a very safe system for making money. Yes, he said, I'm sure of it. That roulette is a good way to make a little spare money.

So the next night, Victor went back. Due to his new-found confidence, he was successful in winning a net nineteen dollars—a profit for himself. That was three weeks wages for a hired hand. It was not a bad wage for two nights of work.

"Here's your twenty," said Victor, "Plus the ten you wanted me to make for you." Bon took the money, folded it carefully, and put it in his shirt pocket.

"You did very well tonight."

Victor, who was rather pleased with himself, couldn't have agreed more with what Bon said, and was in a distinctly jovial mood after his night of monetary advancement. He longed to get back to his horse and canter down the main street of town until he got to Magnolia Avenue, where he would transition into a gallop and race home. The feeling of the night air against his flushed skin would have an extremely exhilarating effect, in which he could somehow express or show his feelings in a very private way to some invisible audience, who he imagined was always watching him.

"Thank you," said Victor in a voice that rung of humility.

"You could make a lot of money here," said Bon, as another man from across the room was motioning him, Bon, to transverse the smoky den and listen to his urgent information.

"If you have money, it's easier to make money."

"Exactly," said Bon as he started across the room, when he paused momentarily and turned his head back towards Victor, "If you ever need help with a stake just come to me."

"Thanks," said Victor, but Miles was gone; vanished into the haze which seemed to be as natural to the establishment as the fading finish on the walls and the warped floors. *I am a Stuart*. The affirmation pulsed through Victor to the groves in his fingers. *I am a Stuart*. Once again it resounded throughout his being as his fingers brushed through his long, light brown hair, charging the strands with the electricity of this new profound sensation that he was a part of something—perhaps the saving part, chosen to regenerate the whole. What the whole was: whether it was his family, his town, nation, or even his place among men, he, Victor Stuart, felt uniquely chosen to be the one who was to lead a future way of being. The invisible audience was applauding vigorously as Victor smoothly walked outside and unstrapped his horse to ride home. There were no worries. Money, future, the all of what a person may worry about when financial status is in peril had been particularly enormous for Victor. Now they neither affected him or occupied any place whatsoever in this new frame of consciousness. He mounted his horse and, in perfect accord with his vision, started his horse through its paces.

Victor found that he could be moderately successful, though not abundantly so, playing roulette, when one day about six months after he had started playing semi-full time, Bon approached him a second time with another proposition.

"I've heard you like automobiles."

"Yes, my father has a friend who owns one and frequently I get to drive it. They're very fast. I like speed, I think it feels natural."

"Well, there's a fellow who will be in town this weekend and he wants to spend the afternoon at the races, only he doesn't like to drive and asked Bill if he would try to find someone who would drive him."

Miles paused as he took a long drag from his dangling cigarette. "It would mean five dollars. Would you be interested?"

"What kind of car does he have?" asked Victor, who really was quite excited at the prospect of going to see a horse race, as well as drive the car of a fellow who was rich enough to pay someone five dollars just to drive thirty or forty miles. But the most exciting prospect to him was what kind of vehicle he would be driving, and could it go fast.

"Hudson, I think."

"Fine. I'll do it," replied Victor immediately, trying to hold back his enthusiasm for the project, but this act instead resulted in simply a rather strange sound, though Miles appeared to take no notice.

"Good, be in front of the hotel at ten o'clock Saturday morning."

"Ten. Right. I'll be there."

***

The first day at the races didn't disappoint Victor. He roamed the grandstands while the gentleman he had chauffeured was sitting with a rather select group inside an enclosed box at the top of the track.

The tote board and the betting—the entire atmosphere seemed very hospitable, almost familiar to the boy, as he had taken along fifteen dollars just in case he wanted to win some money in a few carefully placed wagers. But the whole system of betting seemed sufficiently complicated that the prudent side of his character bid him wait until he had discovered a "system," as he had in roulette.

However, by the seventh race, all this caution had suddenly dissipated in an attitude of confidence that young Victor had acquired as he sat and watched others making bets. Victor watched others winning and losing—the various conversations and how they reacted. He was also struck by what seemed to him to be an extraordinary similarity between roulette and gambling on the magic tote board.

There were a few mechanical problems that he hadn't worked out; for example—why the odds kept changing over the loud speaker, until just before posting, and how he could take the best advantage of these miniscule pieces of information to better his chances at winning. This led him to conclude that since the odds were continually changing, it would be best to place one's bets only just before posting so that one could get the final odds. He decided to use his "hedge" system so that he would never lose everything nor get the greatest return, either.

Victor bet the entire fifteen dollars in the seventh race and ended up losing three dollars, though he gained back one of those dollars in the ninth and last race (he didn't bet the eighth, as he had trouble finding where to cash in his tickets).

On the way home, the important gentleman asked if he, Victor, had done any betting.

"Well, not a lot really," started Victor, unsure at just how to respond to this stranger.

"Have you ever been to this track before?"

"My father and I have come to look at horses."

"Your father's interested in horses, is he?"

"Yes, you might say that he raises horses (on the side, that is). He runs an estate in the eastern part of the county and that takes most of his time."

"Horses, you say. Well, I'll have to meet this father of yours sometime. You see, I'm a person who buys horses, and I'm always interested in seeing what local people have. Sometimes you can get your best buys from someone who works on a smaller scale."

Victor didn't know how to respond, and so he continued to drive, attentively watching the road. Finally the other said, "So you've never been to a track?"

"Well, not for the races," replied Victor, somewhat troubled at this probe into his personal life, forcing him to reveal a point of inexperience which a boy of his age often takes to be the admission of some grave personality defect.

"How did you like it?"

"It was all right."

"Did you bet?"

"Only the seventh and ninth races."

"Tote?"

"Pardon?" said Victor, as he didn't understand to what the gentleman was referring.

"You bet tote, I mean the track betting. You bet where they gave you the tickets."

"Yes."

"Hum, that's not a very wise move, you know."

"What's wrong with betting 'tote'?"

"Well several of the things you did, actually. For one, you should never bet on the last three races at a small race track like that, because they are always fixed, and if you don't have inside information, you are going to get the raw end of it. Also, when a track features a daily double, bet the first race and not the second. In the first, the favorite usually wins, so that the people who buy the tickets can get their hopes high, but in the second, the favorite never wins—it's generally someone from the middle of the field. The best races to bet are the middle ones, unless you have information.

"Your second mistake was betting where you couldn't make a lot of money. How much did you make today?"

"Two dollars," said Victor, as he was ashamed to admit that he actually lost that same amount.

"Two dollars? Well, if you had bet that off-the-track, then you would have probably made five dollars."

"Really?"

"Certainly, it's much better, cause they don't have to pay any taxes on their earnings, and other things like that, so their overhead is very low; they can afford to give better odds."

Victor had no idea why the off-the-track betting gave better odds, or why they were exempt from taxes. The thought that they might *not* be a legitimate group never entered his mind, but because he was so impressed by this rather easy gentleman, he immediately resolved to go to the track the following week, and try to find the off-the-track betters, and make a little money for himself.

"Do you want to see how fast this thing can go?" asked the gentleman, as Victor, in all honesty, had forgotten that he was driving, so intent was he upon his plans the following week.

"Pardon?"

"The car, do you want to test her? I don't mind."

"All right," Victor responded with a smile as he depressed the accelerator slowly but steadily to the floor.

***

In the months that were to follow, Victor found this off-the-track betting to be much more profitable than roulette. And soon, when Miles Bon offered him an opportunity to get some inside information in exchange for a certain fee and the duties of placing bets for Bon, Victor readily accepted. Throughout this time, it never entered Victor's head that he was doing something illegal. Certainly he knew that there was something a little hushed about the operation, and that it wasn't something that he would talk about with other people—not even to his own father, who Victor knew would be against any form of sustained betting, and was strangely enough ignorant of his son's activities. Now this might be due to Victor being a rather secretive boy who easily kept his affairs hidden or, more precisely, undiscussed on the domestic front. In Victor's own mind, what he was doing was slightly ungentlemanly or seamy, but not illegal or criminal.

And so Victor continued to bet and acquire a small pot of money as he continued to tour various racing courses to place bets for both himself and Miles Bon.

Victor continued to gain, though as he became more accustomed to this activity, he also, by degrees, saw the dangerous element that lurked behind its façade of easy money. But perhaps because he did see it only in small increasing increments, the slow exposure meant he was never shocked and his basic view of the entire activity was not altered: that of it being a common, pedestrian way to acquire capital.

This growing bank that Victor now had first went to furnishing him with some new clothes, and then he had plans of buying his father's horses (secretly) and operating a partnership with a stable owner—that is, Victor would provide him with a horse or two, and the stable owner would keep it and find mounts for the horse. Any prize money would be split, proportionally, first making sure that the stable's expenses were covered. This scheme offered a perfect way for Victor to help his father and to get the family into better financial straits, as well as provide a more stable source for his income. The plan would be implemented once Victor, after several years, could finally accumulate enough money to put it into operation.

***

"Victor? Victor?" Jason's voice called.

Victor turned his head. His mind was very unclear. He was tired. Often in the past few weeks he had felt an enormous tension that never abated.

"We won, Victor, we won," cried Jason in jubilant tones. But the news failed to really cheer Victor, as he was still half in his meditations. Why couldn't he free himself from these oppressive invisible visions that plagued his mind and attention, down to the most common and trivial tasks? He found he was able to deliver himself from these fits of anxiety less and less, and only occasionally when he forced himself into a near frenzy—a solution which itself was becoming harder to induce even at crises situations.

***

Then there came a series of losses. These confused Victor.

"We'll make up that money yet, you just wait and see," said Jason as he left to collect the winnings.

"Hurry back," said Victor weakly.

Why had he gone to the track last week? It was one of the poorest moves that he had made. With no information from Miles, he had lost heavily a few weeks previous and had hoped to win it back the week before.

"There won't be any problem," Jason had said. "I've never seen anyone with as much feel for this sort of thing in my life."

Victor knew that Jason was only complimenting him, but still it *was* nice to hear someone confirming what you had thought for quite some time.

"I don't like going to the track without the tips. I think that the races are getting large fields, and that makes blind betting very hard. I think we should hit the cross-country race that I'm riding in on Sunday."

"You know those two bit races, there's no money in them. Why, the only race that has any money besides the tracks is the Varner's Junction race, and that's not for quite some time. Wouldn't you rather try and get some of it back right now?"

"Can't win any of it back if I lose again."

"That's true enough. If you don't think you can handle it, I suppose you know best. After all, it's your money."

Those words rang in his head. "It's your money." Over and over. Didn't he know that it was his money? Who else would it belong to?

Jason was right that the places to win money were the larger track races, but they were also where he could lose, too. He was at a critical position financially: after his horse investments and helping his family, his own reserve had dropped dangerously low so that he couldn't afford another losing week, but still expenses were mounting as the stable owners were coming up with all sort of hidden fees that Victor had never imagined, being relatively new in business dealings of this type. And so the need for ready money was quite imperative.

"Yes, well, I'll tell you what I think later," replied Victor. But in the end he went and lost more money than he actually had. This put Victor in a bind, as he had only a certain amount of time to make good his debt, and they wouldn't allow him to bet more than a certain amount on credit. It was a difficult situation. Then Victor remembered what Miles Bon had said to him about money a long time ago, and Victor wondered whether he could get some money out of Miles, though this seemed a rather dubious possibility, as for some reason, Bon had not been betting for the last several weeks. The reason for this was naturally completely unknown to Victor, but the least he could do was give Bon a try.

"I really don't have much right now, Victor. You see, we're preparing a room for some show girls and all our extra money is going into that."

"But it's really urgent. You see, I've run into a little cash flow situation. I need capital to get me right again. And I remember that you once said to me that I could come to you for money if I were ever in a bind."

Victor felt almost as if he was begging, an action far beneath the dignity of the Stuarts—*I'd sooner starve than be said his debtor*—but Victor knew that it was essential that he get some money so that he could pay back the track betters, and make a little back.

"Well, I tell you, I do remember that conversation. I did promise you a stake. But as I told you, we are in a bit of a spot. I'll give you a certain amount under special conditions, which of course, I'm sorry to have to impose, but as we do operate under supply and demand, and as demand is high and supply low, the commodity will have to be purchased at a price."

"What kind of conditions?"

"How much do you need?"

"Five Hundred."

"Five Hundred? Well you are in a bit, aren't you?"

Victor stepped forward with clenched fists.

"Hold on there, Victor. From the sound of things, you aren't in a position to be rude now, are you? Someone who owes five hundred dollars isn't exactly in the best bargaining position, now is he?"

Victor wasn't sure whether he should follow his instincts and level Bon right there on the spot with one blow, or flail at that arrogant black face that was taunting him. It was because he was so furious and couldn't decide what to do, rather than any self-restraint that kept him from entering into a physical altercation at that moment. "If you can't help me, just say so, but don't give me any of this crap," snapped Victor, who couldn't see that these words were not the most advantageous that he could have delivered.

"All right, I'll give you your money. Come on with me to the back room."

Victor didn't know why he had to follow Miles around like some kind of trained dog that was supposed to heel when called. The entire thing seemed utterly out of proportion. Why had he gone to this little worm in the first place? The entire idea now seemed to be ill-conceived. No money was worth the degradation that he was going through. He wanted to level this impudent little rodent and feel the life flowing out of that smart-talking little mouth.

Bon sat down at a table, the book in front of him from which he transferred certain numbers to a separate sheet of paper. After a few minutes, he handed the paper to Victor to sign.

Stuart snatched the paper and read it quickly. "What kind of terms are these? Five percent per week! Why, that's robbery!"

"If you get your money back this weekend, then you'll have only five percent to pay back. Try to get a loan from someone else at five percent. It's really a very good rate."

"But this is five percent a week."

"It was my understanding that you only wanted the money for a week—until you could get it back?"

"But how am I supposed to be able to make anything when you take it all in interest?"

"Think of it this way, if you paid taxes, you'd have to give back a certain amount of what you made."

"But I don't have to pay taxes."

"I told you before that our money is tight around here. Here's my offer. I really shouldn't be making it, but I like you Victor, hot temper and all. Do you want the money or not?"

Victor knew that Miles understood his situation and that any further talk was simply useless. Victor was in no position to bargain and the other knew it; worse yet, Victor knew that Miles understood.

"I'll take it," said Victor.

***

"Who do you want to bet on in the seventh?" asked Jason, returning from the bookie (off-the-track bet receiver).

"I don't know," said Victor. "How do we stand for the day?"

"Well, we started out with three hundred of your money and I started out with fifty. I lost mine in the first two races, and you kept relatively even. Let's see—you're up about twenty dollars."

Twenty-dollars. It was awful, but somehow Victor couldn't get very excited or frightened. He felt too numbed by his cumbersome situation. He had paid his debt of two hundred dollars, but he still owed Miles Bon five hundred dollars, plus the stable men eighty dollars, plus the 5% per week until he paid the balance to Bon. It would be necessary to try and come in on a long shot. Often in the late races, the long shots would come through as most of the money would be riding on the favorites.

"Do you have the form that I made out?"

"Yes," replied Jason, handing Stuart the sheet of paper.

"That's right. I think we'll put our money on 'Lucky Lady' to win, about two hundred. And sixty five each on 'Pie-in-the-Sky,' and 'Sleeping Beauty' to win."

Somehow, Victor's mind was focusing on these bets. They seemed as if they might be just the thing to turn the tide. The two smaller bets were on four-to-one and the big bet was a seven-to-one. If it came in, then Victor's problems would be over, for the time being.

"I think that I'll go with you this time," said Victor, feeling anxiousness through his drifting mental uncertainty.

"Do you think that's wise?" asked Jason, referring to the rule that anyone who had registered as a licensed rider was not permitted to bet on horse racing. The risk might come with a cost. If Victor waited for the Bella County cross-country race (or other larger local events), there might be less scrutiny. A bet in those conditions might be safer.

However, there was always someone at the track from the state racing commission, and if he saw anybody connected with racing (except big horse owners), then there would be an investigation.

Because of this, one did not want to ever win "big" or they might draw too much attention. This was the reason that Jason had taken over the role of placing Victor's bets for him; there could be no other. Victor was oblivious to Jason's reference.

On other grounds, Jason had convinced Victor that he should always allow him, Jason, to place his bets for him as the off-track betting was shady and because of this it would not do for Victor to be investigated by the racing commission. And so Victor allowed Jason to do Victor's errand running and phone-in (when the bookies weren't near-by). Or Jason could go himself when they were near-by to place Victor's bets and deliver his money to him. This work Jason gladly did, as he endeavored to ingratiate himself with young Stuart.

"I don't care. I just want to go and make the bet in person."

"What's the matter, don't you trust me?" said Jason, laughing.

"Oh, shut-up and get going," said Victor.

When they got to the little house, only a hundred yards from the track where the bookie worked, the two pushed their way inside amidst the tide of human flesh toward the counter to place their wagers.

The man behind the counter recognized Jason. "You haven't had too bad a day," he said, referring to the fact that Jason had indeed won some money for himself that he hadn't told Victor about.

They placed their bets and waited for the results. They were positive, bringing Victor's total to $260.

"Let's go," Victor said in a very low, almost inaudible voice that Jason didn't hear, so that when he saw his comrade leaving, he said, "Where are you going?"

But Victor didn't answer, and only continued in his path toward the fresh air.

"I'm going back," replied Stuart when Jason finally stopped him and wanted to know why he wasn't staying to win back his money. "I'll go with you," said Jason.

"I'd rather go alone, thanks anyway. There's someone I have to see."

Even as he uttered those words, Jason knew that he was talking about Julia, and he felt the conflict between self-restraint and passion (a battle which in Jason's case was no contest in favor of restraint).

Victor knew that the bet had been a stupid one. It seemed that once someone was in a crisis, it somehow became harder to win. Using his system, winning should be an easy **and** steady thing. Stuart didn't believe in luck, so he attributed his bad showing to the fact that he was trying to get too much back too quickly. It couldn't be done. *I should rely on the system. I should have waited for Bon to have resumed his betting. In the past, when Bon stopped as he did from time to time, I always stopped as well. But with this investment of mine. . . . Still, I should never have abandoned the system which has created what's left of the wealth I have.*

Victor knew that he must see Julia. She was the only calm thought that he had; the only thing that he could depend on. He needed to see a way out of the horrifying miasma that he found himself in.

He found Julia in the kitchen, kneading some dough on top of a large wooden board.

"And so the young maiden is slaving in the kitchen," said Victor when he entered.

"Hello Victor," said Julia, who didn't mind having some company as she was engaged in the arduous task of culinary preparation.

"What are you doing there? Making supper? I thought you had a maid for that, or are you just keeping in practice?"

"Actually I'm baking some fresh bread for Mr. Beauchay's birthday. Our families have always been close, you know, and ever since his wife died, we've always given him a few freshly baked loaves of bread to help him enjoy the day. He adores bread, and this year I volunteered to do the honors."

"That's very touching. What a pretty little homemaker you are in the kitchen with your apron on, tackling a big project."

"Oh, bread isn't that big a project."

"I suppose not, but it's just nice to see a woman where she belongs, and with you, it seems so natural."

This statement might have been taken as a compliment by many women, but Julia was rather taken aback by it and somewhat put off as the tone implied that he, Victor, would love to lord over his little slave (or so she was convinced that Victor would like to make her) and beam in his satisfaction over her subservient role.

Why couldn't Victor simply pass conversation without trying to make his little innuendos about his eventual ownership of her?

Couldn't he see that she was in no way desirous of this? Victor was a nice enough young man to pass the time of day with, but why did he have to spoil a potentially pleasant *tete à tete* with his possessive clamoring?

"Perhaps, if you like," started Victor again, "we could take it over to the Beauchay's ourselves when it's through. It's a lovely day for a walk."

Julia knew what Victor would want to do if they went out for a walk together, as the situation had occurred previously where he tried to force himself on her by putting his arms around her to kiss her. Now normally, perhaps, Julia under other circumstances wouldn't have minded being kissed by gallant Victor, the most popular young man among his peers in the county. But her heart was elsewhere, and she felt that to love one person and to kiss another would be to do her love (that is the feeling as well as the rational disposition) a disservice. She was a one-man girl. To act otherwise would be to harm herself and the goals she had set out for herself.

It wasn't a question of actually disliking Victor, in the way for example that she disliked Jason, but that her heart was already engaged. Had there been no John Dow, or if she had no feelings for him, she would have permitted Victor to escort her to the Beauchays.

"Yes, it is a lovely day, isn't it? I so like the middle-late summer. Everything's so peaceful, don't you think?"

But Victor repeated the question. "Would you like to take that walk then?"

"Well, that might be a nice idea," she began tactfully, "had there not been provision for the bread already."

"What do you mean?" asked Victor, slightly confused.

"What I mean is that the Beauchays have already arranged for someone to pick up the bread. They're sending someone over. In only a couple of hours, the messenger will be here. I really must hurry now, or young Mr. Dow will go away empty-handed."

"You mean that black twit is coming over here?" Victor laughed.

Julia was furious at herself for having mentioned John's name in front of Victor. She knew that he would just make a mean joke; he always did. But the temptation had been so great. For though she had no idea who the Beauchays were sending over, she had hoped that it would be John and that hope had slipped into a sentence, which now was causing her acute distress.

"You shouldn't say such things about our neighbors. You know how close our families are," said Julia, trying to change the subject, but also determined to put in a word in defense of John, as she felt that she couldn't passively let his name be slandered.

"But he's not a part of the Beauchay family—not really, I mean."

"He is in every important sense, I think," started Julia, as carefully as she could, wishing that Victor would stop talking about her sweetheart. "At least our family has always considered him so. But then I suppose you must be thinking about the big race coming up."

But Victor wouldn't be sidetracked so easily until he had managed to get the last word and so he replied, "You know you'd think that a fellow like that, illegitimate I mean, would be appreciative of the fact that a kind family took him in and treated him with Christian charity. Such a person, had he any shame, would not insert himself where he doesn't belong."

Julia didn't reply, but returned to her bread.

"You know, rumor has it that a girl that he's been going with in town is pregnant."

"How can such rumors get started?" said Julia, who became very agitated by this news, and wanted to believe that it couldn't be true.

"Don't worry, I have it from very good information. She isn't exactly, what you would say, the most discrete young slut in town."

"Well, Mr. Stuart, it seems that you must have little regard for me either, as you burden me with such salacious gossip. You must have a low opinion of me to think that I'm interested in such lascivious gossip. Excuse me, sir, but I must leave just now." And so Julia left the kitchen, her bread still on the counter in a lump.

Victor was beginning to understand that perhaps it wasn't his recounting of the story itself, but *who* it was about that was the cause of her departure. Events in the past began to arrange themselves in a new order to fit this new possible interpretation. It could account for many things. "But how could a girl of her breeding like, *like* a—" Victor could not bring himself to say the words.

Chapter 6

"In which Several Accounts are Woven Together"

"Oil," said Ed.

"Oil?" the other two repeated in amazement.

"Yep."

"How can there be oil?"

"Don't know, but that's what I heard."

Ike came out from behind the counter, rubbing his hands together as he appeared to be engaged in some momentous contemplation.

"What's on your mind?" asked Jake at last, knowing that Ike was probably bursting to tell them his ideas, but unwilling to offer them unless asked.

"Oh nothing much," replied Ike, who couldn't keep a straight face as he let his fib go for a moment. "Jist that I was thinking of O-klee-homa."

"O-klee-homa," said Jake, repeating these cryptic words from which he assumed that Ike thought that the boys could guess the source of that animated expression on Ike's face.

"Sure, haven't you two never heard of the story of O-Klee-homa?"

"Bunch of Indians made some money on oil. Is that what you mean?" put Jake.

"Not only a bunch of Indians, but a bunch of clever white men, as well. There was a drummer who comes in here one day and tells me all about it. They has this big boom in oil and ails of a sudden everyone in the town is rich, see, and then some dudes who run the concessions jack up the prices so that they are in keeping with the new salaries."

"You mean that if a man earned eight hundred farming and then paid a regular price for supplies, then if he's earning ten times as much his supplies are going to cost him ten times as much?"

"Well, almost. You can't go up exactly in the same rate."

"That ain't fair, Ike. What abouts the people who doesn't get rich? Ain't they goin' to have to pay the same exorbitant rates as the others?"

"Ed's right, you know. Unless you charged a different price for each customer, and I don't know how you could do that. You'd be putting regular people in the poor house."

Ike's smile disappeared. It had seemed so simple. Just like that feller had said. Everyone made money in a boom—even the shopkeepers.

"You know, all we got is that someone says that they was lookin' for oil," said Jake.

"I heard 'em right," replied Ed defensively.

"Ain't doubtin' your word 'bout that, Ed, but supposin' someone was just talking through his hat?"

"And suppose they wasn't?" responded Ed, who rather didn't like the insinuation that the information that he had gotten might, in any way, be doubted.

"Doesn't matter wither they is or isn't fer this example, Ed, cause what I'm sayin' is that there is a one-in-two chance that the story you heard is just that: only a story: somebody jis a talkin'. An' even if it is fer real, then how does we know that they actually finds oil on that land? Lots of guys go a courtin', but they don't always git what they see, if you catch my meanin'."

"What you're saying is that we only has a one out of four chances of being right, is that it?" asked Ike.

"A twenty-five percent chance of thar being oil on that land, which 'taint very good odds where I bet," responded Jake.

"Still, you know, I've always thought thar was something valuable about that land. When we was a watchin Beauchay all them nights, out there a diggin' holes in the ground. He ain't no fool; I think he know'd something—I mean why else would he buy that worthless land, taint good for anything, 'cept growin' weeds."

"You may be right, Ike, but what you aims to do about it?" put Jake after the other's triumphant speech.

"Maybe we can buy an option on some of the rights from him."

"But why should he want to sell us anything, when he can have it all fer himself?"

"Diggin' fer oil costs money," put Ed, who had been the silent member of this conversation.

"Yar, but I don't suppose that the Beauchays are too strapped for cash," responded Jake.

"You never can tell. Don't think thar are very many people in Bella County that are that far away from going broke. Remember, takes a lot of money to run one of them large places. A couple of bad crops and I think jist about anyone round here would be finished," responded Ike.

"Still, even if that was true, what you suppose would make him want to sign in with a bunch of small time rubes from the town?"

"We might not have much, but I got a guarantee of this store as security," said Ike.

"You mean as an' underwritin'?"

"I guess you would call it that."

"You can do what you want, but it's too risky for me," finished Jake. Both men looked at Ed, who was slowly shuffling the cards.

***

As John walked to town (he didn't want to ride, preferring the time that he would have to think if he walked) he couldn't get over the strangeness of why Cindy hadn't told him of her condition before now, as she must have known it for at least a month or so, as he, John, had been gone camping from the later part of June to the later part of July. *She must have been worrying all the time I was gone*, he thought, *and I just merrily went on my way and selfishly went camping. How she must have suffered for my sake, not telling me because perhaps she didn't want to ruin my camping trip, or perhaps she hadn't been sure before, but now she was.*

Over and over the conflict raged within between his responsibility to Cindy and his responsibility to himself. *I don't really want to marry her for myself*, he decided, *at least not now. But my actions have been so heinous that I ought to make some restitution for what I have done. I suppose that in time, I could grow to feel a love for her like I felt when I first met her*, yet as he thought back on it, that hadn't really been love at all, though it had all the trappings. He had felt tenderness and a desire, but somehow something seemed to be missing. John tried to think back on the conversations that they had had, and was hard pressed to remember any. All that they talked about were silly things like the night and the beauty of the other person. It had been like light lace that had been so carefully sewn that it flies so free in the wind. The lace was so soft and delicate, every stitch carefully conceived; and what lovely shapes the body of lace portrays when billowed in the late night breeze—shapes that could bewitch and mesmerize. But when a gust of wind finally blew the lace with force against a wall in the morning light, the mystery was gone, and all that was left was a flat piece of cloth held fast against the wall by the wind—held flat without any deceptions.

So now what was to be done? In a sense, they must start all over again. It would be almost like meeting another woman, as the old one had died, blown away. And what did Dow owe to this new woman? For it would be she and not the old one to whom he would be making a commitment. It would be the new one with whom he had never even spoken a word. How strange to marry a woman that one doesn't know. How wrong it seemed, and yet just moments before, how certain he had been that it was right.

As John approached Sawyer's Bridge, he heard loud voices. At first he smiled to himself, thinking that it must be some pair of lovers enjoying the night, in a way that he would never enjoy again, but then he realized that he recognized the voices that were talking—though he couldn't make them out. So Dow stopped and crept down the path, every step dreading that he would identify the voices, but at the same time compelled to ascertain whether his suspicions were correct.

As he got closer, he could see a clearing. It was a clearing in which he and Cindy had spent many an hour. Now his ears identified the voices, but it was necessary for his eyes to confirm what his ears had perceived. His apprehension was frightful. But in a moment all was confirmed; in the clearing was Cindy with another man, Billy Thompson.

"But I'm going to have a baby!"

"Well, what do you want me to do about it?" replied Billy.

"Some man you are. I tell you that I'm having a baby and you just sit there."

"Well, what do you expect me to do? It's not my problem."

"Oh yes it is, Billy Thompson. You're the father."

Billy laughed very hard when Cindy gave him this bit of information. "And how are you going to prove that?"

"I have my ways," she replied.

"Bullshit, you do. There must have been four or five guys you were sleeping with, and with a track record like that, you couldn't prove a thing, and you know it."

"Not the last two months; you were the only one, Billy. Everybody was gone on one thing or another, and you were the only one."

"You don't frighten me with your idle threats, you cow."

"Listen, Billy, don't take this too lightly. I could slap you with a mighty big law suit, you know. I have just enough evidence to make it stick."

"Like hell you do."

"Listen. A woman kinda knows when something might have happened, so after I had that feeling I made sure that at least three persons saw us go out of town together for two weeks running in July.

"You see," she paused slightly to try and achieve a maximum effect, "I made sure that I had witnesses so that you wouldn't be able to get away without either marrying me or giving me a big settlement."

"*Why* you little –" began Billy as he swung his hand at her, but Cindy, almost as if she knew by instinct what to do, checked his hand.

"There are witnesses that saw us go out here tonight, Billy. Now it wouldn't look too good in my law suit for me to have been beaten up by the unfeeling father of my child, now would it?"

"You little slut. You can't sue me, and you can bet your girdle that I wouldn't let a tramp like you on my estate, let alone even conceive of marrying you."

Billy got up to go.

"Remember what I said," she advised in the same sarcastic tone.

"You haven't got a prayer, and you know it. Those laws were designed to protect innocent young girls who might get shafted by some unfeeling bastard. They weren't made to be exploited by the likes of you. You have to be crazy to think that a whore like you could get anything from a court in Varner's Junction, when a good portion of the jury has probably slept with you at some time or other themselves."

"You laugh, you little asshole, but you just wait. You just wait," said Cindy, standing up as Billy walked away.

From the distance she heard him say, "Good-bye, queenie."

All this time, John sat still in utter amazement at what was transpiring. It was as if he were watching a play. How could he have misjudged Cindy so? What could he have been thinking? But then he saw the girl alone in the clearing. She was desperate. This is the woman to whom he had bestowed so much of himself, and now she was in pain. He stood up to go to her. Cindy needed someone, and he wanted to comfort her. He could forgive anything at that moment, so great was his compassion for her suffering.

"Who's there?" said Cindy, suddenly hearing something moving in the bushes.

"It's me, John."

"Now you're spying on me, is that it you little screw?"

John didn't understand her antagonism. Why was she so angry, and vulgar? John suddenly realized that part of the intense feeling that he was experiencing was a strong revulsion, an aversion to himself as well as the girl who had deceived him so cruelly. All the jests that people had made suddenly took on a different light. They had been laughing at him. He had seen Cindy only as he had wanted to see her, and not as she really was. But who was she? What was she?

"Please Cindy, I want to help."

"Oh shut up and go ride your horses. I don't need you—any more than I need that little fart, Thompson."

John had never heard Cindy use such crude language, and it bothered him to feel the hurt and bitterness that must be driving her to say such things.

"Please, Cindy."

"I said get the hell out of here, do you hear me?"

"I wasn't spying. I mean I was, but that's not what I was intending to do. I was coming to see you and then I heard—"

"Get out of here, do you hear me?"

"I heard voices, and then I thought I —"

Then Cindy rushed at Dow and slapped him across the face. John saw the blow coming, but made no attempt to block it. His head jarred to the right and then to the left; as her arm thrust forward into his sternum, his legs reeled and he fell down backwards against a tree. Cindy was standing over him now. Her eyes and mouth distorted in a mania of animalistic fervor as her entire character (the character he had known) was transformed into that of a mad wolf.

"All of you are shit, do you know that? You're shit and you can go to hell, every one of you, damn you, goddamn you all." As she said these words, she seemed to John to be near the breaking point. Her voice was hardly in her control. She seemed at the point of hysterical laughing or crying, all the same. She ripped open her purse and took out a five dollar gold piece and tossed it at John's chest, but she must have accidently aimed low, hitting John in the groin.

"Here," she said after throwing the coin. "Take that and give it to your brother, Jason. Tell him it's a present from me." By now she was panting very heavily, and obviously very tired, but still she stood above Dow, exuding that extraordinary energy that seemed to possess her, but which now was yielding to the near collapse of that small body.

Suddenly, her eyes changed expression. It seemed to John that her eyes were almost pleading. Then they changed to despair as she shook her head and muttered in a barely audible voice, "No. No more. Please get out of here. Please leave me alone." She inhaled and in a louder voice, but still much softer than a speaking voice, she managed, "Please, leave me alone."

John got up, took a step toward her and stopped. He knew she didn't want him, so he turned and stumbled back through the undergrowth as if he didn't know the terrain at all; as in ignorance he tripped and slid as he made his way back through the forest he had once known so well.

Chapter 7

"Further Details on Victor's Unfortunate Habit"

"But you don't know the spot I'm in," said Victor.

"If I had the money, you know I'd lend it to you," said Jason.

"I'm desperate."

"Oh, you'll pull through," said Jason, who really didn't know how desperate Victor's situation was. He imagined that Victor still had a few thousand stashed away somewhere that he didn't want to touch because it was his reserve, and Jason thought that if Victor wanted to continue betting, that he would have to dip into his reserve. Jason looked at his rival. *How deceptive he can be,* he thought. *Beneath that handsome smile is a crooked soul of treachery. How wrong it would be to let the likes of him have Julia. But brains will always win the day.*

***

And now Jason saw his opening to take his rival down. Jason was smitten with the gambler's vice. Jason would tag along to the track. There Jason would observe everything.

He would carefully list the various people with whom Victor talked and how and where he made his bets. All these things Jason industriously pursued so that he might not suffer for want of information.

It was only after he had scrupulously studied his quarry that Jason approached young Stuart.

"Hello Victor. You've done very well for yourself at the tracks, haven't you?"

"What, what gives- you the idea—"

"Come now, Victor, old friend, you needn't be shy around me, I'm your old playmate, remember; I saw you the other day when I was there myself. We both bet with the same bookie."

"I don't know—" started Victor, who didn't know quite what to make of this overture from Jason.

"You know, however, you had a very close call last week. I was going to warn you, but as you squeezed through all right, I didn't think there was any need to spoil your afternoon."

"Close call, what on earth do you mean? You're talking in riddles, you know," Victor replied, though now he was somewhat apprehensive of this fellow who knew so much about him when he had been completely unaware of his presence. It struck him as creepy. It was as if someone could see through his new clothes and was laughing at his nakedness.

"The racing commissioner."

"What do you mean?"

"Well, you're a registered rider, right?"

"Yes, I just registered because my father found out that registered riders get higher prizes than non-registered, amateur ones."

"Well there is a regulation, in case you didn't know, that prohibits riders who are registered jockeys in Georgia from participating in pari-mutual or other forms of betting in the same state. Now I know that off-track isn't pari-mutual, but whereas no one is very strict about enforcing the regulations on bets between friends, *they* are quite strict on keeping registered riders away from the windows.

"And that includes off-track betting. And the local commissioner is from where you just rode in a steeplechase, if I'm not mistaken, and so would know you very well."

"I've never heard of that rule," said Victor firmly.

"Well, look for yourself. All you have to do is go over to the records office and ask them to get you the statues concerning 'The Control and Regulation of Horseracing in the State of Georgia.'"

"What did you say this rule is called?"

"I don't remember the number, if that's what you mean, but I do know that it carries a five thousand dollar fine or one year in prison or both, as well as a lifetime suspension from ever racing or betting in Georgia again."

"Sounds pretty stiff."

"It is stiff; the intention of the law I guess was to keep the separation between the gamblers and the riders, so that the sport could be kept as free from outside influence as possible."

"That's a laugh."

"None the less, the new state commissioner is determined to make his political reputation on cleaning up the state racing system, so I'd stay clear if I were you."

"Fat chance of that, I'm not about to throw away going to the track for some stupid regulations."

"No, I don't blame you. There's a certain excitement about betting and seeing your horse pull through."

"That's the truth."

"I don't know too much about racing really," said Jason, in a bashful voice, as he changed the speed and fluency of his speech and started to pause and hesitate, as if he were embarrassed to admit to Victor that he really didn't know very much after all. "I've only been to the track twice, and I've just learned where everything is, but I don't have any idea really of how to make bets to one's best advantage. I imagine that there must be some inside knowledge that helps. But you know, I lost all the money that I brought to the track both days."

"It is rather difficult," said Victor, now confident as he felt really happy to pass along some help to this other person, who was now readily admitting, or acknowledging his, Victor's, knowledgeability on the subject area of racing and betting.

"I found that when I first went to the track, things were happening so quickly that it seemed impossible to ever be able to manage, or even comprehend all the subtle actions and signs that are a part of the racing life," put Victor. "That's just now I feel; hopelessly lost."

"Yes, it's tough at first. Luckily, I had someone explain a lot of what was happening to me, and what he didn't tell me, I soon found out for myself—but it takes a while. You can't expect to know everything at once."

"Yes, but how does one 'break-in?' Does it just happen automatically?"

"No, you have to find out a few basic facts first. Now I heard you mention off-track betting and pari-mutual. You know what they are, I take it?"

"Yes, I know that one is supposed to pay more, and that technically it isn't allowed, but I'm not very certain of when and how to make bets most advantageously."

"It's a bit tricky, and difficult to explain right now, but I tell you what; if you want, I will take you with me when I go up next Saturday, and show you a trick or two."

"That's great. I would really appreciate that."

"Don't mention it. Besides, if that racing commissioner is around, then you can carry my bets for me, so that he doesn't get wise."

"Sure, anything," replied Jason as he waved good-bye to his friend.

***

Jason went to the track that next Saturday with Victor and let Victor give him the tour of what was going on, complete and only excluding a few of the secrets of Victor's own private betting theories, which he wished to keep for himself. Jason was amazed at how much money Victor earned that day (two hundred dollars), which Victor explained was a better than average day, and that sometimes he had poor days and so they, to some extent, cancelled themselves out. Victor didn't want Jason to get the idea that he was worth too much money; but then, perhaps because he had been considered so poor by so many of the other land owners for such a long time, he also wanted to let Jason know that he wasn't in any way struggling, and that he lived quite comfortably on the money that he made and that he could clear a couple thousand on a good season, of which some money went to such things as clothes, food, and an occasional trip to Savannah (which Jason took to mean cat houses).

Jason was impressed that Victor seemed to be quite solvent (though he sometimes complained to the contrary), and that it would be difficult, in the short time that he had, to do anything that would put him off-balance to the extent that he would not be in a position to steal his Julia when he, Jason, was away at college. The only thing that he could do, if he couldn't damage Victor's solvency, was to fill him with ambition for what he could buy with his money, and thus keep him occupied with the task of earning enough to satisfy his dream, which Jason was confident would be more than enough to keep him away from any thoughts of marriage—for Jason was sure that even more basic to a man's heart than a woman and children, was the acquisition of wealth and power which somehow enhanced one's feelings about one's self. To imagine the self in a position of greater power than one's peers, in a position which would be the greatest actualization of any realistic dream, would be the highest exercise of the will and power of a man.

How to put these ideas into Victor's head would be another problem, but Jason, who didn't necessarily think that everything need be planned out in minutest detail, especially when this was impossible, tried to play the situation in an impromptu fashion during talks between himself and Victor at the racetracks.

"I hear that the Macklins are willing to sell their eastern field—you know the one that they just use for hay," said Jason.

"Really, that's certainly a waste of good land. We used to own that land before we ran into hard times. It prospered under our direction."

"I've heard that things are getting better for everybody these days."

"Yes, prices are up."

"Do you think that you'll buy back any of that land that you sold, or rather, your grandfather sold?"

"I don't know. It would be nice in a way to return the old place to the way that it was meant to be. Dad would certainly like that. I'd gladly lend him a little money if he wanted to try, but you know he hates loans. He says that they're deceptive, and give other people control over you. I suppose he's overreacting to the fact that he's had to take a number of loans, plus the ones that he inherited from grandfather. He's really done a remarkable job, considering what a botch of things he had to start with."

"And maybe, when it's your turn, you can turn things around even more?"

"I think that perhaps if I had the land to use as I wanted to, I'd turn the whole thing into a stable to raise horses. The South produces the best horses in the country, you know, and I think a stable would be quite a profitable venture, besides the fact that I would be doing something that really interested me."

"You need lots of land for that, don't you?"

"Not really. What we have now would be adequate, but of course extra land wouldn't hurt." Victor rather liked talking to Jason, the only one it seemed he could talk to about his ideas of the future. Jason respected him, and Victor (who was well-liked by most of the boys of the county, but not always respected as a thinker) appreciated being put in the role of diviner of his own future—a future that he was sure would be a bright one. How he would love to own such a stable. His father enjoyed horses too, and would take pleasure in producing a fine breed of animal. It wouldn't take too much money to actually start such a concern—as they already had several fine horses that they raised as a hobby. If they could get a little operating capital. . . .

Victor liked Shylock, their finest horse. It was the one Victor often rode. If they could get a good mare for Shylock, then perhaps that could be a beginning. But all of these ideas required capital, something that Victor had in a small quantity, but not in proportion to the scale needed to realize his dream.

"Why are the odds changing all the time?" asked Jason.

"Well," started Victor, still thinking about his stable, "you see there is so much betting going on and the odds reflect how the track is wagering at the moment. That's why we always make our bets at the end, just before posting. Now the reason for this is . . . ."

Victor never finished his sentence.

Chapter 8

"A Painting of a Still Life: A Pause in the Fair's Activities"

—*Excuse me young ladies*, *I have to get up to taste your pies— did you hear that, young ladies, why I--now you listen Ed Lambert, flattery will get you—that little devil, why I feel like a young lady at heart, don't you Maybel--I swear Cynthia, I don't know how anyone's going to beat your cherry pie—well, I did get lucky with the crop this year, I think it's very good, but that's none of my doing--well God didn't see fit to give me decent blueberries this year, so I had to make a current pie, mind you I've never made a current pie before, but I—Oh now you're just being modest, and you know it--now, stop talking like that or you'll turn my head — well as long as we're turning heads, look over there, it's Max and Frank doing their two man band—aren't they ridiculous--I rather like it, what would the fair be like without several appearances of those two clowns, I swear, it's a gift from God, the wag that they can make those children laugh, just look--I don't mind admitting that they make me laugh too, I guess I'm just a child at heart--why I remember when I was young, there was a couple of men like those two who used to do a juggling act with anything they could get their hands on, I mean anything—oh yes, what were their names? Marshall or something like that--I don't remember—who are you two talking about—oh it was before your time--I guess that dates us pretty well, doesn't it--well, anyway, I remember one day my daddy had won a stuffed animal for me and my brother and we were walking along eating cotton candy, and suddenly this man comes hopping in front of us and asks us if we wanted to see our teddies dance, and so we gave him our bears and he took colored saucers from out of his enormous pockets, they were red, I think, a very happy color, and so he started juggling the two saucers and the teddies, and darn if they didn't look as if they were dancing in the air; I remember that I laughed so hard that I felt as if I was going to burst; after that I always tried to make the bear dance myself, but you know it was never quite as grand as when that man, clown, came up to me and my brother and made our toys come to life—*

"Please Daddy, can we try, can we?"

"Well, you knew what I said, you each have five tickets, and you can use them as you please," said the father, seriously, but with a smile.

"Step right up—and see a little monkey that actually dances! Just push the bubble and watch him dance!" The barker demonstrated as he depressed the rubber bubble of air that forced a current through a rubber tube that made a rubber monkey dance, or rather jerk about his little tree (real wood). All about the huckster were ten or fifteen children squealing with delight as they watched the animal hopping about. "Buy one today—only a quarter."

"Only a nickel for two throws to knock over the milk bottles with this big softball," said another barker, holding up the large ball for all to see. It looked so easy, thought the little boy. That big ball and those small bottles, and there were only six of them. Why, they'd all topple over with ease. The boy remembered how he had tried, at various times, to pile various items on top of one another and now invariably they all would come tumbling down with no help from himself. In fact, just looking at those wooden milk bottles standing there seemed to invite someone to blow hard, much less throw a large softball twice, and so knock them down and gain a stuffed bear.

"I want to try, daddy."

"All right. Well then, here's your ticket. Go up to the man and give him your ticket."

The little boy made his way to the counter and stretched out his arm high above his head so that the man would see it.

"Very good, we have a young contestant right here. Are you ready to try your luck, young man?"

The boy nodded, very sincerely.

"Well, this is a ten cent ticket, here. I'll let you have a go at it and see if you want to try another. Otherwise, I'll give you one of these five cent tickets in change."

The boy didn't respond, but stood at attention waiting to be handed one of the balls. It felt smooth; it was a new ball, or at least not very old, and so the boy had a difficult time getting a grip as it was slightly too big for his hand. But he found that by digging his nails into the seams he could hold it reasonably well. He reared back and threw the ball with all of his might, but at the last minute, it slipped. The ball struck against the tarpaulin backstop and rolled to the ground. He had missed everything. He had only one more throw. This time he didn't throw the ball as hard and he knocked all but two of the milk bottles down. If only he hadn't been wild on his first throw, he thought, it would have been so easy to pick-off those remaining two bottles.

"Nice try young fella, do you want to try again or do you want—" But before the barker had finished his sentence his question was answered for him as the little hand thrust up in the air in the direction of the softballs.

"That's what I like to see," said the man, "a fella with gumption. Here you go." The barker handed the balls (this time both of them at once) to the boy, who aimed again at the bottles, which had been quickly restacked by a little boy, who he took to be the barker's son.

This time the ball was older, it displayed the black marks of age that softballs, used around their natural environs, seem to attract. As they were older, they seemed more manageable in his tiny hands, yet these things did not preoccupy his mind as they had before, no rather, all his thoughts were directed towards what he saw as a "sweet" spot right in the middle of the stack, which he was sure that if he hit, then all the bottles would come tumbling down. The boy aimed and threw the ball—it was a good throw heading straight for its mark. The little boy's soul was in that ball, and he could feel the air parting as it flew through the air. Then at impact, the boy internalized the sounds of the ball crushing the wooden pins tumbling backwards against the leather. One bottle was spinning around. If it fell it might take the other bottle with it.

But instead, two bottles were left standing. They were quite near each other but not touching. The throw had been a good one, hardly missing the sweet spot by more than an inch or two, but somehow there were still two bottles left standing. It seemed wrong somehow that all the bottles hadn't fallen, as it had been precisely planned and executed so well: the results didn't seem at all commensurate with what had preceded it.

But the fact remained that there were two bottles standing and the boy had but one more ball to knock them over. Somewhat shaken by what seemed to be an unbelievable set of circumstances, the little boy aimed again, determined to end this stupid game once and for all. He threw quickly and struck one bottle dead center and the other off center. The first bottle spun backwards into the tarpaulin like a wheel, while the latter bottle spun on its base as it wobbled near to the edge of the board where it came to a stop, just inches from falling off.

"Oh too bad, young man, you gave it a good try," said the barker to the boy indirectly, and to the crowd of potential buyers. "But I'll tell you what, because you gave it such a good try, we'll give you a little consolation prize." And with that, the barker handed him a little sucker. It was very small, the kind that could be purchased two or three for a penny. The boy took the sucker and ran back to his father.

"Well, you almost got them there," said his father cheerfully. "And you got quite a nice little treat there. You really threw that ball well, I don't know if I could have done as well, myself."

But the little boy tried not to listen. Even though deep inside he knew that his father was only trying to be nice, it still seemed to him as if he were mocking him and his wasting a ten-cent ticket on such a silly game. Then his brothers tried to grab his sucker so that they could see it, which seemed rather stupid to the boy as they had seen hundreds of suckers like these before, and had bought them in the stores themselves, so why they were so anxious to see one just because it had been given away to make him feel better, a purpose which it did not fulfill, he did not know.

—yumm you know the best part of this competition is when we get to sample each other's pies, when the judging 's over--you know I think it's a wonder that some of these judges don't get indigestion eating all those pies, and some of them judge other contests as well—they don't eat very much, you know—I understand but still I'd think that they'd need some baking soda when they got home after a day of sampling all these rich foods--o, ho, one of the men heard you, I saw him turn his head when you said baking soda— let him, I'm not embarrassed—oh Jenifer, you are such a terror—

The park was filled with families who were now getting ready to eat their noon-day meal, which many brought with them, while others bought hot dogs covered with catsup, mustard, and relish and washed them down with a cold soda. It was a colorful picture: all the families variously dressed in the noon-day sun, some with hats of different shapes and sizes and a few with parasols. The sun was also involved by pausing for a rest at the top of the sky before starting its long trip over to the west. The noonday light brought the composition to a bright intensity. The whites and yellows of many of the men and their wives were complemented by the assorted bright colors of the children as they scurried about, giving a pallet knife texture to the reds, blues, and violets that rotated about the stable centers of whites and yellows. They all lay over the greens and browns of the grass, which only appeared openly in small patches, though the underpainting could be felt throughout the visual presentation. Not to be forgotten were the spotted tents that were arranged in no discernable order about the grounds, and the three large trees that stood, quietly smiling at the bustle and confusion that was temporarily subsiding. It was almost as if the large protectors were puzzled at how all these colors had madly raced about in the morning in blurring pastel while now they sat, except for the children who continued to rotate and revolve about those quiet masses of white and yellow as if in constant constellation, defying Kepler's Laws. They must have been puzzled as their idea of motion was so different, their time located according to some other system of calculation, pitching different degrees of measurement. It was over this scene, glazed with light green as the breeze blew through creating dancing shadows, that rose-colored conversation and blue-purple cries (from the hot dog man delivering his alert to everyone and to no one) that miniature accents could be detected that added to the ensemble.

One detail in this composition was at the milk bottle throw. The forlorn little boy reached up on his tiptoes and got a softball and tossed it at a partially fallen pyramid of bottles. The bottles had been in a peculiar position and as the ball hit them, it caused one of the bottles to jump sideways and out of the booth. The boy rushed over to pick up the bottle to replace it, when at that moment the barker was returning with his son.

"Say now, what are you doing?" said the barker, seeing the little boy throwing the ball and one of the bottles going outside his booth. "This booth is closed for lunch. You come back later and pay your money if you want a try."

The little boy picked up the bottle, but then it struck him that the bottle wasn't at all as he'd expected it to be; it was heavy. He turned the bottle over in his hands and could tell that it was weighted on the bottom. That's why I couldn't knock it off. They weight the bottles. The bottle seemed grotesque to the boy.

"Say now," said the man, picking the bottle out of the boy's hand.

"Give me my bottle, now you go on to your parents," said the man as he jerked the bottle from the boy's hand, who gave no resistance.

"These kids, I don't know what gets into them," said the barker as the little boy walked slowly away.

Chapter 9

"A Short Hint of Various Important Decisions and Revisions"

"It's only a week away," said Rodney.

"Yes," replied his sister, who was busy with the final pillow in her set of four that she had been making for the fair.

"Are you going to enter that?" asked her brother.

"Yes, I was planning on it. Why, is there anything wrong?"

"No, nothing wrong. It's just that I don't think you can finish them in time. Look at that one you're working on now, you've barely started."

"I've done most of the work," protested Julia, "it's only the scene I have to finish. A couple of quick seams and it'll be ready after that."

"But that kind of work takes ages, I don't see how you'll ever get it done in time."

"It's the last one," she said, "but one thing's for certain, I won't get it done if you keep talking to me."

"Oh, I'll let you do your work, if you want, but I don't see why you continue," teased Rodney. "There's only one Vanderkamp who's going to win a prize at the fair, and it's going to be me." Rodney put his hands to his waist, drew out his elbows, and stuck his chest out.

"Oh is that so, mister big britches. Well, we'll see about that," said Julia, hopping up and running over near to where her brother was standing and she picked up an old cushion and spanked him with it on the backside. "That's the only thing I see your britches are good for: spanking!"

Then Rodney grabbed hold of the pillow and pulled it free from his sister's grasp. When Julia saw she was going to lose the pillow, she let go and ran across the room.

Rodney started in chase, but the quarters were too tight for his less than graceful lumbering, and so Julia was able to keep well ahead of her brother. Then Rodney, holding the pillow over his head, threw it successfully at his sister and said between his laughing, "That'll show you what a good shot I am."

Julia retrieved the pillow, and smiling, walked over to her work and picked it up to leave.

"Where are you going?" asked Rodney.

"I haven't time to give you a real licking," said Julia, "and if I start, I'll never finish this sewing."

"I like to see a woman who knows when she's beaten," said Rodney triumphantly.

"Well then, you must not be happy at present, but if you really want to see a person who knows when he's beaten, there's a mirror in the washroom."

***

It was a beautiful afternoon as the sun was just swaying to the west, over their (Beauchay's and Vanderkamp's) side of the county. Julia walked out past the lake along the river to a quiet place where she often went when she wanted to be alone.

Her heart felt full of many things. The scene she was embroidering was one of a young man with a fishing pole and a red cap, angling in a forest lake. The fisherman, of course, was John. She had so many conflicting thoughts about him of late. It seemed that she would never have him, as he had possibly gotten that girl in town pregnant and then would marry her.

There was something about his spirit that was so wild and free that she longed to give up everything that she had and join him somewhere in the woods far away from all people. He seemed so honest and sincere, something that came not because he made religious pretensions like Jason, or because he was consciously gentlemanly like Victor, but rather simply because he was so intense about everything that he did so that he could be nothing but honest, because to be devious would somehow soften this fierce inner desire to live that she sensed he possessed. He wanted every little detail to be important; to consume each moment as if he might have no others, so that small and large alike took on ultimate importance to him.

But all these musings were futile, for it could never be, as he was in love with another. The noise of the water was soothing to the spirit, she thought. How she loved to play with her thoughts and amuse her own soul. There seemed such a storehouse of quietude within those magic noises, which water, no matter where it is, makes as it splashes a voice that seems to imply an eternity of patient endurance. So she sat with her sewing in the shade of the trees by the river.

And not very far away, John Dow, too, was alone walking his horse who also was tired as John sorted his mind. Telling Jefferson about what he had found out about Cindy hadn't been as hard as he had feared. He hadn't wanted to go into a lot of details that would have been insignificant to what he really wanted to say.

He had so seek out Jefferson.

"I found out that I wasn't responsible," said John, to Jefferson alone.

"You mean you weren't the father?" replied Jefferson.

"Yes, that's what I mean."

There was a pause, and then John added, "I know it for a fact. My discovery happened while I was walking in the woods."

"I thought that it might have," responded the other.

"I don't love her."

"No?"

"At least not *now*. But truthfully I didn't know what I was doing."

"No."

"I don't know if I ever did or not. I don't know if it was what you would call love."

"Perhaps it doesn't matter what you call it," said his mentor, putting his hand on John's shoulder.

"I suppose that's right. I don't know really but I was never lying to myself. There was a lot I didn't see, but at least I didn't lie."

Jefferson didn't respond, but put his hand on the cross that hung around his neck.

"You know, it's funny how people can be so stupid," said John.

Jefferson's eyes changed momentarily, so John added, "*Funny* isn't the word; I'm not saying it very well, but then I've never practiced, you know—it all comes through the tangle of the words—"

Jefferson smiled. It was a comfortable expression that told John that his mentor understood and that he didn't have to say anymore.

Their eyes had really done all the talking, the words had been useless—not completely useless, as the tones helped define the eyes in subtle hues; but the signs were never the words themselves.

The two went their separate ways.

John felt the heat of the sun as he was walking west, but at the same time his nerves that were on the surface of his skin were relaying a tactile tingling from groping in a future that just moments before had been firm and knowable. Suddenly there was none of that, all that searching was thrown back on himself—but what to think about? There was nothing, only that tingling, and his consciousness of it.

That was all.

Then John thought he saw an ivory dress. He imagined it was the ivory dress that he so admired on Julia. Why was he thinking about that just now? He felt so confused. Jefferson had always told him that life wasn't worth living unless you constantly ask yourself why you are as you are and whether you should change. This was very hard advice.

Was it a mirage?

The only way to know was to hide and sneak up. And so he moved himself carefully into position and then sprung out, making a loud noise as he leapt. Julia was so startled that she couldn't even cry, but merely gulped in air so quickly that the sound of the moving air gave a sort of verbal expression of surprise. John came leaping from the bush as he grabbed her about the waist and the two tumbled to the ground. Julia's crochet ring went up in the air, flipping around several times before it came to rest precariously on a rock adjacent to the stream.

Somehow, Julia *knew* that it was Dow, though she didn't actually see his face until they were on the ground, with him lying on top of her, laughing at his practical joke. It was unusual for John to play such a joke as to surprise someone else, but the circumstances of the past days along with what seemed to be the most comical of situations, someone sitting alone in intense concentration on such a day that cried for activity, combined to inspire him.

"John Dow, you little rascal," said Julia in mock seriousness. "Do you make a habit of going about scaring young girls half out of their wits?" added Julia as she gazed up at John, as his head was blocking the sun so that the edges of his hair sparkled.

Dow put his right hand behind her head and his left around her waist as if to help her up, but for some reason he paused as he sensed the lightness of her body. It felt so delicate, more precise than he had ever dreamed a woman's body could be.

Julia paused too, not getting up immediately, but lingering just a moment under the weight of her welcomed intruder. But this moment soon passed all too quickly, as she started to get up and John, whose hands were already in position, helped her to her feet.

"I hope I didn't give you too sudden a start," said Dow with a smile.

"Well, I'm not accustomed to being startled in the midst of my sewing—my sewing?" Suddenly she remembered her work and the thought of it floating irretrievably downstream brought a flurry of emotion that occasioned an instant frantic search.

"What's the matter," asked Dow.

"My crochet, where is it?"

"What does it look like?"

"Oh, I know that's its gone. It's floated downstream forever."

"Is that it?" said Dow, pointing to the ring, which balanced precariously upon a rock, ready at any moment to descend into the river.

"Oh dear, it's going to fail into the river," said Julia as she started towards the rock. But John motioned her to stop as he adroitly stepped into the stream with one foot and lifted the precious needle work successfully from its delicate position.

"Very good," said Julia. "Now you've righted what you did when you gave me such a start."

"I'm sorry, but I saw you sitting here all alone, in such deep thought on such a bright and happy day, that I felt that it was my duty to break the spell and set you alive to the day."

"I'm quite alive, thank you. But you know, it *is* nice out," said Julia looking about her, this time seeing green in everything. "It's just that I have this needle work to do for the fair, and I have to get it finished."

"Oh, there's always plenty of time for that," replied Dow. "Days like this are rare. They almost beckon one to explore."

"Explore, yes I suppose so. I like exploring. But I do have this work that needs to be done."

"Hang the work, and let's go exploring," offered Dow.

"Well—" started Julia hesitantly.

"Good, we can start out with a little riding, though not too much as my horse gets tired easily on days like this—I mean I would too if I was carrying someone around on my back on a day when I could be eating oats in a nice cool stable."

Julia laughed and John took her hand to lead her through the tangle of flora that guarded her bower.

"All right, but just for a little while, I really must finish my work; it won't finish itself."

"You have my word, my lady," said John jokingly. It seemed to him almost like when they were children and they would put on all sorts of accents, as they played roles ranging from pirates to kings and queens.

When they got to the horse, John lifted Julia up to the saddle. She was so light, and his hands felt almost as if they could reach around her slender waist. Then John hopped up and they were off—at first at a slow trot, but then John slapped the horse's side (his signal to the horse to go faster) and suddenly the horse took off into a gallop. Julia threw her arms around John's chest and clung to him lest she fall off.

Soon they stopped, and John got down. "This is where we cross the river. It's very shallow. Do you want to ride the horse across? Or shall I carry you?"

"It doesn't matter, perhaps it would be easier to ride the horse."

"Well I don't know," said Dow. "The horse is pretty tired, I think perhaps it would be better if I carried you."

"But won't I be too heavy?"

"No trouble at all."

And with that they crossed the stream, Julia in John's arms, followed by the horse.

They walked a while, until John declared, "This is one of my favorite spots, because of all the different types of moss."

So they stopped. John opened one side of his saddlebags and took out a large sandwich wrapped in oil cloth and an apple.

"Do you want some of the sandwich?" asked John.

"No, I don't think so," said Julia when she saw the size of the sandwich that had three layers of meat and two of tomatoes. It seemed impossible that a person could actually get that into her mouth, she thought. "But I will have a bite or two of your apple." And so they ate. John addressed his big sandwich (which took him very little time to finish), and Julia consumed part of the apple before handing it over to John.

When they had finished, John asked, "Are you getting excited about the fair?"

"Yes, I suppose so. I like to see all the people all doing different things, and all the unusual smells and whatnot that make the fair what it is. Though, in all honesty, it is not the same kind of anticipation that I had as a little girl, but then I'm no longer a little girl." Julia paused momentarily, "What about you? You must be looking forward to winning some contest or other. I know all the boys talk about entering this or that. I suppose they want to win a bouquet of flowers to give to their sweethearts. Yes, all the boys who come over to our house have talked of nothing else for weeks."

"I don't know. I hadn't really planned on entering anything. I haven't any reason to, really. I'm not that excited about contests and I could care less about the flowers as I've no one to give them to." John spoke deliberately as he dug up the dirt by his heel with a little stick.

"Oh, come now, that's hard to believe. A handsome young man like you with no girl?" said Julia as she watched John's expression.

"No, I haven't anyone—at least, not now." John looked up and smiled as Julia dropped her eyes in embarrassment. "I'm alone, but I don't really mind. It's not such a bad state, actually." Then John paused and wondered about Julia. For the first time it entered his mind to want to ask about Julia, and whether she had any beaus who would give her any flowers if they won the competitions. But somehow the question seemed indiscrete. It was something he should not ask. Of course she had beaus, why hadn't he heard that half the county's eligible young men paid her a visit each month? She could pick and choose. Yet the more he tried to repress the question, the more he wanted to ask; he desired to know.

"I suppose you're looking forward to the dance?" asked John, as he felt that in this way he could indirectly find out who she might be seeing (whether singular or plural). John thought that perhaps by asking questions about who she was going to dance with he might obtain the desired information.

Julia, on the other hand, took the query as implying a leading question that would proceed to an offer to escort her, or at least for a request for the best dances on her card. However, she didn't wish to seem too anxious so she replied, "Yes, I like dances, do you?"

"They're all right," replied John, who wasn't prepared for that particular comeback. Surely she could see that he was trying to find out who else she was seeing. Not that he could ever hope to find any of her time free for himself, for what would she want with him? "The girls I always want to ask already have their cards filled, so that I rather end up dancing with someone who nobody else wants— or just leaving."

"You must ask a girl early. Everyone keeps her card open until the first day of the fair, but many girls have their cards filled by nightfall."

"I'll bet you get yours filled in the first hour," said John smiling.

"That, my dear John, is a woman's prerogative to know and not to tell."

Why wouldn't she tell him? Was he that insignificant that she wouldn't even honor him with the slightest piece of information concerning the men in her life? *But why do I deserve such consideration?* Here is a woman who is so kind, and interesting to talk to (not like Cindy, who didn't know *up* from *down*, thinking for some reason that men found a witless girl more attractive). And as Julia was rather good looking, a fact that he had not really thought about until just now (not that he had ever thought of her as unattractive, but simply that he had not given any thought to it, as other of her characteristics, such as her love of nature and science, seemed to come to mind first in his conception of her). But she *was* rather good looking, and as he thought of it more and more, she struck him objectively as being beautiful. But John wasn't sure whether it was her actual beauty that he was seeing, or a composite picture with her face as the base and over it superimposed all of her character and personality traits that he had always admired so that what he was seeing might not be her mere physical comeliness, but somehow a combination of everything.

Julia became somewhat distracted by John's stare, which soon caused color to rise to her face. "I think it's a pity that you don't enter any of the competitions when you are such a good marksman and rider. At least, that's what we've heard over on our estate."

"I'm not too bad, I suppose," said John, not wanting to be overly bold or too humble.

"You might have a good chance of winning something. There's a cash prize, you know."

"Really? Since I've never entered before, I didn't know."

"Sure. That's part of the reason that most boys enter. You know that Rodney is entering both the rifle and riding contests."

"I didn't know Rodney was a marksman," said John, as Rodney had never talked about such with John, though John hadn't seen much of Rodney since he was gifted his father's rifle.

"Well, I don't know whether you'd call him a marksman, but he's entered shooting competitions ever since he was in the juvenile division." Julia smiled as she looked into John's face, "I think he does it more for the fun of it rather than because he's especially good at it, which makes sense to me."

"I agree, a person should enter those things to have a good time and not to try to win, because then everybody but one will end up disappointed," said John.

John took the apple core and made a little hole for it with his stick. Then he dropped the core into the hole and covered it up with dirt with a motion of his shoe. "In fifty years, there'll be an apple tree right here."

"I really think you ought to enter at least one of the competitions; it'd be a shame to let Billy and Victor win so easily. Rodney tells me they are favorites."

"I may enter, but it'll be just because of your persistence, and not because I want to."

"Oh, you shouldn't do it for *my* account, I only encourage you because I think you'd do so well."

They sat in silence for a while, when Julia said, "I really have to get back to my work."

"Why don't you do it here; there's plenty of light."

Julia didn't object, so John got up and got her work out of his other saddlebag. As he brought it over to her he happened to notice that it was a scene of a fisherman with a red hat. A hope rose in his heart, an impossible coincidence that made him look again to confirm what his eyes had just witnessed. Could it be that there was a similarity between his red fishing hat and the hat of the figure in the scene? Could he be the subject of her artistry? The thought brought a feeling of tenderness and hot emotion that captivated his entire being, as he handed the needlework to Julia.

There was something thrilling about being alone in the woods with such a woman. Why hadn't he noticed her before as a woman? How could he have been so blind? Here was his childhood playmate. As children there is no real difference between boys and girls except superficially: *they* wore dresses and *we* wore pants. But now things were different. *Really* different. Why had he been so backwards? He gazed at her with new eyes, and it was exciting. And it was just possible that she felt something for him as well—as was evidenced by her work. Or could have been just a coincidence?

He had to know, but hadn't the nerve to pose the question. "You know I like to fish a lot," began Dow.

"Yes, you've gone with Rod several times."

"It's such an exhilarating thing to be fishing, especially on a day such as this."

"If you want to leave, don't let me keep you. I can find my way back," said Julia, who thought that John was trying to tell her that he wanted to leave her to go to his favorite fishing spot. But John again was surprised by this response, as Julia was either missing his message, or was deliberately giving him a hard time.

"No, I didn't mean that; I'm going tomorrow. It's just that—" John paused, he didn't know quite what he wanted to say. "Well maybe you will change my luck, next week," he said referring to the dance, but Julia thought he was still talking about fishing.

"But I thought good fishermen make their own luck. I've heard you say that to Rod many times."

"I'm not talking about fishing."

"Then what are you talking about?"

"Don't you understand? I'm talking about the dance."

"What?" replied Julia, who was so surprised by this comment that she stabbed herself with the needle.

"I want you to change my luck on getting dances from a nice girl, that is if you'd save me a spot on your card."

Julia, needless to say, was pleasantly unsettled by this declaration. She had come to accept that, in all probability, John would never notice her as a woman. But despite her confusion, she remained calm, a trait which she possessed in great quantity (that is when she was the most upset and nervous she appeared to be the most calm). "Well, you know it is the custom to never promise a particular dance to someone before the first day of the fair, but I will say this much to you, that if you find me sometime in the early part of the day, I will make sure that my card isn't completely filled."

Such a guarded response was still more than John had hoped to receive (since a part of hope is pessimistic, least one inflate one's expectations too high and precipitate a fall). But she seemed to be saying that so long as he got to her in the morning there would be a place for him!

"I'll seek you out,'" said John, "you'll know me because I'll be wearing a red carnation." Referring to a joke that the two of them shared when they were children.

"Splendid," responded Julia, " and I'll be smoking two cigars."

They both laughed when John noticed Julia's finger was bleeding from where she had stabbed herself with the needle.

"Julia, your finger!" he said, taking her hand and putting the finger to his lips to stop the bleeding.

"Oh, John, it's really nothing," protested Julia, though she said nothing more as the feeling of Dow's lips against her skin did more than adequately deal with any minor discomfort she may have been experiencing.

Then John put Julia onto his horse and took the bridle in his hands and so took Julia home.

Chapter 10

"In which Victor puts his Back to the Wall"

"Listen, I'll get it all back—who's going to beat me?" said Victor in a raised voice, that didn't portray the heightened anxiety that he was experiencing, as he knew that if it did, the chances for the loan would be shot.

"And what about that five hundred that you said you would pick up last weekend?" asked Miles with a smirk.

"I made some mistakes. I tried to win it all back too quickly, but I know better now. . . . Anyway that's not the point, I'm not asking you for money to bet at the track, but simply to bet on myself on winning the cross-country race. There's a difference; nobody can beat me."

"Well, I wouldn't say that it's impossible."

"I am. And I'm willing to bet on it."

"And what are you going to bet? Some of those pretty ladies that take a fancy to you?"

"Listen Bon, don't give me any of your guff."

"Oh, you're getting a little sensitive, eh? Now you shouldn't get sensitive, especially when you're so dependent upon the generosity of others." Bon pulled a cigar out of his pocket and bit off the end, then licked it slowly with artful precision, and finally put it into his mouth and lit it.

Victor wanted to strangle Bon. His temper was almost out of control. What made this little nigger think that he could tell a Stuart when to dance? This uppity little blackie ought to be tied to a tree and hung a while so that he could feel more at home and get some sense into his head, or wherever niggies kept in their little brains.

"You know there's nothing like a good cigar," said Bon, blowing smoke into Victor's face.

"Stop dogging the issue, Bon, will you give me the money or not?"

"If you put it that way, the answer is 'no,'" replied Miles calmly.

Victor picked up his hat and spun around and charged towards the door.

"Cause," Miles added slowly in a carefully modulated tone that was designed to make Victor stop. "If you ask in that manner, then you'll never get anything."

Victor stopped. He knew that this was his last hope, but how much more could he take of this arrogant little bastard?

"Now the way I figure it," said Miles to Victor, who had stopped just short of the door, facing the street, "if you go now, then you ain't ever going to get any money from me, and when you lose me as a friend, buddy, then you haven't got anybody left."

Victor spun around, "Are you going to give me the money?"

"How much do you need?"

"A thousand dollars."

"A thousand dollars, well, well, little Victor is moving into the big time. A thousand dollars, well, well. . . ." Miles took out his cigar and turned it slowly between his thumb and index finger. The ash was getting big, but the man made no attempt to knock it off, but rather watched it with interest as it clung to the partially-burnt cigar. "That's a lot of money, Victor."

"I know how much it is," said Victor, who so badly wanted to punch the face of that little laughing idiot so that all his facial bones would become just a soft pulp.

"You know, when you play for big stakes you take big risks."

What was this, some bad dime store novel? What was this flat nose Ubangi trying to do, audition for a movie? Why wouldn't he either give him the money and cut the by-line, or simply say cram it? Victor's hands were at his sides, fingers fully extended so that the tendons were bulging.

"What game are you trying to play, Bon?" said Victor scornfully. He might be in the inferior position financially, but he would make it known that in every other way, in *every* way, he was Bon's superior.

"Just this, my boy," began Miles, picking up every intonation in the other's voice. "I'm not a charity. I didn't get to where I am by doing people favors who couldn't reciprocate. You see the game I play *is for real*. I deal in money and other commodities, which amount to the same thing, and there's only one rule to my game, and that is to win and win big *every time*. I have to make a killing every time, Victor, or you see I might just fade out of sight, and I wouldn't like that to happen. So listen, white boy," began Bon, walking towards Victor, "if I lend you some money I expect you to pay it back," Bon was now so close to Victor that their clothes were touching, "and pay it back with generous terms." Then Bon grabbed Victor's collar and pulled down the other to his height and softened his voice to a whisper, "because we're in this *game* for one reason, to make a killing, and don't you ever forget that. Do you hear me— Victor?" Then Bon let Victor go. The loan shark then turned around and strode back to the bar where he knocked off the ash on his cigar.

"Now if you'd like to follow me?" said Bon.

Victor was beside himself. His breathing was heavy, he couldn't control that. His mind was focused upon one and only one thing but that was something *felt* and not *thought*. But soon he shuffled forward through the sawdust as he followed Bon's trail to the box of green life.

***

It was a bright morning as the sun was burning off what was left from some low clouds of the day before. Jason was riding into town to meet Victor when he saw what appeared to be Victor in the distance driving up in a car.

"Say, where did you get that?" asked Jason.

"Want to get in?" asked Victor.

"Sure, but what'll I do with my horse?"

"Oh, yeah, that is a problem. Say why don't you ride him into town and tie him up, and you and I'll go out for a drive."

"Sounds like a good idea," responded Jason, who had never ridden in an automobile before.

They drove toward town and went through the motions.

"You know," started Jason. "I've never been in one of these."

"Really?" said Victor, astonished, as many of the citizens of the town (half of them farmers) owned a Model-T.

"Yeah, father doesn't approve of them. He says they choke up the air with toxic fumes!" The two boys laughed at this foolishness.

"I'm afraid that my father is just a little behind the times."

"How did you get this? Is it yours?"

"Gracious no, where would I—" Victor stopped.

He set his jaw and then pointed to a group of birds who were frightened by the sound of the motor and flew away. "All sorts of animals are scared by these things."

"It's the motors, I think," said Jason. "They're a little loud, especially when they make those little explosions, kinda like gunshots."

"Backfiring."

"Is that it? Well anyway, those things can be a little disconcerting to say the least—at times."

"You want to know where I got it, well, a friend of ours, who owns it (and has for the past several years), lets us use it when we want. Usually we only take him up on it when something big or important comes up."

"Well, you've certainly got something big coming up."

"What?" said Victor in mock surprise.

The two of them sat awhile as Victor demonstrated to Jason the full range of capacity that the automobile could handle. Jason was a bit nervous, but didn't say a word.

"Jason?"

"Yes?"

"Do you think you can handle my bet for me on racing day?"

"Sure, whatever you say."

"I'll give you an envelope in the morning and I'll tell you who to give it to, and then just hand it over to them. There won't be anything to it. Everything will be inside the envelope."

"Sure Victor, no problem at all."

Then Victor downshifted as they approached a hill.

"If you think we were going fast before, just watch her now. She's going to fly like there's no tomorrow."

Chapter 11

"Containing an Account of Prizes and Competition"

Though it was early in the morning, even the first day of the fair had the park buzzing with people. Some of the workmen were putting finishing touches on their masterpiece as the sound of hammers finishing the work that was essentially started the day before, namely transforming a serene park near the cemetery into the arena where everyone would be changed somewhat, as the townsfolk returned in a yearly migration to this spot for two and a half days and their lives became transfigured.

Among the first arrivals were Julia and other women who were entering the embroidery contest, the first to stage in the new pavilion. There were only five women entering and so this event, like all the others, was positioned according to the projected interest and given a time accordingly. By the time that judging for the contest was over and the ribbons were awarded, most of the fair-goers would be just shuffling in.

At the Beauchay estate, Jason was up very early and walking about nervously. He was considering whether he could execute his plan of action. The consequences of this plan were serious indeed and might forever alter events in Bella County.

***

The grass was still dewy as the judging began, however already two boys had seen Julia, and one had asked her for a spot on her dance card, which she granted, as she was of the opinion that after reserving a certain number of special places, the rest should be allocated on a first comer basis, as was the custom.

It was twelve-thirty when John finally woke up. Jason, in his contemplation of his scheme, had probably just forgotten to wake John. There could be no other explanation for his failing to fulfill his promise.

John didn't know what time it was (as his drapes had been pulled shut) and lazily got dressed thinking that he had all the time he wanted to wash and eat and still make the one o'clock initial round for the rifle shoot. When he saw the clock at the bottom of the stairs, he thought that someone must be playing a trick on him, probably Jason, as it read twelve forty-five, and he still hadn't washed or eaten, but when John saw how the light was angling through the window, he became convinced that indeed he had overslept and that it really was a quarter to one.

Instantly he bolted towards the barn to get a horse and make his way to town. Unfortunately, Jason had taken their fastest horse. Not only that, but as everyone had left except John, there was nothing left except the old plug that rarely got ridden (being mostly a workhorse) except when everyone else was gone with the other horses. *I'll never get there on time*, he thought.

John mounted the horse and tried to elicit some speed from the tired old animal, but to no avail. The horse had one speed, and that was slow, and no one was going to make it go any faster.

"I could make it faster by running," said John aloud. So he tied up the animal (they were still on the Beauchay estate) and took off at full speed. Now John, though he was a very proficient rider, was not an experienced runner. He didn't think that if one had a certain distance to go that it might be best to pace himself.

Instead, John ran at near to full speed until he was exhausted (as he was also carrying his rifle, which didn't make running any easier). Breathless, John stopped when he got to Highway 3. *I can't go any further*, he felt. His chest heaved as his stomach was irritated with tense knottiness, partly from hunger and partly from his mad dash. He plopped down by the side of the road. "Now I'll never make it." He looked at his rifle.

"What things you could have done old sport," he said to the proud firearm.

Then another thought struck him: *Julia*. What if she's already got her program filled? This thought disturbed him and prompted John to get up again and try his aching legs once more. He started out when he felt a stabbing pain in his right thigh. It felt as if all of a sudden his muscle had contracted and would not relax. John stopped and braced himself with his rifle. The pain was excruciating. He couldn't do it.

He could barely walk, much less run, no matter how much he wanted to. It was impossible. Dow started to madly massage the muscle to try and restore it, but to no avail, when he heard the sound of an automobile. About three hundred yards away was an old jalopy moving very quickly as the dust that trailed it attested. John hopped into the road and put up his hands. The car will have to stop or hit me, he thought. What Dow didn't consider in his request for a ride was the added incentive of his holding a rifle (which in his excitement over getting into town, he had entirely overlooked in his appraisal of the situation). This had to enter into the driver's mind.

The car pulled to a stop. ""Take me to Varner's Junction?" asked Dow.

The man behind the wheel was not local and had never seen Dow, nor was he especially looking at him now either as his eyes were focused on the barrel of the Winchester in John's hands.

"Sure, buddy, anything you say," said the man.

John got in and after a while said, "I hate to ask you a favor, but you see I'm in quite a hurry, and if you could go as fast as you think you can, I'd certainly appreciate it."

The man didn't respond, but floored the accelerator so the car was going so fast that it was beginning to noticeably rattle, but John didn't say anything as he wanted to get there and the driver didn't say anything as he could still see the rifle out of the corner of his eye.

Then they were in town where John needed to be.

"Stop here," said John.

"Sure, buddy. Anything else you need?"

"No, thanks a lot."

The driver let John out, and then made a screeching U-turn and headed away as quickly as he could towards his Savannah weekend, which he had been saving up for after nearly a year of scrimping (he was relieved to get away with his money, his car and his life; in that order).

As it turned out, John was a little late and had some penalty points added to his score, but as this was only a preliminary round, it was not too serious. Dow, with four others, qualified for the finals which were to be held later that afternoon.

If I find that Jason, I'll let him have a piece of my mind, thought John. As he hobbled over, his leg was still very painful. *I had asked him to wake me up*—just then John saw Jefferson.

"How are you doing, John?" asked Jefferson with a smile (Jefferson was one of the few blacks who was allowed in the "white" portion of the fair, as most blacks were confined to the gambling and drinking areas on the theory that that's all that would interest them anyway).

"My leg, I've hurt a muscle."

"I can see that, you've quite a limp there."

"It'll work itself out, I'm sure."

"Well, let's hope so, we can't have you limping about like that, especially when all the hard work will start in a couple of weeks," joked Jefferson. Then he added, "Have you had anything to eat?"

John remembered that he hadn't thought about it as his mind had been occupied with other matters, however, even now, though he was quite famished, he still couldn't allow himself to be overcome by this suggestion as there were other things that took precedence in his mind. "Have you seen Julia Vanderkamp?" asked John.

"No, but she should be easy enough to spot. Just look for the greatest conglomeration of boys and there she'll probably be," put

Jefferson, again in the light vein. But John didn't particularly like the joke, as he only knew too well of Julia's popularity. Though she was never a flirt, she still seemed to attract many to her, especially on this first day of the fair when the young men were scrambling for a position in the written hierarchy of acquiring desirable partners at the dance the following night.

John didn't respond to Jefferson, but bowed his head and kicked a stone with his feet.

"I think she may be over there," said Jefferson after a quick survey of the park. Sure enough, Jefferson had spotted Julia, who was at that very moment besieged by three boys who all wanted to become engraved upon her card.

John followed with his eyes to where Jefferson was pointing, and observed his Julia surrounded by others, just as Jefferson had said. Dow was overcome by a feeling of independence. *Why should I have to go over there and compete with those others for her? If she wants them so badly, then she can just go and have them.* John put his head down again. *I'll go back to the rifle shoot and pace off the course and maybe relax my leg so that it doesn't bother my shooting.*

Just then it came to him that the only reason he was in the rifle competition in the first place was to impress that girl who was being bothered by all those others. He was fooling himself if he tried to pretend that he could just turn around and walk away from the situation, from his Julia. So he took one step in the direction of Miss Julia, when he stopped and turned to Jefferson. "Thank you," he said.

John wasn't sure what he was saying thank you about, whether it was all that Jefferson had done for him recently, or whether he was merely thanking him for pointing out the girl. John, who usually didn't make such introverted gambits, was struck by his own ignorance of his meaning.

"Good luck," replied Jefferson, smiling almost as if he knew what was going through John's head. John studied the other's face for a moment and wondered to himself for the first time in his life about how much Jefferson really knew him.

What was he seeing when he smiled in that manner? These questions weren't exactly in line with the way John reacted to the world. They propelled him into another realm, one of thoughts and endless ambiguities, which caused him to answer rather hesitantly, "Yes, thanks," as he turned and walked toward the crowd and Julia.

Julia was having a rather a difficult time as several boys were talking at the same time all about different subjects (though in one sense it was the same subject—in other words, themselves). Each wanted to make some kind of impression that would enable him to gain the precious few openings which might yet be vacant, though none of them wanted to ask directly in front of the others and so tried to turn the conversation onto their own ground and so drive away the others. The main area of difficulty in this strategy was that each was carrying out his strategy in a similar manner.

Then suddenly, Victor burst into the circle. He was a formidable figure to most of the other boys, who stopped their conversations, giving dashing Victor the first opportunity to say or do whatever he liked. Indeed, Victor was more awe-inspiring to them than usual because of his harried expression and an uncharacteristic darkening below his eyes. This made him seem more terrible than normal.

"Hello Julia," he said politely in a quiet voice, as he bowed his head slightly.

"Hello, Victor, how are you this afternoon."

"Well I would be fine if you will consent to give me the first dance at the party tomorrow night."

Everything seemed to the bystanders (the other boys) that the scene might have been written in some play, so natural it seemed for gallant Victor to approach and take the hand of fair Julia.

"Well, Victor, I'm so sorry," began Julia, with hardly a moment's hesitation.

"I have already promised that dance to another."

"Another!" screamed Victor. How could she have done that? Certainly, it was the custom to give out dances to most anyone who asked for them in order of asking, but certainly the first dance did not fall into this category, as it was one dance that was reserved for someone who one cared about. And everybody knew that Julia and he were a couple, so how could someone else have had the nerve to have asked for his dance? And after that, how could she have accepted?

Then Victor managed, "Well, then, if I can't have the first dance, can l have the last?"

"No, I'm sorry, that's promised too. But I do have one vacant space on my card for the third dance if you like."

"The third dance," said Victor, not wishing to show his vulnerability in front of the others. "Well, if that's all you have, then I will certainly take it, for I could not turn down an opportunity to dance with the prettiest girl in the county." Victor's words came smoothly, though not easily from his lips.

"So it is," she said, taking out her card and marking it so that no one else could see.

Victor wanted to ask her who it was who was rude enough to impose on her kind character and ask for the first dance, when everyone in the county knew that there was only one logical, natural choice for that position, namely, himself. But again, pride proved to be the father of restraint, and he kept his silence.

Now, John had been walking toward the group when he saw Victor approaching at a brisk pace, making no secret of where he was heading. John stopped and shuffled quietly out of range so that he might not have to talk to that poisonous tongued Victor, who never had anything nice to say to him, and also, perhaps primarily, because he wanted to give Julia the opportunity of signing someone who would make a far better match than he would on her card. Victor, he thought, was everything that he was not, except as a rider, which he hoped to show the other in dramatic fashion the next day.

After Victor left, the group itself dissolved and Julia was left alone to complete her journey to her parents, who were sitting under the shade. But before she could go very far, John hobbled over to her.

"Hello there, Julia," called John.

Julia turned, but recognized the voice even before she saw the face. "Hello John," she cried in reply when she noticed his limping. 'What's the matter with your leg?"

"Oh, I just hurt a muscle coming over here this morning."

"Is it serious?" asked Julia, who wanted to gently rub his leg so that it would feel better, but who naturally would never commit such an action in public.

"No, it's not too bad. It should be all right tomorrow for the horse race."

"Then you decided to enter," she said, in a tone that revealed her obvious contentment as she had been the one who had suggested that he enter the competition.

"Yes, and I've entered the rifle shoot, also."

"How did the morning round go?"

"Well four people in my group qualified for the finals. I was in the last group. I couldn't see whether Rodney made it or not, but then he was in the first group. My group was mainly for guys like me who've never been in the rifle competition before."

"And the finals are this afternoon?"

"Yes," said John as he became aware of how beautiful Julia looked in her dress, which was very simple, but yet seemed to reinforce her basic goodness.

"Well, I shall certainly make an effort to go see it."

She could have said that she wanted to see it because I was in it, he thought, *or say that she wanted to see her two men (me and Rodney). But instead she makes such an ambiguous statement that I cannot tell why exactly she wants to go—is it to see me or her brother—or someone else?*

Then John remembered that Julia had been in a competition herself, just that morning. "How did you do?"

"What?" replied Julia, somewhat startled by this oblique question.

"With your sewing."

"My needlework? Well," began Julia slowly. "I was very lucky and won first prize."

John adored the simple, matter-of-fact manner in which she described her success. She neither flaunted her achievement, nor had she employed that other tool people often use, namely false humility, which ends up as more of an egoistic adventure than bragging as it requires the other to pull it out of the fortunate one, who all the time is being built up by the original feat as well as the new laud of being so humble about the entire operation.

This feeling of initial warmth blended into one of admiration and pride over her endeavor. "That's very good. I'm very happy for you," said John, scarcely knowing what words were falling, though they reflected his feelings. John's communication was like drops compared to the flood of her achievement. Why couldn't he just say this?

"Thank you, but it always helps to have a good subject for one's work."

John understood this reference as it confirmed his suspicion—that indeed he had inspired that scene of the fishing. What he didn't understand was that he was the center of all the scenes.

"Are you walking somewhere?" asked John.

"Well, I do have to get back to my parents, but I have time to talk a little if you do."

John smiled. *What else would I do with my time than talk to such a lovely woman, who seems to like me, and whom I adore passionately*? "I don't suppose you remembered our conversation the other day," began Dow after an awkward silence.

"Yes, I remember."

"Well, I talked to you about, well, a little problem about dances—do you remember?" said Dow, wishing that Julia would get the hint and not force him to complete the question. John had a rather hard time asking other people to ever do him a favor of any kind as he never wanted to cause any inconvenience to others.

"Yes," said Julia.

"Well," began John, seeing that he would have to go through with it. "I was wondering whether you still had any openings on your dance card, and if you did, whether you would give me one?"

Julia smiled. "I have four, the first dance, the last dance, the second dance, and the tenth dance. Which one would you like?"

"Well, to tell you the truth," began Dow with a laugh, "I'd like all or any of them."

Julia looked at John for a brief instant, as their eyes met in a moment of intense communication. Then Julia took out her card and wrote something down. "Very well, John, you have me for four dances. I hope you don't step on my feet, for I shall have to put up with you four times."

Julia's voice is light and rhythmic, Dow thought, *so much different than my ramblings*. How quickly she threw that statement off to him. It seemed so unbelievable that he could have all four dances, and yet her voice had been so light that perhaps it wasn't the demonstration of affection but merely the rendering of the information.

"I should be very delighted," replied Dow.

"So shall I," responded Julia in the same tone so that John couldn't tell whether she was seriously showing him her feelings, or merely being polite. Had he been too crude in his remark that he wanted all of the dances? Was her response merely the proper social response required, or was there some other combination?

"Well, I should get back to my family, as they are waiting for me to begin lunch, and Rodney is awful when his lunch is late," laughed Julia.

"Goodbye," said John as it seemed to him that his voice just lingered in the air as she turned and disappeared into the dots of color.

***

That afternoon, John found that he was scheduled to shoot last in each of the three rounds. Billy Thompson was first and had quite a following among the crowd.

After the first two rounds, it was fairly even among the eight contenders (except for Rodney, who was deep in last place). Billy was leading by only a few points. Then on the last target, Billy got six points away from a perfect target at the furthest distance shooting off-hand (standing). This was greeted by those in attendance as an indicator that the contest should be stopped then and there and the ribbon and cash prize be given to Mr. Thompson. Indeed, his father came out of the crowd to shake his hand, as did his friends. Off-hand is the hardest to score maximum points (in comparison to the other two positions, laying down and kneeling). When the targets are moved back to the furthest point, this usually means a drop in score. And as Billy's closest opponents would have to have a near perfect target to beat Billy, it did seem almost silly to continue and only embarrass the other contestants. But for formality's sake, the match continued as one after the other made their futile attempts (though one fellow actually tied Billy's feat of six away from a perfect score, drawing applause from the crowd, though he started from a point hopelessly far behind).

As Dow took the line for his final turn, many of the people were walking to the prize stand in the park so that they could get a better view of Billy when he got the award. Dow's leg was twitching slightly, but he didn't notice it as his mind was fully upon the target.

"Bullseye," said the scorekeeper on John's first shot. *All I need are nine more*, thought John, who needed to get three from a perfect score on his last target to tie Billy.

"Bullseye," said the scorekeeper after John's next three shots. Most of the people were gone. It was like a practice session. John felt much more at ease in the solitude, as he imagined that everyone had left (which was almost correct, except for six spectators, among whom included Jefferson, Julia, and four drunks, who were foolishly waiting for their turn).

"Nine," yelled the scorekeeper after John's sixth shot. Dow had four shots to go and two had to be bullseyes.

"Nine," called the scorekeeper after the next shot.

John frowned. There didn't seem to be any reason for that shot to have missed. He quickly fired—"Bullseye,"—and again—and again; John fired his last three shots rapidly.

They were all perfect.

John put down his rifle and the scorekeeper rushed out to the target, almost as if he thought his eyes might be deceiving him from that great distance through the glass. When he came back he was dumbfounded.

"Young man," he said. "You have just gotten a near perfect target, just two away." He went back to his figures and started marking numbers down in a frenzy, when he looked up again and declared, "You have beaten Thompson by one point!"

John smiled and turned to trudge away when he felt a hand on his shoulder. It was Jefferson. "Where are you going?" asked Jefferson.

"I don't know," said John. "Home, I guess."

"Don't you want to pick-up your ribbon and money?"

"I'll take the money, if they'll send it to me, but do I have to go to some silly ceremony?"

Jefferson put his arm around the boy's shoulders and started leading him towards the park. He could appreciate what the lad was going through.

"You know you had one more spectator besides those lushes over there."

"On really?" responded John, "who?"

"Miss Vanderkamp was a constant spectator. She stayed until the scorer said that you had gotten an almost perfect score. She left in the direction of the park. I have a hunch that she's by the awards stand right now."

John didn't respond, but then he didn't put up any resistance either as Jefferson led him into the park. At the awards stand, everyone was prepared to give Billy his prize and then go to The Marsh and have a drink on it (it was no secret where the stuff could be obtained). The ceremony had even gone so far as for the master of ceremonies to have just finished delivering a little speech about the winner, and how Billy was a fine young man (even though he was the speaker's nephew) and an asset to the community. That the rifle competition represented everything that this young generation often scorned, namely the respect for tradition and the ways of the past which were so important. And that by winning this competition, Billy was helping to inspire moral virtue in his peers. It was a moving speech which even brought out the handkerchiefs of a few ladies, but when it was done and Billy had already stepped up upon the platform, the scorekeeper came trotting from the range.

"And here is the scorekeeper for the official results," declared the master of ceremonies.

The scorekeeper was out of breath from his run, so that he climbed the platform slowly.

"Would you care to read out the official results?" asked the master of ceremonies. Then without waiting for a response he added, "Would the boys whose names are called, please step forward and receive their ribbons, or prize money as the case may be." These last words were spoken to Billy.

"In third place," started the still winded scorekeeper, "with a total of 243 points. . . is Grant Wilson." There was polite applause as Grant bashfully made his way to the stand and was handed his ribbon. Grant was going to step down when he was reminded that all of them were supposed to stand together (as it was decided some time ago that to stand together was a sign of good sportsmanship).

"In second place," the scorekeeper cleared his throat, "with a total of 254 points is . . . was Billy Thompson." There was silence for a moment as the master of ceremonies started laughing, then stopped as it suddenly entered his head what had just been read, and so he snatched the score sheet to see for himself. Just at this moment, as if the grabbing of the scoresheet broke some kind of spell, there was shouting and demands by the people to know what was going on. They had all seen Billy win and what was this scorekeeper trying to do? Was he fiddling with the figures so that they would come out differently? There were grumblings that 'figures never lie, but liars figure.'

Billy himself didn't know quite what to do; whether to go up and get his ribbon or to walk away in protest of a bad decision. Desperately his eyes searched for his father so that he could see what he wanted him to do.

The scorekeeper, conscious of what might be going through everyone's head, began to shout. "The winner of the rifle shoot," he began, but barely could be heard.

"With a total of 255 points after an almost perfect last target, is John Dow!"

From the back of the crowd there was a clapping that could not be heard, the sound of two small hands against the fury of the crowd.

Then there were shouts of, "Where is this Dow, anyway?"

"Who is that?"

"I've never heard of him."

"Dow, Dow, there's no farmer by that name around here."

Just then Jefferson and Dow appeared. The scorekeeper motioned to John to come forward, so John began walking briskly towards the platform. As the scorekeeper motioned to John, the noise stopped as everyone turned their heads to witness the mysterious winner, who had somehow stolen the prize away from its rightful owner.

As John mounted the platform, there were grumblings as the crowd murmured, "I've never seen him."

"Oh sure that's the boy who works in the casino."

"He doesn't work at the casino."

"Looks like a nigger to me," said one man.

"That he does," said another. "Not full-blood, but he's got in 'em; you can tell."

John took the prize of fifty dollars and the ribbon and stuffed them both in his pocket and started off the stand in a hurry. Poor Billy, in all the confusion, wasn't even handed his second place ribbon.

"You're a rich man," said Jefferson on the way back to the farm.

"Nobody wanted me to win. They all wanted Billy."

"A rifle shoot isn't a popularity contest. Besides, I don't think it was that people didn't want *you* to win, it's just that they wanted Billy, because he's known by more people. If people knew you, they'd have wanted you just as much."

"I wish I didn't have to stand in front of all those people."

"You did fine."

"At least I got the money," John put after several minutes.

"You had two strong fans rooting for you," said Jefferson, but John didn't smile, but only kept checking his pocket to make sure that the money hadn't fallen out.

***

As the rose fingered child of the morning stretched forth a new day, Victor was already up and about. He had heard the results of the rifle shoot, and that Julia had been there clapping for Dow. It had never entered his mind, except for fleeting moments, that Julia could ever like such a disgusting fellow. He remembered isolated incidents in the past and other times he had had inklings of suspicion, but now it seemed quite evident. How could there be anything so degrading than to have to compete with such a piece of black refuse as that bastard who was kept as a charity ward by kind old Samuel Beauchay? *I won't compete. Either she takes me and me alone or she doesn't. That's all there is to it. I won't go chasing after her when she has this oddness about her. I will give her up, rather than. . . .* There was a tearing tension within his breast as he realized what he was saying.

If she'll not have me properly, I won't have her. I've my good name to think about. He knew that he wanted her more than anything else, and this fact disturbed him, but at this point of emotional unrest, each new disturbance now served only to make him tired. *I've got to snap out of this or I'll lose the race today and any chance at financially getting back on my feet again.*

The two young men were to meet in town, however; Jason had beat Victor to it as he sat in a chair just outside The Marsh. Victor wanted to instruct Jason very exactly, even though he had written directions on the envelope. This was because Victor's entire future depended upon his winning the horse race tomorrow, and every cent to had be wagered on his victory. Anything else would be a tragedy.

"There is a man named Bon. Miles Bon is his name. He's a black guy who is mighty mean. He'll connect you to the man taking the money. He sits in a back room behind the poker table," said Victor.

"It's all very simple," Victor said again after a hesitation, "There's a thousand dollars in the envelope. Bet it all on me to win. It's all or nothing." Victor knew he had to pay Bon back or things could get complicated. Only a win with significant gambling money could make this possible.

"You don't look too good today, Victor. Are you sure that you will be able to compete? I mean, you look pretty sick."

"I'll be all right, don't worry about me," snapped Victor.

"Suit yourself," replied Jason. "And your bet is everything on you to win."

"That's right. Don't make any mistake," snapped Victor.

"I won't, but I do wish you'd take care of yourself. I have my own money on this race for you to win."

"Cram your goddamn money," said Victor as he closed his eyes and pressed his hands against the sides of his nose.

***

It was the middle of the afternoon the next day when John saw Julia again. She saw him in the park (fair grounds) and approached him.

"I want to congratulate you on your fine win yesterday."

"Thanks, but I'm afraid that I wasn't the popular choice."

"I was there. I knew you could beat Billy all along."

"Then you did come," said John, pretending that he didn't know.

"Yes, I watched every one of your shots."

John smiled. The afternoon sun was getting rather hot as everything seemed a bit muggy.

"It's been an interesting fair," said John finally, wishing to say something. It was true that he had liked the previous day, but whether it had anything to with the fair itself was a question that he did note.

"Are you looking forward to the dance tonight?" asked Julia.

"Of course, or should I say more precisely, to four dances tonight."

John smiled to himself. That compliment came off rather well, he thought, and he congratulated himself. So often he found it rather difficult to appropriate the correct words for what he wanted to say to Julia, but when he didn't think about what he was going to say, somehow, it always came out better.

The two talked for over an hour, when Julia had to leave to take her shift at the booth for Georgia's charities.

As they parted, at the other end of Main Street Jason was entering The Marsh.

Dear Victor, Jason imagined, would be severely hurt if he didn't win his prize money. It would probably take away all of his loose cash, for at least eight months or so (the time that Jason imagined it would take for Victor to recover the losses he had incurred the past weeks). Victor had looked so tired that it seemed doubtful to Jason that he would win. Jason knew that John was entering the race and that John was a very good rider as well—not as good as Victor in general racing or even cross-country racing, which John was much better at—but considering that Victor was in such bad shape, Jason thought that it was probable that Victor would lose.

It was probably for this reason that Jason declined to bet his own money on the race and bet Victor's money ($250) on Victor to win; $250 on Victor to place (meaning second) and the rest ($500) on Ed Crow to win. Jason must *not* have thought Victor would win, so he placed the bets differently than he had been directed. He could have had no other motive.

"Got it," said the man as he handed Jason a stub of paper that recorded the bets.

In the street, the officials were already preparing the starting line for the race even though it was an hour and a quarter away.

Soon however, the vacant streets were filled with people as they flocked around to see the main event of the fair. It would be safe to say that every single person connected with the fair was at some point along Robert E. Lee or Magnolia Avenues (or about the grounds for that matter, as they were also along the route) to see for themselves what promised to be an exciting race.

As the horses lined up, Stuart looked about for Jason to see if things were all right, but he could not see him as Jason was sitting on the steps of the church a few hundred yards away from the starting line.

Many of the horses were nervous and didn't want to cooperate in front of all the people. Julia was prominent near the starting line in her pink dress as both Dow and Stuart waved to her, though it's needless to say which she responded to with more vigor. But none of these things seemed to affect either Victor or John, who were both determined to do one thing: win the race.

The horses lined up and there was a long silence punctuated with miniscule breaks in the surface tension. Then the gun fired and the race had begun. John's horse reared up at the gun and turned sideways; though Dow was quickly able to rectify this, he had still lost valuable yardage in the precious battle.

Many of the people commented on Dow as his horse faltered. "Isn't that that sharpshooter?"

"Yes, Dod, or Dow or Doe or something like that."

"Does he think he can win a double?"

"I don't know, but anybody that can come from behind and almost get a perfect target like he did, better not be counted out."

"He sure was a good shot, I'll give him that."

"I've never seen such a shot in all my days."

As they passed over the first bridge, Victor was in the lead followed by three horses closely and four more in a pack several lengths back; John was last. The road riding wasn't easy for John, but when the race moved to the fields, then John made a move from the rear to join the first pack of horses.

John was now in fifth place. Victor was riding comfortably in first place with a two and a half length lead. As they entered some woods (actually a windbreak between fields) one of the horses in front of John fell, throwing off the rides and causing the horse directly in front of John to stumble, too.

John couldn't react fully in time, but his horse luckily helped him as he cleared the other two horses with little to spare, just missing the leg of one of the riders. Now, through no real effort of his own, John was in third place about six lengths behind Victor. This area was very familiar to Victor, who was beginning to feel the effects of the fatigue and tension. He rode without thinking.

It was at the first fording of a river that John caught up to Victor as John's horse was an excellent water animal. John knew that he had a chance. They came out of the water at the same time, though John had the inside position on the turn which was to his advantage. Victor bore down when he saw his rival, and applied the stick with force, and passed into an almost delirious sate of concentration and desire to beat this Dow who had become almost a symbol of everything that had gone wrong lately. He felt as if he were racing with something besides another rider; it was something inside him, and outside him at the same time, he couldn't tell. All that Victor could feel was his desire and his will to destroy this Dow and everything connected with him.

As they hit Highway Three, Dow was in front by a full length, but John knew that Victor's horse was faster on the road surface than his, so he endeavored to move in front of Victor to try and block Victor's attempts to pass. But young Stuart was not to be denied, and being an experienced rider he moved to the flank of Dow's animal and when the other moved to block his passage, he hit Dow's horse with his whip, causing it to hesitate just momentarily— just enough time for Victor to pull alongside of John. It's never good to look at your opponent during a race as the jockey is taking his eyes off of the surface and as well loses a certain contact with his animal, but both men were looking at each other as they struggled for the lead over Sawyer's bridge, which only allowed one horse at a time to cross the old wooden structure.

As they got nearer to the bridge, Victor tried to pull away from Dow, but to no avail. John's horse was keeping up with the faster animal at this stage of the race. Then Victor took his whip and turned and slashed at his adversary, causing him to lean to the opposite side of the horse's neck for protection, though it was of little value as Victor again struck savagely at John, and Dow moved his horse into Victor's so that they almost were touching, then rose and caught Victor's hand as he tried to strike John again.

John pulled at Victor to try and take his whip away. Suddenly the two realized that they were at the bridge. One of them would have to give way to the other as there was only room for one horse on the bridge. But neither was willing to do so, for in the final two hundred yards, not much could be done to gain back such an advantage as would be procured by going over the bridge before the other.

John let go of Victor's arm and bore down, determined to be the one who would be first over the bridge. The two horses were neck and neck as they both hit the wood at the same time, forcing a collision between the two animals that propelled them both off the bridge and into the water over, or actually through, the thin wooden railing on the sides.

John was thrown from his horse, but Victor remained in the saddle, as he started his horse across the river. John quickly recovered and just grabbed his horse's saddle as the animal was beginning to cross on its own accord. The water was deep and the animals were straining against the water. Dow was trying to pull himself to his mount and onto the saddle before the horse reached the other side. He made it to his horse's neck when the animal reached the opposite bank. Victor was already climbing the bank, when his horse slipped, momentarily giving John time to get on his horse and start up his side of the bank which was considerably easier.

Behind them they could hear the sound of the other horses who were just hitting the bridge. In another moment, both riders were atop the bank and heading down the final stretch, Victor slightly ahead of Dow. The two were straining as both had lost their riding sticks in the water. They were riding with their horse's understanding of what was expected of them. Close behind were the other riders, who had closed the gap to a half-a-length. Gradually John began to make up the head difference between the two. There was a block to go. The two horses were straining for every inch of ground. Victor veered his horse towards John's, trying to move him off the street, but to no avail, as John used his foot to keep the other away.

A half block to go and John was a half head behind. Both riders were poised in a crouch to keep their centers of gravity low and forward. Again, a veer by Victor, so slight, but it brought the response of John's foot, which was countered by Victor's boot in John's shin. There was a shooting pain in his leg as John and his horse made one final effort at the finish line. They were moving forward! They passed Victor, but now the race was over. Had he passed Victor in time? John slowed his horse as the screams of the people were now becoming apparent to him, and the excitement which had been slowly building was now making him shake. Dow dismounted as Jefferson and Samuel Beauchay were there to greet him.

"You did an admirable job there, John," said Beauchay. "I think you may have nipped him there at the tape."

John didn't answer, but felt rather nauseous and faint.

"Come over here and sit down, my boy," said Beauchay, bringing John over to the sidewalk. All John wanted to do was lie down and sleep, his body was numb and all that he could feel was his disorientation and nauseous stomach.

"I thought that was pretty shoddy the way Stuart cut off your lane there. It looked as if you two were having a kicking match out there. I would have taken my whip to him. Why boy, you're all wet," said Beauchay, discovering that there was something strange.

"I thought all the fordings were rather shallow," he repeated, as if he was trying to get John to tell of his own free will the un- sportsmanship conduct of Victor. But Dow was too overcome by it all to say much of anything.

"Let's take him over and buy him a lemonade or something," offered Jefferson.

"Yes, that's a good idea."

"Do you want to come, or should we bring it to you?" asked Beauchay. John shook his head indicating that he didn't care, or that he couldn't answer.

"We'll bring them here," said Beauchay as the two left.

Though there were not very many people around young Dow after the race, Victor was swarmed with people who were curious at how it had been such a close race.

"What happened Victor?"

"I told you that Dos feller was mighty good."

"That's not Dos, it's Doct."

"You're both wrong, its Doe."

"Well he's pretty good with a rifle and with a horse."

"I'd never heard of him before yesterday."

"Well that's how it is you know, one minute you heard of some guy."

"How are you feeling, Victor? That was a narrow win you had there."

"Yea, you just nipped him, had it been five feet longer, you'd have lost."

"Excuse me gentleman," said Victor, trying to extricate himself from the mob to find out the results.

Then his eyes focused across the street where Dow was sitting alone, when a woman approached him. It was Julia.

"You were splendid," she said.

"Hello," managed Dow, who was leaning against a post for support.

"Why you're all wet," she said, "that's not supposed to happen."

"We decided to take a swim, to relieve the tension," said Dow with a smile. The sight of Julia raised his spirits. She had come to him before Victor; at least he was winning in something.

"It was so close, I think they're having a difficult time deciding who won," said Julia.

"If there's any question, you know who it'll be," said Dow, but Julia didn't take any notice of this, but saw red soaking through his pant leg.

"You're bleeding," she cried. "Pull up your jeans and let me see what's happened."

"I'm too tired," said John.

"Don't you know that it might be serious?" she said, pulling his pant leg from his boot and rolling it up, exposing the gash that Victor's racing spurs had made in John's shin.

Well at least now I have something wrong with both legs," said John with a smile.

"That will have to be cleaned-up," she said as she got up and left.

Victor broke free from the group around him to look for the officials, when the results were given. Victor was proclaimed the winner and John second. Somehow there was no feeling of elation in Victor at having won. It was almost as if he had been expected to win so that winning was not at all unusual, but the narrowness of his win had been, in a way, a defeat of sorts. And to have been challenged so closely by Dow brought his ire to a head. Had there not been so many people around. . . . People were grabbing his hand and slapping him on the back, congratulating him on his showing; everyone's happy when the favorite wins because then the maximum number of people are winners also, as their bets pay off. Stuart started pushing his way through the mass of people, not really knowing where he was going, but simply walking for open space, when suddenly he found himself standing in front of Dow, who was still seated in the same place, leaning against the post.

Victor stopped and stared at the other. John looked up and saw Victor, and then pulled himself to his feet and extended his hand. "Nice race, Victor."

But Victor responded, "Get out of my life nigger," and then spit at John, landing his spittle on John's face, then turned around and marched away.

"I don't think that was such a good idea Victor."

"Do you know who that is?"

"I think he probably does, he just raced against him didn't he?"

"But that fellow is a dead shot, no sense fooling around with the likes of that."

"I like to see good sportsmanship."

"That's bullshit; grow up."

"I still wouldn't fool around with the likes of him. Why, he got a near perfect off-hand target."

***

That night at the dance, before things had started and everyone was still arriving and having some punch that the wife of the president of Alter Books had prepared, as she did every year, and some cookies that W.A.C.K.O. had provided (though they had threatened to boycott this year because of the exotic dancing show, which was the topic of conversation in the stag circles), John hobbled in expecting to see Julia, but she had not arrived as yet. John came alone as Jason did not care to dance (as he thought himself too awkward) and Mr. Beauchay never went to a social function of that nature since his wife passed away. John felt somewhat uncomfortable among all the people. He recognized many faces, but it seemed that no one cared to come up to him and ask him what he thought of something or other. Then he recognized Jake Murdock, and walked up to him, "Hello, Jake."

"I saw you in the race today. You gave a good accounting of yourself."

"I did all right, I suppose."

"All right, you did better than that, I thought you won, but it's hard to tell from the angle which I was watching from."

"Do you have many dances lined up?" asked John.

"About six, how about you?"

"Four."

"Well, it should be a fairly good evening for both of us then."

"Yes, I hope so."

Just then Julia came in and so John excused himself and went over to see Julia.

"I understand that you're to be congratulated," said Mr. Vanderkamp. "Rodney's told us about your dramatic win yesterday, and we all saw how close you came to making it a double today."

"Thank you, sir."

"Perhaps next year you will be more fortunate."

"Yes, sir."

"Well we have got to get some of that delicious punch before it's all gone."

The party passed on to the punch table, except Julia, who lingered to talk with John.

Things seemed to lighten for John when he talked with Julia. It hadn't been a long time that they had been seeing each other and talking as lovers do, but to John it seemed that he knew so much about Julia already that they must have been lovers for the entirety of their lives. There were so many mutual interests between the two, and they each held similar outlooks and dispositions. There seemed to be so many common features that John couldn't believe that this girl had been so close to him all the time and that he had been chasing after someone so far away, who really shared nothing with him except a physical attraction.

"You know I like you very much," said John suddenly and out of context with the conversation.

"Well, that was sudden. When did you decide that?"

"It seems that I've felt it all along."

"Oh really?" said Julia in a tone that said, *if you felt this way all along then what were you doing running around with Cindy Pancroft?*

"Yes. You and no one else."

Julia smiled and looked at him as if he was giving her a line that she wouldn't swallow.

"Well, there was one other, but that's all over. I didn't know what I was doing. And besides, I never really felt anything for her. I mean anything real—real like I feel with you."

But before she had a chance to respond, the band started making noises that meant that it was time for men to find their partners and take their positions on the dance floor.

"Shall we go?" asked Julia. "I believe that you are my first dance."

John smiled, "I'd be delighted," he said in an affected Virginia accent. John was not a good dancer, but it seemed that with Julia he was smoothly moving about the floor in a flowing rapture that had no boundaries. There was John and Julia, and Julia and John, and that's all he had to know on earth and all he wanted to know. In the corner of the room, unseen by John, was Victor Stuart, who had come after the first dance had begun to see who it was that Julia had accepted for her first dance. He had also come to see if he could locate Jason, who had his stub for the bet, which he needed to cash in for his money. After the race, there had been too much commotion for him to get his money (as many people didn't come by for their money until a day or so afterwards anyway), but Victor wanted it that night. The sight of Dow disgusted him.

What was the matter with Dow? Why hadn't he gotten up and engaged a fight when he, Victor, spat in his face. Why had he just sat there and taken it? What was the matter with him? Couldn't he see that *he,* Victor, hated his very being with an all-consuming passion? Hadn't he made that evident?

Then the dance was over and John gave a slight bow to his partner and turned around and bumped into Victor, who was coming to jerk Julia away from Dow, but had been a little late, and instead was bumped backwards a few steps by the stronger Dow.

"Oh, excuse me, Victor," said John as he hadn't seen that anyone was there, as in fact, just an instant before there hadn't been and if Victor hadn't been in such a hurry to get to Julia and try to make a scene of grabbing her away from Dow, he wouldn't have collided with Dow.

"Watch what you're doing, you clumsy oaf," said Victor.

"You shouldn't be walking so quickly about the dance floor, young man," reprimanded Mr. Jackson, the chaperone but Victor didn't respond, and merely walked up to Julia.

"You should be more careful Victor," said Julia. "You might hurt someone."

"And you shut-up, or that person is liable to be you," said Victor under his breath so that Julia could just make it out, as Stuart took her hand and gave it a painful squeeze to show her that he was the more powerful of the two.

As they danced, Victor led forcefully, as he felt a compulsion to almost overpower his partner and grip her until she smothered in his arms. Her light petite body seemed to stoke his desire to dominate completely and consume her entirely. The music drove him to a recognition that he would have to win her by force. She was no longer a little girl simply playing with Dow and little farm animals. Things had changed. This was not acceptable. She must be driven to feel something. She must know that she belonged to *him*, Victor. He would not allow what was *his* to be robbed from him.

It had been known by everyone that he was to get young Julia, and that she was to become Mrs. Victor Stuart. Didn't she understand that she was violating the calm order of things? He had been perfectly willing to go along with events as long as he was the appointed victor? But now she was choosing to violate the rules, and go outside that calm framework where their relationship had been so carefully contrived. He felt perfectly free to use whatever means that he felt necessary to possess his object: Julia.

Victor drew Julia closer to him, but she resisted. What was she doing? Didn't she know that he could throw her to his feet if he wanted to? He could make her grovel before him in abject humility. Here was this loathsome creature who thought she could pit her puny powers against those of his own. What could a mere woman, fragile with her thin neck and hollow bones, do to thwart the desires of a man of destiny? Victor drew her to him again, but by now the music had stopped and Julia pulled away on the pretext of a bow, and John was soon at her arm for the next dance. But Victor wouldn't give up. He put his hand on John's shoulder and said, "What do you think you're doing, lover boy?"

"It's my dance, if you don't mind," responded John as his muscles tightened.

"But I do, lover boy, I do, " said Victor in the same even tone that accentuated the ends of each syllable in exaggerated enunciation.

"I'm sorry, but this is my dance. You may look at the young lady's card if you don't choose to believe me," responded Dow as he took Stuart's hand off of his shoulder and tried to walk away with Julia. Everyone had stopped as they were intently watching the conflict between the two who had fought on the race course earlier and had words after the race, and now were again at it over the most volatile of subjects: love. It was a kind of paralysis that grips people when suddenly they realize that the mood wasn't what they thought it was (i.e., a gay party where everyone was having a good time in light amusement) but was instead turning out to be something much more serious. In their midst, a confrontation of the most serious variety was setting up: a confrontation that nobody knew just how to deal with. All eyes were on John as he turned around with Julia and began to walk in the other direction.

"Come back here, boy," said Victor as his diction took on a more vicious tone.

But John kept on going.

"I said come here nigger before I have to come and get you."

John stopped and turned around deliberately. "You know, Victor, you're making a fool out of yourself. Calm down, there's nothing to get so worked up about. You'll get your chance to dance later; have a little patience. Perhaps you'd like a glass of punch or something to cool yourself off."

"I don't want punch. I want to dance."

"Well," began John who had started to turn around again and said over his shoulder, "If you're so intent on dancing, I'm sure there is someone who will be willing to dance with you, if you care to ask around."

Victor couldn't take any more as he rushed at Dow. That's when the spell of the crowd was broken and several of the attendant men grabbed Victor and pulled him towards the door.

"Let me go, goddamn it, I want to fight that bastard, let me go I tell you!"

But scream though he did, Victor was taken outside and made to get onto his horse and leave. Instantly, the band picked up a fast snappy· number and the couples slowly returned to the spirit that had just been interrupted, and in a half hour it was almost as if nothing had happened. Though there were some murmurings among some of the men—"Don't know what's got into that Stuart."

"Can't you see that other feller, Dod, has stolen his girl, if I'd been Stuart I'd have slugged him."

"I don't know, I'd never fool with the feller who just won the rifle shoot, no matter what he did."

"After all, you may not know it but Julia Vanderkamp has been going with Victor for almost two years. They were almost engaged."

"Really, you mean that guy's stole his girl?"

"Did Victor call him a *nigger*?"

"I don't know, but he does look a little black, doesn't he?"

"I'll say he does. That's probably how he can ride and shoot so well, you know them coloreds are real good at sports like that. Natural hunters, they are, just like in Africa."

"If it was me, I'd have socked him one."

"I don't know, I'd never fool with the feller who just won the rifle shoot, no matter what he did."

As the night wore on, John and Julia talked exclusively at the intervals almost as if there was no tomorrow. Their excitement was that of discovery. Both were so enraptured with every word the other said that they could not keep their bubbling conversation within the limits of any given time period, yet interruptions came during dances, which seemed interminably long, until they were united once again. But soon the last dance was being played and John held Julia in his arms as the music flowed so sweetly. It seemed that he must be on another level of reality. All seemed so peaceful, serene, he couldn't have wished for a more pleasant evening. And when Julia was leaving with her family, John squeezed her hand one last time as the music of the band played on and on in his memory.

Chapter 12

"Some Reflections which Jason has Before his Anticipated Departure to College"

Jason was finding it hard to go to sleep lately, in excitement. True, he didn't have a fur coat, for who would wear one of those in Georgia! But he had everything else ready for college, and would be leaving soon. How long he had waited for this day; how close he seemed to yet one more step in his plan for himself.

He remembered his long hours with Mr. Russel and all the extra work he did, while John simply dallied or had gone fishing. His hard work had finally paid off. He was going to a big name university and would return a polished man of business ready to (at first) help his father with the estate, and any extra capital that he might have laying around (and later) to expand his dreams into the amalgamation of wealth of which he'd dreamed. He would transform the backwards South, which he felt was still living in the Reconstruction, and build himself an empire: an empire of industry.

How often he would awake early dreaming about some great vision of himself, and then he would be unable to go back to sleep as the thought had sallied from the back to the front of his mind where he couldn't wrench it out.

Mr. Beauchay, he would be addressed. Or possibly just J.B.

Yes, he liked that; J.B.--*What do you think we should do J.B.? Shall we move into Chicago? What about the West Coast J.B.? J.B. do you think our Texas holdings. . . .*

Yes, Jason felt he was quite up to the task of leading the state of Georgia back into the Union once again. No longer would the South be pushed around like a group of naughty boys who had been found truant and are made to scrub the black boards while the other children go out and play. No, sir, things were going to change.

Often when Jason woke up in the morning, he would dress and go out for a walk. He would walk towards the east, where the industrial power in the country was; the east, where the sun rose each morning in its enormous energy. Just think, he thought, what a profit a person could make if somehow he could harness some of that wild untamed energy of the sun. That was what it was all about: taming natural, crude energy and fitting it so that it could run efficiently for the good of Mankind. It was all like a giant machine that someone was constructing a little at a time, setting certain parts to running before the entire machine was operational. Man, anyway, but was just a machine. He wanted to control that machine to produce finished products of wealth and power. Most people became so enraptured by the parts of the incomplete machine that they couldn't see that all they were enchanted with, were merely incomplete sections of a giant whole—a giant machine: the machine of industry. For after all, weren't certain reactions continually taking place? Some people foul up their machines with excesses in various areas, so they can't utilize the full capacity of their machines, which is enormous. But a few keep themselves running smoothly, as they carefully plan out every section of their fate and tame that chemical hodge-podge that we call ourselves and then are prepared to control other entities, after the initial conquest of themselves. It is this conquest that takes only a moderate amount of intelligence and perseverance to make a man master of himself, and only people who are masters of themselves can be masters of other things. After himself, a man seeks to master his environment and some person or group of persons. These are important as they allow the individual to assert his mastery of himself and further perfect the whole through bringing others into the machine. The master is the craftsman, putting people and raw materials into their proper places and then setting things into motion.

Many people have it all wrong when they talk about people being good or bad. They are either to be *respected* (that is, if they are masters of themselves) or *used*, if they aren't. It is very simple, really, for the machine will continue to be built with or without any single planner, as it has to be—that is as long as there are any planners left.

And would there ever be an end to it all? Perhaps, but such a question does not deserve any real consideration as it is irrelevant to the present where so much is needed to be done, so many opportunities for large sections of the machine to be constructed.

Thoughts of the machine made Jason impatient, as he wished he could transcend the traditional barriers of time in order that he might effectively put his plans and ideas into effect immediately. But then he would try and offer himself solace in the pronouncement that as he was a planner, he could not allow himself to feel anxiety (in any real sustained sense) over factors which he didn't have direct control. For such factors were illusory, being only one's vision of steps not adjacent to one's progress. Nothing was out of reach, provided he approach it in the proper sequence.

His personal life was all neatly arranged with Victor, Julia's other admirer, now in a financial bind that would prevent Victor from receiving any real consideration on her part until this situation could be reversed. Victor's one chance at climbing out of the hole had been the horse race, but Jason had fixed that, too. By splitting the bets, Victor was only getting a fraction of what he had hoped for. But because Victor had been such a wreck before the race, Jason could easily defend his actions to others.

The net result was that now Jason had some time, a commodity which he desperately needed, for his apprenticeship was not completed, but soon he would be free—free to carry out all of his designs. The realm of the possible loomed before him and made him restless, but the somber contemplation of what he had accomplished by way of various designs already gave him cause for great satisfaction. The time was at hand when all would be waiting for him, and he had to be ready.

Book Six

Sources and Influences

It is a frequent cry of directors that their script is unintelligible in a particular section, leaving them the choice of deleting that part or trying to make some sense of it. I was even told once that the "problems" in a play tell one more about what the author was trying to do than any other passage or set of passages. Now, often I have seen a director struggle with such a problem and finally throw his hands up in despair and simply pick an interpretation from out of the air. But I have detected a more systematic approach from certain other artists who are concerned with what the author is saying, or was trying to say in his script. As the reader knows, my first experience with the stage was in England, having left my native America to make my fortune. I had no idea where I might eventually stop in my journey, and it just happened to be on the first stop in my travels. I have always been cognizant of just how much American theater has been influenced by the British that when I was confronted with the progenitor of my own heritage, I was so captured that I decided that I must stay and come to terms with it. I think that authors are the same in many respects, that is, they are taken with certain books (art, history, philosophy, religion, science, etc.) and try to translate some of what they find to be important into their own work. When such connections can be found in a work connecting it to another work, the prior work can be said to be a source of the latter. What such a determination can mean is that the audience may know just what type of question the writer was dealing with and so be able to put into a context this mediate content material. When it was shown to me the hermetic sources in the work of Henry Vaughan, I could better understand the poet's own differences from Herbert. By knowing the source (e.g. a direct reference to Paracelsus), the reader may determine just how the author is similar to or different from his source. If Herbert is the source of many of Vaughan's themes, a one-to-one comparison can yield valuable information as to what base the author is working from and what alterations have been made. By just quoting a line from another poem, the author brings the entire meaning of the other work to bear upon his own. Often an author will copy a scene from another work with only minor alterations. When this is detected, the careful reader will note just where the differences lie and speculate as to *why* these changes were made, e.g. how is the tone affected, or the theme, or the character. . . . Such close connections bind a particular work to a tradition of other specific works. If one problem has been treated by a series of authors, it is not uncommon for the astute writer to bring the history of the controversy to bear in his own play (as Dryden does in his preface to *Troilus and Cressida*).

With only a few well-placed references, the author has acquired a greater complexity to his work. He can employ the agonizing tortures of Othello with only a line or allusion. Any work that is rich, or that aspires to be written in a high form, will also be rich in references to other works that place the piece in an historical tradition and also bring intense treatments of particular aspects of those previous works to bear upon similar aspects of one's own story. This is not to say that any scene about ill-fated love should make reference to Pyramus and Thisbe, but that an appropriate analogue must be found that is specifically applicable. If I am costuming a seventeenth century play, I will not just use some "standard" costume of the era, but something that applies specifically to this particular production because of its thematic commitments—essential when I am asked to create costumes for a time, place, or culture in which I have never lived. Were personal experience the litmus test for creating and re-creating art, then everything older than fifty or sixty years would cease to be produced—a pity, that.

Influences are broader backgrounds which may affect an author and are also invaluable when trying to decipher a particular meaning that might be in the work (intended or not). The political turmoil of the revolution of 1642 and the return of Charles II in 1660 followed by the Glorious Revolution of 1686 created a background in which any restoration writer could hardly be exempt. Various elements of the political struggle such as side-changing, millennialism, popish fears, and the like can hardly be excluded when trying to understand the milieu of the author, which in turn might explain how Almanzor can go from side to side in *The Conquest of Grenada*. An understanding of what is involved in loyalty to one's liege during an excess of prerogatives can perhaps illumine Aureng-Zebe's actions. No one-to-one correspondence can be found in the case of influences, but just overall attitudes, which are prevalent and might be important in understanding how something works.

However, there are obvious limits. The 19th century attitudes of evolution would not illumine Adam in *Paradise Lost*, who was created under the influence of the static Great Chain of Being. Different influences of particular epochs affect the author in various ways as the broadly accepted common places act as a structure in which the author may compose his or her book. Both sources and influences can be helpful to the audience, and the attentive patron will always be searching for reference to one or the other in any work of art. Whether intended or not, they offer crucial evidence for deciphering the meaning of key passages and may help to untie some of the problems that one finds along the way.

Exhibits:

> Let me powre forth
> My teares before thy face, whil'st I stay here,
> For thy face coines them, and thy stampe they beare,
> And by this Mintage they are something worth,
>> For thus they bee
>> Pregnant of thee;
> Fruits of much griefe they are, emblemes of more,
> When a teare falls, that thou falst which it bore,
> So thou and I are nothing then, when on a divers shore.
>
>> On a round ball
> A workeman that hath copies by, can lay
> An Europe, Afrique, and an Asia,
> And quickly make that, which was nothing, *All*,
>> So doth each teare,
>> Which thee doth weare,
> A globe, yea world by that impression grow,
> Till thy teares mixt with mine doe overflow
> This world, by waters sent from thee, my heaven dissolved so.
>
>> O more than Moone,
> Draw not up seas to drowne me in thy spheare,
> Weepe me not dead, in thine armes, but forbeare
> To teach the sea, what it may doe too soone.
>> Let not the winde
>> Example finde,
> To doe me more harme then it purposeth;
> Since thou and I sigh one anothers breath
> Who e'r sighes most, is cruellest, and hasts the others death.

John Donne, "A Valediction: of Weeping."

Know'st thou This, Souldier? 'Tis a much
      chang'd plant which yet
          Thy selfe didst sett.

O who so hard a Husbandman did ever find
      A soile so kind?

Is not the soile a kind one, which returnes
      Roses for Thornes?

      Richard Crashaw, *Upon the Crowne of Thorns Taken
      Downe from the head* of our *Bl. Lord, all Bloody.*

Slow, slow fresh fount, keep time with my salt teares;
      Yet slower, yet o faintly gentle springs:
List to the heavy part the musique beares,
      "Woe weepes out her division, when shee sings."
        Droupe hearbs, and flowres;
        Fall griefe in showeres;
      "Our beauties are not ours":
        O, I could still
(Like melting snow upon some craggie hill,)
      drop, drop, drop, drop,
Since natures pride is, now, a wither'd daffodill.

      Ben Jonson, from *Cynthias Revells,* "Echo's song"

Love bad mee welcome. Yet my soule drew back
      Guilty of dust and sin.
But quick-ey'd Love observing mee grow slack
      From my first entrance in,
Drew neerer to mee, sweetly questioning,
      If I lack'd any thing.

A guest, I answer'd, worthy to be heere:
     Love said, you shalbe he.
I the unkind, ungratefull! Ah my Deere
     I cannot looke on thee.
Love tooke my hand, and smiling did reply,
     Who made the eyes but I?

Truth *Lord*, but I have marrd them: Let my shame
     Goe, where it doth deserve.
And know you not says Love, who bore the blame?
     My Deere, then I will serve.
You must sitt downe sayes Love, and tast my meat:
     So I did sitt and eat.

     George Herbert, "Love" (III).

Lynching and mob violence under the common law have no technical signification. To the legal mind the terms connote a hodge podge of numerous crimes—riot, rout, unlawful assembly, murder, assault and battery, et cetera. "Lynching has no technical legal meaning. It is merely a descriptive phrase used to signify the lawless acts of persons who violate established law at the time they commit the acts. . . . The offense of lynching is unknown to common law." Georgia Code Ann. (Michie, 1926) Section 964. . . "It shall be lawful for the judge of Superior Court of the circuit in which a crime is alleged to have been committed to change the venue for the trial of said case on his own motion, with or without petition, whenever, in his judgment, the accused party will be lynched, or there is danger of violence being attempted to be committed on said accused, if carried back or allowed to remain in the county where the crime is alleged to have been committed.. . .Section 363. Any sheriff or other officer having knowledge of *a* meeting or assembling together of any citizens of the State for the purposes set forth in the preceding section, and failing to attempt in good faith to suppress the same, either by himself or by summoning a posse as prescribed in said section shall be guilty of a misdemeanor.

James Harmon Chadbourn, *Lynching and the* Law,
(Chapel Hill, N.C.: 1933), pp. 29, 154-5. common law
citation, *Corpus Juris,* Vol. XXXVIII, 328.

An Indiana Case

Almost equal to the ferocity of the mob which killed the three
brothers . . . was the action of a mob near Vincennes, Ind. In this
case a wealthy colored 9.11, named Allen Butler, who was well
known in the community, and enjoyed the confidence and respect of
the entire country, was made the victim of a mob and hung because
his son had become unduly intimate with a white girl who was a
servant around his house. There was no pretense that the facts were
otherwise than as here stated. The woman lived at Butler's house as
a servant, and she and Butler's son fell in love with each other, and
later it was found that the girl was in a delicate condition. It was
claimed, but with how much truth no one has ever been able to tell,
that the father had procured an abortion, or himself had operated
on the girl, and that she had left the house to go back to her home. It
was never claimed that the father was in any way responsible for the
action of his son, but the authorities procured the arrest of both
father and son, and at the preliminary examination the father gave
bail to appear before the Grand Jury when it should convene. On
the same night, however, the mob took the matter in hand and with
the intention of hanging the son. It assembled near Sumner, while
the boy, who had been unable to give bail, was lodged in jail at
Lawrenceville. As it was impossible to reach Lawrenceville and hang
the son, the leaders of the mob concluded they would go to Butler's
house and hang him. Butler was found at his home, taken out by the
mob and hung to a tree. This was the law abiding state of Indiana,
which furnished the United States its last president and which
claims all the honor, pride and glory of northern civilization. None
of the leaders of the mob were apprehended, and no steps whatever
were taken to bring the murders to justice. . . .

The entire system of the judiciary of this county is in the hands of white people. To this add the fact of the inherent prejudice against colored people, and it will be clearly seen that a white jury is certain to find a Negro prisoner guilty if there is the least evidence to warrant such a finding.

Meredith Lewis was arrested in Roseland, La., in July of last year. A white jury found him not guilty of the crime of murder wherewith he stood charged. This did not suit the mob. A few nights after the verdict was rendered, and he was declared to be innocent, a mob gathered in his vicinity and went to his house. He was called, and suspecting nothing, went outside. He was seized and hurried off to a convenient spot and hanged by the neck until he was dead for the murder of a woman of which the jury had said he was innocent.

* * *

John Peterson, near Denmark, S.C., was suspected of rape, but escaped, went to Columbia, and placed himself under Gov. Tillman's protection, declaring he, too, could prove an alibi by white witnesses. A white reporter hearing his declaration volunteered to find these witnesses, and telegraphed the governor that he would be in Columbia with them on Monday. In the meantime the mob at Denmark hearing Peterson's whereabouts, went to the governor and demanded the prisoner. Gov. Tillman, who had during his canvass for re-election the year before, declared that he would lead a mob to lynch a Negro that assaulted a white woman, gave Peterson up to the mob. He was taken back to Denmark, and the white girl in the case as positively declared that he was not the man. But the verdict of the mob was that "the crime had been committed and somebody had to hang for it, and if he, Peterson, was not guilty of that he was of some other crime," and he was hung and his body riddled with 1,000 bullets.

Miss Ida B. Wells, *A Red Record, Lynchings in the United States,* (Chicago: 1895) pp. 34-5, 36, 64.

Mr. Raper. . . . I started to tell you of that case of Elwood Higginbotham. He had some difficulty with a white man who was driving a cow across Higginbotham's land. That night, after he and his wife had gone to bed, someone knocked at the door. He told his wife that was probably someone to cause trouble. The door was broken down and this man rushed in and broke down the door to the bedroom. He was armed, and threatened to kill Higginbotham. However, Higginbotham was too quick for him, and shot-him and killed him there in the bedroom do his house. He was arrested and taken to Jackson for safekeeping. Higginbotham was taken out by a mob and lynched.

* * *

Senator Wiley. You claim that in those three cases the officials in the counties in which they occurred were remiss in their obligations or duties?

Mr. Raper. I have not said that, Senator.

Senator Wiley. Will you take those three cases and show how the particular law we are discussing would have remedied the situation.

Mr. Raper. Let me take 1935.

Senator Wiley. No; you referred to three lynchings in 1939.

Mr. Raper. I have not personally investigated those three. Since 1937 I have not been connected with that work.

Senator Wiley. Take the one instance in 1935. Where was that?

Mr. Raper. Oxford, Miss. in 1934.

Senator Wiley. Now, you are jumping again.

Senator Connally. I think that he should answer the Senator one way or the other.

Mr. Raper. I was just looking at the record for 1934. I do not have a complete record for all those years. The Higginbotham case was in 1934.

Senator Connally. I think he should answer the question about 1939.

Senator Van Nuys. He testified that he did not investigate these cases in 1939, but he had in 1935. Now he says it is 1934.

Mr, Raper. That extends over a period there of 10 years.

Senator Wiley. I wanted to get your testimony as to where and how the Federal courts could better administer such a law than the local judges.

Mr. Raper. May I get my records? I have the whole thing.

Senator Wiley. Yes.

Mr. Raper. The Higginbotham case was in 1935. There was something over 100 in that 10 year period.

Senator Wiley. Go ahead.

Mr. Raper. Higginbotham was in his home one night about 10 o'clock and a rap came on the door. . .

* * *

Senator Wiley. What happened to the parties who did the lynching?

Mr. Raper. Nothing in the world. Nobody was ever punished. I will be very happy, if you want to call me later, to give you full details of that case.

Senator Neely. Did not the grand jury make an investigation?

Mr. Raper. They made what I would call a perfunctory investigation. They said he came to his death at the hands of parties unknown.

Senator Neely. Did you identify the two individuals to whom you referred in your letter to the judges?

Mr. Raper. I said I was convinced they would testify to that if they were willing to testify.

Senator Connally. Willing to testify to what?

Mr. Raper. To what had taken place in regard to that case. I talked with a man there about it.

Senator Neely. What did he say?

Mr. Raper. He said there always had to be arrangements made for these jail breaks, and that was how they got into the jail and took him out and lynched him.

Senator Neely. How did they get into the jail?

Mr. Raper. Either because it was not locked or somebody must have let them in.

Senator Neely. Was there any resistance by the officers?

Mr. Raper. None whatever.

Senator Wiley. On the trial was there any conflict in the testimony as to just how this white man was shot by the colored man?

Mr. Raper. There was evidence given by the wife of the dead man.

Senator Wiley. No other testimony?

Mr. Raper. There was other testimony, but there was no other direct testimony. Two of the jurors felt that the man was not guilty of murder, and that held up the verdict of the jury. It was during that period of time that the mob took him out and lynched him.

Senator Wiley. Ten of the jurors apparently felt that he should be convicted. That causes me to stop and ponder for a moment. What appeared in the evidence that justified the conclusion that this man was shot while invading the home of the other, and rightfully shot?

Mr. Raper. The whole thing seemed to turn on the contention that no Negro had the right to kill a white man, no difference what the situation was, and that a Negro who killed a white man should not be allowed to go free.

Senator Connally. That is a base slander on the Southern States and is utterly untrue. I am surprised that any white man from the South would come here and make such an outrageous statement.

Mr. Raper. I was basing it on the proceeding that occurred.

Senator Connally. You know what I am talking about. I am surprised that any white man from the South would make such a statement. You were talking about the situation in the South.

Mr. Raper. No; I didn't mean—

Senator Connally (interposing). Let me speak for a minute. You said it was the attitude of the people there that they should not be punished, no matter what the facts were. You know that is an infamous falsehood.

Mr. Raper. The Senator asked me, and I was speaking about the Elwood Higginbotham case.

Senator Connally. I do not know anything about that case. You made a general statement, and it was an infamous falsehood.

Mr. Raper. Didn't you ask me what the situation was in that case, whether it was 10 jurors for conviction and 2 against it?

Senator Wiley. No; I asked you what the evidence showed.

Mr. Raper. In that case?

Senator Wiley. Yes. You apparently volunteered the statement. What did the evidence show as to why this man was shot, why this white man was shot and how this white man got into the colored man's home?

Mr. Raper. When this white man came to Higginbotham's door, according to the testimony he said to his wife that maybe he was there for trouble of some kind.

Senator Wiley. You stated that the white man was in the colored man's home.

Mr. Raper. Yes sir.

Senator Wiley. The colored man was in bed?

Mr. Raper. Yes sir.

Senator Wiley. The white man had a gun in his hand?

Mr. Raper. Yes sir.

Senator Wiley. Apparently with the intention of killing the colored man?

Mr. Raper. Yes sir.

Senator Wiley. Apparently there may have been some other factors involved in the case. However, it not so very important.

Senator Van Nuys. Go ahead.

Mr. Raper. One other item I shall have finished. To expect lynchers to be punished, even when lynchers include peace officers, under present laws, is asking the impossible. Lynchers now go unpunished because punishment of their crimes depends upon the same peace officers and court officers whose impotence they demonstrated when they lynched. The officers of the law have already shown their unwillingness or inability to administer justice. To expect these officers that connive at or wink at or permit lynching to arrest and punish lynchers is like expecting a dethroned government to punish those who overthrew it. It has been demonstrated many times that local communities in which lynchings occur will not punish the lynchers. But many local people would be glad to testify, if they could do so without danger to themselves. I am sure in many localities there are many people who would welcome the opportunity to stand up and perform their duty as citizens and testify against lynchers and against public officers for failure to perform their duty as such. . . .

> *Crime of Lynching, Hearings before a Subcommittee of the Committee on the Judiciary, United States Senate, 76th Congress,* Feb. 6, 7, March 5, 12, 13, 1940. pp. 6-11.

More lynchings occur in the summer months than in either spring, fall, or winter. Some Negroes as well as whites, who are close to the situation, feel that there is a relation between the weather and crimes against the person and a consequent relation between the weather and resort to lynch-law. Working and living out of doors in warm weather, mid-summer unemployment, landlord-tenant relations in summer, and other factors greatly modify any all-weather explanation. With the coming of warm weather, the majority of the farm folks work out of doors, the members of the family often being scattered over the fields at different tasks.

During the midsummer months, after cultivating is done and before harvesting begins, there is little to occupy the time of Negro and white workers on Southern farms, nearly two-thirds of whom are wage hands or tenants. During the slack-work summer months, there is a great deal of visiting, loafing, gambling, and general "carousing about", and inevitably an unusually large amount of crime.

* * *

Data secured from the superintendents of state prison systems and wardens of penitentiaries of Southern states for the eighteen-month period ending July 1, 1931 demonstrates conclusively that Negro criminals brought before the courts were not dealt with leniently.

* * *

Of the 3,693 mob victims between 1889 and 1929 in the United States, 1,394 or 37.7 per cent were accused of murder, 214 or 5.8 percent of felonious assaults, 614 or 16.7 per cent of rape, 247 or 6.7 per cent of attempted rape, 264 or 7.1 per cent of theft, 66 or 1.8 per cent of insult to a white person, and 894 or 24.2 percent of all other offenses (e.g. expressing sympathy with murder of white men, offensive language, and alleged disrespectful utterances against President Wilson and others).

* * *

Although a few lynchers have been indicted, tried, convicted, and sentenced, the courts usually deal with them in the most perfunctory fashion. Between 1922 and 1926 grand juries investigated seventeen lynchings and indicted 146 persons. In 1922 ten were sent to the penitentiary; the next year two, in 1924 five were given jail sentences; the next year five received suspended sentences, one was put in jail, and fifteen were given indeterminate sentences of six months on the chain gang to eight years in the penitentiary; in 1926 eight were given sentences of four years, and a ninth, a life sentence. Of the 1930s twenty-one lynchings, investigations resulted in grand jury indictments of lynchers in five instances, forty-nine persons being indicted. In only one case, that of the second lynching near Thomasville, Georgia, were the lynchers dealt with as murderers. Here, life sentences were given to two young white men.

* * *

Five of Georgia's six lynchings in 1930 occurred in the southeastern part of the state where the white people are traditionally antagonistic toward the Negro.

> *Lynchings and what they Mean: General finds of the Southern Commission on the Study of Lynching* (Georgia: n.d.), pp. 13, 18, 25, 29.

STATEMENT OF WALTER WHITE, EXECUTIVE SECRETARY, NATIONAL ASSOCIATION FOR THE ADVANCE-MENT OF COLORED PEOPLE, WASH. D.C.

Mr. White. Mr. Chairman and gentleman of the committee, my name is Walter White. . . I appear her today on behalf of the national office and the 1,627 branches. . . The association has for many years been opposing lynching as a grave danger to the democratic way of life. We have investigated lynchings. I myself have had the experience of investigating some 41 lynchings, and some 12 race riots in the United States and I have done some writing and speaking on the subject.

* * *

Finally, I want to point out that there is hysterical fear in certain quarters in the United States today of Communism. I charge bluntly today that the most dangerous destroyer of faith in the democratic process in the United States is not the Communist, but the Eastlands, the Rankins, the Bilbos, and the Talmadges, who cast discredit upon our Supreme Court and who advocate mob violence. I charge also that those who wittingly or stupidly finance and support the racism of such demagogues are doing more harm to the United States than all the foreign agents who may possibly be at work in the United States.

* * *

Mr. White. Thank you sir (finishing his statement).

Senator Ferguson. Are there any questions?

Senator Revercomb. Mr. Chairman, this is a very able presentation of a viewpoint, ably presented. It is regrettable, however, that the witness in presenting it, whatever his feeling might be, would make any personal attack on a Member of the Congress, particularly upon a member of the committee. I make that comment for the record.

Senator Stennis. Mr. Chairman, am I permitted to say a word on that?

Senator Ferguson. Yes, sir.

Senator Stennis. I was going to say, Mr. Chairman, that I do not know what the practice is here, but I personally object and officially resent the remarks of this witness directed toward Senator Eastland.

Senator Eastland. What was the remark?

Senator Stennis. He called you a demagogue.

Senator Eastland. That is absolutely right.

Senator Stennis. Senator Eastland is a member of this committee and a Member of the Senate, and the senior Senator from the State of Mississippi.

Senator Eastland. Some people might think so. But it is absolutely all right. I do not want to carry on any controversy with a nigger.

Crime of Lynching, Hearings before a Subcommittee of the Committee on the Judiciary, United States Senate, 80th Congress, second session on S. 4, S. 135 and S. 1465. January 19-21; February 1, 18, 20. 1948. Pages 97, 108, 117.

After puzzling our brains for years, we were reluctantly driven to the sad conclusion that it was almost impossible to escape from slavery in Georgia and travel 1,000 miles across the slave States. We therefore resolved to get the consent of our owners, be married, settle down in slavery, and endeavor to make ourselves as comfortable as possible under that system; but at the same time ever to keep our dim eyes steadily fixed upon the glimmering hope of liberty, and earnestly pray God mercifully to assist us to escape from our unjust thralldom.

> William and Ellen Craft, *Running A Thousand Miles for Freedom,* (1849): from part one.

Early the next morning Mr. Flint was at my grandmother's inquiring for me. She told him she had not seen me, and supposed I was at the plantation. He watched her face narrowly and said, "Don't you know anything about her running off?" She assured him that she did not. . . . My grandmother's house was searched from top to bottom. As my trunk was empty, they concluded I had taken my clothes with me. Before ten o'clock every vessel northward bound was thoroughly examined, and the law against harboring fugitives was read to all on board. At night a watch was set over the town. Knowing how distressed my grandmother would be, I wanted to send her a message, but it could not be done.

Harriet Jacobs, *Incidents in the life of a Slave Girl* (1861): 17.

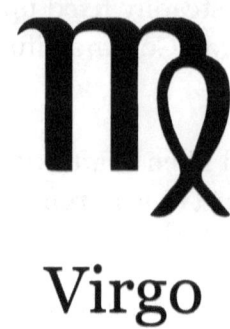

Virgo

Distillation

Chapter 1

"All About Chance and the Terrors of a Bad Hangover"

Victor Stuart's body wasn't found until ten o'clock the next morning, lying hall-buried by garbage in the city dump. Two black men who had had a bit too much to drink the night before were taking the long way home (the dump is right next to the Negro section of town) when they walked, quite by accident, into the dump. One of the men tripped on a metal band that was lying on the ground and fell into a heap of garbage. He wasn't hurt, in fact he was laughing as he fell into a particularly soft place and the noise of his body oozing into the garbage somehow had a comical effect on one who had been drinking for twelve hours or so.

"Dids yasee zat?" slurred the first man as he flopped back in the garbage. But the other didn't answer as he was vomiting while holding onto a fence post for support.

"Willie ah says *Willie*," slurred the first in loud, doleful tones as he flopped over and felt a hand. For an instant he thought it was his friend Willie and a smile stretched across his face, but then he quickly realized that the hand was clammy and not warm like a normal hand. It was cold, and the skin felt like thinly stretched rubber, artificial, pretending to be Willie. The sensation gave him such a start that he pulled his arm away, though he failed to relinquish his grip on the other arm and so pulled it along with his retreating hand.

"Willie!" screamed the first again as he tore his hand free from the deadly grasp of the other. "Willie!"

Willie had just finished and was wiping his mouth on his sleeve as he became aware of his friend's calls. "Amos, what it?" he managed with difficulty as he staggered toward the voice.

"Look Willie," said Amos. "Look Willy, it's a hand."

Willie looked at his friend sitting in the garbage with both his arms outstretched in his pleading. But what was Amos getting so excited about? Here he was, sitting down and telling him that he, Amos, had a hand.

"Dats real sweet Amos, Ise has two of dem, see," said Willie holding out his own hands so that his friend could see.

"Donts ya see It Willie, donts ya"

"Ya Ise sees your hand. Ise sees two ofs dem."

"Not my hand, Willie, Ise thought its was yours, but its not Willie, its a dead hand."

Then Willie saw the arm sticking straight out of the garbage, the hand half clenched as if to grab something. Willie blinked his eyes to make sure he was seeing something that was really there and not some aberration brought on by the intoxicating beverages of the night before. But the hand remained and did not move.

"Ise thinks we shoulds gets out ta here," said Willie as he turned around and started away.

"Willie!" screamed Amos.

"What is it ya wants?" replied Willie as he stopped and turned around.

"I'm stuck, I cants gets out."

Willie put his hands on his hips and looked at his friend sitting in the garbage, trying to move his rather large body.

"Willie!" screamed the other again.

Then Willie walked over and grabbed Amos' hand, being careful that it was Amos' hand, and lifted his comrade from his soft abode. Then the two put their arms over each other's shoulders so as to give each of them the benefit of the other's stabilization and trudged towards their home which was across the railroad tracks. As they got up to the dirt road, they saw the depot master of the rail station going to work. He saw them coming from the dump.

"What were you two doing in the dump?" asked the depot master, as lately there had been people going into the dump late at night and scattering things all over, including onto the rail tracks which could cause a serious derailment and loss of money and lives.

And so the station master, seeing these two drunks coming from the dump in an obvious inebriated condition, was suspicious. But the two comrades, thinking that he must be referring to the dead body (or rather arm, as they didn't make the connection between the arm and it's being attached to something), decided that it wouldn't do to be brought back and questioned so they started walking faster.

"Wait you two," yelled the station master, who took their walking faster as a sign of guilt about something. "I want to talk to you."

"Wese didn't do it!" yelled Amos as the two started running as best they could, which was still better than the station master who was old and had a lame leg.

Failing to catch them, he decided to send some men down from the station to check out the dump and make sure that all was in order.

***

Julia was just arriving at the park as the final judging on some of the livestock and such was taking place. She was coming for her sewing, which she had been obliged to leave as an exhibit. Everything would be closing up in a few hours, and the people would be going to church (as services were moved back two hours to accommodate the fair). She had just picked up her things when the word hit the park: Victor Stuart had been murdered.

"Who did it?"

"I don't know, but he was shot, and it looks like it was a rifle."

"A rifle?"

"That's odd isn't it?"

"What do you mean?"

"Well, you know what a row that Dod feller and Stuart were having during the race after, and then at the dance last night. I wouldn't be surprised that maybe our young sharp shooter got his revenge on our poor friend."

"You think that Dow did it?"

"Do you know of anyone with a better reason? Look, he fights with you with kicking and what-not down the final stretch of the horse race, and then insults you afterwards, and as a final kick in the rear, he steals your girl away from you—now, what would you do under the circumstances."

"I'd get the son-of-a-bitch."

"Exactly, and that's probably what this Dow was afraid of, so he decides to get Stuart first before he had a chance to get him."

"Why that little—"

"Now calm down, it's only a theory."

"Theory nothing, it makes sense to me. I say we go over to the Beauchay's and string the little bastard up right now," several voices piped their agreement.

"Now, you must—" started the man with the theory again, trying to make another disclaimer.

"—Victor Stuart was a decent boy and anyone who murders decent folks deserves the same. I say we go and get him."

Julia quickly gathered her things together as she got onto her horse and rode quickly towards the Beauchay farm.

"Where's John?" she called to Jefferson.

"Why I don't know?" said the tall man. "Why do you want to know?" he responded, sensing that there was urgency in her voice.

"I've got to talk with him quickly," she said. "Is he in the house?"

"I'll go and see," said Jefferson as he put down what he was doing and rushed into the house.

After a few minutes, he came out and told her that he wasn't there.

"Well, we've got to find him, something terrible has happened."

Jefferson didn't know what it was that was bothering Julia, but it must be serious.

"Well, I'll give you a hand. We'll look for him together."

And so the two mounted up and went out in search of Dow. As they were riding, Julia told Jefferson about how Victor had been found murdered and that because of the arguments between the two, everyone thought that John had killed him.

"I'm certain he didn't do it," said Julia.

"So am I," replied Jefferson. "The important thing is to find him before the mob does."

They rode awhile when Julia asked, "He did come home last night, didn't he?"

This question might have irritated Jefferson coming from anyone else, as then it might be construed as an intimation of John's guilt, but as he knew how Julia felt about John and how he felt about her, the question was one rather of constructing the case based on the facts (rather than mere feeling and character prejudice, as others, namely sheriffs and juries, were prone to do in small towns).

"Yes, he came home about twelve-thirty. He said that the dance had been very nice and that he had decided to walk his horse home, and then had spent a long time grooming it, as it had been a rather long day."

"You know the dance got out at eleven," said Julia.

"Yes," he replied. It didn't look good for the case, if John had been an hour and a half getting into the house. Plenty of time, a judge would say, for a young man to kill another and bury him in the dump and then return home. And why had he gone out suddenly as he had, they might ask? Why wasn't he at home? Jefferson knew that it was often his custom after a particularly eventful day to retreat to the woods so that he might better evaluate what had happened to him, but how could that be explained to a group of men who would were wedded to the reason that John wasn't home was because he was hiding out, afraid to take honorable and just sentencing from the law. *Boy we find you guilty—guilty of conspiracy to create a riot and undermine the constitution of the city of Baltimore and the United States of America. You will serve*—Jefferson's arms tightened, "He generally goes one of two places. I'll go here, and you go about a quarter of a mile down and follow the trail until you get to a large rise, on the side. It's a seasonal river, sometimes he goes there as well. If we're both unsuccessful, then we'll meet at the river in an hour or two. Remember to always watch to see that no one is watching you. If someone catches your trail then it's over for John. If they catch him when they're hot, he hasn't got a chance."

They separated, and Jefferson took the low path through the thick undergrowth. If he found John, he didn't know what he would say to him. Would he recommend that he turn himself in and face the fairness of the law? He might get an unbiased trial and then be exonerated, but what if he didn't get a fair trial, and he was sentenced to death? Or even a long prison term which would surely be tantamount to the same thing; the prime years of his life taken away from him: his love, hopes, and ambitions—all, gone. This was a terrible fate. Jefferson sighed.

And yet could he live as a fugitive, always running? What sort of life would it be? To be in constant fear of capture? He'll be like a fugitive slave. Would it not be the same as a jail sentence? Would this constant danger not in itself perhaps constitute a greater risk than being out on a work gang day-after-day with sadistic men who liked to see men's backs scarred from the attacks of their whips? But at least then the time spent would be working towards his freedom, while his life as a fugitive would be useless. At any moment he might be apprehended and then he would have a harsher sentence than if he had voluntarily given himself up. And yet, if the sentence were death, how could it become any harsher? With the recent altercations between Victor and John, the prosecutor would have little trouble showing pre-meditation, which would mean death, unless he pled guilty—but this seemed a perversion of the system. If running away was a violation of the code of Justice, a breach of the social contract, then wouldn't pleading guilty be doing the same thing, as it would be lying to take advantage of the system, that is not acting in good faith? But then wouldn't pleading not guilty, when he knew that such a pled was tantamount to committing suicide, be a perversion of the system as well? The American system of jurisprudence is an adversarial system. It seeks to create fair conditions in order that justice might prevail most of the time. But small towns were often different. Even if one were acquitted, the heat of the moment might precipitate a lynching. Clearly to submit him to such a trial and aftermath would be a perversion of the system, as well. As each alternative seemed to imply a contradiction with the ideological framework on which it was designed to operate, Jefferson decided that he must rely upon his ethical intuition to decide which was the most proper course of action. Clearly none of these routes alone would be correct, but perhaps as circumstances shaped themselves, an opportunity would present itself whereby he could advise John to what he believed to be the proper course of action under the circumstances.

Chapter 2

"John is Forced into a Plan of Action by the People of the Town"

Julia had taken the trail farther up and had just climbed the mound which Jefferson had described to her. It was a quiet Sunday, and the forest exuded the stillness of the heavy air. Even the light was different once one rode into the forest, as the leaves refracted and diffused the light so that it's intensity and quality were distinctly different than the field, giving the area an almost meditative quality. Then she saw a small ravine where a seasonal river might flow, dismounted, and went to the edge to have a look. But there was nothing. I'll have to try a little farther down, she decided, following the crest of the rise until it turned, when there, near the bottom, was a familiar sight; John was giving himself a drink from his cap.

"Hello down there," called Julia, as she dismounted and carefully started making her way down the slope.

"Hello," said John, happy to see Julia.

When she got to the bottom, John dumped out his cap and walked over to greet her. "You know I was just thinking about you. I had such a wonderful time last night that I can't get it out of my mind."

"Listen, John," began Julia in a tone of seriousness, but John would have none of it as he continued to laugh and joke with her.

"Do you remember the time when you fell down the hill and ripped the back of your skirt and demanded that we all walk home in front of you?"

"John," she began. "I've got something to tell you."

Then John ceased talking but could not stop his· mind from its fast movements. In all truth, John couldn't have heard a word of what Julia had said so far since he was so excited at seeing the cause of his intense exhilaration.

"It's Victor—he's been hurt."

"You know you're the best dancer I've ever seen," said John, still unaware of what the other was trying to say.

Julia grabbed John's arms and shook him. "Listen to me, John. It's Victor. John, Victor is dead!"

John stopped. The message was beginning to penetrate. But it was so unthinkable, so horrible, how could it be so? Did he hear incorrectly? No, the words were plain. "Victor dead?" exclaimed John in a whisper. "Who did it? How did it happen?" Nothing could have been more out of place. Dead. Victor was dead. He would no longer—

There must be some sort of sense in this, but what it was? but why, how, what for?? His mind was filled with thousands of interrogative particles which all asked the same and different questions simultaneously. It couldn't be true. But it was true. But it couldn't be.

"They don't know how it happened, someone from the train yard found his body in the dump, covered with garbage. It seems he was shot."

"Shot?"

"Yes, with a rifle."

"How can they tell that?" asked John, who thought it strange that someone could look at a bullet hole and be able to ascertain that a rifle or pistol had been the offending weapon without first cutting open the wound and taking out the shell and examining it, which never occurred until an autopsy. It seemed that if in truth Victor was dead, then anything might be possible, for once the realm of the possible is violated, then all compartments within are no longer held in the same assurance as before.

"I don't know, but what I do know is that they think that," Julia paused, for she couldn't bring herself to say the words, but her expression conveyed what her words couldn't.

"That *I* did it?" asked John in amazement. There was a pause. Certainly there had been disagreements between the two, and Victor had been particularly abusive at the dance, a fact which he had almost blocked out of his mind as a blemish upon a perfect image. But thinking about it from someone else's point of view, I would be the natural one to suspect. *I had all the reasons for killing him, he insulted me several times, we were both fond of the same woman, and we had just finished a hotly contested race in which I had been the loser. Yes, there is a clear motive for me, and if indeed he was killed by a rifle shot, then circumstances also point a finger at me as I just made my reputation as a marksman at the fair. But do people think I really did it?*

"A person could make a good case that I did it," said John. "I had every reason to, you know."

"Oh John, what are we going to do?"

"Julia," began John with a smile. "You completely believe in me, don't you?"

"Of course, and so does Jefferson, and so would anybody who knew you."

"But," supplied John, as he knew that Julia's thought was incomplete.

"But the others—" started Julia.

"The others are convinced by the situation as it stands."

Julia didn't respond.

"But why would I be so stupid as to kill someone after I'd left all those clues about myself?"

"You remember the last murder we had in town," said Julia.

John bit his lip. Again, a Stuart had been involved. *—the shiny yellow car was scaring the horse, causing it to rear back. And Victor had acted recklessly, without regard.*

Still, the fallen woman had been Stuart's mother, and she acted decisively in the open without hesitation, to put a bullet through the head of Lucius Smith, former proprietor of The Marsh.

"Am I under arrest?"

"Arrest? I don't know, but what I do know is that they were talking in town about forming a lynch mob that would ferret you out so that they can—" Julia stopped.

John frowned as he mentally finished her sentence.

"I rushed out to the farm to find you because that's the first place they're going to look."

"And after that?" asked Dow.

"Who knows after that, in the woods maybe, along the roads—probably as many places as they've got men."

John was silent for a moment. "Do you have any paper?" he asked Julia.

"I don't know, I can check my purse, it's in my saddlebag."

"I'll get it," said John as he scampered up the hill. *I've got to write a note to Jefferson,* he thought, *since I can't make a move until I have more information. If things seem calm and orderly, I'll give myself up and let them arrest me if they want to, but if there is a lynching mob, then I'll stay out of sight for a time.*

John found a pencil and paper quickly. He wrote a note to Jefferson, telling him some of his thoughts. Then he folded the note and slid back down the bank to Julia.

"Here's a note you're to give to Jefferson."

"Good, I'm to meet him in about an hour or so. Do you want to come along?"

"No, I think it would be best if I kept out of sight, until I find out just what the situation is." John looked at Julia and then thought about what was happening; it was so gnarled and false. With the events of the past weeks, life had suddenly begun to play tricks on him, it seemed. For just a fortnight before he would have been looking into different eyes when he was alone in the woods with this girl, and his future would have been as open to him as the plain at sunrise. But now everything had changed. It was entirely different, as every decision, instead of being an unconscious mechanism which really didn't affect his basic state of being, now had to be scrutinized as exhaustively as possible so that he might predict the outcomes of various chosen courses of action that were still before him. No longer was it dreams that he was dealing with; the idle fancies of a young man contemplating what it would be like if he did this or that, but instead, the concrete dilemma that demanded urgent solutions on his part before they found their own solutions (which might or might not be to his advantage). He had to act, and act quickly. But the question was: what to do? If he made the wrong decision, then no matter how quickly it was contrived, it would not advance his cause. No, it must be advantageous, that was certain. But what wasn't certain was the nature of such an action taken at such a period of stress. All these problems shot quickly through his body as anxious tremors, which he was trying to suppress. *Whatever I do*, he thought, *I must keep my head. If I lose that, I've given up the ghost.*

"I think," he began to Julia, "that I'll find a place to hide, that isn't so vulnerable as down in this sway here, and then I'll wait for you and Jefferson to kind of feel the situation and see if it would be safe for me to leave. If all is calm, I'll turn myself in and hope that I get a fair trial, but if it isn't good, then I'll have to have a contingency plan of how I am to survive; either around here in the woods, or else by going somewhere else."

"John," intoned Julia with a connotation that couldn't be mistaken—she didn't want him to go away.

"Of course, staying around here would be ideal, as I'd be close to everything so that when the emotionalism blew over, I could make my decision more clearly, but then it might become too dangerous here in the woods as they might start stalking me, seriously. There's some real good human trackers left over from the old days. I'd need my horse, that's for certain, to survive here, as they could get me in a couple of days if I was on foot."

"I can't believe all this is happening."

"Neither can I, but I suppose we have to accept what circumstances offer us and try and make the best of it."

"Of course you're right, but that's little comfort, don't you think?" Julia's face was frozen into a grimace.

"These next few days could determine whether I'm still a living soul or—"

"Oh, don't talk like that. You know this has got to work out, somehow." Julia grabbed for John's hand.

"I hope that it will, but what we need at present is something a little more substantial than hope; we need a plan of action. I'll bring my horse up this hill, and I'll lead you to the place where I'll hide. You come to meet at this place in the afternoon around four or so, bring Jefferson if you like, but make sure that no one follows you. After they find out that I'm not at the farm, they will suspect that I'm hiding out somewhere, and the likely suspects would be you and Jefferson. They might try and trick you into leading them towards me."

"Don't worry, I know when I'm being followed; a woman develops a marvelous sense for that."

"Good, now let's go."

John led Julia up the bank and rode until they reached a stream with a rather steep bank that was six feet high on the other side.

"This is a good place, I think, as the bank on the other side is very difficult to ride over—one has to go down stream about three hundred yards and climb up over there, and the thickets on the other side would hide me well, so that I can see who's coming. I think I'll stay here. When you return, just remain where you are, and stay on your horse gesturing at that tree, that way I'll know that everything's all right and I can come out. If you call my name or dismount or do anything else, I'll take it as a danger signal and take off."

Julia nodded. It was a good hiding place. How she wished to stay with John, but she had to go—for his sake.

"Jefferson will be expecting me," she said.

"Yes, I know. Thank you for coming by and warning me."

Julia didn't answer but took John's hand and gave it a squeeze, then turned and walked towards her horse.

"Julia," said John softly. She stopped, and John approached her and put his hand on her shoulder to turn her around, which he did effortlessly, then with the same motion pulled her to his breast and gazed for just an instant into the somewhat startled, yet expectant face of Julia and then kissed her, putting his lips first so gently upon hers, but then drawing intensity as he soon pressed his lips firmly against hers as their arms locked tightly together. It would be the last time that they might be alone together and somehow there was a powerful sadness in this mutual realization that seemed to make those few moments of their embrace seem both infinite and illusory at the same time.

The sun was already past noon, and the morning dew had completely vanished.

Chapter 3

"Victor Stuart, Sr."

In town, Victor Stuart Sr. had been called and was just riding down Magnolia to the doctor's office where Victor's body was resting.

There seemed to be little expression in his face, the people thought when they saw him ride in. It looked like he had just been awakened in the middle of the night to go outside and perform some routine repair task that urgently needed attending.

Stepping down from his wagon, he turned to one of the many men and women who were gathered outside the doctor's office.

"Is my boy inside?" he asked in a hoarse voice that had a gritty quality to it, not abrasive particularly, but tired. The man nodded.

Victor Sr. walked toward the house, not quickly, but as if each step was being measured.

***

"I think it's terrible, first his wife and now his son."
"He only has Louise now."
"What a poor man."
"I tell you, I think I'm going to join Abe's posse."

"That's a mob, not a posse."

"You're wrong. They're getting the sheriff to deputize them."

"You think that's going to alter their character one bit?"

"The sheriff's going along."

"No offence to our sheriff, but he couldn't stop those men if they decided to string up Dod."

"But that's what the rascal deserves."

"He deserves a trial."

"Yes, the same sort of trial he gave to the Stuart boy. That was a fine boy and a credit to our town. What is this other boy? He's a half—breed, and a good shot—if I had to take my pick, I'd take the Stuart boy, thank you."

"Still doesn't alter the fact that—"

The conversation was interrupted as Mr. Stuart came out of the house.

"Who did it? Where can I find him?" asked Mr. Stuart in the same low voice.

"It was that sharp shooter from the Beauchay's."

"Why did he kill my Victor? He was such a—good son."

"Don't worry, Mr. Stuart, there's a posse being formed right now, and some of us here are joining, too. We'll get your killer for you."

"I want, I—" started Mr. Stuart when his hands began shaking and he slumped against a wall. There was a rush of people to help him to his wagon. "We're on this, Mr. Stuart."

They helped the man to his wagon and someone hopped up with him to drive him home.

"Wait, I want to say something," said Stuart as his voice had such a grainy quality that it hardly seemed to be the voice of a normal man. "Victor was a good son," he said. "I don't know why anyone would want to kill him." Then with a surge of energy he said, "Where is this man, let me talk with him so I can know." His voice cracked as he finished his sentence. "He was a good son."

Then Mr. Stuart swayed slightly as the man who was going to drive the wagon pulled Mr. Stuart over so that Stuart was leaning on him, and started away.

"Well, what do you say now?"

The other man who wanted to bring Dow to trial didn't have a chance to answer as several other voices were quicker.

"Let's get him."

"Over to Abe's posse."

"We look after our own around here."

"This isn't going to go unnoticed."

And with that, the men started over to the sheriff's office to join the man hunt.

Chapter 4

"A Dreadful Incident Causes John to React on Instinct"

I didn't do anything, in case you were wondering. Julia just brought me the news. I'm hiding in a place where she knows. Find some information about what the mood of the town is and whether it would be safe for me to turn myself in, if not, get my fifty dollars that I won yesterday from my room and a change of clothes. Come by with Julia at four.
Yours, John

Jefferson put the note into his pocket, and then he took it out again and put a match to it. *They'll be coming around soon*, he thought. Julia and he arranged to meet at a certain place and then they separated. Jefferson rode toward the farm to get the money and clothes.

It was a successful strike. The Baltimore shipbuilders would have to relent and let blacks organize the same as they were letting whites organize. The union would be formed and no longer would they suffer by getting body fungus from the horrid damp conditions that they had slaved under. It seemed that they had won the battle. It would be a victory for them. He could just imagine the looks on the faces of many of the wives now that their husbands would be coming home at regular hours just like white folks did. All it took was a little patience and determination. After this he would try to find another project by which he might help others. There seemed as if there was so much to do. So much good that could be done for others, it gave his life a firm goal to which he could strive, a worthy object for his labor. With the cat at his side and his wife and child at home, it seemed as if nothing could stand in his way.

How hard it had been to get to the North after his inheritance money had been stolen. Everyone had said that things were better in the North for black folk. All a person had to do was make it to Boston with a determination for hard, honest labor. But that had not been the case. After college and after Peabody in New York City, he had gone through a time of travel. He had little money and rode the rails in boxcar, barely getting by with his feline companion. Then things turned around in Baltimore. He got a real job, a wife, and a future. But he didn't content himself with that alone. His reading in college had convinced him that he had to return to Plato's cave and help other descendants from Africa find a fairer life in America. He decided to become a union organizer and also worked on the labor team at the National Association for the Advancement of Colored People (that was also in Baltimore). The future seemed bright, but life with Marcel Beauchay and the destruction of Peabody had made him cautious in his heart.

***

After Jefferson had collected John's things, he made his way to the road and headed for town. Instead of coming in the normal way (over Sawyer's Bridge and down Main Street), he decided to go around by the flourmill and through the old section of town. The streets in this section of the town were in essentially the same condition as they were when the town was no more than a few houses together and a city hall (which was constructed by Mitchel Evans' great grandfather, as he decided that it was time that the little settlement became an actual town, which of course was achieved by building the city hall, which later became the school house). Now selected streets were becoming smoother in comparison (as automobiles needed smoother roads than horses). It seemed to Jefferson as if he were riding into an area of vast disrepair, which in itself was somewhat true, though the striking disjunction that was felt by comparison was what struck Jefferson. In his mind he juxtaposed the two slapped together with the conclusion that the unknown future had to be regarded with skepticism.

Railroads had been the technological change in his lifetime. Now it seemed that automobiles would be taking over. The telephone and radio were changing the way one confronted distance. Soon, everyone would be riding in a big version of Charles Lindbergh's airplane. Yes, these were new gadgets, yet some things never change. The hatred of most whites against blacks seemed not to end with slavery. And now John, who he thought of as a son, was at risk for lynching. This was not acceptable.

Jefferson dismounted on a quiet side street. He walked up to a group of young boys standing on the corner.

"What's new today?"

"Haven't you heard?" replied one of the boys directly. Jefferson smiled at the boy's lack of inhibitions that might have normally caused such questions to be ignored. Though Jefferson was black (the same as the young man) he was considered by his manner and habit to be rather above most ordinary blacks in caste or station, not because he, Jefferson chose to be there, unless one can say that by choosing to go to college and travelling up and down the east coast as he had done meant that he was responsible for all consequent effects. Rather, Jefferson was considered to be a strange creature: an oddity to all in Varner's Junction. This became particularly clear whenever Jefferson happened to get into conversations with the ordinary citizens of the down.

Was it because he was a college educated man in a town of little education? Was it because he held himself differently? Was it because his hair was beginning to gray? Throughout Varner's

Junction, white and black alike treated Jefferson like he was a class unto himself. He was the man from Mars.

"Victor Stuart was murdered today by John Dod, that fellow who won the rifle shoot on Friday."

"Yeah, he was shot six times in the head and the heart."

"I heard that it was twenty times in the—"

Jefferson knew that this part of the story would not be the most reliable, so he asked, "Did they catch this guy?"

"No, not yet, but they're fixin' to right now. They're forming a posse over at the sheriff's office."

"Much obliged to you," said Jefferson as he left the young men to argue among themselves whether it was thirty or forty shots that had killed Victor.

***

"I tell you, we've got to ride now," said Abe, a sturdily built Dutchman.

"I'd rather get a coordinated effort with the state and local police so that if he's gotten away, we can get him," said the sheriff, rubbing his stiff back.

"By that time, he'll have gotten away. I think we've already wasted too much valuable time. I only wanted to wait until Mr. Stuart came into town to see if there was anything special that he could or wanted to do. But the poor fellow is so broken up that he doesn't know what to do. And who blames him? First his wife, and now his son—what has he got to live for? There goes his blood line just like that."

"I know, but I've got to get this thing coordinated," said the sheriff. "If we don't we'll be working at cross purposes."

"All right, organize, but we have to have some action, and quick. If you'd have seen that boy with that bullet hole in his skull as big as a silver dollar, and his blood and brains oozing out onto his forehead, you wouldn't just be sitting there on your fat ass and would help bring this guy in."

Jefferson witnessed everything out of view, but as the men were making no effort to keep their voices down, he could hear all that was going on.

"All right, Abe, I'll get to it, I'll get to it."

"Be sure that you do, 'cause we're going after him by car and by horse in one hour."

"Yes, Abe, I'll get to it," the old man said as he shuffled across the street in the direction of the telegraph office. "What are we waiting for Abe, let's string the varmint up right now."

"I said I'd give him an hour, and I will, meanwhile, let's make plans on how we're going to cover the ground." Abe was a stubborn Dutchman who didn't like dissent.

Then the men crowded together so that Jefferson could no longer hear. But one thing was for certain, as he had suspected, if they found John, they wouldn't bring him back alive.

Jefferson quickly made his way back to his horse. The sun was falling in the sky; it was Sunday but hardly anyone had gone to church, they were too busy with avenging the blood of Victor Stuart.

As he mounted his horse, he saw another rider coming into town via the same route that he had just taken. The man was in quite a hurry. Jefferson couldn't quite make out who it was though he was a short, black man. Was it the man who ran The Marsh? *Then Jefferson came into the door of their place and found her lying on the ground, she was dead. "Darling?" he cried in a whisper. He couldn't believe it to be true. But it was, and he knew it. They couldn't get to me so they killed my family.*

It was a warm day as Jefferson rode out to the place where he was supposed to meet Julia. The realm of human action and how distant the existence of the holy felt at that moment. It was as if he were entirely divorced from the religious realm and put entirely into a godless world. The heavy weight of responsibility for not only his life, which he felt was wasted, but also John's as well, which threatened also to be one of pain and suffering, seemed unbearable. All seemed to be chance whirling about, searching for the receptacle of wisdom, but where was it to be found? His horse would follow his senses to water and hay, not to truth and beauty. *Whose worldview was more accurate? Do humans delude themselves that they are at the top of the heap? What if they were at the bottom?*

And now John was alone and in danger of losing his life—what could be more important to him than some kind of inner peace, and yet, where was it to be obtained? At the very moment when it was most demanded, it seemed to be most lacking. There was no higher logic to events, and if the people of the town were merely chasing a shadow, their bullets certainly weren't composed of shadows but metal that could rip open flesh and drain the body of the precious blood which carries the spirit of life.

Could it be that after all these years he really hadn't learned anything about life at all? That his fancies were mere ghosts and nothing else, mocking his naive credulity as the babbling of an idiot? Signifying? So many things that had seemed to be so certain in his youth, so clear in their logic, now seemed to be banal platitudes that didn't match with events as he was experiencing them. And after all, what can be more certain than the datum which we register as our primary reactions of what is happening right now all around us?

Isn't the realm of the ethical, the sphere of human action, Man's first concern? For when we are faced with a crisis, what should we do? How do we feel, or more precisely, what do we feel? Is it simply an instinct to survive, or is it an instinct to enable ourselves, or somehow make ourselves seem worthy in our deepest recess of self-evaluation. Is all fear then really fear of death? Or is that, too, an object of self-deception? A lie that we have perpetrated to ourselves because it is part of a fabric that makes life appear to make sense? It could be termed the fallacy of misplaced valuation, infusing meaning into that which is meaningless (the only meaning which it carries is that which we falsely assign it). In those inner chambers of self-evaluation the lie is always seen for what it is, but because we have constructed barriers of consistent, coherent lies, we can no longer feel and thereby know with our whole beings. We are blocked. And at some time when this becomes apparent, we say that perhaps we are simply fearing death, or that as animals we're thrust into a struggle for survival, but this is all modern pollution stemming from a scientific model (science always makes bad philosophy, as we should have learned from Newton). What is really happening is something much more complex in its operation; it is the contest between the forces that desire to know and those that wish to be happy, for the two are inalterably opposed. To truly seek after knowledge is to open oneself to the horrible pain of one's own deceit, as every theory is a deceit, even this one, so that only the tentative half-truths remain. Tools which, when accepted, must lead to a hollow and infinite suffering: a clashing of sameness, the same lacerating itself with joy, and no joy, where two, one, or three don't matter and then . . . .

The cool breeze of the trees relaxed Jefferson as thoughts reverted to feelings, sensations on the skin, basilar vibrations in the ear, spots of light after one closes his eyes; these visceral tremors continued even after Julia got off her horse.

"It is as we feared; he doesn't have a chance in town."

"What shall we do?"

"We'll go to him, what else?"

As they rode, Julia told Jefferson that her father had just heard the news when he had come back from church, and that he forbade her to see John.

"I think that he should stay where he is until we know more about what the developments are. It is possible that they'll find the real killer, and then John will be off the hook."

They finally came upon John's spot and Julia silently looked at the tree and gestured as she had been instructed.

"I was wondering when you'd come," said John with a smile as he sprang out of a bush and into the water. "It certainly gets boring just sitting somewhere when you have to. You know I could have sat the same amount of time somewhere when I wasn't obliged to and have been *perfectly happy,* but when you know that you can't move, then somehow, the same interval gets longer and unbearable."

"Things don't look good," said Jefferson as he handed John a change of clothes and the fifty dollars. "When I left town, they said that in another hour they'd be out looking for you. They should have started by now."

"You don't think anyone followed you, do you?" asked John as he put the money in his pocket and stuffed the clothes in the saddlebag on the horse.

"No, we're safe, I'm sure."

Julia walked toward John and he put his arm around her.

"I brought you some food. I didn't know how long that you might have to be out here, but I thought that something might be welcomed."

"That was very nice of you," said John. "But it won't be too bad, I mean this can't go on forever."

Jefferson turned his head away when Dow said this. Julia got the food and offered John a piece of meat, which he took with pleasure. "What do you plan to do?" asked Jefferson.

"I don't know. It's difficult to say. I suppose basically I'll stay right here until I'm forced to leave or until the real murderer is caught. By the way, is anyone unconvinced that I did it?"

"Not from what I heard," replied Jefferson.

"It doesn't look too good, does it? Well what I suggest is that we plan certain meeting times, say every few days or so, in able to keep up on this thing."

"And I can bring you food," offered Julia.

"Thank you Julia, but you'll have to be careful not to be spotted. You and Jefferson are two people they are going to watch closely."

The group talked a while about various things, but there seemed to be a certain repetitiveness about it that all sensed as their nervousness. At this time, the men on the posse had paid a visit to the Beauchay residence, and found a startled Samuel Beauchay and Jason in their drawing room, reading before supper.

"We thought you might know where he might be?" asked Abe.

"No. I have no idea."

"How about the whereabouts of that man of yours."

"Jefferson?"

"If that's his name."

"I have no idea," responded Samuel.

"Then we'll have to try over at the Vanderkamps," said one of the men.

"Why over there?" asked Jason.

"Because the boy had a row last night over the girl, Julia, I think her name is. It was quite a row, in fact. Perhaps she might have some knowledge of his whereabouts."

It now became clear to Jason that perhaps Julia had liked both John and Victor. His first suspicions had been correct all along.

Victor was dead. The news was really a shock to Jason, but then when seen in another perspective, perhaps it was all for the best, as he would have been frustrated in his main desire; possessing Julia. So that perhaps this was for the best. Victor was out of the way.

Any warm feeling, or thawing of feeling between Jason and John, from the former's point of view, was now arrested as it seemed that in a sense John had been hiding his feelings about Julia all along, as several times Jason had asked John through various indirect means whether he cared for Julia (as he wanted to check his theory about Julia really caring for Victor and not Dow), and each time that he had tested the other, the same resulting negative occurred. Therefore, this new revelation seemed to go against everything that he had been testing over the past year or so.

John had lied to him, and the realization of this reality as perceived by Jason was not at all comforting.

"I don't like to say anything against the person who I've grown up with as almost a brother, and God knows that this is hard for me, but," began Jason, looking at Samuel Beauchay to test his reaction, "I may I know where he might be, but I don't know whether I can bring myself to tell you gentlemen. It seems to be proper, as you represent the law, but then again, how does one measure the commitment to one's friend, almost—brother?"

Samuel Beauchay was touched by the sentiment that Jason was expressing, and had not the other men been around, he would have probably pressed his son's hand warmly for it.

The leader of the posse, Abe, began to tell Jason about how he appreciated the loyalty he felt to his friend, but that for the law to operate, it needed the cooperation of all the citizens, and that it was necessary for justice to be served that Jason reveal to them where John might be so that they could see that the sacred cause might be fulfilled even if it meant great personal sacrifice on the part of the loved one's family. It was for the good of all for Jason to talk. Then Abe gave a brief description of the corpse and the scenario about how depraved a person must have been to do such a thing. They had to get Dow.

This speech must have moved Jason tremendously, as he then offered the men a rather detailed account of where John sometimes went when he wanted to be alone. It should be noted that Jason knew very few actual locations where John went, and did not know the place where he was actually hiding, but by some fluke, he did name a place that was very near to where John was.

Then the posse left, feeling assured that John would soon be theirs. None in the posse knew this land very well. Therefore, it was a stroke of misfortune that it came near to John's hideout. It was approaching six o'clock as the sun was three quarters in the sky and beginning its final descent, which would last several hours more.

The group tried to be very quiet as they entered the woods, thinking that if they scared the rabbit, he might run.

***

"I want you two to know that I appreciate all that you're doing for me. Why, if it wasn't for your help, I might have gotten a new necktie by now."

Neither Jefferson nor Julia laughed at this reference to a lynching, but tried to remain calm, when Julia said, "Be quiet, I think I hear something."

They were all still, but they could hear nothing. The conversation resumed when again Julia asked for quiet.

"You're going to have us tied up in knots with your nervousness," said John as he took another piece of meat and started to eat.

"Hush," repeated Julia.

"What's all this foolishness about—" began John, when Jefferson said, "I hear it too. They must be near. Either they are just lucky, or someone has told them where you are."

"But that would be impossible, nobody knew about this place but me."

Each of them looked at each other in nervousness as if expecting the other to explain this occurrence.

"We've got to leave. It's far easier to find three people than it is one. You'll have to go back into hiding."

John put his food away and gathered his bundles. Then Jefferson took off a chain from around his neck that had a misshapen cross on the end.

"Listen, John, things may be getting a little tight. I want you to take this," he said handing John the cross and chain. "It's stood me through many hard times; I'd like you to have it."

John took the cross and Jefferson's hand and grasped it firmly. The posse was getting closer, they were now fanning out around the area that Jason had described to them and one of these men was only a hundred yards away.

John didn't want to let go of Jefferson. A man was walking in their direction on an angle, and was now only a hundred and fifty feet away. Jefferson held John's hand and then put the cross inside the other's palm and closed his hand over the cross and chain.

Then John turned to Julia. The man was walking carefully with his rifle, ready and loaded. She looked so beautiful, but it wasn't only a beauty of the body, though he readily felt that, but what was more important was that proud independent spirit that he saw. It was a spirit that was in no way submissive, but an autonomous entity that seemed rich with inner resources. He reached out for her hand when the man, who was now only a hundred feet away, stepped on a dry branch that snapped with a loud crack!

The man fell down and his rifle went off.

"They're just over there," said Jefferson as he rushed to his horse. "We've got to go," he said to Julia, who was somewhat less in a hurry to depart. John watched the two mount their horses as he heard the commotion of the other men of the posse rushing to the aid of their comrade, who they imagined had been engaged in a battle with the renegade Dow. John watched his friends leave as he crossed the river to his place of secrecy.

Three men were quickly on the scene and were somewhat disgusted when they could see that their friend had merely fallen down and had discharged his rifle out of ineptitude rather than from an actual battle with the desperate killer Dow.

"On, Sam, you clod," exclaimed one of them, but the other now heard the horses of Jefferson and Julia which were close indeed, as they were attempting their escape.

"Quick, there's somebody nearby on horses," said the second.

The two rushed at an angle towards where the other path made a bend, and began firing warning shots. "Stop I say, or I'll blow your heads off," yelled one of the men, though in truth he could not yet see them and if they had chosen to make their escape it would have been quite possible, but due to the fact that Jefferson was riding with a young lady, he declined to risk such a venture, and slowed up his horse.

Soon the man with the gun stepped forward and ordered the two of them to get down from their horses.

Soon the whole posse was there as three shots were fired in the air, signaling that the others should gather.

"What do we have here?" asked Abe.

Jefferson didn't say anything.

"Why are you holding us at gun point?" declared Julia. "My father wouldn't appreciate your actions."

"Your father wouldn't appreciate you being alone with a nigger in the woods," replied another.

"What were you two doing in the woods?" asked Abe.

"I came to fetch Miss Julia so that she wouldn't be late for Sunday dinner; our families often invite each other to Sunday Dinner."

"That's very good, and so quick too. It must be true what they say, that you're a college man. I've got to hand it to you, boy, you're not as stupid as the rest of *your people*."

Jefferson looked straight ahead. These words no longer affected him.

"I think you were doing something else, though. I think you were aiding and giving comfort to a fugitive murderer. That's what I think."

Julia started to speak but checked herself.

"I don't know what you're talking about," replied Jefferson.

"Oh, then you don't know about the Stuart murder?"

"Yes, I heard about it, this afternoon, from some workers from the fields. But from what they said, there has been no autopsy, arrest warrant, or systematic gathering of evidence. That is what is called the 'rule of law.'"

"You're talking like a damn Yankee. We know how to take care of our own around here. "

Then another said, "You didn't say why you are here in the woods. When we talked to your master, Samuel Beauchay, he didn't know anything about the murder."

Jefferson could have risen to the bait, but instead said, "Mr. Beauchay likes to stay by himself on Sundays. Besides, what does this have to do with us?"

"Oh you'd like to know wouldn't you, nigger?" said one of the other men, who had a prominent scar on his right cheek. Scarface walked up and slapped Jefferson's face with the back of his hand with such force that it knocked Jefferson backwards. The aging man stumbled to his knee. Julia screamed, and Scarface came forward and grabbed her by the arms and started to shake her.

"Oh, does that frighten you, girly girl? Why, I'll show you what I can do to you—"

Then there was a gunshot in the air, and the man stopped. "Let the girl alone. She's the daughter of a respected landowner. I won't have us forget our stations," said Abe sternly so that the man let go of Julia's arms and walked back to his place.

"Now Julia, tell us where this murderer is."

"I don't know what you're talking about."

"You know very well," began Abe. "Where's this Doe?"

"You mean *Dow*? I don't know, but he's not a murderer."

Again Scarface rushed forward and grabbed Julia by the shoulder and spun her around, "Why you little—" he began as she staggered under the force of his grip. Then he ripped her dress at the shoulder, revealing the strap of her undergarment.

Abe moved in a hurry and tackled Scarface to the ground. Then Abe took a pistol from his pocket and held it to Scarface's throat, "If you so much as touch that woman again, you're going to meet your maker. We're not some animals. We are the Law! And don't you forget that. We're after a killer and we have to bring him to justice!" The Dutchman emitted a bestial snarling noise.

"But I only—"

"Did you hear me? I don't want to hear another word from you. That girl is a nice girl and I will not allow you to treat her as if she wasn't, fugitive or no fugitive."

Then he turned to Julia, who had pulled up the shoulder of her dress again, and tipped his hat, "I'm sorry, Miss Julia, for the rudeness of this man. He has been overcome by the passion of the hunt. Will you accept my apologies and kindly feel free to leave? We have no further need for you."

"John Dow is not a murderer; you're making a big mistake," she said.

"I think you'd better go home," he repeated.

Julia looked over to Jefferson. She feared what might happen to him if she left, but he nodded for her to leave. What should she do? With many second thoughts, she mounted her horse and started away with the idea that if she could get back soon enough, she could send someone out to help Jefferson.

As she left, Abe motioned to several of the men (about half of the group) to follow her.

"Unless I'm wrong, she's going to go to Dow and warn him of our activity. Follow her and she'll take you right to him."

Then he divided the remainder of the men into two groups, one to stay with him to persuade Jefferson to talk, and the other to scout the area in case it was here that John was hiding. Abe didn't know whether they had just been with Dow or were on their way to see him. With this plan, he thought that he could adequately cover both eventualities.

Then he turned and looked at Jefferson for a full minute or so without talking. "I can see that you're going to be a difficult case. Why not make it easier on yourself?"

But Jefferson was silent.

Chapter 5

"The Hunt"

Julia could sense that she was being followed and that it would be necessary to shake her pursuers if she was to get help for Jefferson, so she rode at a fast gallop towards the Vanderkamp lake (the one with the island in the center) and when she got there, she tied up her horse on a tree by the water and then ran around the lake so that she couldn't be seen in the twilight. The five pursuers weren't particularly good horsemen, nor were their horses very fast, so they were quite a distance behind Julia and didn't notice that she had gone around the island and then on to her own stables to get another horse.

Instead they saw the horse tied to the tree and assumed that John must be on the island, so they got off their horses and spent some time devising a plan as to how they could get to the island without making a noise and still keep their guns dry. The lake was too deep to wade; they would have to swim. Yet, their bulky clothes, in addition to making too much noise, would be too cumbersome to swim in, so they craftily decided to only take two rifles, which would be carried by the two men who could swim the best (they would swim sidestroke with one hand holding the gun), and strip down to their underwear so as to make less noise, which was agreed upon after a little debate (begun by the three men who didn't wear underwear—who would have to go buck naked). But such details were quickly settled. It was getting darker and the island was very bushy. So the group set to work to implement their plan.

Meanwhile, Julia was saddling up a horse when Rodney came in to the stable to see what was happening (as Julia wasn't too quiet in her task). But as Mr. and Mrs. Vanderkamp were out on their evening stroll, he was the only one who could hear her.

"What are you doing?" asked Rodney.

"I'm saddling up a horse, what's it look like?"

"Want me to help you?"

"If you like."

So Rodney helped her lift the heavy saddle and cinch up the horse when he asked, "Why do you want to saddle up the horse?"

"Because I want to go riding," she replied.

This seemed to satisfy Rodney, until she was just about ready to go, when he asked, "Why do you want to go riding?"

Julia hesitated—should she tell her brother? Could her brother help her? The men with Jefferson thought she was acting only out of a blind passionate love for Dow, and that she was not rational. And wasn't it true that Rodney was quite a capable fighter? And wouldn't it be better for her to have as many bodies as possible to act as an intimidation to the band of cutthroats who wouldn't understand anything except violence? But on the other hand, he could call the whistle on her at any time, and possibly arrest her efforts at saving Jefferson.

She looked at Rodney, who was waiting for a response and quickly answered, "C'mon and I'll tell you, but you better be quick, someone's in trouble and we've got to help him."

Rodney didn't ask any more questions, but saddled up a horse in excellent time and caught up to Julia, who had already started towards the Beauchay estate.

"What's this all about sis? Does it have anything to do with the fuss in town today?"

"Then you've heard," she said.

"Yes, we found out at church that Victor has been killed."

"Murdered, they say."

"Yes, murdered. That's right. But for the life of me I can't understand why anyone would want to murder poor Victor."

"Then you don't know," she said, surprised that her brother hadn't heard the rumors that had been flying around the town.

"They suspect that John did it."

"John Dow?" said Rodney in astonishment.

Julia nodded her assent.

"Why that's ridiculous. He wouldn't hurt a fly, and especially not Victor. Why I remember lots of times that Victor tried to get John into fights, and John wouldn't have any part of it, and even when they did fight, John was always trying to fight defensively; he never liked to fight."

Rodney paused. The entire idea of John Dow killing somebody seemed so utterly absurd that he couldn't understand how anyone with any sense would fall for such a flagrantly outrageous story. "You don't believe it do you, sis?" he said in a slightly different tone, as he wanted to make sure that his sister felt the same way as he did. Rodney was not always conscious of what others about him were feeling about a particular topic, having never been one to concern himself with what others were thinking or the minute variations that they might be experiencing in moods or disposition. He was a very open person, he thought, and why should not others, if they wished to be understood, be as open, i.e., if they wanted something to be known, then why not come right out and speak it plainly? This he believed to be the best course of action, but, alas being somewhat of a realist, he knew that this was not always the case. So often, if he wanted to be certain of what others were thinking or if he suspected that there was something that he was supposed to be perceiving through some extra sense that was not developed in his person, then he would make the bold and explicit statement of his question so that there could be no doubt.

"Of course I don't. And neither does Jefferson, but some of the men in the town have formed a lynch mob and are out after John."

"A lynch mob!" exclaimed Rodney.

"Yes, and I just left Jefferson, as we were overcome by the men who wanted us to tell them where John was. They let me go because I was a woman. But I'm afraid for Jefferson's safety."

"Shouldn't we call the sheriff?"

"The sheriff is an old man. Besides they have the unofficial sanction of the sheriff, who wasn't strong enough to control them. The important thing to do now is to get over to the Beauchay's and get to Mr. Beauchay and try to elicit his help in rescuing Jefferson." Rodney gave his full ascent as they arrived at the Beauchay house and knocked on the front door.

At this time, the men dispatched to capture John and Julia were just making their way to the island, despite sonic complaints about the coldness of the water, which were actually loud enough to have frightened anyone away who might have been on the island, though, of course, this wasn't in the consideration of the men, who were busy trying to negotiate the water (as none of them were really good swimmers, even the ones who claimed to be able to do the side stroke in order to keep the guns dry). The water was cold—especially for those who were entirely au naturel.

"You say they have Jefferson?" answered Beauchay.

"They're an angry mob, Mr. Beauchay, and were going to rough me up, if one of them hadn't come to my aid."

"They seemed quiet enough when they were over here," Mr. Beauchay said, almost to himself. "Of course we must go and rescue Jefferson." These problems were very upsetting to Samuel Beauchay, as he was at present in the midst of dinner, and in a greater context was mentally engaged in other problems which he wished to devote his entire mind towards. It always seemed to him that whenever he was really engaged with a particular problem that there was always something to distract him so that he could never devote himself fully to it. But of course this was serious, as Jefferson wasn't a young man and could easily be overly strained by physical torture. He hadn't really considered that the posse was a lynch mob, or that they might have blood on their minds. He really didn't even consider that John was actually thought to be the one who had performed the murder, though looking back on it it seemed that it must have been made perfectly clear to him at the time. Somehow, everything had happened so quickly and in addition, he had been somehow so concerned with Jason: what he thought or was feeling that he, Samuel Beauchay, had not given ample consideration to his own predilections on the said topic. Indeed, now that he considered it in this new light, it did seem dubious that John would ever have committed a murder. No, John wouldn't have done this. John was a little headstrong at times and not very prudent, but he wasn't a murderer.

What had he been thinking of before? Had he thought that the group headed by Abe was just after John as a witness or accessory, or something minor? He had certainly never considered that they were accusing John of murder, himself! Everything seemed rather vague, as the event previously had flowed so smoothly, *We want to talk to John in connection with—in connection with—in connection with*—did connection with necessarily mean that they believed that John had done the deed? Certainly it was strongly implied, but somehow the connection had not been made by Samuel at the time. He had been preoccupied. He had felt so proud of something that Jason had said that he somehow forgot—it was something that showed his, Jason's, loyalty and trust in John, that somehow he had felt that it was sufficiently clear that he and Jason supported Dow completely. Certainly they didn't consider him to be a murderer!

The entire scene seemed to reiterate to him the recurring problem of something that was trying to divert his attention from his intended sights. His struggling with his distraction (trying, as it were, to make it go away by force of will, ignoring it until it finally pulled him from his appointed task). It placed him in a new predicament. He had been thinking about George Dodson, and his new land and the oil men, but these thoughts had to be tabled as the situation now demanded his full and entire attention. Of course, if the personal safety of Jefferson was now being threatened, and John was possibly being hunted as a murderer, a crime which anyone who knew John must declare him incapable of committing, then he, Samuel Beauchay, must drop everything else and devote himself fully to this new calling,

And so, without too much delay, Samuel Beauchay saddled up and got together some of his hands from the fields to accompany them as they rode out to where Julia was directing them.

On the island, the two men with the rifles climbed onto the bank and checked the mechanisms to be sure that they were operable. They felt sure the guns were fine, but this judgment was more a hope than a considered judgment. Then all of them were on the bank and they crept about the island searching for the renegade couple.

"Are you sure they're here, Clem?" asked one of the men with the rifles.

"Shush, and keep crawling. We don't want to give ourselves away."

"But it might take us forever to crawl around this whole thing."

"Then it'll take forever, now shush."

And so they crawled about the bushes, getting quite dirty as water on their bodies from the traverse had a way of attracting dirt.

***

The crowd of men started laughing as Jefferson tumbled to the ground from the impact of the blow.

"Now, we don't want to get too rough with you, nigga, but we have got to get our information."

"You're no deputies of the law," started Jefferson, his hands tied behind his back, kneeling on the ground, "You're just a group of wild men, who want to take the law into their own hands."

"Wild men, wild men are we?" exclaimed Scarface, who now stepped forward and kicked Jefferson in the ribs, making the man fall backwards and groan as a result of the jarring, dull thud. Then Scarface was about to administer another of the same (as it seemed that he really didn't care about finding any information, but simply teaching this uppity nigger who had gotten an education). Scarface knew that Georgia niggers, no matter how fine they talked, weren't worth any more than a barnyard dog.   He was ready to kill this insolent animal. The moment was ripe.

But then the moment was interrupted by a defiant taunt,

"Hey, you Georgia Crackers come and get me. That is, if you're man enough not to beat upon a man who's worth more than the lot of you. If you mean what you say, come and get me!"

Then John turned his horse and started away.

"Mount up, men, and after him! We've flushed him out," cried Abe. Scarface, still standing over Jefferson, was of two minds. He felt like just staying and beating the tar out of Jefferson, but on the other hand Abe had been strict with him before about the purpose of the posse, but he was sure that Abe didn't love these blacks any more than he did, so he finally decided to stay and gave Jefferson another painful kick, this time in the kidneys. Then there was a rifle shot that whizzed past the head of the eager zealot standing above his quarry.

Scarface spun around and saw Abe atop his horse with his gun pointed at him. "The next shot goes into your head, are you riding or not?"

Without very much hesitation, the other walked over to his horse and started off with the group, leaving Jefferson alone, tied up on the ground in considerable pain.

The appearance of John was not coincidental. He had heard the three warning shots, and figured that it must have been some kind of signal, and so he had carefully made his way to where he could observe what was going on. He saw their rough treatment of Julia, and the threats of what they were going to do with Jefferson, so he, John, carefully made his way back to his horse and untied it, leading it to where he could make a dramatic entrance with as little risk to himself as possible and allowing them a good enough view so that there was no mistake at who it was.

In this way, he had hoped to lure the desperadoes away from Jefferson, who he was sure would never have told them anything. Jefferson, who he regarded as his father, was in the position of grave physical harm. Nothing else mattered to John but to save Jefferson.

John hoped to lead the men on a merry chase on the winding trails of the forest, which he knew well enough so that he could ride very quickly, even at twilight, and which the others would have considerably more trouble, especially when it became completely dark.

There were gunshots that were uncomfortably close as John took a turn that he was certain would fool them as he headed towards Mitchel Evans' farm. By some strange quirk, one of the men in Abe's party took another route, thinking that he could cut the distance that separated them by riding cross-country (a very foolish thing to do in the semi-darkness) but he happened to arrive at the trail that John was to take before him, so to John's surprise, he found himself face to face with a man and rifle as he galloped down this new trail.

John saw the gun and tried to turn his animal so sharply that the horse lost his footing, and the shot that was intended for the felling of Dow met the horse instead. The blood of the animal spurted out into the air; the bullet had hit a main artery and caused a surging flow that was under great pressure. John was pinned under the animal, whose weight was considerable, but almost as if the cumbersome animal knew what was happening, it tried to stand again, allowing John to be free. Then there was no other shot as the horse staggered. John saw that there would be little he could do to save his beloved horse, so he took flight into the trees. There was another shot and John felt a stinging —a sharp stabbing pain almost like a sudden burn, but still he kept running.

The others joined the first and started after John, cross-country on their horses, though this area was quite dense and difficult to negotiate on horseback.

"Let's split up, you three go on horse to the field where this comes out to meet our friend there, and we'll pursue on foot. Remember, take him alive so we can hang him. A bullet is so quick and easy. The noose is more appropriate to his kind."

And with that the group separated, but the time allotted gave John an opportunity to get well out of rifle range, in the woods, as he found a path that he'd never seen and started down it, intending to go back into the bushes when his pursuers had shortened the distance. Suddenly he felt that same muscle tighten again in his leg from a couple days before. He wouldn't be able to run. And with no horse, his chances of survival now seemed to be slim indeed. The land about him was quite flat. John made a mental note of this as he pulled up from his run. The cramp in his leg now made even walking impossible.

The group was about a hundred and fifty yards behind, and now they were carrying torches as the twilight was fading into darkness. Then John stumbled and fell. He didn't move. He couldn't move effectively. His mind raced. Though he'd never had any ambition in his life, still it seemed to him to be very sad that he should die in this manner at his young age. There could have been so much for him to do—so many mistakes he had made now flashed in his mind. He thought of Cindy and what a fool he had been all this time.

Here he had Julia, who was so loving and kind, waiting for him. How much had Julia known about Cindy? Several statements that Julia had made could have indicated that she knew everything. But how could she have known all and still have continued to love him? The power of what he imagined to be such a perfect love moved him almost to tears. How he had violated the trust of the most perfect creature in the world, and then that he had the audacity to make advances, formal and limited as they were, to one so much above him made John feel like the lowest creature on the earth.

Perhaps I deserve to die? He put forth to himself. He remembered his childhood and all the adventures that he had undertaken. It had been so good to be a young lad, with no cares in the world, so that he could go fishing at any time that he wanted to and never have to worry about a thing. John wanted to be left alone. He had the friendship of young Julia, who used to share so passionately his love of animals. Why did he need anything else? All these incidents melded together to create a crushing feeling in his breast as he was falling to the ground and he rolled to the side off into the bushes, which happened to be blackberry bushes with sharp thorns that tore at his shirt and stuck into his skin. But being in the midst of thick undergrowth afforded him excellent cover. He wanted to cry. He wanted to sleep, but something kept him alert, even as the men passed him on the road and didn't notice where he was, partially hidden, off to the side.

He had a reprieve. He would do all those things that he had failed to do in his life up to now, his first life. All his mistakes would be rectified. He was certain that this sign of Providence should not go unheeded. He would be a better person, he told himself as he dragged himself out of the stickers, which, now that the men were gone, were beginning to become painful and irritating.

John knew that he could not take too long as the men would soon be back when they reached the end of the trail and didn't find him there. So John decided to go directly into the woods where he had better cover. After a short while, he stopped to rest. He was a long ways from where he had made his remarkable escape, but still he imagined that he could hear the men in the distance and the image of the faces illumined by the torches made him decide to hobble (for walking normally was quite impossible), as rest would do him no good if he was captured.

***

The party of Samuel Beauchay, hearing the shots in the distance, feared the worst. No one said a word, but the question that was on everyone's minds, though unspoken, was, "Was that shot for Jefferson or John?"

Soon they came upon the place of incarceration. On the ground was the figure of Jefferson lying lifeless. Quickly, Samuel Beauchay jumped from his horse and rushed over to Jefferson and cut the rope that tied his hands, and he put his ear to his friend's chest. He was alive, but was probably unconscious from shock.

Samuel Beauchay took off his coat and put it on his comrade and then took off his shirt to help secure him on Beauchay's horse.

"We'll take him as far as the field, and then you, Rodney, get our wagon. I think that it would be better to transport him lying down in case anything's broken. Also, we'll need some blankets."

They made their way back to the field. Julia tried to help as much as she could, but the older man, Mr. Beauchay, insisted on caring for his friend and could not be separated from his side, even after they had taken Jefferson back to the house and called for the doctor.

"I don't know why he didn't come to me," said Mr. Beauchay.

"There wasn't much time, and you were out," said Julia.

She was right. He had been out inspecting his new land holdings. But if he had only known—he would have been back in an instant. Beauchay hated to see a person he cared for lying supine in the bed waiting for the doctor—waiting to receive the verdict on whether or not he would make it.

Many thoughts and remembrances passed through his mind as he sat by his friend's side feeling that somehow he was to blame for what had happened. Somehow, he wasn't sure how, perhaps that was part of the problem, but there must have been a way that he could have helped, or prevented the awful nightmare from ever taking place.

Julia also waited, though her brother encouraged her to go home and that he would come ask if any new occurrence developed, but she was determined to stick it out, as she felt sorry for Jefferson, but also felt closer to John being near the man who had sacrificed his own physical safety to aid Dow. How she would gladly have allowed herself to be beaten, she thought, to be able to save John from the outrages that the mob wished to inflict.

And where was he now? Safe in his hiding place most likely, she thought. John was too clever to be found by somebody at twilight. He had spent the entire day working out a retreat for himself, so that he would be perfectly safe. But did he have enough food? They had been interrupted too quickly for them to make any plans. Perhaps tomorrow she would ride out with some food for him.

The doctor came and went, saying that Jefferson had several badly bruised ribs, but that no bones had been broken. Further, there was no obvious signs of internal damage, though of course, it was too early to say for certain whether he would be completely all right.

As to his unconsciousness, the doctor said that he would come out of it sooner or later, and that it had probably been induced by the pain and the shock of the ordeal.

After another hour or so, Jefferson sat up quickly—bolt upright, and declared to the startled people in the room, "John's in danger. I can feel it. I can feel it."

Samuel Beauchay, not knowing what to make of this sudden revelation, put his hand on his friend's shoulder and laid him quietly back into bed. "There, there, it's going to be all right. The doctor's been here to see you. It will all be fine."

Rodney motioned for Julia that perhaps it was time for them to go. Jefferson had regained consciousness. But Julia, though she allowed herself to be escorted home after paying her respects to Jefferson, was now afraid of what the other had said. Had they indeed discovered John's hiding place? Was John at this moment lying helpless somewhere as Jefferson was? But if he was, it would be futile to try and search him out. The evening covered the spacious forests with its blanket of invisibility. John could be anywhere—alive or dead.

The thought she refused to entertain was the possibility that he might be dangling somewhere at the bottom of a rope.

***

"I don't think they're anywhere on this island," said one of the men who was getting cold, crawling around without any clothes.

"I agree with Sam, I don't think we're going to find them."

"They must have gotten off the island somehow, without our knowing it. But how?"

Then they heard the noise of a man and a woman talking. They also saw a light in the distance. "There they are. They must have left the island to get something to eat and now they're returning. I say we swim back and get them before they cross."

There was no disagreement to this plan as they prepared again for their perilous crossing. However what they didn't realize was that the pair they had taken for John and Julia was really Mr. and Mrs. Vanderkamp returning from their walk.

The motley crew managed to get back across the pond just as the two were approaching. All of them assembled on the bank and then rushed out from behind the group of trees with their guns, making quite a loud noise.

Now Mr. and Mrs. Vanderkamp had been walking ever so peacefully as they had taken their usual Sunday night constitutional, which consisted of a large turn around some of their land. They would talk over what had happened the past week and what they planned to do the following week, and after they had all of it discussed and decided, then they would pretend that they were young lovers, alone on a summer's evening, feeling daring because they were walking arm in arm. It was in such a mood that they were in when they approached the group of aforementioned trees. Mr. Vanderkamp was carrying a lantern that would make sure that they didn't step into any holes and twist their ankles, as they knew that they weren't as young as they used to be and such an accident could put on of them up for a couple of weeks, possibly. At any rate, the lantern was carried low, so as to only cast light on the ground, and so their faces were largely in the shadows, so that when the men jumped out in front of them, there was a mutual lack or recognition.

"All right, stop right there," shouted one of the men holding his rifle. Mrs. Vanderkamp, who was in the romantic mood described above, jumped backwards in startled surprise, while Mr Vanderkamp lifted his head angrily as he raised the light of the lantern to perceive who his assailants might be. However, much to his surprise (and I might say shock) he found himself affronted by eight men, five of whom were in only their underwear, and three who wore nothing at all! It should also be remembered that they were sopping wet, which added another layer of oddity to their presentation.

"What do you want?!"

The men quickly saw their mistake. Two of them instantly recognized the Vanderkamps, as they knew them by reputation, and surmising the situation for what it was, instantly dove back into the trees and modesty of darkness from whence they had come. The two were followed by five more in their exodus leaving only their leader standing in his dripping underwear holding a gun. However, when he saw that he was alone, he quickly followed his comrades, dropping his gun and running away with as much quiet as he had entered with noise.

Mr. Vanderkamp lifted the lantern higher and saw that the men were apparently gathering their clothes and running away with them.

"Now that was odd," said Mr. Vanderkamp after an elongated pause as he was trying to somehow appraise the situation, without much success. "I wonder what they wanted?"

But Mrs. Vanderkamp could only manage the weak reply in an almost question, "Landsakes! What?"

Chapter 6

"In which Several Personae make Entrances and Exits"

John was stumbling through the woods when he finally came upon a stretch of open field that he recognized to be the end of the Mitchell Evans farm. Only a hundred yards further and he would be to the road. Unknown to John was the group of men who had been guarding the edge of the forest and were only an acre or two away. But John, who was in no hurry, stumbled along relatively quietly, as the closest watchman had gone to search for his comrade, to see whether they should call it a night. Thus, the watchman did not see or hear John as he made his way to the road.

On the road, John was determined to flag down the first car that he saw. *If it's one of the men who are after me, then so be it,* he thought, *because they're going to get me for sure, if I'm out here.*

Strangely enough a car did come, and seeing John standing in the middle of the road, it pulled over and stopped. The driver was the same man who had given John a ride into Varner's Junction at the beginning of the weekend. He had spent his time in Savannah, and now was heading home, poorer, but tired and satisfied. When he saw the man again, who he thought no doubt was still carrying a gun somewhere, he did not argue when he stopped and John got into his car. John quickly recognized the car and driver, too, and asked the man where he was heading.

"Anywhere, mister, anywhere you want." His voice was fast and nervous, for he had no money for John to steal now. He did regard his life in a more tender vein than he had when his bank roll was burning through his pocket. The weekend of sensual pleasure gave the driver a will to live.

"I want to go wherever you are going."

The driver didn't need any more incentive for his conviction that this man was a criminal. The driver thought he noticed dried blood on John's neck. Along with Dow's clothes, which were tattered from the weeds, he certainly did look terrible.

John detected the driver's attitude after an hour or so. They passed from county to county, putting a comfortable distance between him and dear Bella County.

Dow studied the size of the driver, but immediately came to the conclusion that his clothes would be too large. He must buy some new clothes the next morning. Looking as he did, he would be easy to trace, and then they would be on his trail quickly.

"I'm getting near my town. The sign for it was back there, only two miles," said the man.

"Okay. I'll go the whole way."

Now by this John meant the entire way to the town, but the driver took it to mean the entire way to his house, which might include an overnight accommodation.

"Yes sir," he replied and drove into town, when John surprised him by saying, "You can let me out here, that'll be fine."

The driver was so relieved that he said, "Oh, thank you sir, and you don't have to worry; I won't tell a soul."

John didn't like this last phrase, as it signified to him that indeed the other probably would tell the police of his whereabouts as soon as he could. So John got out and thanked the driver, leaving the frightened man to his own devices.

He's probably going to telephone as soon as he gets back, decided John. *I've got to find a train station.* John walked about the streets of the town, which were empty, being about one o'clock, and soon found that the town did indeed have a terminal. On the schedule that was on the wall, however, he found that he could not get a train until ten o'clock the next morning, which would be too late. *They'll have me by then*, he thought, when he heard a train whistle. It was a freight train. He had never tried jumping a freight train, but it seemed so easy, as the cars moved so slowly, that he thought that there would be no trouble.

The train slowed down some as it came through the station area, and after the front of the train passed, John started running as best he could (his leg was still very painful, though the muscle had loosened some). He caught a hold of the attached ladder at the end of the box car. *This wasn't too hard*, he told himself, but how to get inside the boxcar? The task had seemed easier than it now appeared to actually be. What he'd have to do is to climb atop the car and then attempt to open the door from the top and then swing down into the car. He waited until they were well away from the town before he climbed onto the top of the car. He found though that the door was bolted shut with a lever that swung down and was almost impossible to open from his angle. What was he to do? His decision was expedited by the sight of nine balls of lead that were hanging from a bridge close ahead. *They'd knock me right off*, he thought. And so he climbed down the ladder again, this time taking the one that was adjacent to the inter-car coupling. This was really two "J" shaped cast-metal 18" x 18" fittings: one from each car that made the connection. They held the cars together, but they shifted about a bit as there were turns in the track. It was not an easy move, but John didn't feel as if he had much choice. Then John heard someone walking atop the train. It was a railroad man paid to keep the trains free from people like John. Dow had heard of such men and how they beat people sadistically and didn't care whether the poor soul was injured or killed in the process. So John, preparing for the worst, got himself in position to jump, if necessary. Soon the man came into view, wielding a club about the size of a man's forearm.

Their eyes met for an instant, and then John saw the man reach into his pocket, as John was out of range of his club but John didn't wait any longer and jumped from the train with hardly a look, as he thought he heard a gunshot, though the noise of the train made this assertion difficult to claim with any real certainty.

John, luckily enough, landed on the side of a grassy hill and rolled easily down after the initial impact. The grass there was tall and comfortable. After lying there a moment, Dow looked around to see if he could detect anyone from the early morning light of the moon. All was calm, so he walked toward a bush and curled himself around it for added warmth and protection and fell asleep.

It seemed to John as if he had just closed his eyes when he became aware of something cold on his neck. Instinct told him to open his eyes slowly and not to make any sudden movements. His eyes revealed that the coldness was the prongs of a farmer's pitchfork, which was being held to his throat.

"Ah, *Buenos dias*; I sees you is awaking up, there. Have enough *belleza del sueño*?" Then the man let out a sort of cackling laugh that lasted only an instant when the other stopped and asked John accusatively, "What are you, a bum?"

John didn't answer, but motioned that it might be easier to talk if the man would kindly move his pitchfork from his throat.

"Nothin' doin, I want to know if you is a bum or not. Cause if you is, I'm goin ta have ta kill you, and if you is not, then I'm going to put you ta work, cause I got a lot to do."

"I'll work," managed John in a whisper.

"What was that?"

"I'll work," repeated John in the same voice without hesitation.

"Well, then if you is willing to work you must not be a bum, right?" said the man, taking the pitchfork away and lending John a hand to stand. "We is going to have us quite a day of it; *hace mucho calor*, oh yes a very hot 'un that's for sure." John looked about him and saw that indeed the sun was already hot for being so early in the morning.

Chapter 7

"Developing Plans"

"I'll tell you, Ike," began Ed, "I don't know whether eit's me or this here town, but with everthin' goin' on, I gets to feeling my years."

"Yaah, I reckon we've all been feelin' that way what with that shootin' and all awhile back."

"They still haven't caught that boy yet, have they?" asked Ed.

"Nope," replied Ike. "And I bet they never will. I think he's too smart for them."

"Well one thing's for certain, he must be pretty smart to have been able to have gotten away from that posse when they had him right there and all."

"What makes you so sure that the Dow boy did it?" asked Jake, jumping one of Ed's red pieces.

"Don't know. I suspect it's for the same reason as everyone else," replied Ed, taking his eyes off the game for a moment.

"You got some doubts, Jake?" asked Ike.

"Don't know, but seems too odd to me to be jist what it seems. Kinda like that other one we had a few years back with Victor Stuart's wife. Too much is obvious for me, people jist aren't like that; ya can't give 'em simple motives for doing things. And when that is a simple reason, it generally looks like it's a real complicated one. I always say that whenever ya think ya have a feller figured, that nine times out a ten, ya haven't."

"Ya may be right, Jake, but what else is a person ta think?"

"Don't rightly know, twhich is why I ain't offerin' no theories of my own, but what I do know is that it jist don't seem right—something don't jive."

There was a prolonged silence as the men made several tactical moves in which Ed was faced with choosing between two moves which would either give Jake a double jump or a king. After much deliberation he chose the latter.

"Are you goin' to go to Beauchay soon?" asked Jake, breaking the silence.

"I was thinking about waiting a spell for things to settle down some, afore I went."

"I wouldn't waste too much time, if I was you," said Ed.

"You know, oil won't wait fer no man."

Jake looked up as if he recognized some famous line, or something in that vein, but then turned his concentration back to the game.

***

"I tell you all, it will be a splendid idea."

"What makes you so sure?" asked one of the men in the back row.

"As you can see by our graphs, 1929 is an ideal year for investing, all the factors that we normally consider in ventures such as this are at prime moments. If I were you, gentlemen, I'd waste no time in forming into the corporation that Mr. Whren suggests." The thin man who delivered this speech sat down amidst grumblings and assorted hurts of applause.

Then Oscar Whren stood up. "Gentlemen, I believe that the proposal has been adequately put forth. I now propose that we entertain some discussion on the topic. We do not have to abide by any of Mr. Johnston's recommendations if we don't want to, or we may decide to act on any or all of them, but I think that this is something that we don't want to rush into; at least I for one wouldn't like to see us either make a mistake by rushing into something, nor do we want to pass up an opportunity of making money when it could be made."

There was general agreement to this sound advice as the crowd of men began to talk things over among themselves. After a time one man arose. "We've done pretty well on the investment in this casino, you've always paid big dividends. I've been happy. I've always wanted us to bring in a moving picture theater. They make a lot of money." The man cleared his throat and cleaned out his right ear with the little figure of his right hand. He wiped off the earwax onto his trousers and continued, "And now we have to consider *this* deal. You say we'll be able to share directly in the profit. I think it sounds like a good idea to me."

"My question is," another started, "what is our personal liability in such a venture?"

"Nothing," replied Mr. Johnston. "Being a corporation instead of a company, you are exempt from any individual personal liability. If anything goes wrong, they sue the corporation and the insurance company. We're not liable if someone is hurt on the property, and the like."

"What kind of real estate would we be investing in?"

"That depends," began Mr. Johnston, "on how much power you decide to give me. You may want to set up a committee of several men to approve each of my decisions, or on the other hand you may want to give me complete control. With one, you'd be in the say on each piece of land purchased, though the slowness of the process might mean that we'd lose any really hot commodity items where speed is essential. However, the safeguards there provide for greater control. The decision is yours."

"Will it be agricultural or industrial property?"

"That depends on which is the most promising."

"How much money can we expect to make?"

"That also depends on what kinds of risks you are willing to engage in. Obviously the greater the risks, the greater the potential return, conversely the safer the investment, the more gradual the return on capital is. It all depends on which way you gentlemen want to take this."

Mr. Vanderkamp stood and asked, "What sort of outlay is this going to entail from each of us?"

"An initial purchase of at least one thousand dollars of stock per person would be a minimum for any real leverage. However, if you gentlemen would wish to spend more, that couldn't hurt."

There was some discussion about the sum of a thousand dollars being very great. Indeed, many of the men didn't have a thousand dollars in ready money—though they were unwilling to say so directly.

"If there are any of you who would choose to take a loan from the bank," began Mr. Johnston, sensing the sore area, "then I'm certain that we could very easily get the money as this venture would certainly qualify as a bona fide venture that would be accepted. Understand that these would be personal loans to you as individuals, but that as the money was going into an endeavor such as this that the bank would not hesitate to give you the money. And your money would be making more in an annual interest, most likely, in this scheme than any other way, even subtracting the percent that you must pay on your loan."

This last argument was most persuasive to all and soon without much further discussion the new company was voted into existence and the participants signed the necessary legal papers, making them bona fide stock holders in this business venture. It was decided that, at least for the time being, a committee would supervise the acquisition and divestiture of all properly.

Almost everyone left the meeting with a feeling that he was part of a dynamic new venture that was going to make them a good deal of money.

***

There was a single insect flying about in square-shaped flying patterns inside the store. The bug was driving Ike into fits as he tried everything he could think of to rid himself of this pest. But each time the fly seemed to elude his grasp.

Finally, the fly landed on the checker board. Ike hovered above the board, prepared to strike, when Jake motioned to Ike to stop and wait a moment. Jake stretched out his right hand over the fly about seven inches from the table and cupped his hand, then took his left hand and strummed the table with his fingers, moving closer and closer to the fly until the fly started off. Just as it did, Jake snapped his wrist and closed his hand on his captured prey. He then shook it a few times as if he was shaking some dice and finally tossed the stunned half-dead fly into the spittoon, finishing the job.

"Flies always start by going straight up. All you have to do is be ready for them."

"Much obliged," said Ike, putting his rolled newspaper away.

"I thought you were going to scatter checkers all over here," said Ed with a smile.

"I might have, too. I was in jist the mood. That fly had me real riled."

The two of them continued as Ike began straightening up the store. "I went to Beauchay's the other day," he offered. Both the others stopped and watched him.

"What did he have to say?" asked Jake.

"Nothing doing," he said. "He told me that I'd be safer investing my money in that casino project than to spend my money on his oil field. He kept emphasizing to me that tit wasn't finished nor confirmed. And I says I know that, and that's the reason that I expect to get in so cheap. But he still wouldn't have it as he said it was necessary for those two oilmen to come by again and have another look."

"Really, they're comin' back?" asked Jake.

"Yep, that's what Beauchay told me."

"Thar might be something to it, do ya believe us now, Jake?" put Ed in a tone that said, 'I told you so all along.' "I was the first one to find out about this you know."

But Jake only sat back in his chair shaking his head as if he didn't really believe that it could be true.

"I'm not yet satisfied that he's given me a fair shake. I'll give him another try, he's bound to soften. I got a feelin' about that land that it's going to make someone a lot of money, and I want to get in on it if I can."

"So would I, if I could," replied Ed, but Jake didn't reply as he was still leaning back in his chair.

Chapter 8

"Further Details on a Certain Land Deal"

When Julia got the following letter, she could hardly wait to tell someone, but who could she tell?

> *I'm fine at present, meaning that I'm still alive.*
> *I want to try and arrange a meeting with Jefferson some time, but at present, it is impossible. I think often of you.*
>
> > *John*

Jefferson was away, and she dare not tell her father, about whose reaction she was unsure. Rodney was away as he was conditioning for imminent departure to the University of Alabama. There seemed to be no one, and yet she was just bursting to tell someone.

It was mid-day when a figure, long forgotten around the Beauchay estate, George Dodson, came driving up in his new automobile and stopped at the house. Samuel Beauchay heard him coming and dreaded the meeting, though he had expected it for some time.

"How are you, Sam old boy?"

"Won't you come in, George?" replied Beauchay, who didn't like calling the other 'George,' but then there was nothing else to call

him. He certainly couldn't call him Mr. Dodson, or Mr. President—
or anything else really except 'George,' though because of the
familiarity which the name implied, Samuel felt very false and
uneasy.

"Step into my study. I believe you will remember the way."

"I do quite well, thank you," replied the other.

They went in and sat down.

"Let me get right to the point," started George. "You have a
piece of land that is right next to my property and I'd like to expand
a little, you know make my place a little larger, and I think that the
acquisition of this piece of land would be very nice for a small estate
of my own."

Beauchay smiled. Dodson was going to pretend that he knew
nothing of the oil on the land. It was a part of the bargaining and
jockeying for position that was inevitable.

"Well, you know, I've grown quite attached to that little piece
of land myself. It's so picturesque, don't you think? I think it was a
terrific idea to make it into a golf course, as it has such a pastoral
effect. Nine years have passed, nine summers with the length of
nine long winters—" Beauchay looked up. Dodson didn't understand
the purpose of the transposition, or indeed what was being
transposed; it reminded him once again what kind of man he was
dealing with. "What I mean is that I think that I just like the land for
what it is. I get deep personal peace from it, and when that west
wind blows over the overgrown grasses, I feel inspired to write an
ode or an elegy." Beauchay was breaking up inside with laughter as
he finally had Dodson in a position in which he could lambast the
other in a private display since Dodson's ignorance and disgusting
pettiness would let all be dismissed in his single-minded vision.
What a barbarian, thought Beauchay. He rather enjoyed the
conjecture.

"What are you talking about?" asked Dodson. "What is all
this about west winds and poetry and nine summers or whatever?"

"Nothing, my dear George, they are just—how would you
say, my reply to words full of sound and of fury spoken by some
local bank president and signifying –. I seem to have forgotten his

name or what they signify. Oh well, I suppose it was nothing. . . As to the land—"

"Yes, as to the land," repeated Dodson, who gave the appearance of being thoroughly confused.

"I think that I may decide to re-open the golf course. Do you think that there might be much of a market for it?"

"Listen, Samuel," started George in an altogether different tone, as he was aware that Beauchay was trying to play some kind of little game, and so he, George Dodson, would have to put his cards on the table. "I know that there has been speculation that *that* land might have something valuable on it that is marketable."

"I'm not sure what you're talking about," replied Samuel Beauchay.

"Oh, c'mon Sam, you're not going to pretend that that visit by those oil men, mysterious as you tried to keep it, is actually a secret, do you?"

"I haven't made any claims one way or the other, as far as I'm aware. As I'm sure you know, George, a visit by some men from the government doesn't signify a thing, even if they were from, as you say they were, the Department of the Interior, Bureau of Mines. Perhaps they were coming to confirm or deny a rumor; these things are difficult to determine, you know."

"Yes, I'm quite aware of that, which is why I didn't come rushing over here before I had heard that they were going to come out here a second time."

"A second time. I can't confirm that nor deny it, but again the presence of certain individuals doesn't mean that there is actually something of value on that land."

"I think there's oil, and I am willing to take that risk," said George Dodson.

"Oil? In Georgia?"

"C'mon Sam," said Dodson in a tone that Beauchay took as showing his dissatisfaction with Samuel's evasiveness. However, this didn't bother Beauchay in the least, and could not be in any way construed as a form of negative reinforcement.

"Look" began Dodson in a business-like tone. "Farm land around here goes for thirty-five dollars an acre. I'm willing to pay you one hundred dollars an acre for that useless farm land."

Beauchay smiled and opened a box of mints and offered one to Dodson, which he refused, before taking one to chew on. "I don't know what's the point in coming and making me an offer that you know I'm going to refuse."

"Now don't become that way, Sam, I was just trying to see where we stood, that's all."

"I have no time to idly barter away. If you have an offer to make on the land, then do so. However, know from the start that I'm not certain at all whether I'm interested, as I have a rather fondness for the property myself: such beautiful contours, and the way it looks at sunset with the light reflecting the colors in that grass. No, I rather like that land."

"It's especially beautiful at *night*," said Dodson.

"Oh really?" said Beauchay, smiling and helping himself to another mint. "I suppose you'd know, but really I must insist that if you've business with me that you should get on with it. I hate to be rude, but I do have a lot to do this afternoon, you know. This farm doesn't run itself."

George Dodson looked as if he was going to reply, but then stopped and didn't. He cast his eyes down to his lap and then looked at Beauchay. "I'll give you two hundred and twenty dollars an acre, and that's my top—you'd be getting far more than you paid for that dung heap, which won't be worth a cent, unless these reports prove correct. It's quite a risk I'd be taking."

Samuel Beauchay rose and walked toward the door. "If that's your final offer, then I'm afraid I must turn you down, George. As I said, I'm not really in the mood to sell, and it would take quite an incentive to make me part with something which has, in so short a time, become so dear to me."

George shot up but stayed where he was, staring at Beauchay before walking toward the door.

"Good-day, George," said Samuel, but the other didn't respond.

***

It was the next afternoon when Jefferson returned that he paid a visit to the Vanderkamps.

Julia heard that he had come, and went to great him.

"I got this from John," she said, showing Jefferson the letter. Jefferson quickly scanned it with his eyes, then pushed it back into its envelope.

"I've got to arrange a meeting with him," he said. "If you get any further word—please let me know."

"Of course, you'll be the first to know."

***

The room was quite smoky as Mr. Johnston finished discussing his first plans with the committee.

"You think that this home-tract, as you call it, will be successful?"

"It's sure to be. Why, all we have to do is to get the options on this property, which I admit will take some doing, and then we build some streets, pave them with cement and put in street lights. It's all in the package, because by building so many of these houses, we drive down the unit price."

"How big an area will this be?"

"Well, initially, the plan will call for the construction of houses on a fifty acre lot, but there are two other lots that could triple the size of this move if we can get all of them. And, of course, if it is successful, the land that we're buying up around it will increase in value for industrial purposes."

"What makes you think that an industry will want to move in?"

"Let me put it to you this way. There is a lot of industrial expansion at the moment, and companies are looking for places winch will offer their workers good benefits. Now our little proposition will be about the best anyone is going to find, and we can do it for a song."

Michael Boylan   223

"But you said something earlier about buying some land with mineral rights. What has that have to do with this?"

"We buy some West Virginia land cheap that still possesses full mineral rights. The land is next to an existent coal mine. Our experts think that the coal vein extends under our property. Therefore, when the existing mine owners figure this out, they will have to pay us for mineral rights if they want to tap into the vein. We can make a tidy profit."

"Who are our experts?"

"Listen, we're never going to get anywhere if I have to explain every little thing to you men. When I told you I did this for a living, I was serious. Now you gentlemen aren't the only one of these investing clubs that I represent. I can deliver these goods to someone else if you're not satisfied. Of course I don't hire a staff, I let the U.S. government give me my information for free. I have friends in the Bureau of Natural Resources. Does that suit you?"

The man who asked the question felt slightly ashamed at having opened his mouth. There was little to be said when Mr. Vanderkamp, chairman of the committee said, "I've heard enough for me. I think that your graded plan sounds good to me, and I like the way that you are multiplying our money by those special bank loans you described. And as long as you're sure they're safe, then I for one vote to accept the proposal."

The motion was carried and Mr. Johnston assured the group that they weren't making a mistake in their investing, but guarding for the future, as that is something that no one can predict with certainty. He went on and made other remarks that stirred the minds and imaginations of the listeners, but for some reason were of the nature that soon after the meeting they were forgotten, and all that remained was the memory of being so stirred.

Chapter 9

"John Begins a new Trade and Makes some new Friends"

After the farmer put the pitchfork down and John had a chance to get up, he found that the other didn't seem so menacing after all. Without his weapon, or rather with his weapon put to different purposes, he seemed like a congenial enough fellow.

There had been no exaggeration when he said that there was a lot of work that needed to be done. First of all, there were two crops that needed to be harvested, and then some livestock had broken through a fence which now desperately needed repairing, and would require sinking new posts, as the old ones were cracked.

John was told to start with the hand digging of turnips. There were already two women and a small boy who were busily engaged in the task, and the farmer figured that it would be best to have the stranger in a position in which he could be watched or supervised to the greatest extent. The farmer left and went somewhere else. Where, John didn't know nor care, as he almost welcomed a chance to relax and do a little light work as his thoughts straightened themselves out.

Things seemed safe to him on the farm. The people that he observed were in no way wealthy (as their clothes were in the same condition as John's after his many experiences the day before) and so probably would not be on the lookout, or have heard that there was a fugitive in the region last spotted in a town not far away (for John was certain that the man had told the authorities about his strange car trip). The morning passed quickly as John quickly got the routine of digging down and he didn't have to think about what he was doing.

The others who were working included the wife of the farmer and her daughter, who was twenty-five, and a small boy of ten. The daughter of twenty-five looked at John now and again when she was sure that he mother couldn't see. At her age, in her area, she was considered almost past the age of marrying. She was not a pretty girl, but she did have a pleasing figure, which didn't exactly suit the overalls which she wore. She was of Mexican descent. Her father was almost full Mexican and her mother was half-Mexican. It was probably for this reason as much as any other that they had to live in such poverty, struggling with all their resources to just survive on the land which they rented from a wealthy senator. There were many such farms as these, near and around the area, in fact the entire region, excepting the city and the scattered large residences of the landowners, which were very poor. Nonetheless, these people thought themselves not particularly discriminated against. It was a tough world.

The girl's eyes saw a man who appeared to be very handsome to her way of thinking, and strong—not in a brutish way as many men are, but in a graceful manner as his muscles seemed to be just definite enough to indicate their presence, but not overly bulky. This supported the almost innocent quality of his face. Her father had indicated that he was a bum, but he didn't look like a bum to her, but a person who was quite respectable (as bums, people who drifted aimlessly about, usually deserting a wife and family to do so; they were thought to be of the lowest station, as their own fate necessitated loyalty to the family as the only means of survival).

When she saw her father coming with her brothers from the fence work for lunch, she felt an excitement at the prospect of serving and observing this stranger as they broke for the noon repast.

John also felt good at the sight of the man, since John hoped that he might have a little break and some water in the shade. The work had been good, but the rest would also be welcomed. John didn't think he was really very hungry, as his stomach wasn't in pain, but he thought that some cold water might be nice, if there were a well in the vicinity.

"Break time," smiled the old man. "Time to eat."

The woman took this as their cue to walk back to the house, or shack, which would be a better description, and get the food.

John put down his shovel and walked toward a tree and slumped down. He suddenly felt very weak, almost as if he had been working all day without rest instead of only the morning. His mind still refused to arrange things in a harmonious way; his eyes hurt, and so slumped he over his knees, resting his head on his folded arms and quickly went to sleep. This repose, however, didn't last long, as a hand shook him. "Hey, stranger, you—do you want anything to eat?" The voice was that of the youngest son.

John lifted his head. The sun was shining so brightly that he had to shut his eyes again. His face and lips felt so dry that he didn't think he could talk, so he shook his head.

"Are you sure?"

John tried to tell him that he wanted some water, but no sound came out as everything was so dry and there was no saliva to alleviate the situation. John shut his eyes again and felt a stabbing pain over his left eye.

"What do you mean he didn't want any?" asked the old man.

"He didn't want anything, I just asked him. Now let me have his portion," said the boy, reaching for the bowl of beans, but the old man grabbed the hand and picked up the bowl and walked over to John.

"Hey, you, whatever your name is, what do you think we are? Thieves? Like the people who rent this miserable land to us? You did an honest morning's work and we want to pay you, but we don't have any money, so take this."

John remained motionless. It wasn't that he didn't want the food, for now he felt very hungry, but that he was so weak that the effort required to stretch out his hand seemed to be so great that he remained as he was.

"You know you don't look too good. If you want to put in an afternoon's work, then you had better take some." The old man put down the bowl near John and returned to his family.

"Look at him father, he's not even touching his meal. I say you ought to let me have it."

"What do you mean?" said the elder brother, who sensed that he was entitled to some of the beans as well. "I might to get some too, remember, it was me who first spotted him lying there in the field this morning."

"That's enough, all of you, can't you see that the fellow is proud and doesn't want to show us that he's so hungry that he's about to faint. You look at his eyes and you can see it. I tell you that's no bum. That fellow hasn't learnt what it means to accept anything that looks like charity, which means that he isn't a bum. So give the fellow a decent break. He worked hard all morning and deserves some food. Besides if he doesn't eat, then he's liable to collapse on us this afternoon."

Maria, the eldest, suggested to her mother that perhaps she should bring the stranger a ladle of water, as the sun can make one thirsty. The mother agreed and handed her the ladle as she made her way to the stranger.

John no longer had his eyes closed, as· he imagined that it was almost time to resume work and that he had to summon his strength for the task. The girl came over and put the metal of the bowl to his lips, "I thought that you might like some water," she said.

John opened his mouth. The water seemed to rush into his empty cavity with a force that burned as it went down his throat. The water was warm, but it was wet. John could sense the liquid flowing through his esophagus and into his stomach upon which he suddenly had a strong wrenching feeling as he turned away. Thinking that he might vomit as his chest heaved once, but nothing came up, only hot phlegm which felt like acid on the tender tissue.

This was followed by rather heavy breathing as everything seemed to be spinning about, and nothing was in perspective.

"Are you all right?" asked Maria, but John was unable to answer, but merely panted as he supported himself with his arms; a load which seemed incredibly burdensome.

Maria, being an unmarried woman of roughly the age bracket which might be loosely termed contemporary to John (at least it was seen as such from Maria's point of view), felt understandably restrained in the steps she might take to help this fellow who seemed as if he was on the point of virtual collapse. Her heart told her to go to the man and help him back against the tree, to loosen his shirt and give him some more water, while feeding him the beans, but her discretion told her that this behavior would be, under the circumstances, unwise and not something that she ought to do, no matter how much she longed to. And so she rested there, kneeling as she was, torn as to what she should do, when finally she stood and returned to her family, as her mother would not like her to spend too much time with any strange man, even though he was just twenty or thirty feet from the rest of the people.

John was able to roll over onto his side, which he found to be a more comfortable position, now that he was again alone. He took a few bites of the portion that was before him. Though it was cold and the spices too heavily administered for his taste, it still did him good, he thought, to eat.

Those few mouthfuls seemed to fill his stomach, for he felt a slight revival of strength when the others declared their intention to return to work. John got up and began to walk to where he had been working before, when the old man called for him to come with him to work on the fence. This made John happy, though he wasn't sure why. Perhaps, he thought, it was that he was being promoted to a more sensitive area so that he could help, as he had proved, or perhaps (this second reason didn't come to him until several days later) he was asked in order to separate him away from the daughter of the man.

At any rate, work in the pasture was more interesting than digging holes for red roots, and gave him an opportunity to listen to the old man talk, though it did take a few hours for the man to soften sufficiently so that he would say anything.

"It's a hot one today."

"That it is," said one of the boys.

"This heat can sure get to one. Makes me think of tonight, and that cool breeze," said the other. All of them smiled, including John, who thought that he rather liked these people, and might stay on awhile, if they wanted him.

That night, the conversation became even more personal as the old man invited John to dinner and at the table asked him if he was from around the area.

John didn't know what to respond to this question. If he told the truth, then they might become slightly suspicious at why he was drifting, when he was so close to home, or why he appeared to be in no hurry to get back. Of course, John could say that he was on the way back, but that might get a little sticky. Also, if someone came around talking about there being a fugitive from a neighboring town, it would not go too well for John to declare that in fact he was from a neighboring town. Though John hated to lie, and especially to such a congenial family, there seemed to be really little else that he could do.

"No, I'm from Baltimore," said John almost immediately.

"Baltimore, eh," began the old man. "That's a long ways away from here, are you just traveling?"

This last question seemed to be particularly personal to John, though he would not have thought so if he had not so much to hide, but as his circumstances were as they were, he almost resented the question, though he knew that he must not let his questioner detect any of this in his voice.

"We had some bad luck at home, and some of us decided to move on elsewhere." This response, even as John spoke, seemed to him to be a stroke of genius, as he was actually telling the truth, that is if one defined "us" as John himself.

"So you came to Georgia to make your fortune."

"Not my fortune, I guess, just a living, that's all; just a living."

"Know any skills?" asked the old man.

"No, not to speak of," replied John, thinking that this response would be the best, i.e., safest to make.

"If you don't mind me asking," began the old man again, "what did you do in Baltimore, if you have no skills?"

John's mind raced. He had no time to think of how he was being rather imposed upon with this grilling and cross-questioning, after having been invited to the table, but this he didn't consider, as he was too occupied with trying to come up with an answer to the man's question. He hadn't really any experience with the city and now was rather sorry that he had mentioned Baltimore as where he had been from, but it was the first place that had come into his mind. Everything that he knew how to do was connected with the farm, and it would have been stupid to have worked on a farm and lived in the city—horses. He did know horses.

"I worked at a stable."

"Oh that's nice work, I like horses myself," said the old man, apparently satisfied with the answers of the young man. Working in a stable seemed to be a right enough job to him as long as he wasn't a jockey, and he could tell by the physical stature of John that he wasn't a racing jockey.

Maria sat in silence, which the women normally did, except that women generally have their ways of making themselves known when they want to be heard, even in such a strict household where they are not allowed to speak, normally, at the table. However, Maria wasn't even making any signs, but watching the stranger as he ate his meal. She thought that John ate with such delicate manners that he must have been from a nice family, as in fact, John did hold himself (even in his condition) better in points of etiquette than any of the others at the table. But his (John's) was not a flamboyant sort of grace, and so it wasn't noticed by anyone except the girl and the old man, who was watching the stranger and his daughter's reaction to the man.

The old man thought that the stranger seemed like a nice enough fellow, but that never proved a thing as some of the nicest looking people often turned out to be the worst. No, he wasn't taken in by John's appearance (that is, his handsome face and well-proportioned body) nor his easy manner of speaking. All he knew was that John wasn't a bum. In his eyes Dow could be a criminal, or a decent man merely down on his luck. At any rate, he would sleep on it and decide whether he would offer to let the fellow stay on for a while until the work was finished.

The next morning brought everyone up at dawn as they eagerly assaulted the fields. John, who had slept on the outside porch, also was up when the old man approached him and motioned him to step to the side.

"Now stranger, I don't know who you are, but I want to appeal to you that if there's anything wrong with you that you clear out today, because we have more than enough trouble without having someone else around to cause any more."

"I don't want to cause any trouble," said John, thinking that the old man meant disruption of the family or robbing them or worse, but the old man was thinking about his daughter, who, though she was twenty-five and unmarried, he still wasn't willing to let get hurt needlessly, and would endeavor to protect her in any manner that he could (as he always had).

"Good, I just wanted to make that clear. If you stay, you'll get meals and nothing else; not much for a man out to make his fortune."

"I told you," said John, "that I just wanted to make a living."

"Just the same, those are the terms."

"All right," said John.

Then the old man turned around and marched back to work as if the little conference had never taken place.

Chapter 10

"In Which Certain Legal Problems Present Themselves"

After Jefferson came to on the bed, he thought of nothing else but that he had to do something for Dow. Where was he now? He was vaguely aware that John had lured the riders away from him, Jefferson, but this gave rise to the obvious question: did they get him?

Everyone had left the room and Jefferson was all alone; there was no one to ask. He felt too tired to get up, and it would be necessary to get some sleep if he wanted to go into town the next morning—he couldn't wake up Beauchay; that was out of the question considering how long the other had stayed with him until he was sure that he, Jefferson, was well. This worry nagged even as he fell into a very deep sleep.

The next morning, or really afternoon, as Jefferson didn't awaken until nearly one o'clock, he felt much better. The doctor had wrapped his ribs with bandages. This contained the sharp pain to a mere throbbing. Jefferson also felt a quivering in his back. Just a muscle, he thought, *you can't go about as I did yesterday and get kicked around, at my age, and not feel the effects for quite some time.* He tried to sit up, but when he did, there was a stabbing pain in his lower back. *I wonder what they did*, he thought. *I've got to get up, but it doesn't seem as if I can, at least for the time being.* So the man sat back again in his bed and rang the little bell that was by his bed side.

Very quickly Jessy was in the room. "What do you want?"

"Something to eat, and someone to tell me what's exactly wrong with me," replied Jefferson.

"Well, I can get the first, but I'm afraid I won't be of much help on the other."

Jefferson smiled. "Has Mr. Beauchay come in for lunch yet?"

"Yes, sir, he's done come and gone."

"Well, then, when he comes back for anything else, tell him that I want to see him."

Jessy assented and it wasn't too many hours before Jefferson heard the familiar knock on the door.

"Come in," replied Jefferson to his friend.

"Well, if you wanted some time off, you should have just told me instead of going through all of these heroics," said Samuel, smiling.

"You'd never given it to me, you old miser, why you haven't taken a vacation yourself in years."

"That's not so, I go to the Planter's Association conventions every year."

"If you call those holidays, then you are the one that ought to be in this sick bed and not me." They both laughed as Beauchay sat down and changed his expression.

"What happened, Jefferson?"

"You've heard everything?"

"I think so, it's all so confusing; so much at one time. Charles Vanderkamp was just over here talking to me about it. It seems he's worried about Julia."

"That she might get hurt?"

"Well not only that, it seems that he *thinks* that she's in love with Dow, or at least let me put it this way, he's *afraid* that she's in love with Dow."

"And so?"

"Well, he had something else planned for her I think: a more advantageous wedding for the family. I mean, marrying John would be about as low as one could get in his opinion."

"Is that because he may be a black man?" Jefferson felt like saying, but kept silent. Samuel was also silent for a few moments.

"Of course I tried to tell him that he was probably getting worried over nothing, but he seemed to think that the two were in love because they danced together so much on Saturday night, and what he called parental intuition. I tried to dissuade him from making any rash pronouncements that he might regret later, but he was not to be denied."

"He's right."

"What?"

"She does love Dow. What do you think of that?"

Beauchay was silent.

"Of course he's poor and at present a fugitive—I take it he did get away?"

Beauchay nodded.

"But what's that to two people who are in love?" said Jefferson in an almost mocking tone as he looked down to his hands, which were clenched. He had never really had an opinion of Mr. Vanderkamp one way or the other, he seemed as if he was a nice enough sort of fellow, but when he went around making these sorts of judgments, it bothered Jefferson. *What was wrong with Dow (except that he might be black under the eyes of the law)? But then didn't the Fourteenth Amendment to the United States Constitution grant equal protection under the law? Equal, equal--what did it all mean? What did it mean to be equal? Presumably it means to be considered as possessing the same franchise as everyone else in a legal sense. But this ought to hold in a moral sense as well: that is all persons possessing the same actual degree of worth, whatever that meant, as any other. But what was this worth to mean? Was it simply that just because Dow was a living entity that he ought to be regarded as other living entities? Is it that he has some property that he possesses called* worth, *which entails the bestowing of an equal legal franchise?*

If there were such a thing as one person having more worth than another, what would such a claim come to? It must mean that the agent claiming to be more valuable had something that the less valuable lacked. So if the more valuable (x) had such a trait (F) or qualities, what could they consist of? Perhaps wealth, intelligence, color of skin, type of family born into, teeth, eye color, hair texture, length of fingernails, number of hair follicles on the chest, or under the arms, running ability, strength; the list might be very long. But one thing ought to be distinguished, namely those qualities that one possesses as a result of his birth and those qualities that an individual achieves himself. For it seems that x couldn't claim an advantage over y (the less advantaged), for any F that x possesses that was acquired at birth for this is not properly deserved by x. Because how can x be said to be in any way responsible for what his parents did, or who his parents were? X has to accept his situation as it is given to him, and as given, cannot properly be termed a virtue that x has any right to claim merit from, as he had nothing to do with it. It was passed from parents to child. The child begins with a certain genetic situation and a certain environment and from there he can begin to make certain accomplishments that may be said to reflect on him as an agent (though even then this may be modified, as in the case where x is brilliant and becomes famous as a result of being given a superior mental potential at birth, whereas y may have actually utilized more of a limited potential and thereby achieved, in an individual sense, more than x, even though the absolute achievement when judged on a competitive scale may be less. This is to say that some achievements, even though earned in some respect, may also reflect a Natural Advantage, but are surely not a deserved merit. And if achievement is always modified by birth and circumstances which qualify as one's good fortune, how can x ever be said to be deserving of merit more than y? Fx (x possesses properties F) > Hy (y possesses properties H) where F > H and both F and H were bestowed at birth by nature or social advantage. These are statements of luck. Luck is fortunate, but undeserved. What is undeserved is beyond praise or blame.

For how are different accomplishments to be compared? What system of cross-rating is effective? Many people believe that money is such an indicator, but surely this is not the case as money tests for only economic success, which is not representative of the whole person. There are many people who are superb at a particular skill which does not afford pecuniary rewards, while others are mediocre at a skill that is economically precious (as judged by society). Again, this goes back to luck to which no desert attaches.

The good opinion of others isn't a proper measure, either, for the same reasons (random standards and different judging techniques). This is seen all the time: for how many good people are completely misunderstood by their friends, or how often are morally just decisions unpopular? Then perhaps it is impossible (though this cannot be said with any certainty as I may have forgotten many other candidates that might satisfy the question) to make my judgment with any reliability, for there is no real standard from which to judge.

But what is one to think when one poses the questions of merit and desert? How does one answer the assertion that it is impossible to judge the worth of an individual in terms of earned merit? This question is not a philosophical, but a tactical one.

One could argue, or not argue. If he chose not to argue, he could act as if he agreed or not. Clearly the easiest and the most honest would be to be silent, but to not act in any way is taken by others as if one agrees.

Then Jefferson relaxed his hands and looked up at Samuel.

"I've always said that John was a decent sort, and I could never for a moment believe that he killed someone," said Beauchay.

"He's got to be cleared," declared Jefferson.

"But how? If he gives himself up, then you know as well as I that there wouldn't be twelve impartial jurors in this county. Victor Stuart Sr. has been through a lot of hardship you know, and people are sorry for him and would like very much to see this young boy hung to pay for it—even if he didn't do it, they need someone to die for it."

"I think you're right, and that's why I want to have a look around for myself to see if I can find anything."

"But in your condition?"

"What condition do you suppose John is in right now?"

"But the doctor said—"

"Yes, I can imagine what the doctor said, but as soon as I can get out of bed by myself, I'm going to town, and I'm planning on tomorrow—before things cool down too much."

"I don't like it," started Beauchay, "but if you're going, then so am I."

Jefferson lifted his arm and held the other's shoulder. "I was hoping you'd say that."

Chapter 11

"An Unfortunate Excursion Leads to Problems"

After some days in his new abode, John was beginning to get to know the farm land and enjoyed going outside and working. Gradually, his strength had returned. He also was getting rather fond of the family and now and again would talk to the older son who reminded him of a boy he had known on the Vanderkamp fields when he was a youngin. He knew that he would have to leave.

His routine evoked positive dreams, which were what John needed just now. However it was always crystal clear to John that his first responsibility was finding the real killer and catching him so that he could return to Bella County and marry Julia, if she would have him. The future depended upon what he did now, and his only real future lay in capturing the murderer, who was no doubt getting further and further away from detection as each minute passed. But John didn't think of this. His mind only dwelled on what a pleasant time he was having now that he was away from the commotion of his home.

Of course he knew that he couldn't stay on this farm forever, but John thought that it might not be a bad idea to stay as long as he could. He liked the quiet and slow moving life that these people led, and saw no reason why he might not stay as long as they would have him.

"Would you like to go with me to the cantina tonight?" asked the older brother one day.

John took this as quite a compliment to be asked to go somewhere after work and of course accepted with enthusiasm. The slow movement of the hands as they worked against the soil made John think that perhaps this was the most natural life for a man (that being the simple tilling of land without the fancy machinery that Mr. Beauchay employed). There was something so pure in this way of life that brought a peace to John's soul.

At lunch time each day, the women would bring out the food, and now John sat with the family and was called by his name, John, which was the only name that he had given them. It was no secret to any of the family, save perhaps the ten year old boy, that Maria was sweet on John. She took special pleasure in serving him at each lunch, giving him bigger portions than to anyone, save her father.

The brothers would have objected as they liked their food as much as anyone, but they knew of their sister's predicament (being twenty five and not married) and also they basically liked John's easy-going manner.

"Would you like some more, John?" asked Maria, in her plain, but therefore to John in his present state of mind, sweet voice.

"Yes, I could stand some more, that is, if no one else wants anymore, because I had quite a big first helping." John looked around and no one motioned, but John had the feeling that the two brothers would like some, but would not say anything (because John thought they were being polite to him, which, of course, was only half-true). So John took the food and afterwards, put a portion in the bowls of the two brothers, who didn't say anything, but did eat what John had given them. And all the family admired John's generous spirit, and the friendliness which he exhibited. He was no longer a stranger.

That night as Pedro and John were walking to the cantina, Pedro asked, "What do you think of my sister?"

"Maria?" answered John, slightly puzzled at the question.

"Yes, I have no other."

What puzzled John was not the question itself, but why it had been asked. Of course he had feared that it might be asked as he noticed the attention that was given to him by her, but he had always suppressed the thought, thinking that somehow it was all his imagination that she really liked him in an amorous fashion, and that he was merely mistaking friendship for something else—a mistake he did not wish to make, especially in a friend's house. But Maria had caught his eye, or perhaps it would be safe to say that Maria's figure caught his eye, as she had changed her overalls for a dress recently for the preparation and serving of dinner, which was most pleasing to John. But, of course, he didn't remark to this effect as he felt it would have been out of place. Yes, he had noticed Maria, and found her quite attractive. She excited the types of feelings that he hadn't felt in a long time. Maria was so much different than Julia, whose beauty was that of a goddess to him, a regal and aristocratic sculpturing of delicate and rounded white lines and golden hair, but Maria was angular with a comely brown complexion, and though she wasn't *pretty* to John, her other features more than made up that particular deficiency in a way that caused his spirit to throb in a different way than what Julia's brought out in him.

It wasn't that he loved Julia any less, but that she inspired the permanent in him, the longing for a lasting life according to the highest virtues and values that man could derive, whereas Maria made him simply desirous that she was what she was, namely an alluring woman. John wouldn't go into detail with himself on just what this feeling was or why there seemed to be no conflict in his mind when he thought of Maria and pushed the permanent (which did indeed suffer from his situation and his position) far from his conscious thoughts.

"She seems very nice."

"She is. She's a nice girl; a *very* nice girl." The words seemed to John to be almost like a warning, but what the warning was, he couldn't detect—perhaps it was (John surmised) that if he wanted to make eyes at Maria, he'd better be careful.

The two walked further through the dusty streets that passed the crate-wood houses that served the needs of the families who were unlucky enough to call it their home. The smell of urine and feces was so strong that it seemed to take any of the anticipation of the cantina away. Pedro asked another question, "Are you married?"

"No," replied John immediately. Did this mean anything?

Pedro seemed pleased at this answer, but what could John understand by that? Did it mean that he, John, could have free rein at trying to win Maria's heart? Did this smile that had followed his response mean that it was all right for him to speak to Maria more intimately than he had done before? And what would be the limits of such a relationship? The cabin hardly afforded enough privacy for the two to get to know each other very well, but yet, John could not think of going out in the fields—the thought of Cindy Pancroft came to mind, of how he and she had first ventured to Sawyer's Bridge and then to the woods nearby, and how he had gone with fear and many reservations, thinking that he might be rushing into something that he did not wish to rush into, but still he had gone. And he went again and again to those same woods, not because he really wanted to, as he thought back on it—he decided that he had gone because he couldn't help himself. He had just gone, that's all—there was no more to it. But he couldn't treat Maria like that, she wasn't the sort of girl that Cindy was, though John didn't know at the time that Cindy was the kind of girl that she was, either. But somehow there seemed to be a difference.

Maria was so much more a serious girl than Cindy, and yet why did Maria play up to him so? Had she any other lovers, or was he the first? There was something romantic about being the first, he thought, but then on the other hand, if he was the first, then the family might take a different view of things, that is he might find himself coerced to take a step that he might not want to take: marriage.

For even though Maria was able to push thoughts of another person out of his head, she was not able to inspire in him the yearning to be wed, which was something that he associated with only one woman.

When they entered the cantina, John's thoughts were full of Maria, even as Pedro ordered their first drink.

"I haven't had much to drink," said John. "What with Prohibition on and all, where I come from there isn't much available."

"It relaxes one," replied Pedro, as he turned to listen to a man who was playing on a guitar while a woman in a bright red dress was dancing wildly on a platform. Many men were clapping and chanting as the music picked up in intensity. She was moving her feet faster and stamping the platform with her shoes as she carefully lifted part of her dress to reveal her slim legs. They were beautiful legs and didn't escape the notice of Pedro and John as they sipped their drinks.

The tightness that John had felt on their walk after the questions soon disappeared as both men were captured by the frantic mood of the cantina.

"She's quite a dancer," said John after it was finished.

"I'd like to have her in my lap here," said Pedro as both men laughed jocularly at this. The alcohol was beginning to go to their heads.

After that, everything seemed fast and free as the two men spent their hours at that table until the chimes declared it Sunday morning.

Chapter 12

"With Sport on his Mind Rodney goes to College"

"I'm concerned about Julia," said Mr. Vanderkamp to Rodney, as the latter was just finishing his packing for college.

"Oh, I wouldn't be. She's a smart girl, even though she is my sister."

"That's not what I mean. I think she fancies that Dow."

"Well, so do I. So do you, I believe. I don't think he could have possibly done what they say."

"Why did he run?"

"From what Julia told me, they were ready to string him up. Wouldn't you run under those circumstances?"

Mr Vanderkamp didn't answer, but sat on his son's bed and watched him fold his clothes and put them into his suitcase.

"Sometimes I wish you were going somewhere a little closer to home."

"Alabama's not too far."

"Far enough."

"Perhaps, but not too far," repeated Rodney, who didn't mind getting a chance to go a distance away and see what it would be like being on his own for a while.

"I wish you'd have gone to Georgia. The Bulldogs are a good team, you know."

"Remember it was you who—"

But Mr. Vanderkamp didn't let his son finish, "Yes, I know. It seemed the best thing at the time, but now I think that I was a little too hasty, short sighted, I suppose."

"Well, if I don't like it, then I can transfer, you know."

"Yes, I've already thought of that. It's not that I don't want you to go to a good school, but, well, you know, we've just been always so close for a father and son that I hate for you to go away all at once. Alabama is such a long ways away." Mr. Vanderkamp was thinking of how he would like to visit his son whenever he wanted to, but as he was going to Alabama, that would be more inconvenient—and expensive, too. He had half a mind to just flatly tell his son that he had changed his mind about letting him go to Alabama and that he would have to stay at home or go to Georgia. Rodney could get as good an education at Georgia, and the football team was good enough for him to make a name for himself. Somehow, Rodney had never really considered Georgia seriously. And Charles had agreed, perhaps because he had felt that he had to send his son far away for it to be a really good school. He had wanted to show people that he could send his son *away* to school, and if he had chosen a school that had been closer, somehow it wouldn't have been quite the same as saying that his son was in Alabama attending school out-of-state. It was now that very reason that made him balk at the thought, nay the reality of what that decision was actually going to entail. It had seemed such a good thing at the time—it had felt so right, that he had actually persuaded his boy to go to Alabama, but now that strong feeling wasn't holding up under the circumstances that had developed.

A man, in the vigorous part of his life, has to be able to *feel* what's right and wrong, he had always told himself. A good man just *knows* when the decision he's made is going to be a good one or not. And that confidence comes from the *dream*. After all, a person has to go by something when he decides, and if a man doesn't have the confidence in his urges, then he should pack it in and call it quits. The dream is over, and he has to wake-up.

Charles had made the decision concerning his son's education based upon what he had felt was correct, and there was no advantage in feeling bad about it now. The decision had been made. If he doesn't like it, then perhaps he could transfer, but now was the time to go forward: what was best for Rodney had already been decided.

Charles looked at his son and tried to imagine what he was like at that age. He imagined that he was very much the same as Rodney, who was very warm hearted and mannish in all his recreation. Charles Vanderkamp used to remember how comparatively late he had acquired an interest in girls, preferring sports with his comrades, and hunting on the wild land. His youth had been filled with a fondness for those manly pastimes, which now seemed to be degraded by many of the young people, as the young men seemed bent on courting as soon as they reached puberty! What a mistake he thought. How much of the comradery of men they were missing by trying to rush the natural course of things. There would be plenty of time to give one's life to a woman, they (women) weren't going to disappear; so one need not be in a hurry. Instead, a man ought to attune himself with the land, so that he can acquire natural instincts that will serve him in later years when the important decisions of life had to be made.

"Yes, Father, but I'll be all right, I promise you," said Rodney, who could sense his father's worry but still felt that it was time that he gave himself the opportunity to see what he could do on his own. He felt continually under the influence of someone at home—not that he particularly resented it, he adored his family and their way of life, but he wanted to be sure that it was *his* way of life as well, and that he was not blindly accepting something that he wasn't sure he actually wanted. Alabama would give him just the distance that he felt he needed. It would be hard to leave home, no doubt, but then it was necessary. He knew this, but he couldn't elucidate these thoughts to his father because he knew that they would be misunderstood as signs that he, Rodney, was unhappy at home or ungrateful for all that his family had done for him, which, of course, is not what he wanted to communicate at all.

Rodney wanted a time away in which he felt that events would show him whether he was comfortable in a different lifestyle or not. He would be able to see whether basic feelings brought him back towards home or pointed him in another direction. It would take a neutral environment to test his feelings, for they were restrained and prejudiced at home in a way that would not allow the freedom that he desired.

"We'll only have one child at home; it will be strange," said the father.

"Yes I know."

"You don't think she's really serious about that Dow fellow, do you?"

"I believe she's serious in wanting to help him."

"That's not what I mean and you know it."

"She's a little young to be making any other kind of commitment, isn't she?"

"That's what I say, but remember, that's never been a barrier to other women of this county. Sally Lou Thompson married Victor Stuart when she was only sixteen, and that's a year younger than your sister."

Charles Vanderkamp failed to mention, though his son realized it immediately, that he, Charles Vanderkamp, married a girl who was only seventeen, and in fact, most of the girls who married in the county did so before their twentieth birthday.

"At any rate, you can't control a woman," said Rodney, using one of his father's favorite expressions.

"That's what worries me. Not that I have anything against John personally, you understand, I mean about his birth and all. I think that I'm a very fair minded person, but it's just that he has no money and little prospect of earning any. He's not very ambitious I don't think, and even if he were there are certain things that might tend to hold him back." Mr. Vanderkamp was referring, in an oblique way, as Rodney could see, to John's dark complexion and curly hair. Though most subtleties of conversation were generally lost on Rodney, he usually understood most of what his father was trying to say.

"Well times are pretty good right now; perhaps he'll make good after all."

"I think there's more chance hoping that Julia will forget him."

"I don't think there's much chance of that," said Rodney, finally making his opinion known.

"No I suppose not. But you know, Rod, I'm not a rich man. I have a little money, and I'm trying to make it grow through investments, but at the moment, we don't have much loose cash, certainly not enough to keep my daughter and some husband who might be penniless. I wouldn't have it. It's not right."

"I don't think Julia would have it either, do you?"

Charles Vanderkamp had now ceased to think about his daughter and was concerned with his financial situation, which he just realized wasn't in the strongest position. The investment corporation had taken a big portion of his loose cash. Farm prices were down, and he might not have a profitable year. Everything that he knew was connected with his farm: his money and the way of life that the two together provided. To think of having to alter his life style in any way was frightening to him. He was not as young as he used to be. The possibility of a struggle was no longer romantic, but terrifying to him. What he wanted was to have a place which virtually ran itself, and then to hand it over to his son, who would take charge of all the stress that goes with running a place. Then he could just relax and enjoy his life's labors in the peace of a lazy Georgia afternoon. It was *peace* more than anything else that he longed after, and he would not allow any thoughts to the contrary to disturb this dream.

Book Seven

The Text: Where is the Play?

When first venturing to England from the United States when I was seventeen, I was in search of the stage. In my mind there was something that was ideal about this conception in my mind. It was far grander than that which I had known in the States. It was a public experience that carried with it a tradition so that everything associated with a production in Europe would be different than the same lines read in America.

Many of the things that I learned about the stage in Coventry convinced me that there *were* many remarkable things unique to the British stage, but there were also practices which, at the time, made me shudder. There is a coldness about how one has to fight for work when breaking into the profession that many times made me want to turn home. If I had sufficient funds at the time, it is likely that I would have returned, but in time, my illusions no longer seemed necessary to me and the reality that confronted me was such that I became interested in its development instead. By having the fortune of being able to pass through the rough times, I found that I had another scale which in time proved to be an even better one than my original scale of dreams had been to apply to myself as a measure of happiness.

All this is in prelude to an interesting problem that deeply concerns me as a practicing member of a production company:

where is the play? By this question I mean to query if the play exists on the pages of the manuscript presented to the director, on the director's corrected version, or is it what happens after the house lights go out, the curtain rises, and the actors appear. Individual productions vary greatly with the director and his team (crew and actors). If the play is said to be in the actual production, then it seems that there is no clear objective item that can be pointed to as being "the play." It is the adjective "the" that becomes troublesome, as there would be a plurality of "plays" being a function of the number of productions. Any discussion of *the play* becomes meaningless since each production is a different play—in fact, granting the difference between different performances on different nights, there would be a plurality of plays within a given production. Obviously, this is absurd since we speak all the time of *Hamlet* and communication seems not only possible, but unquestionable. However, there are some problems when considering plays in this manner as well. A mere pointing to the words on the page says nothing about that most distinctive feature of a work of art, how it makes us *feel*. By this I mean, how it affects us, emotionally and intellectually. When one makes reference to how he enjoyed a play, he does not say anything about the script, physically? For example, whether the author did not misspell any words? Or does it refer to certain formal elements that made him enjoy it? One enjoys good art. It is an experience. This experience suggests some interplay between the author and his audience. Part of this interplay is that which the author implies, but leaves out of his work. It is impossible for art to be life, so that it is filled with illusions. These illusions *suggest* certain things, but it is up to the audience to supply the rest. They must bring to the work certain knowledge and sensitivity. Seen in this way the work, itself, is important. It does have objective reality and importance, but it is also seen as limited. The work is only an outline of what the story actually is. Art only suggests, it can never fully declare. The script of a play is an outline, which the company tries to flesh out into a more complete illusion, but even then it remains only an illusion, which requires the audience to be active participants in the process of creating the drama. A reader of a book picks up a detailed outline and as he reads, he creates the novel, poem, or whatever. The more a reader brings to a piece of art, the better he will be able to finish the process. The author offers guideposts, and good writers are suggestive in comprehensive ways that stimulate and challenge a large variety of readers.

In answer to the problem posed as to where the text is located, I have suggested that it is located both in the readers' minds (since they create the story from the suggestive outline of the author), and as an objective, physical reality (the printed script) existing as an outline which can be read by many people and among whom certain common objective facts can be said to exist, e.g., the arrangement of words, a set sequence of events, literary conventions, and genres. The book as a whole must be created anew each time it is read and the play is an experience unique to each performance. The work cannot be discussed in good faith without reading it, i.e., going through the experience of creating the story for oneself from the physical text. This, then, is matched against the experience in the theater, which is far more holistic: costumes, set, lighting, and the production itself.

The process of experiencing art is alike the biography mentioned at the beginning of this introduction, one has an outline of expectations and then confronts what is really there and, if successful in completing and creating the work, one can finally know the experience in a unique way. No one else has gone through the experience in the exact manner that I have, though many have had various degrees of similarity to it. Because of this experience, I know what it means to have been connected with the theater in a certain way. Because of the experience of seeing a play, the patron understands a play in a unique way— unique because *he* helped to create it.

Exhibits:

Thus measuring things in Heav'n by things on Earth
At thy request, and that thou maist beware
By what is past, to thee I have reveald
What might have else to human Race been hid;
The discord which befell, and War in Heav'n
Among th'Angelic Powers, and the deep fall
Of those too high aspiring, who rebell'd
With *Satan*, hee who envies how thy state,
Who now is plotting how he may seduce
Thee also from obedience, that with him
Bereav'd of happiness thou maist partake
His punishment; Eternal misery

John Milton, *Paradise Lost,* VI: 892-904

Hail holy Light, offspring of Heav'n first-born,
Or of th'Eternal Coeternal beam
May I express thee unblam'd? since God is Light,
And never but In unapproached Light
Dwelt from Eternity, dwelt then in thee,
Bright effluence of bright essence increate.
Or hear'st thou rather pure Ethereal stream,
Whose Fountain who shall tell? before the Sun,
Before the Heavens thou wert, and at the voice
Of God, as with a Mantle didst invest
The rising world of waters dark and deep,
Won from the void and formless infinite
Thee I revisit now with bolder wing

John Milton, *Paradise Lost,* III: 1-13

All he could have; I made him just and right,
Sufficient to have stood, though free to fall.

John Milton, *Paradise Lost,* III: 98-99.

And grisly Specters, which the Fiend had rais'd
To tempt the Son of God with terrors dire.
And now the Sun with more effectual beams
Had cheered the face of Earth, and dried the wet
From drooping plant, or dropping tree; the birds
Who all things now behold more fresh and green,
After a night of storm so ruinous,
Clear'd up their choicest notes in bush and spray
To gratulate the sweet return of morn.
Nor yet amidst this joy and brightest morn
Was absent, after all his mischief done,
The Prince of darkness; glad would also seem
Of this fair change, and to our Savior came,

John Milton, *Paradise Regained,* IV, 430- 442.

What I offer is an alternative to the standard model of merit by preferment. Under my model merit is a more inclusive concept. It includes the *road traveled* by the individual in question? What part of the puzzle [of life] did she complete by herself (or largely by herself)? [What obstacles did she overcome?] What is the probable trajectory of her development from here on out?

Michael Boylan, *Natural Human Rights: A Theory* (2014): 190.

The negro of Middle Georgia is a creature in whom the emotions entirely predominate over the intellectual faculties. He has little of that shrewdness which town life cultivates in the black race. The agents of the Bureau complained that they had sometimes great difficulty in persuading him to act in accordance with his own interests. If a stranger offered him twelve dollars a month, and a former master in whom he had confidence, appealing to his gratitude and affection, offered him one dollar, he would exclaim impulsively, "I work for you, Mass'r Will!" Sometimes, when he had been induced by his friends to enter a complaint against his master or mistress for wrongs done him, ludicrous and embarrassing scenes occurred in the freedmen's courts.

"Now, Thomas," says the good lady, "can you have the heart to speak a word against your old, dear, kind mistress?"

"No, missus, I never will!" blubbers Thomas; and that is all the court can get out of him.

The reverence shown by the colored people toward the officers of the Bureau was often amusing. They looked to them for what they had formerly depended upon their masters for. If they had lost a pig, they seemed to think such great and all-powerful men could find it for them without any trouble. They cheered them in the streets, and paid them at all times the most abject respect.

> John Townsend Trowbridge, *A Picture of the Desolated States* (Hartford, Conn.: 1868), ch. 64

Overview: Dred Scott was an enslaved individual whose owners moved to a free state. Because of this Dred Scott sued for his freedom. In a 7-2 decision Chief Justice Roger B. Taney ruled that African Americans, free or slave, could not be citizens of the United States. Because they could not be citizens, they could not have standing in a lawsuit. Thus, since Mr. Scott had no standing, the ruling went against him. The court also ruled that the Missouri Compromise of 1820 (that restricted slavery to certain territories) was unconstitutional. It was only the second time that judicial review had overturned an Act of Congress.

"The question is simply this: Can a negro, whose ancestors were imported into this country, and sold as salves, become a member of the political community formed and brought into existence by the Constitution of the United States, and as such become entitled to all the rights, and privileges, and immunities, guaranteed by that instrument to the citizen? One of which rights is the privilege of suing in a court of the United States in the cases specified in the Constitution.

In the opinion of the court, the legislation and histories of the times, and the language used in the Declaration of Independence, show, that neither the class of persons who had been imported as slaves, nor their descendants, whether they had become free or not, were then acknowledged as a part of the people, nor intended to be included in the general words used in that memorable instrument."

DRED SCOTT, PLAINTIFF IN ERROR, v. JOHN F. A. SANDFORD./ SUPREME COURT OF THE UNITED STATES/ 60 U.S. 393; 15 L. Ed. 691; 1856 U.S. LEXIS 472; 19 HOW 393/ March 5, 1857, Decided; December 1856 Term

OVERVIEW: In 1890 the state of Louisiana passed a law that mandated separate accommodations for African Americans and European descent Americans on railway transportation. A test case was created by the East Louisiana Railway Company using an octoroon, Homer Plessy. The railroad wanted to avoid the added expense of having to buy extra rail cars to meet the standards of the law. Plessy was arrested and compelled to pay a $25 fine. A citizen's committee appealed the case to the Supreme Court of Louisiana where Judge Ferguson upheld the fine. The case was appealed to the United States Supreme Court. The Court ruled 7-1 upholding the ruling of Judge Ferguson. The majority opinion was written by Henry Billings Brown. Justice John Marshall Harlan wrote the dissent.

"It is true that the question of the proportion of colored blood necessary to constitute a colored person, as distinguished from a white person, is one upon which there is a difference of opinion in the different States, some holding that any visible admixture of black blood stamps the person as belonging to the colored race, (State v. Chavers, 5 Jones, [N.C.] 1, p. 11); others that it depends upon the preponderance of blood, (Gray v. State, 4 Ohio, 353; Monroe v. Collins, 17 Ohio St. 665); and still others that the predominance of white blood must only be in the proportion of three fourths. (People v. Dean, 14 Michigan, 406; Jones v. Commonwealth, 80 Virginia, 538.) But these are question to be determined under the laws of each State and are not properly put in issue in this case. Under the allegations of his petition it may undoubtedly become a question of importance whether, under the laws of Louisiana, the petitioner belongs to the white or colored race.

The judgment of the court below is, therefore,

Affirmed."

PLESSY v. FERGUSON./No. 210/SUPREME COURT OF THE UNITED STATES/163 U.S. 537; 16 S. Ct.

1138; 41 L. Ed. 256; 1896 U.S. LEXIS
3390/ Argued April 13, 1896/ May 18,
1896

Now, conceding for the sake of the argument that the admission to an inn, a public conveyance, or a place of public amusement, on equal terms with all other citizens, is the right of every man and all classes of men, is it any more than one of those rights which the states by the Fourteenth Amendment are forbidden to deny to any person? And is the Constitution violated until the denial of the right has some State sanction or authority? Can the act of a mere individual, the owner of the inn, the public conveyance or place of amusement, refusing the accommodation, be justly regarded as imposing any badge of slavery or servitude upon the applicant, or only as inflicting an ordinary civil injury, properly cognizable by the laws of the State, and presumably subject to redress by those laws until the contract appears?

* * *

It would be running the slavery argument into the ground to make it apply to every act of discrimination which a person may see fit to make as to the guests he will entertain, or as to the people he will take into his coach or cab or car, or admit to his concert or theatre, or deal with in other matters of intercourse or business.

Opinion of the Court in the Civil Rights cases of 1883, Justice Bradley.

It is I submit scarcely just to say that the colored race has been the special favorite of the laws. The statute of 1875, now adjudged to be unconstitutional is for the benefit of citizens of every race and color.

What the nation, through Congress, has sought to accomplish in reference to that race, is—what had already been done in every State of the Union for the white race—to secure and protect rights belonging to them as freemen and citizens; nothing more. It was not deemed enough "to help the feeble up, but to support him after." The one underlying purpose of congressional legislation has been to enable the black race to take the rank of mere citizens. The difficulty has been to compel a recognition of the legal right of the black race to take the rank of citizens, and to secure the enjoyment of privileges belong, under the law, to them as a component part of the people for whose welfare and happiness government is ordained.

Dissenting opinion in the Civil Rights cases of 1881, Justice Harlan.

Question: What do you know of any combinations in Georgia, known as Ku-klux, or by any other name, who have been violating the law?

Answer: I do not know anything about any Ku-Klux organization, as the papers talk about it. I have never heard of anything of that sort except in the papers and by general report. . . .

Question: Tell us about what the organization was.

Answer: The organization was simply this—nothing more and nothing less: it was an organization, a brotherhood of the property holders, the peaceable, law-abiding citizens of the State, for self-protection. The instinct of self-protection prompted that organization; the sense of insecurity and danger, particularly in those neighborhoods where the negro population largely predominated. The reasons which led to this organization were three or four. The first and main reason was the organization of the Union League, as they called it, about which we knew nothing more than this: that the negroes would desert the plantations, and go off at nights in large numbers; and on being asked where they had been, would reply, sometimes, "We have been to the muster;" sometimes, "We have been to the lodge;" sometimes "We have been to the meeting." Those things were observed for a great length of time. We knew that the "carpet-baggers," as the people of Georgia called these men who came from a distance and had no interest with us; who were unknown to us entirely; who from all we could learn about them did not have a very exalted position at their homes— these men were organizing the colored people. We knew that beyond all question. We knew of certain instances where great crimes had been committed; where overseers had been driven from plantations and the negroes had asserted their right to hold the property for their own benefit. Apprehension took possession of the entire public mind of the State. Men were in many instances afraid to go away from their homes and leave their wives and children for fear of outrage. Rapes were already being committed in the country. There was this general organization of the black race on the one hand, and an entire disorganization of the white race on the other hand. We were afraid to have a public organization; because we supposed it would be construed at once, by the authorities in Washington , as an organization antagonistic to the government of the United States. . . This organization, I think, extended nearly all over the State. It was, as I say, an organization purely for self-defense. It had no more politics in it than the organization of the Masons.

Reports of the Committees for the House of Representatives for Affairs in the Insurrectionary States, 42nd Congress, 2nd Session, 1871-2, I, 449-52. Testimony of General John B. Gordon.

Question: What did you see?

Answer: I saw men out there standing with horns and faces on all of them, and they all had great, long, white cow-tails way down to the breast. I said it was a cow-tail; it was hair, and it was right white. They told me they rode from Shiloh in two hours, and came to kill me. They shot right smart in that house before they got in, but how many times I don't know, they shot so fast outside; but when they come in they didn't have but three loads left to shoot. I know by the way they tangled about in the house. . . . By the time the fellows at the back door got in the door, these fellows at the front door busted in, and they all met in the middle of the floor, and I didn't have a thing to fight with, only a little piece of ax-handle; and when I started from the first door to the second, pieces of the door flew and met me. I jumped for a piece of ax-handle and fought them squandering about, and they were knocking about me with guns and firing balls that cut several holds in my head. The notches is in my head now. I dashed about among them but they knocked me down several times. Every time I could get up, they would knock me down again. . . . They surrounded me in the floor and tore my shirt off. They got me out on the floor; some had me by the legs and some by the arms and the neck and anywhere, just like dogs string out a coon, and they took me out to the big road before my gate and whipped me until I couldn't move or holler or do nothing but just lay there like a log, and every lick they hit me I grunted just like a mule when he is stalled fast and whipped; that was all. They left me there for dead, and what it was done for was because I was a radical, and I didn't deny my profession anywhere and I never will. I will never vote that conservative ticket if I die.

Ibid., 482-3.

Question: You had no ridings about at nights?
Answer: None on earth.

Ibid, General Gordon.

Question: When they proceeded to carry out the objects of the organization, did they do it in numbers, by riding in bands?

Answer: I do not know; I never saw the organization together in my life; never saw them out in any numbers, or anything of the kind.

> *Ibid.* testimony of General Nathan Bedford Forrest, Grand Wizard of the Ku Klux Klan.

"One cannot help feeling a little contempt for the people who here in the South make themselves needlessly unhappy about 'social equality.' I was amused at a sensible planter—a Democrat, and a native Georgian—who said to me, 'It is absurd in us to make such a fuss. There is scarcely a man of us whose children are not suckled by negro nurses; our playmates were negro boys; all our relations in the old times were of the most intimate; and, for my part, I would as soon ride in a car with a cleanly dressed negro as with a white man. It is all stupid nonsense, and makes us absurd in the eyes of sensible people.'

The feeling takes the most ridiculous forms, too: for instance in Atlanta and Augusta colored people are allowed to ride in street-cars; in Savannah they are forbidden. Why the difference? Is a Savannah negro less clean, or is a Savannah white man a more noble being, than those in the other two cities? There is still in many counties some prejudice against colored schools, but it constantly decreases . . . The superintendent of schools told me that there was less prejudice against colored schools in the southern counties, where negroes are the most numerous, than in the northern part of the state."

> Charles Nordhoff, *The Cotton States in the Spring and Summer of 1875* (New York, 1876), pp. 106-7.

It is asked, said Henry Clay, on a memorable occasion, "Will silvery never come to an end?" That question, said he, was asked fifty years ago, and it has been answered by fifty years of unprecedented prosperity. In spite of the eloquence of the earnest Abolitionists, poured out against slavery during thirty years, even they must confess, that, in all the probabilities of the case, that system of barbarism would have continued its horrors far beyond the limits of the nineteenth century but for the Rebellion, and perhaps only have disappeared at last in a fiery conflict, even more fierce and bloody than that which has now been suppressed.

It is no disparagement to truth, that it can only prevail where reason prevails. War begins where reason ends. The thing worse than rebellion is the thing that causes rebellion. What that thing is, we have been taught to our cost. It remains now to be seen whether we have the needed courage to have that cause entirely removed from the Republic. At any rate, to this grand work of national regeneration and entire purification Congress must now address itself with full purpose that the work shall this time be thoroughly done. The deadly upas, root and branch, leaf and fiber, body and sap, must be utterly destroyed. The country is evidently not in a condition to listen patiently to pleas for postponement, however plausible, nor will it permit the responsibility to be shifted to other shoulders. Authority and power are here commensurate with the duty imposed. There are no cloud-flung shadows to obscure the way. Truth shines with brighter light and intenser heat at every moment, and a country torn and rent and bleeding implores relief from its distress and agony.

Frederick Douglass, "Reconstruction," *Atlantic Monthly,* 18 (1866): 761-5.

I know what the caged bird feels, alas!
    When the sun is bright on the upland slopes;
When the wind stirs soft through the springing grass,
And the river flows like a stream of glass;

When the first bird sings and the first bud opes,
And the faint perfume from its chalice steals—
I know what the caged bird feels!

I know why the caged bird beats his wing
      Till its blood is red on the cruel bars;
For he must fly back to his perch and cling
When he fain would be on the bough a-swing;
      And a pain still throbs in the old, old scars
And they pulse again with a keener sting—
I know why he beats his wing!

I know why the caged bird sings, ah me,
      When his wing is bruised and his bosom sore—
When he beats his bars and he would be free;
It is not a carol of joy or glee,
      But a prayer that he sends from his heart's deep core,
But a plea, that upward to Heaven he flings—
I know why the caged bird sings!

"Sympathy" Paul Laurence Dunbar (1899)

Libra

Sublimation

Chapter 1

"In which John Experiences the Grub and his Tactics"

There is a sense that to work with another, or with a group of people, is one of the most intimate episodes that humans ever experience. So much can be communicated through the movements of the muscles engaged in a task. When this task is involved in a common goal, there arises a consciousness of the presence of others, as well as the emphasis on getting finished that brings people together. But perhaps most important of all is the open acknowledgement of the shared state of suffering. There are so few times when people can readily express the anguish of what it means to be in pain. This is because there are many inhibitions concerning this subject.

The problem amounts to one in which one person is forced to be the giver or taker, and the other takes on some other role, perhaps listener, or minister, or deaf ear. But each of these roles requires a transformation into someone other than what the person who trying to express himself is at that moment. Perhaps the only way in which pain can be adequately discussed in an open way is through mutual suffering in the heat of a Georgia summer afternoon in the sticky red dirt of the fields. It is a type of communication that is essentially non-verbal; it is sensed in all ways, but never spoken.

It oftentimes is an experience that one is conscious of, though that is not to say that the people involved aren't conscious of what is taking place, but simply that they don't think of the experience as a dialog concerning human suffering—it's not that they think it's something else, but simply that they don't make any categorization at all. It is merely felt as a surging visceral feeling in the pit of the stomach, which reinforces the sense of pride and accomplishment that they feel as a result of finishing their task.

John was experiencing just such a feeling as one day was drawing to a close after his weekend with Pedro. In one way, he felt as if he had known the Martinez family all of his life, as he was so natural with them. He had a sense of belonging, yet he was also estranged by his own inner recognition of his current situation. They knew nothing of him, really. No one in the family knew his *real* history; it was all a lie. They believed in a lie. But somehow it didn't seem like a lie. He was natural with them and they with him. How could that be a lie? How could any human relationship ever be termed a lie? Especially one in which the parties were so natural with each other? And yet, what did they know about him—what he liked, how he thought—did any of them know him one hundredth as well as Jefferson? But how much did that matter? Was that type of understanding really necessary? Perhaps all that is needed is to feel natural. It seemed so as he worked alongside Pedro, his friend. Here were people who had no illusions about themselves, as so many of the people he had known in Bella County had. They were simple and poor. It seemed to John that they were among the happiest and luckiest people in the world. He could gladly bear their lot for a lifetime, he thought, and be grateful for the experience.

"Well it's about time we called it a day," said the old man.

"All right, papa, but let me finish what I'm doing first," said Pedro.

"I'll see you back at the house," said the old man as he and the younger son left Pedro and John together in the field. Soon Pedro finished and then sat down and picked up a grub with his fingers. "You know sometimes we get so mad at these little worms and their friends, but you know I suppose we don't make life any easier for them now, do we?"

John laughed at this. Pedro was such an easy fellow. He had no axes to grind or points to prove. John always knew that he could trust Pedro and not be deceived or ridiculed.

"You better watch what you say, or he'll tell his friends in the other fields that Pedro is soft on insects and then you'll really be in for trouble," said John, trying to return the joke.

Pedro grinned, "Well maybe then I could hire myself out as protection for all the fields, and have them pay me to keep the worms away for a fee."

"We'd better get back to the house, before you start thinking too seriously about it," returned John.

The two got up and as they walked back they could see a light green Ford parked near to the house. Pedro said something in Spanish that John didn't understand, but took to be an expletive of an untranslatable character.

"'What's the matter Pedro?" asked John.

"It's the grub who collects the rents. He's here; that's his car."

The full significance of this statement was not accessible to John, but he did feel rather disturbed by something in Pedro's words. His friend said no more, but the two approached cautiously as the man came out of the house with the old man behind him shouting. "He is an evil man, that one," said Pedro.

"Why? What does he do?"

"He tries to change the bill, and at this time of the year, we have no money, and so he demands that we pay him or he will charge us interest on what we don't pay. But it's impossible to pay before we're even paid for our own crop. What are we to pay with? By making us pay interest, he gets a higher rent for his land than he should."

The green car pulled away as the boys approached the house, but scarcely had it gotten out of sight than another car came into view—a police car.

John froze. How could they have known that he was here? All the quietness of the life on the farm now instantly seemed a thing of the past. They were too close for him to run now; where could he go? What could he do? When the two got to the door, John declared, "I think I'm going to stay out here for a while."

"Suit yourself," said Pedro going inside.

Out here, John felt he had a better chance than he would have had in the house. He decided to go over to the well and appear as if he were drinking, as he could sit down out of sight and, if spotted, could have a reasonable explanation.

The police got out of their car and went into the house.

Soon, however, they had gone and John thought that all must be fine again. All the escape routes and plans that he had thought of in the last few minutes now seemed to be unnecessary, unless the people inside had told the police a lie, or perhaps the police were planning on coming back later on that night to get John in his sleep—but no, that was ridiculous. If the police had wanted to get him, they would simply have walked over and taken him. After all, they had guns, and John didn't—but did they know that? All the same, it seemed to John that the police must not have been told.

Soon Pedro came outside and spotted John sitting.

"Why don't you come in and eat? It's almost ready. Maria cooked it tonight *alone*, I think you'll like it."

"The police didn't stay long," said John in the most off-hand manner in which he could muster.

"No, they just came to warn us that there have been some disturbances on the farms around here with gangs the past nights."

"Gangs?"

"I wouldn't worry about it, I'm not. Perhaps someone broke a few windows or something."

"'Windows?"

"Yes, that's what I say. It's a laugh, isn't it? *We* don't have any glass windows."

John tensed his lips into a smile and was persuaded by Pedro to walk with anticipation into the house. Inside the old man was ranting in a quiet voice.

"What's the matter?" John tried to ask Pedro in a low voice so that the man could not hear, but he heard.

"The matter?" he replied. "First we get some robber over here who is trying to get more money from his land than it's worth and then he's sending his thugs around here to try and enforce it."

"Thugs?"

"Yes, you heard what the sheriff said," the old man snapped.

"No, he was outside, father," replied Pedro.

"Oh, yes," grumbled the old man.

"He's just in a bad mood today because of the green car," said Pedro. The old man didn't respond.

The dinner was splendid, as Maria made some delicious dishes that were spiced just to John's taste. It's amazing how well one can eat on so little, thought John, as he had only been used to the cuisine at the Beauchay estate, which was far from meager.

After dinner, the old man sat out on the porch and smoked a cigar while John and Pedro went for a walk to the railroad tracks.

"It's funny how many trains go by here every day," said Pedro. "When I was little, I often wished one would take me away." John was silent. It seemed to him that Pedro was telling him something highly personal, and he felt rather uncomfortable.

"It's funny how young men like to get it into their heads that anywhere is better than things at home. It took me a long time to get it through my head that I'd never be anything except a dirt farmer."

John looked at his friend. Their eyes met, but the stare was too difficult for John, and he looked away. He wanted to tell Pedro that there was nothing wrong in being a dirt farmer, and that the last weeks or so since he'd been with them had been among the happiest in his life—but how could he tell that to Pedro; how could he even open his mouth? All that John could do was stare at the post that he was leaning on and the barbed wire that kept the cattle in. It had been through such a fence (then damaged) that he had made his way to his bower of sleep that first night.

If the fence hadn't been broken he might not have stopped when he did, nor had the experiences that he had, but now the fence was back up again at its full strength to keep what's inside in and what's foreign out.

"But it's funny that I was such a headstrong kid that I had to find out for myself. So I hopped a train right here and rode it to Atlanta where I stayed for about a month doing what I'd always wanted to do, but it didn't take me long to realize that I didn't fit there. You see I'm a dirt farmer, and dirt farmers only belong in the dirt, and so I came back and haven't left since." Then Pedro paused and looked out to the moon, "You know, papa never said a word to me about where I'd gone or what I did—all he asked was, are you coming back. I said 'yes,' and that was the end of it. There was not another word was ever mentioned about it. I kind of think that papa understood. Maybe he did the same thing when he was young, I don't know, except that he came from Mexico and picked crops a few years, before he decided that that life here wasn't good either. I guess a person has to move about a bit before he's ready to put on the harness himself."

"And you're ready?" asked John, hardly knowing what he was saying.

"Ready—why I've already put it on for some time now. Papa knows it; that's why he depends so much on me. He says that I should get married, but I say that I can't afford it. It takes money to get married, and that's one thing that I don't have.

"I guess the main difference is between pulling because you have to and taking the yoke yourself (knowing that you will, because you want to or because you see that there's nothing left to do). A man's got to live."

"And couldn't you live in the city?"

"I could have made money, but I couldn't have lived."

Then there was a long silence as John could feel the night and its mugginess as everything was settling down. In the distance they could hear a train approaching.

"Let's wait for a train, and then head back," said John.

So they stood waiting for the slow moving freight train that carried endless cars with all sorts of secrets inside past them towards some market and buyer somewhere. When the last car passed them by, the two men headed back. When they were about halfway home they heard the noise of a car skidding along the roads, then a screech of brakes. The sound paralyzed the pair for a moment.

"What's that?" asked John, but Pedro just stood still for a moment longer, listening. Then he broke into a run.

John looked around for a stick or something, but there was nothing. He followed Pedro, though the other was running much faster than John. When Dow reached the house he saw Pedro fighting with a fellow out front and the noise of people screaming inside the house. John looked over to the car; it was empty. He couldn't believe his eyes: here were his friends being savagely beaten by some hoodlums, just as the sheriff had warned them, and all for the want of some filthy money.

John rushed to the car and found assorted metal bars, but no guns. If they had any, they were in the possession of the thugs inside. John picked up a medium sized crowbar and rushed for the house. As he got to the porch the man who had been fighting with Pedro pulled out a knife. John lunged at the man, but the man spun around and caught John's head with his forearm, and then slashed Pedro on the arm and stuck him in the chest. Pedro fell backwards as John scrambled to his feet and swung the crowbar so that it caught the man before he could stab John. The force of the metal bar hurled the man against one of the posts on the porch, where he hit his head and was knocked senseless. John moved to Pedro, but the other was already standing, so John wheeled and opened the door. Inside he saw the horrible sight of two men standing before Maria and her mother, with the old man tied to a chair so that he could not move. The little boy stood beside him.

The intruders had tied the hands of the two women to the table legs and had them lying on their backs on the table, one man was standing next to the mother with a knife to her throat and Maria's eyes were glued to her mother. The tops of their dresses (those dresses that had taken so long to make; those dresses that had been brought out only to please John at the special meal) were soiled and ripped so that part of the mother's bosom was exposed and her daughter lay supine with virtually all of her dress ripped down to her hips, though it still stayed on, due to her posture. The men were laughing and making gurgling noises in their throats like animals. As John burst in he could hear one of them say, "Now you be a good girl, or your mother's going to die."

John burst in and the man with the knife looked up and lifted his weapon. Instinctively, John swung his metal bar, and the man threw his knife. John tried to swing at the man, but he dropped out of the way so quickly that John's swing missed him; however, the motion of the crowbar was such that it intercepted the flying projectile and deflected it from its course. Then in the same motion, making a loop with the crow bar, John stepped forward and struck the man who was preparing to rip off Maria's dress in the back, and dealt him a blow across the shoulders. The man who had had the knife leapt at John, and they were soon both on the floor, tumbling about. The knife, which had missed its mark, was lying only a few feet from the men. John felt an enormous surge of energy as he struggled with the man when he felt a sharp pain as the other's knee met his groin with a force that instantly made John feel weak, when only moments before he had felt strong. John rolled over and the man made towards the knife that was lying on the floor.

The thug took the knife and lifted it above John's body, about to stab him, when the miscreant fell backwards, and dropped his knife—Pedro had thrown the knife that had been used on him in order to dispatch the foe.

John got up slowly. The man with the knife wound was not dead, so he would have to be tied up, but first, the old man was released, and then John dragged the two men outside so that Maria and her mother could modestly clean up after the damage.

Pedro stumbled outside. His wound had not been deep, but still he was bleeding on his arm and stomach where it had drawn blood.

"Those dogs; let me kill them. I've got to, did you see what they were about to do to my mother and sister?"

"No, we mustn't kill them," said John, restraining Pedro.

"No!" said Pedro in an almost blind rage. "I want their lives. I deserve their lives. They attacked my family. Now they're going to die."

"We can't murder, too."

"It's not murder; it's self-defense. Who could say that it was any different?"

"*We'd* know."

"I want them," repeated Pedro, pushing John against the pole and putting a knife to his throat.

John offered no resistance. "I'm not going to let you kill them. They're not harming us now. To kill them now would be murder."

"You're crazy. What are you? I tell you I'm going to have their lives, do you hear me?" Pedro pressed the steel to John's throat. Pedro was panting heavily, and knew that John would not give way.

"I'm not going to let you," managed John in a hoarse voice.

"How are you going to stop me?" screamed Pedro. But seeing that there was no fear in John's expression, Pedro dropped the knife and ran into the night. John felt his neck. It was bleeding slightly. Then he knelt down to finish tying up the men, as they were coming to, and he had to attend to the wound of the fat one, who had taken Pedro's knife. They would all live, but John felt little compassion for them. He wouldn't have minded if they died, but he wasn't going to be the one responsible. They were live human beings, and as such deserved not to be murdered: they possessed their right to live, but John wasn't going to give them anything more. How ugly the men were, not in their appearance so much, but in what they had done.

John felt very tired.

Behind John, unseen by him, was the old man watching. He had seen the entire scene between Pedro and John, but had not uttered a word. He had been the silent witness to it all.

Chapter 2

"John Declines an Amorous Invitation"

John had not been sitting with the men overly long when a light flashed; Pedro had gotten the police.

"What have we got here?" asked one of the officers. John was nervous, but there was nothing that he could do under the circumstances but wait. There was no time to run or to hide. Besides, he told himself, the sheriff was investigating one particular crime at the moment and wouldn't be thinking of looking for a fugitive when there were three men to be taken in for attempted murder and rape. John remained kneeling by the men, two of whom were conscious now and struggling with their bonds.

"They attacked the house," John began.

"Yes, we've heard all that," answered the sheriff as he walked past John to the old man.

"What happened here?" he asked the old man.

"The three of them took us by surprise. They overcame me easily enough and the boy, then they knocked around our things, and were going to –to molest my daughter and wife, when these two came to our rescue and stopped them."

"I see one of them got cut," said the sheriff.

"Yes, it was part of the struggle; my son got cut also."

"Too bad you didn't finish the job; it'll just cost the tax payers more money now to try them and hang 'em."

The old man didn't reply, but stood by and watched the sheriff walk past the men and kick each one with great force in the ribs or kidneys—wherever his foot happened to land.

"Do you have any idea who sent them?"

"I don't know," said the old man. "We've only had one visitor, besides yourself recently, and that was the rent collector."

"Yes, it seems he's been busy lately," said the officer with a scorn in his voice. Then he lifted one of the bound thugs up by the hair and, pulling his head back over the officer's knee, the miscreant's neck was stretched so that he could hardly breathe.

"Who put you up to this, eh?" Then the officer laughed in loud, diabolical diction as if he knew all along, and had just been playing a role for someone's benefit: a someone who he was content to keep anonymous. Predator and prey had a meeting of the eyes, and then it was over. The miscreants were taken to the police car by the deputy.

"Thanks for all your trouble," said the officer to the old man. "I'll need you all to come down to the station tomorrow to make statements about this."

"But we have much work to do in the fields."

"That's all right, come in the evening."

And then the man left, taking the three with him. They didn't seem to mind going with the officer. It was almost, John thought, as if they felt safe and secure with the policeman. As if they knew him as a friend.

And then it was quiet again. John hesitated to move, not knowing what to do. Pedro walked up to him and lifted him up by the arm, but didn't say anything as he then went inside.

"Why don't you come in," said the old man to John.

"I think I'll take a little of the night in first," he responded as he walked towards the well.

Going to the police station would be a dangerous gambit to undertake. The policeman didn't recognize him now, or ask any questions, but what would he say when he had had a night of reflection about it? Wouldn't he want to know where John had come from? And even if John told him the same story that he had told the family, which he, of course, must do, as he would be in their presence at the police station, perhaps there might be a hole in the story, or perhaps the policeman might have a fresh bulletin on John at the station and if he just happened to look at it, he might decide to bring John in for questioning and hold him there until someone from Bella County could come and positively identify him, for Bella County wasn't all that far away.

John had never been inside a police station, but he imagined that they had the pictures of all the wanted men up on the walls so that the officers could memorize the faces and descriptions of the criminals. There would be a tremendous risk.

But perhaps all this was being too fearful. This was a community of very poor people. It was very probable that the sheriff didn't know who was a regular resident, unless he had been there for quite some time. People probably drifted in and away very regularly. It probably wasn't unusual for a newcomer to happen by for a while and then disappear. There would be nothing to be suspicious about—nothing at all: just another face among other faces. And if the sheriff was like most whites that he, John, had known, he didn't pay much attention to Mexicans or dark skinned peoples. They were invisible. And was he, John, not dark skinned? And yet, compared to some blacks and Mexicans, he was lighter and more Caucasian in appearance. Wouldn't that in itself be reason for suspicion? What would a white be doing amidst these others? Why wasn't he with his own kind? John stuck out. His situation was suspicious by nature. Because of this, the sheriff might get a little nosey and begin probing—a process that could do John no good: perhaps he was thinking now about John and how he didn't fit in, though the situation and the shadows might have mitigated this slightly. But the question was how much and for how long would he continue to escape this sheriff, who knew that there was someone living with the Martinez's who was whiter than he should be to be with Mexicans.

But if he were to leave, how should he do it? He couldn't just walk out, could he? After all that they had experienced together? He would want to tell them why he was going, but how could he? How could he tell someone else that he was a suspected murderer and that he was fleeing from the law? How could he look at Maria after he had made such an admission? The entire scheme seemed so utterly incongruous. Why did such a situation have to come about? What was the sense of it all? The timing was terrible: just when he found a place that was comfortable, he would have to go.

The night had settled down and a slight breeze was cooling the waves of hot, damp air so that the old day would settle away into another realm of experience, remembered experience—memories felt and lived without immediacy.

Maria came out of the house and walked over to John at the well and put her hand upon his shoulder.

"They said that l should come to see if you were all right," she said. Her voice was so rich and exciting. Even after all that had happened; it never lost its special quality. John turned his head to look at her.

"I'm fine," he replied. "And what about you?"

She looked down, "Thanks to you, nothing is—*damaged.*" She pronounced this last word very distinctly so that the meaning might not be lost to him. He had seen her bare chest, as had those brutal men, but he, John, had prevented anything else from being exposed or violated.

"I'm just glad you weren't hurt," replied John, trying to make it clear to her that he didn't think any less of her because she had undergone this ordeal. Even if it had gone farther, he wanted her to know that it was not anything that *she* should be ashamed of.

"I just wanted to thank you for what you did."

Why was she saying this? Didn't she know that it was unnecessary? What did he want thanks for—didn't they know each other better than that? He only did what he did because he was there and had the opportunity to do so. It was his duty to help. One doesn't thank another for performing his duty.

"It wasn't anything," said John sincerely.

"But it was, and we're all grateful. Pedro, especially, wanted me to tell you that."

So Pedro wasn't angry at him; this made John feel very good. He was afraid that after the way he acted with him on the porch, that the other might despise him. It was very good to hear that Pedro was still his friend.

"I'm happy that no one was seriously hurt. How is Pedro's wound, is it deep?"

"No, it will be fine, Mama has already bandaged it." Then she said in a voice that bespoke her family pride, "We are made of rugged material; we don't tear easily."

This pride made all the emptiness of the previous moments subside as her words freshened his spirit. What beautiful people, he thought, how I should like to be like them in their faith.

It seemed to John that it was almost getting chilly in the open, as the wind began picking up force. He was sitting on the ground and Maria was kneeling next to him. There was nothing more to say. What could he say? It had all been said. The pause made him uneasy.

"The wind is picking up, you'll be cold staying outside like that," said John, wishing that she'd leave, not because he didn't like her, but because he didn't know what was happening or what she was thinking. This uncertainty instinctively made him uneasy. Perhaps her parents would begin to wonder why she was spending so much time out here with him, when all she had to do was tell him a few things and then be back. He did not wish to anger them. There had been enough upset for one evening.

"I'm fine. It's not cold," she replied almost immediately, then she added after a long pause, "Papa and mama told me to stay with you as long as I liked, and to help you, comfort you in any way that you wanted."

Then John looked into her face and he knew; she was offering herself to him, if he wanted her, and with her parents' consent. Her face, which normally didn't seem overly attractive to him, now, in the queer light of the night, had an almost irresistible appeal to it. Her dress, which had been mended after a fashion, still revealed much of her round, full bosom so that he turned his eyes away, so as not to embarrass her, but she wasn't embarrassed, and he knew it, and this only added to the confusion that he was feeling.

He wanted her, and he knew that, but there was a reservation. Maria was the kind of girl who deserved a husband, and John knew that he could never be one. But what kind of reservation was this? He had never given such a thought about Cindy Pancroft. No thought of the future had ever entered his mind, why should it now?

This wasn't like him. He used to be a believer that if one stared good fortune in the face and did not act, then it would quickly go away and offer itself to someone else. All of this was changing. He no longer simply saw and then acted. His desire was mixed with something else, something foreign. He had felt it when the sheriff had come. He was being forced to become calculating about his actions, but did he want this? Was it good?

Maria put her hand to his cheek and stroked it gently, "What's the matter? Am I less of a woman to you?"

What was she saying? She must be referring to the incident on the table? But how could that make her less of a woman, unless she held such things with such reverence that they meant whether *she herself* might have been altered by something that happened to her body, something over which she had no control. And yet if it was so dear to her why was she offering more than that to him right now?

"You musn't say such things. You're no less of a woman. Nothing happened of any consequence, and even if it had, you weren't responsible. Any reasonable man can see that."

She smiled. "Then why don't you wish me?" she said with a purity that made him ashamed of any desire which he was feeling for her.

"Maria, Maria," John tried to begin, but he didn't know what to say. How to tell her that he could never marry her, even if he might want to, as he was a fugitive from the law and would have to run constantly. But he couldn't bring himself to say this, but perhaps something else to the same effect. He wanted her, why shouldn't he have her; fortune was offering her to him.

"You see, I'm a traveler, and I can't have a wife."

"You are already married?" she asked immediately.

"No, but I have to keep moving, and that's no life for a woman like you, who should have a husband and raise a family. I could never be your husband; there's no future with me."

She didn't reply at first, but then after a long interval responded softly, "It doesn't matter. I wish you anyway."

What could he do? He couldn't tell her of how he really did wish to take her lovely body in his arms and squeeze it tightly so that he felt his spirit going from himself to her and that they might unite as one, but something was holding him back. But perhaps the only thing that was holding him back was fear. Was he about to make this woman, who wants him so, unhappy just because he is afraid? Is the only reason that he doesn't take her because he is a coward? It seemed almost a matter of whether he was a man or not as to whether he would take this woman right now, a woman who had been honest to him, and in return he had been honest to her. But how could he do that?

The situation was clear. This kind and generous woman wanted him desperately, with all of herself, and he wanted her, and the parents inside the house wanted the two lovers to have each other as well. So what was the problem? He would take her, he decided.

John turned to Maria and put his hand on her face and brought her head towards his to kiss her, but at the last moment, he pulled her head to his shoulder instead. He held her head close to his shoulder for a few moments, then took her hand.

He couldn't do it.

Whether it was fear or principle, he didn't know, but what he did know was that he couldn't bring himself to go through with it. Something inside said "*no,*" and it would be wrong to go forward against the "no." He knew that somewhere in his head. What he was doing *in his restraint was best*: best for him and best for Maria.

"I think it would be better if we went back to the house," said John in a quiet, but not weak, voice. He felt like her brother, or protector, and he had to take her back to where she would have a future, where she might yet find a husband, if that's what she wanted. At any rate, where she could live her life honestly, without lies and façades that prevented intimate sharing. Her only hope to happiness lay not with him, but with her family, as she was.

"They'll wonder what happened to us," said John, smiling, but not laughing, or mocking, but trying to communicate the high regard that he held her in.

Maria obeyed, and they walked back together, apart, as Maria felt sad, but not rejected.   She sensed something of what John wanted her to feel and it made her both confused and elated.

Chapter 3

"A Medium-Sized Chapter with an Important Episode"

"Not even a kiss?" asked the mother.

"No, he said that he could not be my husband and that it wouldn't be right."

"A fine fellow," said Pedro, who liked John even more, every day.

"A strange fellow," said the old man.

"Yes, indeed strange," replied the mother.

John was outside cutting wood for the family as they discussed their guest.

"We owe a lot to that strange fellow," put Pedro, not wishing his friend to be slighted in any way.

"Nobody is saying anything against him, Pedro," replied the mother. "It's just that sometimes it's hard to understand how he acts."

"He attacked those men with such enthusiasm, almost as if he wasn't in a fight where he might get hurt, but in some wrestling match," said the old man. "I don't know whether he's brave, just young, or foolhardy."

"Maybe a little of all three," replied the mother.

"Well, I think he's brave," replied Pedro. "He saved my life."

"He saved all our lives," replied the old man. "But he didn't want our daughter."

"Even without obligation," added the mother.

"It is odd to me," said the old man.

"He's a good man," repeated Pedro as John walked in with the wood.

All that day John felt that he was being watched by the others. What were they thinking, he wondered? It was difficult for him, for at the same time he knew that he must decide what he should do concerning his date with the police that evening. In addition, his thoughts often strayed to Maria and the scene the night before. How had he been such a fool? But in another sense, he was very proud of himself. He knew that he had done the right thing.

Where was Julia at that moment; what was she thinking? Had they found the real killer? Perhaps he was a free man and he didn't even know it—the thought tantalized him. How could he ever know whether he were free or whether he was still to be on his guard? He must write a note to Julia, but how, if by some chance it was opened, the postmark would give him away.

They would come to the town and find out where he was. John knew that he had to go. It would be necessary to depart from this fine family because he didn't want to implicate them; because if he were caught, they would also be charged with something. John cared too much for them, as well as considering that when he went to the police station that night, he might be discovered. He was taking grave risks by staying in one place for a long time. He would have to leave, but how could he do it? These questions were more easily solved intellectually than put into effect. He could sneak away, but then the family might think something had happened to him and might spend much fruitless time looking for him as well as alerting the authorities about his whereabouts, enabling them, the police, to better know just where he was and making his chances of survival much less.

No, there had to be another way, but how could he admit the truth—especially when the truth would involve an admission that he had lied to them before?

Pedro came to John when they had broken for lunch. "I just wanted to tell you that you were right."

"What?" replied John, not knowing what Pedro was talking about.

"Last night, when I wanted to kill that fellow, I'm glad that you were there."

"Forget it," said John, somewhat embarrassed.

"I won't forget it. Thank you."

Pedro put his hand on John's shoulder and the two walked towards the food.

"How's the wound?" asked John.

"Oh not too bad, thanks."

"You took quite a lot of steel."

"It was only a scratch."

John slapped the other on the back for his understatement as they sat down to eat.

That night, after dinner, John had gathered up his things, and as they were so small as to fit in his pockets, it was not noticed. The old man was sitting at the dining table counting out his money to see whether they had enough to make a payment on their rent so that they wouldn't have to pay any interest.

"Forty-two, forty-three, forty-four. . ." the old man was counting his pennies.

Then Pedro stormed out of his chair, as if he had been simmering for a long time in his seat watching his father and now it was more than he could bear.

"I don't see why you pay them after what they did."

"Fifty-one, fifty-two, fifty-three. . ."

"Did you hear me," said Pedro yelling, "they almost killed us last night and now you're going to give them your last cent? I think it's disgusting."

"Sixty-five, sixty-six, sixty-seven. . ."

"*Why* don't you say something? We can prove that those hoodlums were sent here." But still the old man continued to count out loud and stack the pennies in stacks of ten. "You're contributing to them and their kind by paying that, can't you see?" Pedro was so enraged that he struck the table and caused several of the money stacks to fall. The old man stopped counting, and took off the spectacles that he had put on, spectacles that were cracked in one eye—spectacles that the old man had probably found somewhere, put them on, and found useful. Yet they marked the demarcation between his business-self and his personal-self, so that it was natural for him to take off his glasses when addressing his son.

"There is no way we can prove that those men had anything to do with the rent collector."

"But the rent man threatened us and that very night we were roughed up like he said we would be, isn't that evidence?"

"No one heard the rent man except me, and my word isn't as good as his in a court of law."

"But we were all there."

"You didn't hear, but even if you did, *all our words* would not be about equal with *his* in a court of law; they want cold evidence, not circumstances. As for paying the money, what would you have me do, wait until he sends someone else who will not be as kind as the three last night? They were nothing: amateurs. If we get them mad, we had better go back to Mexico, because there won't be anything left of *us* if we stay."

"But you're giving in to them."

"What do you suggest I do, fight? I'd be quite a foe, eh? An old man with a wife and daughter and small boy. Nice sentiment but not very practical, Pedro."

Pedro turned away in anger and disgust.

"I know what you're thinking, Pedro, we are a proud people, and we don't like to be dirt under other people's feet. We have a choice; we can either stay or go. Because if we fight, then surely we will lose, and it will be for nothing. And if we leave, where shall we go, now that the crop is not even in and we haven't got our money that we put in yet? And besides, even after the harvest, do you imagine that it's any better elsewhere? I've been all over, and though I admit that it's been a few years since I stopped roaming, I still know that one place is as good as another, and it's foolishness to think that you will make it better by leaving. Perhaps we have it very good and don't know it, as we are spoiled by our prosperity.

"You must understand me, Pedro, I don't like this man any more than you do, and if it were in my power to do something that would be fair, I'd do it, but I can't. Anything that I do will be repaid to me many times over in cruelty, even if my intensions are only for justice. We must accept that. It's ugly, but it's the only way we'll ever survive."

Pedro turned and looked at his father a moment, then walked for the door.

"We leave in a half hour, Pedro," said the old man, referring to the police station.

John followed Pedro outside. They walked over to the well.

"You must not be too hard on him," said John.

"But he doesn't understand!'" exclaimed Pedro.

"He's lived a long time," replied John.

"It doesn't matter; I still may be right."

"I don't know anything about who's right, but I do know that the only chance people have is sticking together against people like the rent collectors."

Pedro turned and studied John's face. "You are my reason. You can always cool my temper," said Pedro in an emotional voice as he hugged Dow.

The two were silent for a time, when John said, "It's hard to get by when people try to change the rules."

Pedro didn't reply, but took out a cigarette and lit it. He rarely smoked, as it was too expensive, but at times he permitted himself the luxury if the occasion was right. And now, he thought, was one such occasion.

"You know I have a little money that I got by chance that I'll give you, if you'll take it, to help with things."

"What kind of people are we that we must accept charity?" said Pedro, somewhat offended, though in another sense, he knew that the money would certainly be welcomed, though he could never accept such an offer from a friend such as John, no matter how much it would be beneficial.

"I want you to have it."

"Certainly not, and that's final."

"But I don't see why you have to be so bull headed about it, I have lived in your house and eaten your food, and you have given me your friendship, and now you will not accept my gratitude, a gift which I freely give."

"For your food and board, you have worked more than enough long hours in the sun, and as for our friendship, it is not something which we put a price tag upon."

"Of course I wasn't trying to imply that," said Dow. "I only want to help."

"Well, thank you very much, but we cannot accept such an offer." Even as he said these words, Pedro's mind was equivocating, though his heart was resolute. The family did *need* the money, and perhaps John could give it in the form of a loan, so that the family wouldn't have to pay any interest. It certainly would be in the family's well-being to do it, but he still didn't know how he could make the suggestion now that he had been so firmly said 'no.' It would be wrong, he decided. John is our friend and we shall not use him. We will not make any demands upon him.

Pedro took a few more drags on his cigarette when John said, "There's something else that I have to tell you. I couldn't tell everyone, because it would have been too difficult, but I'm leaving."

"Leaving?" said Pedro repeating the word, but not grasping the meaning immediately. How could John be leaving? I didn't seem possible—he, Pedro, had never given any thought to John leaving. He had thought that John would stay with them for a long time and become very good friends, and then might marry Maria someday. After all, hadn't he been a perfect gentleman to his sister, and what man would do that unless he had the respect of a man who wanted to court a woman? Besides, John had never mentioned anything of this before; it was so sudden. What was the cause? Did he or anyone else in the family do something that offended John?

Could the other night have bothered him sufficiently so that he would want to leave? All this confused Pedro, so that he began to cough as he inhaled too much smoke.

"I don't want you to think that it's anything against you, or any of your family, because I've really enjoyed it here—more than you can know. But it is necessary for me to go."

"But why?" asked Pedro in an amazed tone that seemed to say that he had considered John to be' his friend, and why does one have to leave their friends?

"I can't explain except to say that I am running away from the law for something that I did not do, and if they catch me, I'm sure to get an unfair trial. So I'm fleeing. I stopped here for a while hoping to find some refuge, but I now know that it's too risky here for me, and if anyone begins asking any questions about me, as I'm sure the rent man will, after I helped subdue one of his men, then you all stand in danger as being guilty of harboring a fugitive. I couldn't put you in such danger."

So that was it, the trip to the sheriff's office. Several events seemed to go together in Pedro's mind, as it made sense. But how could John be a criminal? Of course he couldn't; John must be telling the truth, he must be innocent—but what harm could there be in harboring an innocent man? They all loved him so that he was sure that his family would put up with the risk for John's sake, but then the rent man could make it rather difficult on them. They might lose their land, have a bad name and then where would they be? Of course, John was right, again, he must leave, but even this realization brought increased sadness and yearning for John to be able to remain.

"When are you leaving?"

"Tonight, before you go with your father to the police."

"It will be sad without you here. We all like you very much."

John tensed his lips into a smile. He could not tell him what he felt; it would be impossible.

"I wish I could have stayed," said John.

Pedro nodded.

"How would you like to buy me a drink for the road?"

"At the cantina?" asked Pedro. "We have no time."

"Give me your purse, and I'll take out enough for you and me, and I'll drink both of them and remember you with them."

"All right," Pedro laughed, handing John the leather pouch where he kept the small change which he had.

John took the purse and fumbled about and took out a quarter, at the same time placing the folded fifty-dollar note into the purse.

"Please explain things to your family for me," said John. "And if you can help it, don't let the police get suspicious of me, as I need a head start to get out of town. Perhaps they will never ask any questions, but if they press you, protect your family first."

With this John slid off the well and waved to his friend and wandered towards the railroad tracks. Pedro watched him go as so many things seemed to be fading with his friend into the night.

John caught a train, which he rode until he came near a major road, when he jumped down and hitched a ride into a nearby town. The Martinez place was now quite far behind him. For a man on the road, thought John, there is no turning back.

Chapter 4

"In which the Reader Returns to an Old Friend at Work"

On Tuesday after the murder, Jefferson managed to lift himself out of bed. He wanted to get a chance to go into town and try and keep his ears open so that he might acquire some sort of idea of the mood of the town, and whether there were any leads towards finding the real killer.

The town was quite quiet as Jefferson rode in. Things had changed from the mad fury that had been the scene only two days before. From the tone of conversations that Jefferson was able to pick-up, all seemed to be much quieter than before. Maybe it was that John had gotten away, or perhaps that it was now the work week and people had less time to get excited about something when the serious business of earning a living was at hand.

Jefferson went to the sheriff's office.

"Well, I'll tell you," began the sheriff, "we've not been able to capture him as yet, but there is an all-points-bulletin out on him all over the state, and he should be caught eventually. These men can't run forever."

"What about that lynch mob that was hunting for him Sunday, and all the damage that they did, what's going to happen to them?"

"Well I know that they might have had a bit too much enthusiasm—"

"*Enthusiasm*? Why they were ready to string up anyone in sight, just to satisfy their lust for blood."

The sheriff could recognize that Jefferson wasn't like other blacks as he had a better manner of talking and spoke with much more authority and more perception, but he still didn't like the idea of a Negro, no matter who he was, to be accusing any group of white folks of doing something which was *not* in the interests of the law. It was something that he would not tolerate.

"You have a complaint to file?" asked the sheriff in a tone that easily portrayed his thoughts.

"Not at the moment, but I may just have one, later on," said Jefferson as he took the hint and headed for the door. "Oh, by the way," he said, stopping and turning around at the door. "Did you ever make an investigation to determine whether John Dow was the actual killer or not?"

"We all know who the killer is," said the sheriff.

"Wouldn't it be ironic if you were hunting the wrong man, and the real murder was right under your nose?" said Jefferson as he walked out into the street.

The day was not as hot as usual. As Jefferson walked down the street he felt at a loss about what he should do. There had to be some way that he could help John, but what could he do? Where to begin? He decided to take a walk to the city dump to see if he could find out anything.

The smell of garbage on even a temperate afternoon in August isn't pleasant, so Jefferson had to make a special effort to concentrate as he picked his way through the debris to where someone had told him the body had been found. Why the dump, thought Jefferson, if I were to kill someone, why would I choose the dump of all places? Perhaps the killer was inept, or perhaps he wanted the body to be found—but why had they had chosen the dump? The thought puzzled Jefferson. Was there a reason to it? Or had the dump merely been the closest place handy, for disposing of the body? Nothing seemed clear to him as he rummaged through the piles of junk and waste. There were no clues to be found here, only more questions—questions that didn't seem to lead to any conclusions or even possibilities.

He decided to stroll over to where Victor's body was being examined to see if there was anything to be found there. The doctor, who also was the coroner, was a man known to be not adverse to imbibing some during the day, to help him with his tasks. So it was, that he was a highly unpredictable man, who one day might be very friendly and the next highly irrational and irritable. As it happened, this was one of his better days and he received Jefferson cordially.

"I wondered if I could look at the Stuart boy, if I could."

"You have a writ?"

"No, I just want to have a quick look," replied Jefferson, fearing that it was one of the doctor's off-days.

"I'm not supposed to let anyone look at the bodies unless they have a writ—" The doctor stopped in mid-sentence, almost as if he just realized something. "Say, didn't I just treat you a few days ago for some bruised ribs and internal bleeding?"

"Yes, Sunday."

"And then what in tarnation are you doing up and about when you should be back in bed?"

"Well, I—" began Jefferson, but he had no time to continue as the doctor was about to lecture Jefferson, and he was not to be interrupted.

"How am I supposed to be able to treat you people in this town when nobody does what I tell them to do? You are risking further complications by moving around—I suppose you even rode in on a horse—huh?" The doctor looked at Jefferson over the rims of his gold wire rimmed glasses. Then shook his head several times slowly while he made disapproving noises within his closed mouth.

"You're just asking for it. Why I have half a mind to make you lie down right now, and stay here until you're better, but then you'd probably get antsy and want to go gallivanting about as if there were nothing wrong with you until you drove me crazy. No, I know your type, you estate people are all alike: work, work, work, no matter what's wrong with you. That's why you die so young, did you know that? It's true, if you keep up a pace like this you'll be dead in another year or two, and don't say I didn't warn you."

Jefferson tried to control himself, but his mirth was too great, and his face revealed a smile at the doctor's worrying.

"Now up with your shirt, I'll check those bandages, see if they're all right."

Jefferson protested, but the doctor was not to be refused, and so Jefferson let the doctor check the bandage, upon which the doctor decided to add a couple more layers for added support as he grumbled something about people with broken ribs riding wild horses just to test his, the doctor's, bandages.

After the doctor had finished with his work and pronounced Jefferson fit, admonishing him again to take his advice and get a little rest, he turned around and put some things into his bag as if he was preparing to leave.

"Doctor?" began Jefferson, fearing that the doctor had forgotten about the real purpose of his visit.

"What do you want now?" replied the doctor, "I have to go out and make some calls."

"But you remember the body of the Stuart boy?"

"Yes, what about it—oh, yes, well, I'm not supposed to, you know, but I'm already late, so hurry up, and don't take anything."

Jefferson thanked the doctor and went into the other room where the body was lying on a table covered with a white sheet that still had some stains of blood, indicating that they hadn't changed the sheets since they drained the blood.

The body was pale, and mannequin-like in its coldness. There was one bullet wound in the forehead, which had been cleaned up so that it wasn't as messy as it had been when the corpse had first been brought in. He would be buried soon. Jefferson noticed some bruises on his arm, discolored black, indicating that the skin must have been damaged.

Jefferson called the doctor and asked him what those marks indicated. The doctor lifted up the arm, and declared that the man must have been in a fight as in addition to the arm there were spots of something under the fingernails that the doctor said might be blood.

"What do you make of it?" asked Jefferson.

"Well, it's obvious that he must have been in a fight or something which would have given him the opportunity to get those stains under his nails."

As the doctor took another look Jefferson noticed the clothes on the dresser in the corner. He walked over to them and went through the pockets. There was loose change, and a few toothpicks, and nothing else in the pants, and in the shirt he found a small ticket. Must be a betting ticket, thought Jefferson; probably for the cross-country race. He must have made a bundle; I wonder how much he bet.

Jefferson examined the ticket to try and see how much Victor had bet. The card indicated the numbers of the horses betted, and the total amount of money. Jefferson was surprised at two things: first, the amount of money involved, and second, that Victor would choose to bet on several horses. It seemed odd that someone would bet against himself on some bets and not put the whole thing on himself—especially since he was the favorite. But there was something else that bothered him about the ticket that made him lift the piece of paper again, even after he had put it down. It was the signature at the bottom of the stub: Jason Beauchay.

"What happens to all these things, doctor?"

"Well, normally they are given to the relatives, but since this is a state case, they will be kept until the murderer is brought to justice."

"Are they kept here?"

"Oh heavens no, I'd have no room here if I had to do that, I'm cramped enough as it is with all that I have here without having to store something else. No, they're taken over to the Sheriff's safe. Now, if you'll remember, I have some rounds to make that I should have started forty five minutes ago."

"Yes, thank you for all your time, and the extra bandages."

"You remember to take it easy, or it won't matter how many bandages I put on. You've got to slow down, remember you're approaching the prime of life, not your adolescence."

***

"I don't know what you're talking about," replied Jason.

"I think you do," affirmed Jefferson. "You placed those bets that were on that stub, and must have seen Victor on the night he was murdered."

Jason was taken aback at all this. Certainly this was not what he wished or expected to occur. He had been quite surprised when he had heard that Victor had died, but he in truth had not given much thought to the question except to acknowledge that he was in the clear as John was the man that they were looking for. He, Jason, was now without a rival for Julia. But what sort of accusation was being made against him now? He had been at home the entire evening, as his father could attest to. There could be no possibility that he was being suspected of any foul play, for indeed, what had he done? True enough he had placed a bet for Victor, but what had this to do with anything? He saw no reason why he shouldn't tell Jefferson that he had made a bet for Victor that day. There was nothing unusual about betting. It was an annual institution at fair time, so that his betting could not be the source of Jefferson's consternation. There could be nothing that he could reveal that would make himself seem to be guilty. Jason had nothing to fear on that score, so he saw nothing dangerous in answering Jefferson's question, though on general principles, he would tell as little as he could so that he could ascertain what exactly Jefferson was up to with this gambit of his.

"I don't understand."

"Come on Jason, don't play games now, I'm talking about something that is very serious. How did Victor come to have the stub that listed bets in your name?"

In truth Jason didn't know the answer to this question, as he was as much in the dark on this as Jefferson. He still held the stub of his transaction in his room. How had Victor gotten a hold of it? But Victor couldn't have it, because he had checked it when he heard that Victor had died, and so somehow, Victor must have gotten a hold of a copy of the ticket. This made Jason feel uneasy. What would Victor have thought when he saw the ticket? Jason had planned never to show Victor the ticket and tell him the bookie had made a mistake in his records, but he didn't know that there had been a copy of the ticket somewhere. He needed time to think this out, but Jefferson couldn't be led to believe anything that might prove in any way injurious to himself, so he tried to answer the other as quickly and sincerely as he could sound.

"I don't know. I suppose he got it when we made the bets."

"You bet on the race with Victor?"

"Yes, just a few small bets on my part, but I seem to remember that Victor made considerably higher bets."

"Yes, they were on the ticket."

"Well, as you know I lost and he won."

"But why was your name at the bottom of the ticket that had the large amount of money, if you said you didn't bet much?"

"I don't know, perhaps there was some mistake. Maybe the tickets were made out wrong or something; they switched the names or something."

Jefferson didn't reply. He knew that Jason was being less than candid with him and he didn't want to expose too much of his hand by asking too many questions now, but it seemed clear that this innocent bystander wasn't really so innocent after all.

Jason was biting his lower lip with his upper front teeth in quick, rapid movements.

"One more question, you might excuse my ignorance, but I never bet, where do they usually make the bets for the cross-country race?"

Jefferson knew the answer for this question, but wanted to see the manner in which Jason would answer.

"In The Marsh they have a table and a man there to take the bets. You go in and make your bet and then leave."

"And the pay-off is that very day."

"Usually, unless someone is dumb enough to forget."

"So someone like Victor with a winning number wouldn't have had that ticket in his pocket if he had collected his money, right? That seems strange for a winner or a race that bet so much money on himself, isn't it?"

Jason didn't answer at first but then said, "The murderer must have gotten to him first."

"Yes, apparently," said Jefferson as he left Jason alone with his thoughts.

There wasn't much to go on, but there was something. A discrepancy in a ticket issued by Miles Bon and what Victor would have been normally expected to do. Perhaps the numbers on the tickets could be of some value to him. He would go back to the doctor's office and try and get the numbers and check them with the numbers of the horses which ran.

As he rode into town, he couldn't help being overcome by the anxiety that he was on the wrong track, that perhaps all this was nothing—but then again, it was all that he had.

The doctor wasn't in so Jefferson decided to try The Marsh, to see whether they might not have anything that could be of some help.

"Sorry, can't help ya," said Miles Bon.

"Perhaps if I could talk to Bill?" offered Jefferson.

"Bill isn't around today. Anyway, I do most of the managing of this place myself. I can tell ya that it's no use, the records aren't here, and even if they were, you couldn't see them as they're confidential."

"But I could see a bet that I made, couldn't I? A person can see what he did, or not, say if he lost his receipt, couldn't he?"

"Look," started Bon, who didn't know Jefferson from the man in the moon, "these records aren't open to anyone. They aren't my affair."

"That's why I wanted to talk to Bill, so that—"

"They are not Bill's affair either, the betting doesn't have anything to do with us, it's a separate outfit that comes in and rents some space from us to make book; that's all."

"But you see, I have some money that they owe me. It's a ticket that I couldn't redeem because I was sick, so you see, I want to get a hold of them."

"I thought that you lost your ticket," said Miles.

"I did."

"Then you couldn't get your money anyway. There's no money ever given without a ticket."

"But I have a ticket; I mean I bought one, it's just that I misplaced it—I'm sure if I could only speak with someone in charge that I—"

"Listen," began Miles, now rather irritated, "I've told you several times that I was in charge. Now you seem like an intelligent enough sort. Don't starts actin' like some common nigger that can't get an answer through his head." Miles took something out of his pocket, it was a ticket. "Unless you have something that looks like this, you can't claim anything, besides, the fellow's already gone back to Savannah by now; you are out of luck. Why don't you just go home and forget it—try better timing for your illnesses. You can't do anything except make yourself a pain in the ass, which you are becoming very readily at present."

Jefferson stared at the ticket. It was different than the ticket that he had seen in the pocket of Victor's shirt. What was it? Perhaps the color, the writing—something, but it wasn't the same.

"And I have to have a ticket like that to win."

"Why don't you go on home?"

"And all the tickets are the same?"

"What do you think, that they come in different flavors?" Bon put the ticket back into his pocket where he returned it to its mates, as he turned around and walked away. "Come back some time and try gambling here; coloreds can play from four to seven every day."

Jefferson didn't respond, as he watched the other depart. The lanky man set his jaw, shook his head and left the establishment. He had to see that other ticket again. This time he would wait for the doctor to return. Things were beginning to happen, or maybe it was just his imagination, but at any rate, it was a something that he was going to follow out.

Miles walked to the back room where he poured himself a drink. Business was slow after the fair, as people were practicing a bit of economy after the large expenditures of the weekend. Soon Bill Marsh came in from outside.

"Anything happening?" asked Marsh.

"Nothing, pretty dead," replied Bon, pulling out a chair for the other. "A young kid wanted to buy some cigarettes, probably did it cause some of his friends dared him, I don't know, but hell he was he scared when I told him that they could arrest little children for buying cigarettes." They both laughed. "And there was a colored fellow that came in here trying to cash in a ticket for last Saturday's race."

"Trying to cash it in on Tuesday?" said Marsh in amazement.

"Yep, and not only that, but he didn't have any ticket, he'd lost it?"

Marsh's expression changed. "What did this fellow look like?"

"He was tall, medium hair that he slicks over; I don't know, he talks with a northern accent, almost like a white man, why do you ask?"

"What did you tell him?" asked Marsh immediately.

"Nothing," said Bon, quite surprised that Marsh was acting so peculiar.

"Are you sure?"

"Sure, I'm sure." Miles tried to pour Marsh a drink, but the other put his hand over the glass. "Say, what is all this?" asked Bon.

"You know who that was?" asked Marsh.

"Yea, some dumb nigger who was trying to cash in a ticket late, and hasn't done much gambling before."

"It was a Beauchay."

"Beauchay?"

"He works there, as much as runs the place, for that doddering old southerner reformer who still thinks he's in the Civil War."

"So?"

"So! What do you mean *so*, do you know what that means? He wasn't just asking you dumb questions; he's on to something about Stuart's death."

"I don't follow you."

"Come here," said Marsh, in a patronizing tone, "and I'll explain it to you."

***

Sure enough the tickets were a different color, and not only that, but the ticket that had been in Stuart's pocket was imprinted in carbon: it was a copy of a ticket. If that was the copy, then who had the original? Jefferson didn't *know,* but there were two people's names on the ticket: Victor's and Jason's. He had seen Victor's carbon copy. The original must be with Jason. Jason must have placed the bets and given Victor a copy.

Jefferson hadn't told the doctor what he had been looking for, but now it would be necessary to bring him in on it. This ticket could be valuable, and mustn't be liable to the frailties of missing evidence that were common with the sheriff.

"Doc," began Jefferson as he slipped the ticket into his pocket, "what would you say if I told you that there was a valuable piece of evidence on that boy's person that might convict the real murderer, who isn't the man whom they are looking for now, but that it was very important for me to take that piece of evidence and compare it with some other clues that I know of—would you let me do it?"

"Couldn't; it would be against the law."

"But what if I was sure that this piece of evidence would become lost if left to normal procedures."

"I still couldn't allow you to do it," said the doctor.

"Then would you make sure that all the evidence gets into the sheriff's safe properly?"

"Yes, but that's also my duty. After being in the business as long as I have, a man gets to learn what his duty is."

"Thank you," said Jefferson as he walked out. The precious ticket copy was safely in his pocket. Jefferson had wanted to do everything in his power to act within the established guidelines, but failing that, he felt that this ticket was certain to be lost unless he acted as he did. If it turned out to be nothing, he would return it, but in the meantime, he felt that it was his personal responsibility to take any risks necessary in order to serve justice. But how far did this go? How far would Jefferson go in order to obtain what he felt was a just conclusion to the case? He couldn't keep the ticket, that was certain—but what he could do was to take a photograph of the ticket together with its mate (Samuel Beauchay owned a Leica I camera), if it was where he thought it might be. He had until the next morning to complete this piece of work, as then the body would be taken to the funeral parlor for services on Thursday, and the clothes would be the property of the state.

Jefferson was on very shaky ground, and he knew it. He was defying the ethical. He had done it when he let John go free and not told the posse where John was. And now Jefferson was doing it again with his purloining of the ticket. Was this making him as guilty as the offending party in his illegal means at trying to protect a man to whom the law would have dealt, he felt, most unfairly? What if John were guilty—not that he murdered Victor, but only perhaps got into a fight and shot for self-defense? But the nature of the wound suggested that the shot had been fired at very close range and as John was a good shot, he could have always shot to wound and not to kill—there could be no plea of involuntary manslaughter. But Jefferson felt certain that John had nothing to do with it, but upon what was this judgment based? It was on his knowledge of the man.

But was this knowledge of character or simply a reflection of tenderness and friendship? How much can one person be said to really know another personality so that they can say that such and such potential action is really impossible—not highly improbable, but really impossible? How could one make such a claim about themselves, much less about someone else? And yet, he felt that he knew; yes he felt sure. The question to this would have to be: how valid is this understanding, and upon what is it based? He already admitted that he had no idea as to the origins of his feeling. *Certainly they weren't entirely rational, even though they had a strong rationally defensible dossier of evidence, such as character behavior, attitudes towards people who had been antagonistic to him, his disposition etc. But even though these things might tend to suggest that John was not the type of person to murder or kill, they did not prove that he couldn't have done it.*

For one thing, a new set of circumstances might have elicited a new response never observed by Jefferson before (and it must also be emphasized that Jefferson had not seen John in every mood. Therefore, Jefferson, could not make the claim that he had complete knowledge, even by observation, of John's behavior, much less any real indications of what thoughts and imperatives the other used to determine what he should or shouldn't do). It is entirely possible (logically) that the future should not mirror the past, but may bring something quite new. It seemed clear to Jefferson that he could lay no strict logical claim to his feeling about John's innocence.

But even if it weren't logically necessary, did this necessarily mean that Jefferson was wrong or that he should abandon his quest and return to the realm from which he had so recently departed?

No, indeed, he thought, *as the realm of human actions was so often filled with so many variables that it would be impossible to act if one needed justifiable truth claims each time that one wished to act. What was peculiar to the arena of ethical conduct was that it depended upon the assessment of one person by another, however sloppy this might be, rationally speaking.*

One makes certain leaps of faith when talking about people and their affairs at all. There are a large number of issues that are accepted, which if on a different level, say a discussion of metaphysics or ontology, would not be acceptable as the more delicate and pure (non-empirical) nature of the subject being analyzed requires a far more precise measure of accuracy in each of its claims. But when entering into questions concerning the ethical, there are a large number of assumptions that must be made which, if questioned in the same precise manner, would preclude any discussion on the subject. In ethics it is necessary to assert that other people exist in a messy way whose clutter belies exact categorization, a claim which isn't so easily made in another type of discussion. But for the sake of discussing any ethical problem, it is made so that the problem at hand can be scrutinized.

Thus, once admitting that there are many types of questions that are left unanswered or suppositions that are not argued, but only assumed, and most often never even stated, but only implied, then where does that leave the realm of logical consistency as a basis for determining validity and soundness? Could it be that it is rational to assume that oftentimes the individual must make a decision concerning whether he will follow the ethical, according to his duty or perhaps a sense of contractual obligation, only when it (the ethical) is adhering to its declared aims, i.e., if a system of justice varies from its purposes in particular actions, then is the individual freed from his duty or contractual responsibility to adhere to that which he sees as a rule or action which is contrary to said aim? If all obligation stems from the execution of certain felt objectives or primary principles, then it seems that when the resultants of that primary principle do not support it, but in fact undermine it, then the responsibility of the individual reverts to the upholding of the first principles, even if it means contradicting the laws supposedly enacted to promote those first principles. Also axiomatic, is that since this is an individual task of judgment, that the individual may be wrong, or his view may be distorted (though the validation of this is quite unclear) in which case (in the eyes of the majority, who themselves may be wrong) the party who has taken it upon himself to alter the rules must be prepared to suffer at the hands of the unjust statue, though they are under no obligation to overtly sacrifice themselves, as then they would be supporting the very unjust rule they wish to subvert. Rather they must resist, with every power they can, and endeavor to alter said regulation in any way that they think appropriate (e.g., it would be inappropriate to cause civil unrest over some very minute action unless it had real, tangible, symbolic significance—that is otherwise, the disobedience should be in scale with the degree of injustice, however that can be measured: suit the action to the word and the word to the action).

Thus it was that Jefferson struggled with the real turbulence that he experienced as he rode to the farm. He was putting himself above the law; taking it into his own hands, and this was dangerous business, it was an occupation which frightened him. His uneasiness made him conceive of various ways in which he could return the ticket without being noticed. Was there any turning back? Could an individual cross the line, but later return, or was the decision irrevocable? Didn't it mean that if he tried to come back, he would lose any moral justification that he ever had in making his action? He would then become a criminal, not only to the world, but to himself—which was worse.

He thought of John and where he might be. They said that he had been wounded, and that there had been blood found at a point in the wood, and so they speculated that he might have bled to death, but most thought that he was still at large. John had his entire life in front of him—but it was more than that—something else that Jefferson felt, something else that was compelling him on. It was a drive that he could not explain to himself, nor did he really want to; its presence was readily felt so that it didn't require rational exposition. Jefferson reached for his chain, and then remembered that it was gone.

Chapter 5

"A Chapter which Begins with Samuel Beauchay and Ends with a Contract"

Samuel Beauchay sat in his study. He had before him a police report that said that John had been sighted in two places since he had disappeared several weeks before. But the topic which was on Beauchay's mind at present was the implementation of a committee recommendation that the farmers of Georgia take collective action to prevent a further drop in farm prices, which had plummeted in the last few months. For some reason, this seemed to Samuel to be one of the most important moves that might be made in his lifetime. It meant that perhaps farmers might once and for all be entitled to a steady market price for their products. The problem that is particular to farmers is that they must make large expenditures each spring without knowing how much they are going to get for their crop in the autumn. This made things particularly difficult as in an average year they were running on a marginal profit anyway, and if the market dropped off a bit, they were faced with large losses. This could all be prevented if there were some foreknowledge of what prices would be for their products.

This could be accomplished if each farming area gathered its resources and eliminated the dealings between the individual farmer and large scale food and cotton distributors, and instead, let the large collective businesses deal with the large collective agricultural cartel, which would be able to better fix the prices of their commodities as they would represent large sections of the country, e.g., the South, and would be able to say, you either give us this price or you're without these products. By collectivization, the farmers could fix a reasonable, steady price for their goods that wouldn't be subject to the vicious cycles of the commodity markets.

This proposal had been placed by Samuel before the organization many times and gradually it was gaining some degree of acceptance, but minds were slow to turn to new ways. If only he, Samuel, had more time to devote to this project he could get it done in very little time. But something always seemed to get in the way. Something that would stop him just as he thought he might succeed. But this time nothing would stop him; his plan would receive a more receptive hearing as the times were right for it.

All his life, Samuel Beauchay thought that he could be more than just be a simple estate owner. He had considered politics once or twice, but as the system was so corrupt, he felt that he would not be able to endure it. After the World War and Wilson's illness, he had become very discouraged, and then the twenties had brought the Republicans, those protectors of industrial fat cats, back to power and the stench of the Harding administration, that killed the president, had turned the country's eyes away from politics and back to their own affairs. It seemed that all Coolidge wanted to do is to go to Dakota and dress up in Indian costumes.

Economics and politics were both so allied to the power structure in the country that oftentimes they couldn't be separated. What he was striving to do in regard to the farmers was in the realm of economics, but it was really the exercise of power, the idealistic power that he had learned from his father. It was what every true Southerner had in his heart, though the South had been for many years in no mood to do much about it. They had tried once, and were still licking their wounds. Samuel Beauchay knew that he was getting on. He was sixty years old, quite advanced for a Beauchay male, but not so old when compared to the age of many Southern Gentlemen. There was still much time left for him to realize those strong feelings to which he had aspired. At this point in his life, all he was focusing on was this one last task, to help restore a spirit of idealism—a true culture to the state. He wanted to aid his fellow southerners in some way to show them what is possible.

Outside, was the sound of an auto approaching. Beauchay knew that it would be the president of their local bank paying him another call concerning the property. George hadn't been making any new coups lately. It seemed that he might be cooling down, but Samuel thought that Dodson needed at least one giant letdown to show to everyone that they didn't have to be bullied by someone who thought that he could just come in and take over.

"Let me get down to the point."

"Please do," said Samuel.

"I'll offer you three hundred dollars an acre. Now that's an outrageous price for land that probably won't have anything on it but a lot of sand."

"But you know as well as I do that you wouldn't pay that kind of money for sand."

"It's my gamble."

"Yes, that's right. But as long as you're in the mood for gambling, make it four hundred and you've got yourself a deal."

"Four hundred! That's outrageous."

"It's cheap for oil."

"Three hundred and five."

"Four hundred."

"Three hundred and twenty."

"Three hundred fifty."

"Three thirty five."

"Done," said Beauchay. "I'll sell it to you for three hundred and thirty-five dollars an acre. I'll have my lawyer draw up the papers today and send them to your bank for signature tomorrow?"

"Agreeable."

"I'll want half down, and you can pay me the rest over two years if you like."

"I can pay you all at once."

"Well, that's even better. My, you have moved up in the world."

"Yes, Samuel, a little—just a little."

***

As Jason was putting his things into his suitcases for Yale, which he would be heading to over the weekend, he started to sift through things carefully, trying to find something. He was searching for the ticket that he had taken for Victor. It had been part of his records, but he could not find it. He had been keeping it since he had talked to Jefferson several weeks earlier and thought that he might have to produce it in order to clear himself, but as things had apparently calmed down, he had forgotten about it and now was frantically searching for it.

He couldn't have thrown it away. He knew that he would never have done something like that, but where could it be? After looking through everything twice he sat down and tried to reason it out, going backwards in time, but quickly his mind skipped ahead to college. He was excited about the prospect of meeting so many wealthy heirs and future business leaders. The extravagant luxury of the place appealed to him as well. His future seemed very well in hand, he thought. His father was getting on in years and would soon die, probably just after he graduated, so he could acquire his money and land and be able to put the theories that he would have learned into practice. He could also go away safe in the knowledge that his Julia would not be married as now her suitors were out of the way. Things seemed to be very good, which made Jason's heart race in excitement. He lay back on his bed and dreamed of possible future scenarios of success as he forgot completely about looking for the ticket.

***

"Well I'll be," said Jake as Ed burst into the shop with the news.

"He's really sold the land—to Dodson?" asked Ike.

"Yep, the news is all over town."

"Never thought he'd do it," said Jake.

"Me neither," said Ed as he was too excited to sit down and so paced about rapidly.

"I never thought he liked old Dobson," said Ike.

"Never did, from what I could tell," replied Jake.

"I wonder why he did it?" said Ike, who was a little put off that Beauchay would deal with someone whom he considered as a bitter enemy while he spurned the offer of a friend, or at least a neutral like himself.

"I heard that he spent plenty for it too, some say close to twenty thousand dollars."

"No, really?" said Jake in real surprise. "Why that land isn't worth that, unless it's got oil on it, which nobody knows yet—why I wouldn't give more than a couple thousand for it."

"I wouldn't even give that," said Ed, wishing to sound shrewd.

"But that Dobson's no fool, I wonder why he paid so much fer that land? He must know something that we don't."

"Remember, he's just a feller, jist like us, he can get snookered jist like us," added Ed, now happy that they knew so much about what was going on.

"Tits true Ed, but he hasn't been taken yet, and I'll believe it when I sees it," replied Jake.

"I don't know what you gents is talking about, if thar's oil on that land, I'd say that Dobson got a bargain."

"Yes, I suppose that's the question," said Jake as Ed finally sat down to play some checkers.

Chapter 6

"The Lumber Trade"

When John's train approached a random town, he got out and found a park in which he could sleep. The next morning, he went to a dime store and bought an envelope and a piece of paper with some of the loose change that he had, which was now about a half dollar, and wrote the note to Julia. Then he posted it, and started on his way out of town. He knew that he could probably spend another two days at the most on the road before he would become too tired of traveling, but that should go as far as he could so that he felt safe. He didn't know what sort of town he was looking for, but somehow he felt that when he saw it, he would know that he had arrived.

He hitched another couple of rides and finally got picked up by a log truck that was stopped at the side of the road fixing a flat. John lent a hand and the driver obliged by giving him a lift.

"Where are you going?" asked the driver.

"North and east, wherever there's work."

"Looking for work, eh, well this is your lucky day. I happen to be going to a town where there's plenty of work. I can get you on at the mill if you want."

"Lumber mill?"

"Yep."

John had never done any kind of work like that, of course, but he thought that he could use a little extra cash. "Thank you, I'd be much obliged."

And so John signed on at the lumber mill. The town was very small and didn't have a railroad station of its own, so the lumber had to be taken out by truck after it was cut. The mill was the only industry in the town and supported the shops and such, which wouldn't exist otherwise. It was a very small community of less than five hundred people, and it seemed to John that he might be able to get on for a while there if he didn't make himself conspicuous.

"You're a little dark," said the foreman, "what are you, a wop or something?"

"My parents were French," said John, using Beauchay's family as his own (though he did not give them any surname). He knew he'd never stay on if he told them he was colored.

"French, eh, well that's all right. Just as long as we don't gets any of those Eye-talians around here, them Guineas just sit around and lap up the sun and don't do a bit of work, and at night run after our women folk—you don't do any of that do you?"

John didn't answer but shook his head a little, as one of the other men laughed at this accusation. "What do you expect him to be, Jimmy, queer? Of course he likes girls, how do you expect a gent to answer a question like that? He's a square guy, I can tell; give him a break."

"I just want him to know the score, that's all," said Jimmy, walking away.

"Don't mind him, he just had his daughter run away with a son-of-a-bitch from Chattanooga. That's why he's a little touchy with strangers, that's all."

John nodded indicating that he understood, but he began to wonder if this was really the best place for him to be. Dow worked at the end of the assembly line helping to load the finished wood into piles which would be later loaded into trucks. It wasn't a bad job. It had hard and slack times, as the machines operated in such a way that twelve boards at a time were finished, and these were loaded onto long dollies in blocks of thirty six, so that a dolly of thirty six would come out to Dow (and the man who worked with him) and they would take it over to the other end of the yard and stack them. When the trucks came for the lumber, it was also John and Pete, his co-worker, who loaded the timber into the waiting cargo area. Oftentimes they would be working solid for three hours, and then they'd have an hour or so when they didn't have much to do except sit around and wait for another dolly, or group of dollies, to come rolling down the ramp into their waiting arms. It was steady work, but very hot as they had to wear long sleeve shirts and gloves to prevent splinters, which oftentimes defied their protection and pierced their way to a soft spot of skin, in spite of all the gear.

After only a week, John was feeling quite at home on the job. He felt as if he knew what tasks were expected of him and how to carry them out without anyone having to explain it to him. As it turned out, he had a pretty much solo-type occupation. That is, he did his work alone and Pete did his work separate from him so that there was very little contact between the two.

"Say what's with that new fellow anyway?"

"What do you mean Jimmy?" asked one of the others as they were seated in the shade enjoying their lunch.

"Well, he never eats with the rest of us, but is always goin' off by himself. I tell you I don't think everything's right about that guy."

Several of the other men had noticed the same thing that Jimmy had but had never said anything about it, but now that Jimmy had opened the subject there was wide speculation on what was the matter with the new man.

"I'll bet he's a little off," said one.

"What do you mean?"

"Why I think he's not all there, have you ever noticed how he never talks to anyone?"

"That's because he's stuck up. I think the guy's got a big head. Thinks he's too good for us or something."

"Have you guys ever given him a chance?" asked Charles.

"Sure he's got a chance. As much as any of us ever has had."

"I wouldn't be so fast to jump on him, after all I remember when some of you first came here, you weren't so all fired friendly. Have you ever considered that we might not be the most friendly to him either? Sometimes it's hard for a guy to make friends, especially when the rest of us all know each other."

"But do you see the clothes he wears? The same ones every day, and he smells too. I don't think he ever takes a bath."

"Where does he live?"

"I don't know, do you?"

But nobody knew. They had just assumed that he must live somewhere, but nobody had inquired as to where this might be. This stimulated a few of the men to make casual inquiries around town to see who was putting him up, but no one seemed to be able to find out where he lived.

Finally to settle the controversy, one of the men decided to follow John home after work. John walked his normal route, but sensed that someone might be following him. He turned around, but saw no one, so he continued to walk up the side of the hill that sheltered the town. It was full of new growth trees, which were growing back from where their ancestors had been butchered *en masse* ten to twenty years before. There he stretched out next to a log near his little lean-to that he had made from scrap crates that he had gotten from the waste bins of the mill and the local store at night. John had straightened the nails and hammered it all together with a rock, two layers thick with leaves in between to help make it waterproof. At night he would roll up his coat as a pillow and snuggle down in the small hole that he had made for sleeping and lined with dried leaves.

As it never got too cold this time of year, he was fine. All this economy was required, as he wasn't paid until the end of the month and his fifty cents or so had long since expired so that he was living on wild plants and water until he could get some money to buy solid food.

"Why he's living like a savage, he is," said one of the men who saw John stretch out in his comfort. John liked to sleep a long time as it took his mind off his hunger and also his body didn't function very well on his local vegetarian diet. This had the effect of often making him dizzy. Sleep gave him the most relief.

When the two men reported their findings to the others, there was a mixed reaction.

"I told you he lived like an animal, you can tell just by looking at him."

"Maybe we can find some reason why he can no longer be with us? What do you think?"

"It's damn strange if you ask me; a man living like that, all alone."

"What's the matter with you men?" said Dumont. "Can't you see that the man hasn't got any money to live on? Here he comes to work every day and puts in a full day of work and you men are denying him a chance, because he doesn't come around here at lunch time and beg for scraps of our food. I think the man's got guts, if you ask me. He doesn't bother anybody, when he's got more right to than any of us. Only wants to do an honest day's work for an honest day's pay. Lots of places pay by the week—some even by the day. But our skinflint owner only pays us once a month. When you're flat broke, having to wait a whole month to get what you deserve, it isn't easy.

I don't know about any of you, but I'm ashamed of the way we've been treating him—a man in such straits."

This speech made quite an effect on most of the others and there was little talk about the new man. This change in attention was also occasioned by an industrial accident as a worker, Bill Mason, got his fingers caught in the gears of the feeding mechanism and had to have his entire hand taken off.

The whole plant stopped working as there was concern over whether the bleeding that resulted would be stopped and whether any infection had set in. Dumont knew some first aid from his mother who had been a healer. He was able to stop the bleeding until someone with more experience could take over. The town didn't have a doctor.

The accident was jarring but soon the shock of it all turned to outrage.

"Those feeding shoots are dangerous; we've known that for a long time; they should be changed."

"Damn right, and if we don't do something about it now, somebody else is liable to lose his hand or arm next time. Maybe he won't be so lucky and bleed out before Dumont can help him."

"It's because the damn owner of this place is so cheap that nothing like that ever gets done."

"Fred Miller's a reasonable man, I'm sure he'd install safety devices."

"Oh yeah, trying to get money out of him is like gettin' blood out of a rock."

"He's the tightest man I've ever seen, why he barely allowed his wife to have a midwife when she was pregnant; thought it was an unnecessary expense."

"He doesn't care whether we all drop over dead so long as there is someone to run this cursed mill of his. Bill gave up his hand. What's he going to do with a stump of a right arm?"

"I think the only way we're going to get Fred Miller to listen to us is to strike."

"Strike?"

"It's time we stood up for something around here."

"But none of us are rich men, how long could we last?"

"How long can Fred Miller last?"

"But maybe he'll listen to reason. We ought to try."

"Of course we'll try, but you know as well as I do what the answer will be."

During this conversation, which was just after work, Charles Dumont was absent as he was talking to John.

"Did you hear about the accident?"

"Yes, it was terrible, wasn't it," replied John.

"My name's Charles Dumont."

"I'm John, ah John Brown," quickly added John in order that it might not seem odd that he didn't offer a last name.

"I don't want you to think I'm nosey or anything, but I've noticed that you don't mix too much, and I thought that it might be because nobody had been friendly to you."

John didn't respond but looked at Dumont and wondered what the other had in mind.

"For instance, you've been here close to a month and I've noticed that at lunch you often go off by yourself, and you know, don't really get a chance to know someone—well, what I was wondering was whether you'd like to come to eat at my house tomorrow night."

John didn't know quite what to say. He had made a promise to himself that after his experience with the Martinez family that he wouldn't allow himself to get close to anyone until he could honestly enter into some kind of relationship. Otherwise, he thought, it would be better to be by himself, alone and out of the way. But now what this man was telling him was that by trying to be out of the way, he, John, was actually making himself conspicuous. He could not allow that, for in the same way that would call the type of attention that might prompt someone to do some checking on him and that might prove to be disastrous. He was very hungry, and he knew that he would actually enjoy a meal of solid food that was warm, but he didn't have anything to wear, and it would be offensive to go in the clothes that he wore to work every day, that smelled of sweat because he didn't have any way to wash them. No, he couldn't go to someone's house smelling like an animal.

It didn't matter at work, because he was alone, and no one was near enough to speak with him, much less smell him, but a person's house was a different story.

"It's very nice of you to ask me," began John. "But I don't think I can come—you see, I ah, don't have ah, something right to wear for something like that."

Dumont suspected that John might say something like this, and so he replied, "But it's going to be a barbeque outside, and if you don't mind a little smoke, we'd be glad to have you—it's nothing fancy, why you could come as you are, I'm going to wear some easy clothes myself."

There was little that Dow could do in the way of argument to this liberal proposal. A refusal would be an insult, and yet if he accepted, he knew that he would inevitably feel out of place. There didn't seem to be a solution that would be right. These types of dilemmas were always difficult so John added, "I generally go to bed fairly early."

"Well I'm sure that you don't go to sleep before the sun goes down, eh?"

John smiled and shook his head, this man was trying very hard to be agreeable and there was little that John could do except reciprocate.

"O.K., you have yourself a guest, I guess."

"Fine come by around five thirty or so and help me start the fire." They discussed the route to Dumont's house and then the two departed.

Back at the log, John thought about the tightness of the situation. His solitude sometimes made him elated as he became almost euphoric over little things that he usually didn't notice, and at other times he would become very melancholy, usually before he had to go to sleep. It was almost like the process of sleep was one of suicide and that by relinquishing his consciousness each day he was also giving up his life, or a part of his life. As the darkness came and the stars filled the sky, John would imagine what it would be like to be able to fly in an airplane to one of the stars. He wondered how far they were from earth, and whether such a journey was humanly possible. It was at these times that he would often try and imagine what a small piece of everything he was, and yet there was a sense, a point of view in which he was the master of it all and that the whole universe depended upon his looking at it and infusing it with awe and mystery.

His life seemed so confusing and incomprehensible that he could never really calm his spirit sufficiently to allow himself clear thought. Had he done the correct thing in leaving the Martinez's? Most likely nothing would have happened, and yet, he had felt that he was becoming entangled in his own deceit as those people were honestly reaching out to him for a relationship of some permanence and meaning, a relationship which he could not now enter into. But how could he have ever told that to them without telling them the truth, which he had only partially done to Pedro when he had left. It was important that they understand that it wasn't *them* who prevented the relationship, but actually himself, or more precisely his actions, for now John was beginning to disassociate the two somewhat. He knew himself, or at least thought he did, and had a particular mental picture of who he was, and yet, at times his actions seemed incongruous with this picture. What did this mean?

Life just weeks before had been so simple. There had been none of this complication. All had been easy, there was little need to think about things, to plan or to scheme, but now he found himself thinking and mulling over things more and more—why? Before he had always been content with relaxing and giving himself completely over to simple pleasures like fishing in the sun, where there was nothing to think about, and only the pleasant sensations of the body would occupy his mind. He had fish to worry about, but that wasn't real worry, but a game between him and the fish, to see which was smarter—people are mistaken when they think that fish are dumb. On the contrary, they provide some of the best game sport; a fair test for anybody. Yes, there was the fishing, the riding, the running through the fields until his muscles ached and his side throbbed, when he would tumble to the ground and roll through the hay. What more had life to offer than this? Why had he polluted it with the greed of adding to this ample pleasure, and thus ruin that elysian realm of innocence.

Now, actions couldn't be done, or undertaken without first deciding what exactly he was doing and what might happen afterwards. Everything was being examined time and again, and yet in the end it was the same quick decision as before. What was the purpose of it all? Simply to engage in decisive action? In the end it came down to one moment like when he turned around and walked away from Pedro. It lasted just an instant. And then in one more step his life's journey had changed direction.

The stars made him long to return to the days when he was a child and he didn't have to worry whether someone would call him dark, or wonder if he was, was different from the rest *—what's that? —a present, a book—a book? what about?—history, you said that you liked history, so I found this book that I had. John took the* *book and opened it and flipped through the pages of the book – it's long, how will I ever get through it—you should try. There's nothing for nothing in this life.*

Everybody was the same once the light left the sky. Then all differences vanished, except the outlines of things, like the trees. One could see their very structures silhouetted against the starry sky. And the bushes, animals—all were shadows that seemed to move together as parts of a consummate organism.

John felt his heart racing. Whenever it began to speed up there was no stopping it, and the more that he thought about it, the more difficult it would be to control.

He had to sleep, but he knew that the more that he tried, the harder it would become. He tried to blank his mind, but this only brought the disparate events of his life into sharper focus as he could sense the seething tempests. They were beckoning him from the rising stench that was his dirty clothes. How he wished for the comforting touch of some beetle or fly to come and alight on his skin so that he could communicate his miseries. But there was nothing; he was alone.

Chapter 7

"A Very Short Chapter Indeed"

With the money that John had left them, the Martinez family was able to pay two months' rent on their land. John was never discussed, though the reason was never explicit. Perhaps it was out of respect to Maria, who still loved him. Or perhaps it was that they felt somehow that he was an angelic blessing upon their family and because of his extraordinary nature it would be a blasphemy to say anything. For these or other reasons, no one brought up John's name, but that does not mean his presence did not inhabit their hearts.

One morning about ten days after John had left, the sheriff had come to their place.

"You know that boy you had around here?"

"Yes," responded the old man, with Pedro behind him and Maria and the mother coming to see that was the matter.

"Did you ever catch his name?"

"No," said the old man. "If I did, I've forgotten."

"Why do you want to know?" asked Pedro.

"Oh, nothing, it's just that I'm checking up a bulletin from a town a little south of here that said a fellow matching the description of that fellow might be coming this way, and I wanted to know whether he'd already passed through, or whether we had to be on the watch. That's all."

"Is this man a criminal?" asked Maria.

"Yes, ma'am; the worst kind. He's a murderer."

"Convicted or accused?" asked the old man.

"Don't rightly remember, accused I think, but it amounts to the same thing in the eyes of the law."

There were no more questions.

"Well, I guess that he probably hasn't come through yet, so I'll just give you all a friendly warning to say put at night for the next few days until this thing blows over."

The report that the policeman had given was from the man who had given John his first ride and had been afraid to tell the police for a month as he had been afraid of what John might do to him, as he imagined that he was still in the town where he dropped him off (20 minutes south by train). But that report plus the one from Varner's Junction created a travel direction which was forwarded on up to the state line (should he have continued along the same northwest direction).

The family all knew that the man described had been John, and that he was an accused murderer.

"He never killed anybody," said Pedro.

"I know he couldn't have, he was innocent; at least now we know why he left."

"He told me that he didn't want to implicate any of us."

But no one answered this as the old man leaned against a hoe. "I saw him that night, and his eyes were not those of a killer, he had a respect for death, the kind of awe that one loses when one kills another."

"I think he was a good man," said the mother, "a very good man." There was nothing to add to this as they all separated with all their minds on the same topic as they returned to their work.

***

When Jefferson arrived back at the house, he luckily found no one at home, and so he stole to Jason's room and went inside. Quickly and quietly he searched the dressers and closets until he found the matching ticket. Jason had the original. Victor had a copy in his pant pocket. This meant that Jason had been not only *in* on the transaction, but was the sole person who had done the deed. He had the original ticket.

It seemed that Jason placed the bet for Victor, if the story that Jason had told him before could be molded with the facts. Or perhaps, Jason had made the bets with his own money, and if he had, then how did he get the money to make the bets?

Jefferson decided to ride back into town and ask around about how the betting system was operated. However, when he got to town and just dismounted he heard a rifle shot and the sound of a bullet ricochet against the adjoining wall. Quickly he hit the dirt and rolled behind the wall at the corner as several more shots whizzed in the same direction.

Why is someone shooting at me? There was no doubt in his mind that he was the target. He had somehow stumbled onto the right track, and the gunman, by missing, had demonstrated to him that he had been correct in this assumption. Jefferson had to make two trips, one to the local racing track to try and get some further information, and then to Savannah to find this man, and try and draw him out. Jefferson winced at the pain in his ribs. This was not going to be easy. But then nothing in Jefferson's life had ever been easy.

***

On the weekend, Jefferson left on his first trip, which would last only a few days. It was relatively successful as he found out that the name of the man that he was looking for was Georgia Tom, who handled the book for many races, and also lent money to smaller agents. But no one knew just where he could be found. However, this little bit of information would prove invaluable in the tracking of this character, who he would start after as soon as time allowed.

Chapter 8

"John goes to a Dinner Party which isn't All that it Seems"

"Hello, John. Why don't you come right on in here," said Charles Dumont, extending his hand for a hearty shake. John stepped inside. His clothes were still a little stiff as he had attempted to wash them in a stream. He used the time-tried method of gravel and stones to knock out the dirt and stains. Then he tried crushing some sweet smelling herb to give it a neutral smell. The water in the area was very rich in minerals. This left clothes washed in it very stiff.

"We'll go out back and gather the wood for the fire," said Dumont as he led his guest to the back yard.

John knew that he would feel out of place, as well he actually did. *There is little in common between us*, he thought, as Dumont began to tell John all about his house and his children and how they were doing in school and what their favorite subjects were, etc.

All of this might have been interesting if John really liked Charles Dumont, but he actually didn't. It wasn't that Dumont did something that irritated John especially, it was simply that they had different interests and put their priorities in different areas. All the time that was spent for the proposed purpose of starting the fire was full of chit chat—thus was extremely dull to John, as he shuffled about in his stiff clothes wishing that he hadn't washed them and wondering how long it would be before he would get to eat.

"You see John, we really came here from Kentucky and I suppose we're still Kentuckian at heart, aren't we sport?" said Dumont to his large dog who barked and jumped about. Then his children started running across the back lawn screaming at each other in some sort of game. John never minded the yelling of little people playing, but these children seemed as if they were whining loudly all the time. Soon John could tell that they were playing Cowboy and Indian, except they couldn't agree who was to get the coveted position of Cowboy. John was reminded of how Jefferson had told him once that he had some Creek in his own bloodline a generation back.

"I want to be—"
"You were last time."
"I want to be—"
"So do I."
"I want to be—"
"I'm telling daddy."
"I want to be—"

Then they started rolling around on the grass screaming, not yelling, but making noises that were odd even for the high pitched voices of children.

"Go straighten them out, would you John?" asked Dumont.

John got up slowly. He didn't fancy doing this, as he didn't have a real liking for these boys, and it was always bad for someone to assume an authority role, John thought, who doesn't really like these people over whom he's to have authority.

"C'mon boys, let's get up."

The one who was on the top was about to offer a smart alack remark, which was even rolling off his tongue, when he turned his head and saw the figure of John. There was something that made him stop—*the history book wasn't an ordinary history book, but one that--"I don't want it," John intended to say, but instead modified his statement, "Why should I be interested in this? We aren't studying it with Mr. Russel?"*

Then the boy swallowed his remark even as he was speaking. John felt peculiarly uncomfortable, as if a ten year old boy could make him feel self-conscious. But John wanted to leave the scene more than ever, and he felt his muscles tighten as he consciously straightened his body and returned to his chair.

The two boys noiselessly went back into the house. Dumont, all the time, had been arranging the metal grill so that it fit over the fire and hadn't noticed a thing.

"Sounds like you did a good job there."

"Can I help you?" offered John.

"No, I can manage," said Mr. Dumont.

Soon the meat was cooking and the two men were sitting close to the fire with their bucket of water to ensure that the meat didn't catch fire— what with the fat dripping, causing an occasional flare up.

"Nothing like good Southern grown beef, I always say," said Dumont.

"Do you do a lot of cooking in the back like this?" asked John.

"Oh, I like to get out once or twice a month, but sometimes I don't; it depends on how much energy I have. But I always think that a meal tastes better when it's cooked over good wood, and a nice flame, don't you?"

"It certainly gives a flavor to the meat," said John, shutting his eyes as the smoke had blown in his direction.

"That wind sure is something, isn't it? I think it likes to follow you around the fire; that's what I think," Dumont laughed as he referred to John's inconvenience.

The meal started. The meat, though it had been slightly overcooked, was still plentiful and John, though at the beginning of the repast was careful to watch that he didn't indulge too heavily. He didn't want to be an overly indulgent guest. But when he saw the abundance of food and what was just sitting after seconds had been taken, he took a plentiful third helping.

This made his tummy feel very tight as it had shrunken over the past months by his rather anemic vegetarian diet. Still, he did the best he could, which wasn't too bad in comparison. The food was so good that it outweighed the banal comments of Dumont, who was a nice enough fellow, John thought, but just not his type.

"And so I said to Reverend Phillips, you were wrong about Jesus changing the water into wine, he couldn't have done that, or the Yankee Feds would have been on his tail!" At this Dumont laughed heartily at the conclusion of his own joke, and John, out of politeness, each time, felt obliged join in the joviality.

"And then the Yankee comes up to the Reb who was with Jesus and says, 'I surrender,' but then the Reb, who was aching for a good fight, as all good Rebs are, became furious at this Yankee for giving up before they had a chance to do combat and said angrily, 'You surrender, you swine? You can't do that; this means war!'"

Dumont bellowed and so did his boys who had the rather obnoxious habit of laughing with their mouths open so that food sprayed onto the table when they responded to their comedian father.

Mr. Dumont was the life of the party, except John felt that he had gotten his invitations mixed-up and had appeared at the wrong party— perhaps Halloween instead of a back-yard cookout.

"Say, John, did you hear the one about the cannibal who threw up his arms?"

John didn't perceive that the joke was already over and so responded simply and honestly, "No, go ahead."

This however was taken by Dumont and the rest of the gang as a topper to the joke, which they all found quite amusing, more so than the original joke. John, however didn't quite understand what they were laughing at, but thought that as long as they were, that he ought to also, and so managed as best as he could.

Toward the tail end of the meal, while they were eating dessert, the boys started fighting, as they weren't accustomed to sitting in one position for such a long time, and so began to generally rock the table.

"Boys," said Dumont gravely, but the boys were too high-spirited to listen to their father at this point. They still saw him in his former role and didn't understand that a father has the right to switch from role to role whenever he likes, without giving anyone advance notice of his intentions in doing so. Consequently, they were both rather surprised when the long arm of daddy Dumont reached across and threw both of them backwards onto the lawn.

"There, if you want to act like little animals, you can't sit at the table."

John never liked to be involved in family altercations, especially when he didn't know the family at all. But in an instant, all was better as papa shifted successfully back into his previous role and the children ran off, hardly ruffled by the reprimand.

Charles leaned back and smiled as if he had never switched roles at all. The two men took their coffee to the lawn chairs looking out toward the blue haze of the hills at twilight.

"You've heard about what happened at the plant yesterday?"

John nodded.

"Did you also know that they called a strike effective Monday?"

"No," replied John.

"They talked to Fred, the boss$_y$ and he wasn't too keen on the suggestion about getting a new chute with safety features to prevent a reoccurrence of Friday's tragedy."

There was a pause, as if Dumont was waiting for some reaction from Dow, but as there wasn't any, and John sat perfectly still, staring at his shoes, the other continued.

"So on Monday no one will report to work until Fred promises to fix things."

"You mean that everyone's going to strike until the man replaces the chute?" asked John.

"That's the size of it, at least we're hoping that everyone strikes; we don't have any union or anything, but it's been pretty well agreed."

"But there's only three days left in the month," said John thinking about his paycheck which he could so badly use at the moment.

"So what? Are you saying that it's a bad time to strike?"

"What I'm saying is that people would be able to last longer if they had another paycheck freshly in their pockets."

Charles Dumont didn't imagine that John was mainly talking about himself, and took the question for what it was, an alternative proposal.

"It might not have been too bad a proposal, except for two things: first we've already called the strike and we can't very well back out of the thing now, and second, it might call into question our sincerity a little if we waited to strike, working three days after the accident just to get our paychecks. Something like that would only make Fred meaner and tighter than he already is."

There was a silence as both men sized-up each other. John was wondering how much resistance he would get if he went to work for three days and got his pay check.

"Is there a lock out?" asked John.

"No, Hansen said that anyone willing to show up to work would be given a day's work and a day's wages, same as before." This question irritated Dumont; surely this new fellow wasn't going to spoil the unanimity of the strike, which might undermine its effectiveness, would he? If only a few scabs went to work it would prolong the strike for everyone. The total suffering would be worse than if there were solid backing to the strike. John's attitude must be turned toward the workers.

"You're joining the strike, aren't you?" asked Dumont.

"I don't know," said John, "I'll have to think about it."

"Think about it? What is there to think about? There is a strike and for it to work everyone must be in it."

"I know that there's a strike, and if you had called it a few days later, there would be no question that I would join it, but you see, I'm a little down on my money at present and I have to get it from somewhere."

Dumont had forgotten momentarily the extreme poverty that John lived in. If only it was in his power to lend John the money to tide him over until the end of the strike, but Charles didn't have an overabundance himself, and if the strike was prolonged for any reason, he would be scrimping himself. Was there no one who could lend John the money, who both had the resources and the desire to come through and enable this man to make ends meet until he could log in enough days to get his first paycheck? But he could think of no one. Everyone in the town would be in the same situation as the town relied completely on the mill, and when the money dried up from the mill, then nobody had extra money. The strike would be a city strike, not just a strike of the mill, as everyone in the town would suffer in their belt tightening.

"I can sympathize with your situation, John, but we're all in the same boat. I'd lend you the money, if I had it, but I need my spare dollars to keep us in food until this thing blows over."

John didn't reply, because he knew that it would only bring antagonism from this other man, who he didn't want to antagonize. He was the only person who'd shown him any warmth since he'd arrived, but on the other hand, he couldn't very well go along with something that he'd no part in if it would make him starve. All month he'd looked forward to the end of the month. This meal, he figured, would last him a couple days, and then he would get those pains again and the light-headedness; it would be too much to endure for an indefinite amount of time. He had been able to last a month, because he'd known that it would only be a month. But now when it was almost over, and the goal was clearly in sight, someone tries to take it away, replying that he'll have to practice a little economy for a while! It was too much to ask, and John wasn't going to lie about it.

"I know that you probably have it hard, but we all do. You just have to gut-it-out," said Charles Dumont.

"Well, it's getting a little late, and I think that I probably should be going, remember, I told you that I go to bed early."

"Yes, I remember, but John, remember that people in this town don't fancy someone trying to break up their strike."

"One person wouldn't break up a strike. He couldn't do anything. There would be no production at all. One person can't lift a log and operate a saw."

"That's not the point," started Dumont, his voice getting louder. "It's the principle of the thing. If one person goes because he needs the money, then when someone else needs the money, he'll go and then another and another, until there *are* enough people to run the mill—though not perhaps on anything like full scale, but the strike will be broken when that happens. Then we'll never be able to tell Fred anything again because he'll know that when the chips are down we aren't the kind of men who can hold fast to our convictions. You see John, it's a matter of convictions; this strike isn't about more money, but simply that we can work in safety—that we care enough about ourselves as human beings that we think we deserve to work in safe conditions and not have to risk losing our hand every day for some lousy job. What about that lost hand, John?" Dumont's voice was now shouting passionately. "Who's going to give back that lost hand? What is he going to do about that stump of an arm that will never be able to grasp anything again? And don't you think that the rest of us deserve conditions that won't allow that to happen to us? John, it's a serious matter that we're trying to settle. It comes to the security of us all, and we can't allow one person to not support us in our efforts. We can't John.

"Now I'm not a violent man, John, and never a man to make threats to anyone, but I do know that there are men who work in the mill who are violent and will not bat an eye at keeping everybody in line using whatever they think necessary to do the—do you follow me?"

John didn't respond in any way. "I think it's getting rather late," he said again.

"Yes, it is, and I don't mean to talk politics," began Dumont now in a congenial tone again, "at a dinner party, but I just wanted to let you know the score, so that there wouldn't be any misunderstandings."

"Thank you for the meal. It was delicious. Say good-bye, and compliment your wife for me."

"I'll do that, good night, bye, bye, good night."

Chapter 9

"A Light-Hearted Examination of the Expression: 'Figures never Lie'"

"We've come for our follow-up visit," said the small man in his Department of the Interior blazer that had a buffalo on the breast pocket. His thick wire-rimmed glasses magnified his eyes, giving the impression that his eyes were much larger than they actually were. Beauchay thought that it looked as if the little man could see more than was normal for one man to see, as the eyes seemed to penetrate and inspect inside things in a most disturbing fashion.

"Why we're here. I don't know, I think our report was rather clear, but we have been sent a directive, and as you know, a government official does not ignore an official directive."

The vibrato of his voice seemed to reinforce the strident message he was trying to convey.

"Well gentlemen, I can show you the land, though in a day, I will no longer be the owner as the deed has been sent to the state for official transfer and is due today or tomorrow."

"I don't think we'll require much of your time," said the little man as he wheeled and started for the door in his strutting gait while the big man merely looked embarrassed and followed his partner as he waddled behind.

This time the two did not descend and walk about very carefully but simply stood up in the carriage and looked out. There wasn't even the pad of paper, as they seemed content at clearing their throats.

"We've seen enough," said the big man to Samuel.

"Too much," gulped the little man.

"Now Red," cautioned the big man.

"Where would you like to go?" asked Beauchay.

"Back to town would be fine," snapped the little man.

So Beauchay drove them back to town, and they were off on the next train.

It wasn't more than a week when the word came to town that there was no oil on the Beauchay—now Dodson property.

—*what do you think about that?—about what? —well you know that land that was supposed to have all that oil on it?—no, what land?—haven't you heard anything?—are you talking about somewhere in Texas or something?—no right here—you mean there's oil right here, you mean we're going to be rich, all rich, because there's oil here, my Lord I've got to go tell my husband— wait, wait, that's just it there's no oil--no oil, but I thought you just said—that is just the point, there is no oil on the land around here— what's the matter with you Maybel, are you daft, l could have told you that, everyone knows that there's no oil around here, honestly, sometimes I just don't know about you*

"Now Gentlemen," began Johnston. "What I want to convey to you is the situation that is at hand. We've made some very good buys, but as you also know, credit is getting much more expensive at present as the stock market is having some trouble."

"I'll say," said one of the men in back.

But the men in the room were in no mood to laugh. Money had gotten tight all over and many of these men were depending on the money that they had in their investments to tide them through rough times.

"Some of the property we bought on margin: that is we paid only a small fraction of the cost of the land. This is like a down payment. We had hoped to sell before the year was out and thus recoup our money and make a tidy profit. But as things have turned out, this land has taken a downward slide along with everything else lately, though I must emphasize this to you that I am confident that it will prove to be a very good investment if we can only sit tight and not get worried."

"Well I'll tell you; I'm getting worried. I heard about an Atlanta bank that went under last week, and if that kind of thing happens there, just think what's going to start happening here in a few months. I've taken what little money I have left out of the bank before it collapses, too."

There were general grumblings after this speech in which the tone was definitely sympathetic.

"Now, listen, you've got to believe me, this mood that you're describing is precisely the kind of thing that we look for on real estate dealings. It means that we will be able to buy property dirt cheap and when prices go up again we'll make one hell of a killing. I'm telling you that what looks like gloom to others, is really brightness to people who've banded together like us in a company. This is the way to beat the thing, not by hording your money in a mattress at home. You have more chance of losing it in a fire, than you have losing it in real estate investments."

"Then why haven't we gotten our money on the properties that you were talking about if it's such a gull-dern-good-buy?"

"As I explained to you, we had to use a lot of credit to purchase the land as we hardly have what you'd call a large operating capital—"

"Seems pretty large to me, why I put in almost everything I had into this fool company."

"Sir, when we speak of large we aren't referring to fifteen to twenty-five thousand dollars, but two hundred and fifty thousand dollars—that's the kind of money required to make real gains in land investment." Johnston paused to see whether he'd effectively silenced his opposition, which he had, and so confronted with the quiet of assent, he continued, "What has transpired is that we have been requested by the bank to demonstrate that we can handle a larger proportion of our financial responsibility, that is, by law we are required to cover twelve and one half percent of the purchase price in order for a mortgage of this size so that we can be lawfully given the property. However, the bank often times makes exceptions to this rule and we, gentlemen, were such an exception. Now, we aren't being called upon to pay the entire difference, but only a fraction to show that we are a solvent company that won't be affected by these new hard times."

"How much did we pay?"

"What do you mean, sir?"

"What percentage did we pay on the property, and what is the difference that we must pay now?"

"Well we've paid twenty thousand dollars against the original purchase price of two hundred and fifty thousand that I told you about when we purchased the properties—"

"I don't remember you telling us that it would be that much."

"You may have been absent or you may have-been inattentive sir, but I have the sheets with all the figures that I passed around at our first meeting, and I will show them to you after the meeting if you care to see them."

The man was sorry that he'd asked the question, but he was concerned at where their money was going, for in reality none of the men, save Jackson and Vanderkamp, knew anything about financial matters outside of paying their bills each month and picking up their pay. And so they were confused by what seemed to be fiscal mumbo jumbo. And we are not really calling Mr. Johnston a liar, as he was seeming to imply, but merely wanted something explained to them instead of being made to look like fools for not comprehending what was going on. They had voted for a committee to make the decisions, but as far as they were concerned, one person, Mr. Johnston was the one who was, in fact, calling the shots. It seemed at times that they would be just as important as if they'd stayed home than come to the committee meetings where they didn't really understand what was going on anyway.

". . . which means that we ought to have paid $31,250 for our mortgage, but we only paid $20,000, which leaves a balance of $11,250 to be paid if we were called on to pay up all at once, but we are only being asked to pay $5,000 now, which means that we are money ahead, if we consider that the rest of our money is free to invest at a higher rate of interest until we are called upon, or shall I say *if* we are called upon to make up the balance at some future date. Now is that clear to everyone?"

"I have a question," said Charles Vanderkamp. "Why did you put us in such a precarious position, when we only had so much to spend, it seems as if you slightly over extended our money, doesn't it?"

"Not at all, Mr. Vanderkamp. I tried to get the best deal that I could. If I could have gotten it cheaper, I certainly would have, but as it turns out one must pay the market price for land, and that was that."

"But why didn't you simply pay the market price for cheaper land?"

"That, of course, sir, is a moot question, as the land has already been purchased and we are the owners. However, if you and the others wish to sell at a substantial loss, which would be entailed by such an action as not backing the money required by the lending institution, you are, of course, free to do so. However, sir, if such an action was undertaken, I must say that getting further credit for any future ventures would be quite difficult as our record for other lending institutions would not be, as you might say, a good one because they only make money when money is kept for some extended period of time, and when such investments are terminated early, then they don't look upon these clients in what you might call a very favorable light. However, as I've always maintained, the decision is entirely in your hands."

"How much of a loss would we have if we all sold at once?"

"The precise figure I couldn't give you as it would depend on how much a buyer would, in fact, be willing to pay, but I'd put the figure close to twenty five percent per person."

"Twenty-five percent! What's the matter? Our money's lost like that?"

"Not at all, it's only lost if you fold and call it quits. As long as you own the property, then you haven't lost a thing. If my calculations are right, in two or three years, you gentlemen would have doubled your money, that is if you're willing to wait that long, and can stand the small increments such as this, which call for added expenditures of money, to meet the conditions of the current market."

"You mean we can double our money?"

"I think that would be a safe estimate for a three-year holding, which is what I recommend. Of course if conditions change, as they often do, then perhaps the time period could be sooner—who knows?"

"And we could lose *more* than we have already, don't forget to add that," put Charles Vanderkamp.

"I don't think that's very likely."

"But it is a possibility, isn't it?"

"Yes, it is a possibility. In investment, we deal in probabilities, and the probability of such an occurrence is, in my opinion, quite remote."

"And did you predict that things would be as bad as they are now?"

"Well, to tell you the truth, yes, I thought that the stock market was going to get a bit shaky because the index was too high, I could have told you that. This only supports my claim that real estate is a better investment than ever now in these troubled times."

"Well, if you ask me, we're in a spot, either we accept a loss, which none of can afford to do, or we stick it out with more money, which none of us can afford either. I think if we could be sure that we'd get our money back, we'd all go to the hilt to support this thing, but the problem is, that we just don't know." Charles Vanderkamp cleared his throat. He was unsure about what he should recommend that the others do. But as he was the most glib and persuasive member of the committee, he felt sure that whatever he did, the others would follow him, so he felt an added responsibility not only to his stake (which was his own, and would support his family and the men who worked in his fields), but also for the other people whose money was tied up in this venture. The weight of it all was not conducive to sensing that impulse of what decision to make. He stood silent for a moment, trying to feel what he should do, for the answer to be somehow presented to him. But there was no answer.

He had been so sure at the start of the project, but now things seemed to have changed. Was this an indication that they should get out while they could, while they still had seventy-five percent of their money? Or was he being called to stick it out until he either *won* or *lost* it all? The stakes were high, and became increasingly more so when he considered that he wasn't merely betting for himself but for countless others, the leading men in the town, so in effect for the entire town as a whole since they would all be affected gravely if the outcome should be adverse.

There was no answer. He felt things for both sides, felt advantages in both courses of action. There was always much to be said for the conservative course of action; you never became ruined, and it was the way he had always known, but was it the way of a Southerner? Had his father and grandfather been conservative when they had built up the estate? No. They had gambled time and again with their lives to try and gain something better for themselves. No sir, a Southerner never played it safe, but took his flying leap over Hell's flames, even when he wasn't sure there was another side to jump to, because he knew that was what the South was all about. A Southerner, when all was said and done, was always ready to risk it all, because he wouldn't compromise: his character wouldn't allow it—there was too much pride, too much heritage, too much downright pig-headedness. A Southerner would spit at the devil himself because he's a free spirit who won't be anybody's slave—ultimately the only thing that made it worthwhile.

All this was felt, and not thought, by Charles Vanderkamp as he stood pausing in his speech before the others. The hairs on his arms felt as if they must be standing on end; he turned to face his fellows, and didn't even notice that a breeze from the window had stirred the Confederate Flag that was hanging on the wall.

Chapter 10

"A Chapter to Reassure those Readers who have been Wondering about Julia"

Julia Vanderkamp's aunt, who lived in the Buckhead section of Atlanta, in a very nice house that wasn't luxurious, but still very comfortable, was entreating her niece to come and visit her. Now Julia had only visited her aunt once before, but the experience was enough to convince her that she didn't wish to spend more time than she had to with this particular relation. Julia's father didn't like his sister much either, as she was an old spinster who loved the social circles of gossip and backbiting that cities oftentimes afforded to the correct client. Margaret Vanderkamp, in fact, did love society, but didn't consider herself to be a snob in the least, nor affected. It seemed perfectly natural to her that a woman buy clothes that were in style, i.e., according to the designers in Paris and Rome, and that she might smoke cigarettes in a silver cigarette holder—or that she wear lots of makeup and all the jewelry that she could afford (oftentimes all at once). This didn't seem at all unusual to her nor the least bit pretentious. In fact, she wondered at those who found fault with her. As for gossiping, she never used the term, but did admit to trying to keep up on what was happening to her "friends" around town.

At any rate, she wanted Julia to come out to Atlanta. Julia had no intention of *coming out* at all, but out of politeness would answer every one of her aunt's letters as politely as she could, which was taken as a sign of encouragement by the aunt who was determined to introduce her niece to Georgian Society, herself.

Julia's mind was more concerned with what was happening to John. It had been some time since he had written his short letter. The only other word she had received was the rather contradictory "sightings" that were reported back to the police in Varner's Junction. She knew that Jefferson was leaving town every so often, but he refused to tell her where he was going or what he was doing. He said it was better that way. Julia didn't think it could be better in any way, but she didn't argue, as it wouldn't have any positive results. Instead, she only waited.

Things were quiet at home now that Rodney had left. He had written one letter saying that things were fine, but Julia knew the anxiety of her parents about their son. Sometimes she felt a bit nervous about Rodney since he was not a very self-sufficient sort of boy. But as he was a member of the football team, perhaps there would be someone who would be watching out for him.

Outside, the autumn was bringing a chill to the air, and everyone seemed determined to shift into high gear now that the summer was over. Fall was a time when everyone seemed especially busy with the things that they had meant to do all during the summer but had put off. But now that it was fall, they had collectively proclaimed that they would wait no longer. So it was that in the town, the movement was furious and in the fields, the crops were being harvested as groups of migrants came in camps to help with the work, and soon they would move on. These migrants were strangers with no roots and no money. They were forced to move about aimlessly during harvest season to stay alive. At times, Julia felt confused as she saw such people working their fields. She wanted to go and be with them in order to do something productive. But she knew that she could do nothing so long as she was a part of cadre who owned the fields and indirectly contributed to their misery.

"If we didn't hire them, they'd have that much less money," said her father. "God knows that we don't have any money to spare at the moment. I'm just making expenses as it is—and no more. Prices aren't what they used to be."

And there was a sense that he was right, but also a sense in which she felt partially responsible for the misery of each and every person in the field; but this must only be an intellectual or superficial sorrow, she told herself, for if it were genuine, then why didn't she do something?

Of course, she told herself, it wasn't that easy. Her gaze turned to the bright colors of the corps of pickers in their various clothing and colors of skin. There was a rhythm to the picture—it swirled, not in rough texture, but in soft cross hatchings of a delicate brush that outlined all the figures with halos of complementary colors so that they stood out against the scenery, and yet the middle ground was of a light shade of color that seemed to aspire upwards, while the workers in the foreground were of deeper shades that were heavy and inclined downwards. All the lines of the workers were slanted down to reinforce the color effect, while the crops gently curved upwards in the style of late Italian Renaissance romantics.

It was a sad painting. Though the colors were warm at first view, the annihilation of the upward lines by their opposites, and the consequent twisting of the downward as a result of their desperate toil made one despair with a fixed gaze. Here was a recurrent scene, painted with a smooth, easy technique that was subtle in its violence, such that a casual observer might pass by it on the way to José María Jara, where their lusts might be quickly sated, thinking that it was merely another pastoral landscape like so many others, and yet though its turbulence didn't catch the eye as a roughly textured Van Gough might, it contained and emanated a violence so disturbing that the eye was captivated and not allowed escape until all of the horrors and secrets of the whole were discovered.

The painting of migrant workers working in a *de facto* economic slavery deeply disturbed Julia. She lifted her eyes to the sky. And who was *she*? And what if John never came back? The questions were too difficult. She resolved to go visit her aunt.

Chapter 11

"Concerning a Certain Trip Undertaken by Jefferson"

Jefferson had to do some work for Mr. Beauchay, as it was one of the busiest times of the year for them, but he decided that he had to go and try and find out about Georgia Tom. So after a business trip that he had to make to South Carolina for the farm, he detoured on his return trip via Savannah.

It had been too many weeks since John had been gone, but Jefferson felt that every minute he wasted was that much less chance for John to succeed in gaining his freedom. When he arrived in town, he went into a small cafe that he thought might be a place where some toughs hung out. There was a group of young black men playing snooker in the back and making quite a noise as they made their shots, got mad, and slammed down their cues.

"What'll it be mister?" asked the woman as Jefferson sat down at the counter.

"Coffee, with sugar," replied Jefferson.

The waitress looked at Jefferson with a peculiar stare and went to get him his coffee.

"That'll be a nickel," she said.

Her tone was one of disdain, Jefferson thought. He saw a youth alone in a booth. He decided to walk over and talk with him.

"Say there, I wonder if you can help me—" began Jefferson.

The youth turned and looked at Jefferson with an expression of fear and surprise.

"I'm looking for a man—"

"I don't knows no one," said the boy getting up and walking away.

Jefferson didn't know what was the matter. He wandered toward the back of the cafe where the snooker tables were, and didn't say a word, but just endeavored to listen. But when he arrived and it was apparent that he wasn't going to go, the conversation became less and less raucous as it dimmed to pianissimo. Then some of the boys started leaving so that soon Jefferson was all alone.

"Say, why don't you beat it," said the girl. "Nobody likes a cop."

"I'm not a cop. There aren't any black cops. What makes you think that?"

"You're not a black man," she said.

"Sure I am. Are you blind or something?"

"Your skin may be the right color, but you're not colored."

Jefferson thought that perhaps she was referring to his accent, or perhaps his vocabulary, or demeanor, which might sound a little strange to someone who wasn't used to it. But upon reflection, he decided that he had been simple enough and that it couldn't have been that.

There must have been something about him that made the others feel uneasy. This might pose a problem, he thought, he wouldn't be trusted by the blacks because they thought he was different, and he certainly couldn't find this Georgia Tom any other way than with the help of the local populace. The only thing that he could do was to try again. So he did. But this time, he asked the waitress if she knew a fellow by the name of Georgia Tom.

"No sir, I've never heard of anyone byes that name round here." She hurried away almost as if the mentioning of some forbidden name might somehow endanger her in a direct way if she lingered in his presence.

Jefferson made a couple other inquiries of people in the back.

"Get lost, cracker," said one boy.

The group laughed. When one person showed such defiance, then the others rallied around and posed an ominous front. Jefferson repeated his question.

The young man turned and pulled open a gravity knife.

"Listen cracker, you can clear out of here, like a good mister cracker, or ya can stay and feel my blade tween ya ribs."

There was a hushed silence as Jefferson looked the young man in the eyes and then slowly turned around and walked for the door, when suddenly he stopped and said, "I've got a hundred dollars for anyone who can get me in touch with this Georgia Tom. I'm not a policeman; I can assure you." Then Jefferson left.

What was it about him that made them accuse him of being white? The question was intriguing, but he didn't have time or the will to pursue it as he approached some young boys pitching pennies.

"I've got a quarter for one of you," said Jefferson.

The boys stopped playing and eagerly gathered around Jefferson, grabbing at him for the money.

"Not so fast," replied Jefferson. "I'll give a quarter to anyone who can tell me if they know of a man called Georgia Tom."

All the boys looked dumbfounded, and claimed that they never heard of such a man.

"Okay, then I'll give the quarter to whoever can tell me where men go to do their gambling."

"Lots of places," they chimed in unison, and then they started describing different places that Jefferson might go all at the same time so that the result was a hopeless confusion.

"Wait, one at a time. You, why don't you tell me," said Jefferson pointing at random to the boy who looked as if he was more intelligent than his comrades.

"It's on Viceroy, three blocks down and to the left. That's the biggest place."

The little hand thrust itself forward.

"What is its name?"

"Name, I don't think it has a name." The lad looked to his comrades to corroborate his story.

Jefferson tossed him the quarter and started to walk to the place. There was only one place on Viceroy that even approached anything but storefronts, and that was a little doorway that was below the street level with an oaken door. There was no sign to mark it, but he thought it might as well be worth a try and so he started down, when he heard the rather discordant remark, "Hey thar, what ya doin?"

The noise startled Jefferson as he had been so intent on descending the stair to engage the intrigue at the bottom, but instead this voice had called him just at the moment when he had made up his mind to go. The question shocked him out of his mood and concentration with a sudden abruptness. Jefferson turned to see an old man, who was drunk, and appeared that he liked to stay that way as often as he could.

"Don't ya know that it ain't open till eight?" slurred the man, as he leaned on the railing.

"Ah, yes, of course, but I was supposed to meet a friend here, and he's not arrived. Maybe you've heard of him—Georgia Tom, he's called."

"Tom, Tom? No, I've never heard of anyone by that name round here. Say could you spare an old man a quarter?"

"He's in gambling, and his name's Georgia Tom."

"Nope, don't do much gambling myself, I prefer a safe bottle of booze. Say, how 'bout that quarter."

"How do you know that this place opens up at eight if you never gamble?"

The man held out his hand. So Jefferson tossed him a quarter. "They serve drinks; that's why."

"And does a man named Georgia Tom or any big wheel gambling types hang around there?"

The man held out his hand again, so Jefferson gave him another quarter.

"I don't know, they might, but I'se sticks to the bottle."

Jefferson bit his lip and then left. That evening, about nine o'clock, he made his way back. He knocked on the door and a little window in the middle of the door opened revealing a face.

"What do you want?" asked the man. Jefferson realized that the man must be waiting for some kind of word that he should say to get inside, but as he didn't know it, he couldn't say anything.

"I'm looking for Georgia Tom."

"He's not here," said the voice and shut the window. Jefferson knocked again.

"Look beat it or I'll send some boys out who'll break you," said the face reappearing at the window. Jefferson walked back up the stairs. It didn't look good. He'd have to return to Varner's Junction that next day. He could return at midweek, and then perhaps he'd have better luck.

Chapter 12

"A Brief Account of a Long-Feud Between Two Men Competing for High Stakes"

"I never thought I'd live to see the day," said Ike.

"Yeah," slurred Ed. "Old Dodson being outfoxed. I tell you I think it's funny."

"I thought you liked the fellar so much," said Jake.

"Well, I used to think he wasn't too bad, but I guess I don't like the way he's kind of become a little god up thar in his big office and all. Men who know him say he's changed too. T'ain't just me whose thinks so."

"I never liked the man myself," said Ike. "Sose I'm especial glad that he gone bought that land fer so much money and now finds out that it's worthless!"

"It certainly lets the wind out of his sails," said Jake as he was jumped by one of Ed's red checkers.

"I bet it really put him back a bit too. Can't tell me that Dobson's *that rich*," said Ike.

"I don't know about that, Ike," said Ed, as he made another move. "Folks say that he bought that land fer cash on the nose."

"That may be true, but even ifs he did, doesn't mean that he's got lots more. I'd say that must have set him back a bit."

"Well," put in Jake as he jumped a red, "pile thing's for certain, he ain't going to make any money out of that land, thar's no oil and it ain't farmland."

They all laughed heartily as a woman came into the store and bought some calico. Ed got two queens and was chasing Jake's one queen, the last black piece.

"You know, I'll bet that Beauchay was planning that thing all along. He knew that Dodson would go out thar and watch, probably jis like we done, and got himself curious," said Jake ignoring the game.

"Yeah, and when those men came here he must have been excited by the news and wanted to buy right then and thar, but old Beauchay kept aholding him off driving up the price, and when those two men came a second time, then that cinched it," said Ed.

"But if Beauchay rigged it all, then how did he get those fellars from the government to come out here, I mean if thar was no oil and he jist rigged it all," said Ike, who was a little defensive about being taken in himself into thinking that there had been oil on the land, and not convinced that he had been outwitted as well.

"Well," began Ed, as he jumped Jake's queen, "what Randy told me at the records office is that sometimes a man like Mister Beauchay who has a little influence can get people to come out just by pulling a few strings."

"You mean those oil men knew before they came here that thar was no oil?" asked Jake

"I don't know whether they knew about it, but someone in the government did."

"Well, if you're right, then old Dodson sure got bamboozled," said Jake as his last piece was jumped.

"That was some scheme," said Ike. "He really had me fooled."

"You and half the town," added Jake.

"I hope that puts old Dobson down a few pegs," said Ike.

"Want to play another game of checkers?" asked Ed.

Book Eight

The Scope of Art

It wasn't until I lost my first job in London and failed to land a job at the Old Vic that I first considered what I ought to be doing in my line of work. What should a good costume be? Should I resort to easy stereotypes as many other designers did, or create some intricate set of personal criteria as some of the art-nouveau designers were predisposed to do? I actually came upon an answer that was personally satisfying when I visited The Flask, a pub in Highgate, and listened to a conversation between two writers there. The first writer (a Scottish man with a birth mark on his forehead) was arguing for an art which communicated in a public way to all people in the vernacular of the script and production as set out in a traditional way (viewing the author as the ultimate authority). The second (a lithe lady who pulled her hair back and tied it in a blue ribbon) thought that there might be some flexibility in the way fiction might behave.

Art, they both agreed, should be able to be recognized by all or it has no rationale. If the first cause (I take it that he meant the *Aristotelian final cause*) of art is to communicate something to someone, then an art which does not communicate violates the first dictum of art. The Scot said that it must say something recognizable. The lady (who was a university don) agreed to this, but said the question is to whom is one going to communicate?

Hegel had a very limited audience, yet he has influenced the way in which we think through a "filtration" system. That is, one man affected perhaps a thousand thinkers capable of fully understanding him. These thousand, affected five thousand doctoral students, who in turn affected hundreds of thousands of college students, and finally millions of people. Also, he (Hegel) affected other great, single minds, such as Feuerbach and Marx directly, and they filtered their thoughts down to the masses. Hegel could keep his thoughts pure and complex, and at the same time, indirectly affect all of humanity.

There is a difference, said the first, between philosophy and literature; philosophy is primarily analytic and literature is always synthetic. Therefore, by its very nature, philosophy must (as in all analytic scholarship) speak to a very limited audience. Literature, on the other hand, has a much broader base because it has *imitation of nature* as its starting point. Being imitative, it does not seek to break things into component parts, but to find relationships that exist between things and construct some unity. Literature, then, has an entirely different purpose from analytic sciences. Instead of taking things apart into pieces and setting them down again in a pretty pattern, it takes what is given, whole, and arranges it into a pleasing display.

I was thinking that there are, of course, costume designers of both ilk. The first sort generally displays at fashion shows and people say, "Interesting, that. I'll bet no one wears it to the theatre."

While the second group remarks, "Where can I buy that? Do they have a reasonable ready-made at Marks & Spencer?"

Of course, this skews things a bit toward the practical. But costume designers in the theatre have to be that way.

Here's how I relate this to the pontificators at *The Flask*. It turns out that they were both academics. He taught in University College London in the literature department, and she was a philosopher at the Royal Academy of Art.

They were talking about how various plays might be construed as "philosophical." One approach is to take a play that everyone knows like *King Lear* and try to ascertain what it might mean, given the script and production at hand. When someone asks a question like, "What if Goneril and Regan had decided to bring Cordelia into the picture and set out a retirement scheme for their father that would allow for him to rule as long as possible and then move him down by degrees until a painless succession might occur? The estate might become a living trust in which all were beneficiaries."

"No, no, no!" cried the man. "This is *not* how one engages in literary studies. When one wishes to bring in various *theories* that will help elucidate the text as it is agreed to be, then these are one of many windows on the existent text so that we see it from a new angle."

"Au contraire, mon ami, it is not the *text* but the *philosophical claim* that is taken as a given. The text is merely one expression of it."

"The text is *sacred*," replied the gentleman don.

"*Ideas* are *sacred*," was the philosopher's retort. "The only way to get around this is to make application to common experience for it is here that *ideas* reside in everyday living."

The gentleman cleared his throat and ordered another pint of lager.

***

"Your notion of common experience is perhaps mistaken," said the first. "My analogy to philosophy was mistaken, but certainly there is no reason for literature to imitate common experience. Why not say 'experience' or 'nature' (to use your earlier words)? Such a declaration would allow for very personal or idiosyncratic events. Even though it may be construed as experience, so that art which imitates thought (even if *the thought* is analytic) is proper according to the definition that you have just offered. I suggest that we are no further than when we started."

"What you are doing?" said the literature chap in response. "You confuse several different audiences. There is the creator, and a group of peers who understand the minute technicalities that are involved in the work, and then there is the general audience who will receive the final product. Finally, there are the critics who live with the audience and the author in a symbiotic relationship. They both need each other for existence."

"But why," interrupted the philosopher, "must there be a general audience? I see no reason why they should be allowed to dilute the power of art to say complex and intricate things simply because it must cater itself to the illiterate peasant who cannot read nor write."

"There are two reasons for this, first and foremost art is meant to be pleasing; entertaining. Art arose among general audiences, and it has only been in decadent periods that art has become so detached from its touchstone: daily life. Second, it must understand that it is not essential to the basic needs of physical survival. In order to continue, it must depend upon the patronage of society. When the base of art becomes too narrow, it will cease to be understood or enjoyed and so lose this foundation of support."

"I agree," said the philosopher, "that art must, at present, be monetarily self-supporting, but that is a fault I believe in the society. They should support their artists so that they don't need to depend upon selling their art for survival. Money and art are entirely disconnected (and often are at odds). Financial dependence creates an art that prostitutes itself for pound sterling. There is nothing in this process which makes for good art, only for financially successful art."

"But if art is to be generally pleasing, then what pleases most people will also be that art which is purchased."

"This sounds like economics. I thought you taught literature," replied the philosopher.

"Everything is economics, but that's a different discussion. Here, I'm talking of the opinions of Everyman. Art should appeal to Everyman."

"That would be true if all consumers were independent critics," replied the philosopher, "but they are not. They depend upon tastes of the previous generation, while artistic progress changes. That is why great artists remain poor until they are old. It takes that long for tastes to change. What a way for society to treat its artists! It starves them to death and praises them after they are gone."

The conversation went on, but I already had more than enough to think about. Both dons had positions that I agreed with to some extent. The literary don was concerned with maintaining literary traditions and not tampering with the texts because these texts have been tested over time as ticket-sellers made their choices. And that in the end there is something very democratic about theater, and that is as it should be.

The philosopher was rather more keen on ideas and using the plays as occasions in which to discuss the underlying ideas contained within—even if this meant hypothetically re-arranging the plot, characters, set, lighting—even the costumes! For her it was all about the interplay of ideas. (I wonder if she ever worked with Dame Iris?)

I decided that while I wanted to adopt some of the idealism of the philosopher, it would be wise to combine this with some of the pragmatic virtues of the literary chap. And so, now I work with both codes in mind, neither entirely right nor wrong, but both working when its particular insight into the nature of the artistic process seems appropriate to me. But I have to admit that it really excites me that the possibility that all the elements of the play (including costumes) might occasion *ideas* that can be bounced back-and-forth by the audience and critics. Does this mean the play is only an *occasion* for ideas and subsequent discourse?

I decided to walk back to my flat. I had to think this one out further.

Exhibits:

Ah, fading joy, how quickly art thou past!
     Yet we thy ruin haste
As if the cares of human life were few,
     We seek out new:
And follow fate, which would too fast pursue.

See how on every bough the birds express
     In their sweet notes their happiness.
     They all enjoy and nothing spare;
But on their mother nature lay their care:
Why then should man, the lord of all below,
     Such troubles choose to know
As none of all his subjects undergo?

Hark, hark, the waters fall, fall, fall,
     And with a murmuring sound
     Dash, dash upon the ground.
     To gentle slumber's call.

       John Dryden, From "The Indian Emperor"

The Trojan who is master of a soul,
Let him to battle, Troilus has none.

       John Dryden, *Troilus and Cressida* (Act I, ii).

My master heard me with great appearances of uneasiness in his
countenance, because *doubting* or *not believing*, are so little known
in this country, that the inhabitants cannot tell how to behave
themselves under such circumstances. And I remember in frequent
discourses with my master concerning the nature of manhood, in
other parts of the world, having occasion to talk of *lying* and *false
representation*, it was with much difficulty that he comprehended
what I meant, although he had otherwise a most acute judgment.
For he argued thus: that the use of speech was to make us
understand one another, and to receive information of facts; now if
anyone *said the thing which was not*, these ends were defeated;
because I cannot properly be said to understand him, and I am so
far from receiving information, that he leaves me worse than in
ignorance, for I am led to believe a thing black when it is white, and

short when it is long. And these were all the notions he had concerning that faculty of lying, so perfectly well understood, and so universally practiced among human creatures.

Jonathan Swift, Gulliver's Travels, IV, 4.

See, through this air, this ocean, and this earth,
All matter quick, and bursting into birth.
Above, how high progressive life may go!
Around, how wide! how deep extend below!
Vast Chain of Being! which from God began,
Natures ethereal, human, angel, man,
Beast, bird, fish, insect, what no eye can see,
No glass can reach! from Infinite to thee,
From thee to nothing—On superior powers
Were we to press, inferior might on ours:
Or in the full creation leave a void,
Where, one step broken, the great scale's destroyed:
From Nature's chain whatever link you strike,
Tenth or ten thousanth, breaks the chain alike.

And, if each system in gradation roll
Alike essential to the amazing Whole.
The least confusion but in one, not all
The system only, but the Whole must fall.
Let earth unbalanced from her orbit fly,
Planets and suns run lawless through the sky,
Let ruling angels from their spheres be hurled,
Being on being wrecked, and world on world,
Heaven's whole foundations to their center nod,
And Nature tremble to the throne of God:
All this dread order break—for whom? for thee?
Vile worm!—oh, madness, pride, impiety!

Alexander Pope, *Essay on Man*, #8.

We drove between a pair of decayed gateposts—the gate itself had long since disappeared—and up a straight sandy lane, between two lines of rotting rail fence, partly concealed by jimsonweeds and briers, to the open space where a dwelling-house had once stood, evidently a spacious mansion, if we might judge from the ruined chimneys that were still standing, and the brick pillars on which the sills rested. The house itself, we had been informed, had fallen a victim to the fortunes of war.

> Charles W. Chesnutt, from *The Goophered Grapevine* (*Atlantic Monthly,* 1887)

Hair—braided chestnut,
     coiled like a lyncher's rope,
Eyes—fagots.
Lips—old scars, or the first red blisters,
Breath—the last sweet scent of cane,
And her slim body, white as ash
     of black flesh after flame.

> Jean Toomer, "Portrait in Georgia" from *Cane* (1923)

These letters too were like a dream. Sometimes on dreams strange, impossible and incredible dreams; on awakening you remember them and are amazed at a strange fact. You remember first of all that poor reason did not desert you throughout the dream; you remember even that you acted very cunningly and logically through all that long, long time while you were surrounded by murderers who deceived you hid their intentions, behaved amicably to you while they had a weapon in readiness, and were only waiting for some signal; you remember how cleverly you deceived them at last, hiding from then; then you guessed that they'd seen through your deception and were only pretending not to know where you were hidden; but you were sly then and deceived them again; all this you remember clearly. But how was it that you could at the same time reconcile your reason to the obvious absurdities and impossibilities which your dream was overflowing? One of your murderers turned into a woman before your eyes, and the woman into a little, sly, loathsome dwarf—and you accepted it all at once as an accomplished fact, almost without the slightest surprise at the very time when, on another side, your reason was at its highest tension and showed extraordinary power, cunning, sagacity and logic?

And why, too, on waking up and fully returning to reality, do you feel almost every time, and sometimes with extraordinary intensity, that you have left something unexplained behind with the dream? You laugh at the absurdities of your dream, and at the same time you feel that interwoven with those absurdities some thought lies hidden, and a thought that is real, something belonging to your actual life, something that exists and has always existed in your heart. It's as though something new, prophetic, that you were awaiting, has been told you in your dream. Your impression is vivid, it may be joyful or agonizing, but what it is and what was said to you, you cannot understand or recall.

Fodor Dostoevsky, *The Idiot,* Part 3, ch. 10. tr. Constance Garnett

I saw a book in Khusrau's royal hall, Writ in the pahlavi, for so they call That ancient tongue—the great arch-priest of fire, Had placed it there—chief of the learned choir. Within the book in varied tale were told The deeds of ancient kings and heroes old. There too the Zandavasta's sacred line, Was traced, holy Zarthushta's book divine; And there the story of his wondrous birth, And all that marked the sage's stay on earth. Time-worn the volume and mystic page, Was veiled in doubt, and dim with mists of age.

> John Wilson, *The Parsi Religion* (Bombay: 1843): 447ff.

The main symbolism, which the evolvers of the Simon-legend parodied into the myth of Simon and Helen, appears to have been sidereal; thus the Logos and his Thought, the World-soul, were symbolized as the Sun (Simon) and Moon (Selene, Helen); so with the microcosm, Helen was the Human soul fallen into matter and Simon was the mind which brings about her redemption.

> E. M. Butler, *The Myth of the Magus* (Cambridge: 1948): 75.

1. I speak not fictitious things, but that which is certain and true
2. Whit is below is like that which is alive, and what is above is like that which is below, to accomplish the miracles of one thing.
3. And as all things were produced by the one word of one Being, so all things were produced from this one thing by adaptation.
4. Its father is the sun, its mother the moon; the wind carries it in its belly; his nurse is the earth.
5. It is the father of perfection throughout the world.
6. The power is vigorous if it be changed into earth.
7. Separate the earth from the fire, the subtle from the gross, acting prudently and with judgment.
8. Ascend with the greatest sagacity from the earth to heaven, and then again descend to earth, and unite together the powers of things superior and inferior.
9. Thus you will obtain the glory of the whole world, and obscurity will fly away from you.
10. This has more fortitude than fortitude itself, because it conquers every subtle thing and can penetrate every solid.

11. Thus was the world formed.

12. Hence proceed wonders, which are here established.

13. Therefore I am called Hermes Trismegistus, having three parts of philosophy of the whole world.

14. That which I had to say concerning the operation of the sun is completed.

The Precepts of the Emerald Table of Hermes.

Mercury	Sulphur	Salt
Metallicity, liquidity	Inflammability	Uninflammability
Volatile, but	Volatile, and	Found in the ashes
unchanged in the fire	changed in the fire	changed in the fire
Spirit	Soul	Body
Water	Air and Fire	Earth

The Tri-Prima of Paracelsus

The conception of the Philosopher's Stone was the mainspring of alchemy. It provided an unexampled motive power, a kind of alchemical perpetual motion, which animated some forty generations of alchemists. . .The nature of the quest was expressed succinctly by the celebrated alchemist and physician, Arnold of Villanova, at about the opening of the fourteenth century, in the following words: "That there abides in Nature a certain pure matter, which being discovered and brought by Art to perfection, converts to itself proportionally all imperfect bodies that it touches."

John Read, F.R.S., *Through Alchemy to Chemistry*, (London: 1961): 28.

The preparation of the philosopher's stone according to Pernety took twelve steps, relating to the signs of the Zodiac, Aries, the ram (calcination), Taurus, the bull (congelation), Gemini, the twins (fixation), Cancer, the crab (solution), Leo the lion (digestion), Virgo the virgin (distillation), Libra, the scales (sublimation), Scorpio, the scorpion (separation) Sagittarius, the archer (ceration), Capricornis, the goat (fermentation), Aquarius, the water-carrier (multiplication), Pisces, the fishes (projection). Thus is the process that will take place in the Hermetic vessel.

I direct you to take quick silver in which is the male potency or strength; cook the same with its body until it becomes a fluxible water; cook the masculine together with the vapour, until each shall be coagulated and become a stone.

Then take the water which you had divided in two parts of which one is for liquefying and cooking the body, but the second is for cleansing that which is already burnt, and its companion, which (two) are made one. Imbue the stone seven times, cleanse, until it be disintegrated, and its body purged from all defilement, and become earth. Know also that in the time of forty-two days the whole is changed into earth; by cooking, therefore, liquefy the same until it become as true water, which is quicksilver. Then wash with water of mitre until it become as a liquefied coin. Then cook until it be congealed and become like to tin, when it is a most great arcanum; that is to say, the stone which is out of two things. Rule the same by cooking and pounding, until it becomes a most excellent crocus. Know also that unto water desiccated with its companion we have given the nave of crocus. Cook it therefore, and imbue with the residual water reserved by you until you attain your purpose.

The Turba Philosophorum, tr. Arthur Edward Waite
(New York: 1896): 79-80.

Scorpio

Separation

Chapter 1

"In which John is Faced with a Difficult Decision"

As John awoke, he lifted his eyes to the valley, which stretched before him forlorn and wild. It was his seat of desolation, void of the light of dawn, child of the morning whose rosy fingers had not yet brought her glow to the eastern light of the future which would soon illumine the nascent shadows. The pre-dawn darkness, which extended long and far like a diabolic tempest, also promised to usher an immanent vitality to formless potentialities. This light which he fully expected and hoped for, as one always fully expects past laws to continue in their lordly circadian repetition, was not there yet. But its upcoming reality was something that John depended upon. It was his hope.

And so he sat, not moving, except involuntarily. His mind was not within his cranium, but was floating free amidst the dewy leaves and sleeping spirits of the silent wood. It would be necessary to do something about whether to strike or work a few days to gain his fifty-dollar monthly pay. If he were not flat broke and often so hungry of late that his mind was given to unsettled delusions, then he would certainly join ranks with the strikers. But that was not his situation. He must make a decision. There was no escaping it.

The chill of the autumn day made his body stiff.

And now, John slid out of his bower bed and tried to coax life into his body as the cold morning air started his blood to rush to all parts of his being and bring that vital tactile stimulation: the realization that one is alive and about to experience another segment in his life.

He had no food, but there was some water with which to wash and drink. The day had come and he would be ready.

***

At the mill, some of the workers had assembled themselves to see if Fred Hansen would make any last minute moves in either conciliation (which they doubted) or retaliation (which they expected). It wasn't until seven forty-five (fifteen minutes before the plant was scheduled to open) that a car pulled up and both Fred Hansen and the sheriff got out. Fred walked over to the door of the stripping room, and unlocked it and then turned to the men who were standing below him on the bank.

"Any of you who want to work, I will gladly pay you to remain loyal to me. You can be sure that I shall not forget people who have been loyal to me. You needn't be afraid of being harassed, as the sheriff here has guaranteed the safety of anyone who wants to work today."

The sheriff stood behind him with a Winchester 30-30 poised for any confrontation that might occur.

However, despite the offer, nobody moved or made a sound, until Jimmy yelled his reply, "There's one easy way to get us all back to work, you miser, and you know it."

Another yelled, "All we want is safe conditions."

"How would you like to work on that old junk?"

"Why don't you try it? Try running the factory yourself."

But these streams of comments were silenced by the arrival of Dow. He came up the road and tried to push his way through the people, which he was able to do until somebody got it into his head that just possibly this fellow was going to try and report for work, when he felt several hands on his limbs tugging him down.

Then there was a gunshot as the sheriff fired the Winchester over the heads of the men and started walking toward them. The hands that had been holding John suddenly let go and he dropped to the ground.

"Now you gents step aside and let the man through. If he wants to go to work; that's his right."

"But Mike," said Jimmy in a tone that suggested that the sheriff ought to let them tear John limb from limb for daring to interfere, especially as the strike was a just one. Surely only the lowliest of villains would dare to oppose it—and on the first day too! It was a flagrant pretentiousness that could not be allowed to go unchecked.

"The man has the right to work. The law has to protect that right, and I'm the law around here," said Mike in a seriousness that revealed that he actually believed everything that he was saying.

The others sensed that and so, reluctantly, stepped aside and let John rise and start again for the mill. John had just climbed the bank when a stone came flying and hit the bank just near to John. It hit with a muffled thud, which was followed by the sound of a rifle cocking.

There were no more stones.

When John had just reached the door of the stripping room, someone yelled out, "Scab!"

After that, there was much shouting and animated discussion by the men at the bottom of the bank for a while until they finally dispersed.

"Well, have you come to work?" asked Fred Hansen.

John didn't answer, but just stared at the other man. He didn't particularly like the big grin on his face, it made him want to walk over to him and push it into the wall. But John remained motionless staring at the other man.

"Well, at any rate, I'm glad to have you aboard." Fred extended his hand, but John merely sat down.

"What do you want me to do?"

"*Do*, why there isn't much to do," began Fred, apparently not offended that John didn't take his hand. "You can't run the plant with one man."

"I want to do something. I don't like getting paid for nothing," said John tersely.

"Oh, we'll get you to do something. I like an attitude like that; you know you might be foreman potential. How would you like a job like that?"

"I like the job I have."

"Which is?"

"I'm at the end, in the docking area."

"Docking? Why that's the lowest paid job in the plant."

"I wouldn't know, you've never paid me."

"New?"

"Will I get paid if I work?"

"Certainly. It'll be just as if you never left. I don't believe in penalizing a man just because his comrades are unreasonable. I'm a very accommodating man, I'm sure that you'll find that out. And I don't forget favors; *no*, I remember men like you—what did you say your name was?"

"Brown."

"Just Brown?"

"John Brown."

Hansen gave a slight start at the name, almost as if this man might be the abolitionist. But that was ridiculous since that man swung from a tree almost seventy years ago. Hansen didn't really respect a scab—especially one who seemed independent. "Well, Brown, I think we'll get along just fine. You just do whatever you want to today. Tidy up, whatever, I'll be back from time to time to make sure that you're busy, and to try and persuade some of your comrades to join you."

"I don't think you'll have much success," said John.

Mr. Hansen didn't reply but turned and left. The face of Fred Hansen seemed to reflect his personality, John thought. It was light and clear with bright blue eyes and medium short light brown hair that was cut by a very good barber, probably out of town. His clothes and body were immaculately clean and on his face was pasted a large toothy grin that had an imperious ring to it.

John didn't like Fred Hansen.

John spent the day cleaning up around the plant, and generally working at a low level of efficiency so that he wouldn't exhaust the amount of work too quickly. The sheriff left when it became evident that the men weren't coming back and John felt that the mill, which had always seemed interesting as a bustling center where things got done, now seemed lifeless. It was lonely, not just to be by one's self, or even alone when the place was always bustling, but all of this combined with the fact that every worker hated him for being there. They hated him. It didn't matter, he told himself, a person has to be *someone* if only to himself, but somehow this realization didn't bring him much solace. To be completely alien to all of them, not only for something that he was or might be, but for some stupid idea they might have that what he was doing was evil, shook John to his core. What could he do? He was slowly dying in the woods and none of these self-righteous strikers would lend him money to eat, and he would become sick soon if he couldn't get good food.

Theoretically, he could hunt in the forest, except that he didn't know the area at all, and secondly he didn't have a gun. Besides, John had never liked to hunt, and much preferred fishing, but even that was closed from him as he had no tackle, nor a stream big enough to get fish. *You can have Dow —that's okay, you take him —no you take him, we don't want no darkies on our side.*

John was halfway through sweeping the floor. There was something very depressing about sweeping. Things looked much better when they were scattered and dirty, much more like someone lived there instead of a place where gears resided. The machines didn't hate him for cleaning up. He was making it easier for them to operate. But somehow he preferred people; they were his own kind. Machines might have feelings, he wasn't going to deny it, but if they did, they certainly didn't show themselves in the same way that people did. The machine was silent because it was gloating in haughty superiority, or was it merely afraid? The machine knew that it was different, if machines knew anything at all.

How did the machines like being manipulated by people all day, and then when they hurt someone by accident, everyone is angry. It seemed unfair since the machines can't change the way they are. They go "on" and they go "off." Would that people got angry when people *hurt* other people. People have more options than machines.

But of course the individual machine couldn't think or feel the taunts that men carried with them, as they laughed at the ugly nakedness of sharp metal lines and crude gears that emit such a noxious smell, combining oil and sawdust to form a black perspiration that the workers would rush home to wash from their clean, white hands.

Oh, ugliness, how foreign you are—how strange and different: how ugly and deformed. John's sweeping sounds sang these words of scorn as he felt almost like attacking the machine and destroying it forever so that it wouldn't sit there and remain as it was, but this passion was overcome when he realized that by the clock, he was off work, or more precisely he had worked overtime by ten minutes.

John dropped the broom where it was and started home. On the trail leading down the hill, Dow was grabbed from behind. He offered no resistance as he was pulled to the ground and hit with a piece of wood.

The next thing that John knew, he felt cold water being poured over his face. He opened his eyes to see a man leaning over him with some water in a canteen.

"Open your eyes, lazy, and stand up," said a high dissonant voice that had a quick smoothness to it, but there was also a sharpness to the voice that would not permit one to think it at all comforting, even in its most tender moments.

John blinked and focused on the fat horizontally oval face that was emitting the sounds.

"What do you want, who are you?" gasped John in disorientation.

"C'mon, c'mon, stand up and cut the chatter, we haven't got all day."

John wondered whether he was in some sort of dream. What was this fat face with the sharp voice that seemed distinctly congruent with its appearance, doing over him when just minutes before he had been pulled down from behind and wrestled to the ground. Who had attacked him? Was it some of the men from the town? What was this man doing now? What was happening?

"My, my you are a slow one aren't you? Even for a big'un, you seem to be very dull. Don't you know that they'll come back and get you?"

"Who?" managed John, as he couldn't understand what was transpiring.

John felt a tug on his arm that was pulling laterally so that John would either have to move, or be wrenched in the shoulder by the lateral force. He stood up. The man let go of his arm, and John could see that the man with the strange voice and fat face was a dwarf.

"Let's go now; what do you think this is?" The little man talked sharply and started scurrying through the underbrush and John, still dazed, began to follow.

"Now I know you can go faster than that, quickly, I hear them coming." The little man was quite animated, and John obediently began walking faster. He didn't hear anything, but somehow he felt entranced by this little gnome who he imagined was leading him away from danger.

"Down here, quick," said the man, tugging John's arm. John was beginning to be more responsive. John hid in the bush with the dwarf.

John could hear the men approaching as they stopped where John had been lying. Among the men John could recognize a few faces, but the first voice to speak he knew was Jimmy's.

"I thought you said he was out cold."

"He was, Jimmy, I thought that we might have even killed him."

"Wouldn't have been any loss in my book," said Jimmy.

"I don't know where he could have gotten to," said another.

"Well, obviously he's gotten to somewhere, because he isn't here."

"I'm glad that he's all right," said another voice that John recognized as Charles Dumont.

"Yes," agreed another, "I don't go in for these rough tactics. We don't have to sink to the level of our opposition."

"We have to keep the strike loyal."

"But the boy only wanted to work a few days so that he could get enough money to buy some food. You can't fault a man for wanting to eat."

"There are some things more important than eating," replied Jimmy.

"And murder isn't one of them," replied a third.

"He isn't murdered; that's obvious," said another, "or he would still be here, wouldn't he?"

"Maybe, and maybe not," replied Jimmy.

"What do you mean?"

"Suppose Hansen came back here and found him like that, lying in open view, and took his body over to the sheriff's—even if he wasn't killed, still he'd have quite a case against us, now wouldn't he?" This was met by silence. "I tell you, if you're going to do a job, you should do it right. Now we just wanted to rough him up a little, teach him a lesson, but you clods either killed him or pretty close to it, and then got so afraid that you high tail it back to town without hiding the poor slob so that he might be found by any Tom, Dick, or Harry that happens to come along named Fred Hansen. You guys are just plain dumb. I can't do everything around here, you know."

"They were doing their best," defended Dumont.

"Well, their best wasn't good enough, was it?" retorted Jimmy. The leader's mind was working quickly as he paced the ground, before saying, "Bill and Ed, you look down the bank over there," he pointed to the opposite direction to where John and the dwarf were hiding, "and see if he might have rolled down there, and the rest of us will return to town and let Hansen make the next move. I tell you, this whole thing might be lost because of the stupid moves made here today. But we're not going to give up without a fight at any rate."

Then the men left and when the two searchers had also departed, the dwarf got out of the thicket and gave John a tug by the collar. "Come on, are you hungry or not?"

John, who was very hungry, but hadn't really thought about it until the dwarf suggested the idea, readily turned around, convinced that this fellow must be someone to trust as he'd already gotten him out of one jam, and so followed the little man into the trees.

Chapter 2

"In which some Rather Unusual Events Transpire"

"I know for a fact that you are starved, but don't bolt your food. It isn't good for your growth," said the dwarf as he laughed a Mephistophelian howl that made John feel very uneasy. They were seated on a log and the little man had a sack in which there was lots of cold roast beef and a fresh loaf of sourdough bread. John set at the food, despite the caution, with tremendous vigor. The dwarf only ate a little, and mostly watched John eat. When Dow had had his fill, he took the canteen and finished the water that was inside. He was comfortable, but as the food began to settle a bit, he became aware of a pounding on the side of his head.

"A present from your friends," said the little man. John turned and looked at the fellow. The dwarf was an extremely ugly person to behold. His fat face had two almost red eyes that drooped very low and his nose was shaped like a pig's snout. Most of all, the thing that bothered John was the mouth of the little man which was misshapen so that it could not be closed entirely and he drooled every so often. He drooled uncontrollably, a fact which he made no attempt to hide or compensate as he let the saliva drip onto his shirt and trousers where it happened to fall.

"Are you done?" said the dwarf, noticing John's stare. "Then let's be off."

"Where are we going?" asked John.

"You do ask a lot of questions don't you?"

"Well I do want to know what I'm doing and where you want to take me."

"Why you ungrateful little pig," replied the little man. "My name is Martin, that's all you need know."

And with that he turned. John had reservations about following Martin, but as he felt that the other could not out do him in a match of strength, he felt secure that Martin would plan him no harm. So he followed. They walked a long time, and John realized that they were circumscribing the valley via the woods and had gone quite a long ways when the forest stopped and they came onto some grassy fields. About a quarter of a mile off, John could make out an outline of a house.

"Are we going there?" asked John.

But Martin made no reply. John felt that he was rather getting to dislike the manner of this little fellow. And though he didn't hold anything against Martin because of his figure, even though he was slightly nauseating to look at, he did take offence at the manner of the fellow. John found him to be highly impertinent and arrogant.

They got to the house and John could see that it was once a very fine house indeed, but now was in decay. The paint had almost completely peeled away, revealing the weathered wood, now gray, which was warping and falling away. The windows were almost all boarded up and broken glass was everywhere on the ground. John was certain that no one lived there, except perhaps this dwarf who apparently must have found it to be as convenient place as any for him to stay.

The two walked down some old stairs that John felt sure would give way at any moment, to a lower door, and went inside. It was just as John had expected it would be: dark, dirty, and full of the signs of age. There was a strong odor of mildew. John stopped and took in as best he could all that was about him as his eyes were adjusting to the dark. He did not like the place. If the dwarf wanted him to stay here, he would politely refuse, as his old place was much better than this, even though it was only a few boards in the woods.

"Come on, don't just stand there like some kind of feeble minded idiot," snapped the little man.

John reluctantly started forward. When they went into the next room, the dwarf walked over to the fireplace and pulled out two bottom bricks and then grasped a wooden handle that was behind them and pulled it towards him. The handle was attached to the bottom molding, which the man took off with speed revealing two more handles, which the dwarf pushed with one foot, causing the entire wall to slide like a large door hiding another chamber, or set of chambers.

"Come inside, and quit gawking; you look like a stupid half-wit going to wet his pants."

John was fascinated. Inside was a large room and a corridor which were in no way like the rest of the house as they were bright and clean and lighted with large torches. John followed the man to a room and went inside when the door was opened. But as soon as John had entered the dwarf did not follow, but shut the door and bolted it shut. John was trapped. He tried vainly to open the door, but soon gave up and decided to explore the room.

It was large and regal in decor, trimmed in red with velvet chairs and elegant Venetian furniture. On the bed were some clothes that appeared to be laid out for him. Also by the bed was a decanter of what appeared to be wine and beside it, a fifty-dollar bill.

The whole scene was very unreal to him as his head was spinning from the blow earlier. He cleared the clothes from the bed and climbed on it and quickly went to sleep.

When he awoke, the dwarf was sitting in the velvet chair smoking a cigar.

"What are you staring at, haven't you ever seen anyone smoke a cigar before?"

John's head felt funny, almost as if he had been drugged. He didn't seem to have control of himself. He wanted to tell the little man that he wanted to go, and whereas he appreciated all that he had done for him, that now, he, John, wanted to be free, and that was more important than any comforts that might be afforded him in this house, or odd annex, or whatever it was, but instead all that he said was, "I'm hungry."

"Of course you are, and that's why I brought you your breakfast." The little man handed John a silver tray that was covered with another sliver dome designed to keep the food warm. Inside the dome were bacon and eggs and sausages with orange juice and coffee. It was a monstrously huge breakfast—one like he hadn't had since he had last tasted Jessy's fare. As he ate, the little man hummed to himself and puffed on the cigar. John thought that the cigar seemed abnormally long, but that could have been, he explained to himself, because the smoker was so short.

When John had finished, he put his tray on the floor. "Why are you putting it on the floor? Do you expect me to pick it up for you?"

John was surprised by this outburst by the dwarf.

"I suppose you think that because I'm closer to the floor, that I can reach it better than you can?" Martin walked over toward John and gestured with his cigar as he kept pushing the lighted end in the direction of John's face, three inches away.

John wanted to react, but somehow he felt rather weak and unable to move his body at all. It was as if he was just falling to sleep and someone was trying to wake him up, but he knew that he wasn't asleep. But then why couldn't he move? Why were his limbs so heavy and his head so dull? Could his fall have had anything to do with it?

"I saw the way that you looked at me, it was as if to tell me that you didn't want me around while you were eating because you don't like to look at me. Well, let me tell you something mister, I don't like to look very much at you either. You with your dark skin, I suppose you're part nigger, too? That's true, isn't it? Well, you know in the South what that means? You're *all* nigger. And so now get this straight, nigger, you aren't going to turn your nose up at me, because I'm your superior, remember that. It's only by my permission at all that you'll ever get to see your lady. Remember that, only by my leave." Then the dwarf took John's arm, which he couldn't very well refuse (being hardly capable of controlling anything). And then the little man put out his cigar on John's arm, causing a round circle of blisters to appear as a result of the burn.

What was meant by 'never see your lady'? Did he somehow know about Julia? But how would that be possible? On the other hand, how was any of this possible? His mind was so heavy and drowsy. He only wanted rest, but yet, could he rest? He tried to sleep again but found himself unable to completely relax as he was drifting in a limbo state between the two. His arm was throbbing, but John was insensitive to the pain. All that he could feel was an increased sensation of his skin against the harshness of the sheets. How rough they felt, almost as if they were tearing at his skin, and then he imagined that his skin was sticking to the sheets and being pulled off his body as he moved about. So he endeavored to remain perfectly still, but the more he tried not to move the more he was compelled to flop about, as he imagined that all his skin was being ripped away from his bones, leaving him with only tendons and muscles protruding. *A Book of Negro History.*

Sounds, too, were magnified in bright baleful colors and tastes delicate, yet raucous as ear splitting quiet rolled loosely about his tongue and dissolved with bravado into his gums. *I don't want to read, I don't want to read, he said knowing that he couldn't read it he* couldn't—for he was laying with his eyes closed as the dwarf sat smoking another cigar.

Chapter 3

"Jefferson Tries Again"

There were many duties on the farm during the fall that required Jefferson's presence. He had made several trips to Savannah, all without luck. Now that the harvest was finishing, he could devote full time to his efforts of locating Georgia Tom and trying to solve the mystery that was now consuming much of his spare thought. It was becoming an obsession with him. He needed to find that man. Was it just to save John and give him a clear name so that he could live the kind of life that he wanted, or was there some more personal motive? Jefferson often wondered indirectly about this, but refused for some reason to ever seriously consider the question, as such.

Now that things were finally over at the farm and the New Year was approaching, Jefferson made yet another trip to the city which had proved enigmatic in his previous attempts. He checked into the same hotel that he had used each time that he came up and then went walking toward the center of town. He took a different route this time, and passed by a place that appeared to be a billiards parlor. Jefferson rather enjoyed pool, playing it when he used to live in Baltimore, as he learned the game at college.

So he went inside to see what might be at this particular establishment. It was quite dark inside and the room was thick with smoke, though the smells were strange, like an old, musty flavor that never cleared but only accumulated. Jefferson stood in the center of the room, trying to let his eyes adjust to the light.

He could make out that the lights were just above each pool table and at some of the tables there were small crowds of onlookers. Jefferson went toward one such crowd of people.

There was a fat white man with a half, unlit cigar in his mouth. The man had the table (meaning he was the reigning champ and was taking on all and any paying challengers). He was playing a young well-built black man, who was looking on rather nervously. The older fat man knocked in the last two balls that apparently signaled the end of the game. The fat man took his money and then looked around for another challenger. A very young boy, probably only fourteen, stepped forward and wanted a try but the fat man only laughed. Then the boy showed him his money and so the fat man stepped back for the boy to break. It wasn't much of a contest as they were playing eight ball, and the young lad only got in one ball before the older man won by hitting the cue-ball into the two-ball which knocked in the precious eight-ball. One shot, one buck.

Jefferson could see that the fat man didn't have much cue ball control and no object ball control. Also the fat man was using a very unorthodox hand bridge, which made his stroke subject to irregularity. This meant that he might be one to choke in a crisis. Jefferson stepped forward and put a silver dollar on the table.

"Oh we have another sucker," said the fat man, as some of the people walked away, apparently bored with seeing another slaughter, as the last game had been. "I take them all ages, old and young," said the fat man chewing on his cigar.

They played the game and it was rather close with each player getting down to one ball before the fat man sunk his last one to win the game. The victor stepped back and pulled up his pants and scratched his stomach, which was covered with a pink undershirt and was stained in several places. The look of the face with the cigar was one of smugness and pride that he had beaten all challengers to the table. His look changed to surprise when Jefferson put down another dollar.

"Change the game?" asked Jefferson.

"My table, my game," replied the man.

"Suit yourself."

This time Jefferson lost badly as the fat man was somewhat angry that Jefferson had dared to suggest changing the game at his table. There was a look of immense satisfaction on his face when the game finished in quick order and he started to walk away, apparently to get a drink.

"I'll play you again for twenty-five dollars if you change the game," said Jefferson in a quiet voice, but just loud enough for the man to clearly hear his proposition. The man stopped.

"What did you have in mind?" asked the man.

"Straight pool to fifty."

"Straight pool, eh?" said the man in a voice that didn't know quite how to react, whether with satisfaction at an easy way of winning twenty-five bucks, or with suspicion as perhaps this stranger was just setting him up for a killing. It did seem strange that a man who had just been beaten so badly would want to play immediately for more money. This spook wasn't drunk, he told himself, so why would he want to play unless to beat the pants off himself. But on the other hand, if I don't accept the challenge, I will lose the table to this dark stranger. This was a situation that didn't at all appeal to him—especially as he didn't like this cocky fellow.

"All right, sambo, I'll play you as soon as I get myself some whiskey."

They lagged for a break with the fat man winning so Jefferson broke very well, sending the two required balls to the cushion and then almost back again to the pack where they left, almost no shot for the other.

The fat man put down his whiskey when he saw the shot. It wasn't the work of some rube who was just trying to let off steam. This fellow had played straight pool before, and knew something about the game; experience that the fat man didn't have as he almost invariably played eight ball at his table so that there could be a quick game with a decisive winner and time for more drinks. It wasn't a serious game in the sense that one had to concentrate at all times, but was sufficiently relaxed so that one could enjoy the company of the players and the drinks without seriously impairing the course of the competition.

But this game, straight pool, was different. It was a somber game that was rarely played in pool halls as it required total concentration and skill, something that didn't mix very well with the loose boot-legging atmosphere of the dark smoky hall.

The fat man tried a very difficult shot and succeeded in only opening the table for Jefferson, who proceeded to run thirteen balls before missing. It had been a long time, and consistent runs take practice, but at any rate he was up by thirteen.

They were on their third rack, with Jefferson holding a big lead, when Jefferson thought he'd ask the fat man the question that had been on his mind, "Say, fat man, have you ever heard of a fellow named Georgia Tom?"

The fat man didn't answer, but leaned over his shot, which wasn't too difficult, and took more time than normal, for him, to line it up. There were a few people watching this match as they thought it might be humorous to see their local champion get beaten. The fat man stroked the ball very hard and missed everything, it was a table scratch, then he righted himself and threw down the cue saying, "What you go asking questions like that for in the middle of a game?"

"I'm just looking for a man, that's all. I thought that you might know him."

"I don't have to listen to all this double talk from some spook. You know, I've had it. As far as I'm concerned the game's off."

There was a groan in the slight audience at the fat man backing out. In the ethos of the pool hall this was forbidden. However, there was also some antipathy to this stranger—obviously a ringer who was trying to sting the local favorite. But there was one sympathetic noise for the home boy over this stranger. It was from a tall man who wore a brown fedora.

Jefferson didn't contest his leaving, but merely leaned over the cue ball and stroked it, knocking in what would have been his next shot. The people dispersed and when Jefferson had finished with the table, there was no one who was willing to take him on.

The tall man with the fedora sat down for a few minutes and then left. He had had some diversion and it hadn't cost him too much, though he was sorry in a way that he didn't have some winnings in his pocket. He had bet on Jefferson.

The night was foggy and there was a slight mist in the air. It was often like this in the winter as low clouds blew in, covering everything in a thick, protective blanket. As Jefferson walked down the street, he noticed the street lamps as they illumined the fog around them so that they looked as if they had halos. About the halos were shadows.

"Hey friend," called a voice from the shadows. It was a low voice, one that Jefferson didn't recognize.

Jefferson stopped but didn't respond. Waiting for a further communication, but hearing none, he proceeded on when again, "Wait a minute, I've heard that you're interested in locating a certain Georgia Tom."

Jefferson stopped again and this time responded, "Who are you? Why don't you come out where I can see you?"

"Do you want to see Tom or not?"

"Yes I want to see him."

"Then you follow me into the alley over here."

"What's the matter with right here?"

"You ask a lot of questions for someone who wants a favor," said the man. Jefferson didn't like the idea of going into the alley, where he might be black-jacked, or rolled for his money, or possibly knifed by some irate personage from the pool hall who didn't like the way in which he played billiards. But then it was true that he *did* want something and since he did, he would have to accept the conditions that were imposed if he were to get a shot at that information.

Jefferson shuffled towards the alley when he felt someone grab his right arm and twist it up into a half-nelson and push a pistol into his back. "Now move, I'll take you to see your Georgia Tom."

They seemed to walk forever. Jefferson was very uncomfortably twisted. Soon, however, they went inside a building and up three flights of stairs. There was nothing unusual about the outside that he could detect except a strange glow of some sort that he noted from the outside. Inside there was the heavy scent of perfume. The stairs were old, and Jefferson knew that their entry could be detected from anywhere in the building. Finally, they arrived at a door. Jefferson was pushed inside.

"I've heard you've been looking for me," said a man wheeling around in a swivel chair behind a rather flimsy desk in a dimly lit room.

"I can't talk very well with my arm being twisted off," replied Jefferson.

"You little—" began the man holding Jefferson as he began to twist his arm even more.

"Let him go," said Georgia Tom, lighting up a cigarette.

Jefferson's arm felt very stiff from being in that position for so long, so he began to rub the blood back into it. Finally, when it was feeling some better, Jefferson put his hand into his pocket and took out the ticket that he had purloined from Jason and tossed it in front of Georgia Tom.

"I think you owe me something," said Jefferson.

Tom lifted up the ticket and squinted to read it. "Are you Jason Beauchay?" he asked.

"The ticket isn't for Jason Beauchay," said Jefferson.

"Oh, yes, so you're right, it's for V.S.—you must be V.S." Tom put down the ticket and rubbed his nose. "Well I'm sorry to tell this to you, but you know that ticket is too old to be any good even if the horses you picked were all winners. I couldn't pay you now for a race that occurred months ago."

"The debt's still fresh," replied Jefferson.

"Fresh, what are you talking about? I told you that you couldn't collect so why don't you go back to wherever it was you came from and we'll let it pass. Show him the door, Poke."

A man put his arm on Jefferson's shoulder and started leading him towards the door when Jefferson spun away. "There's still something that I don't have that I want," said Jefferson.

"The ticket? You want your ticket back? Well, I don't normally do that, but since you didn't get to collect on what appears to be a substantial loss, I'll give you your ticket back."

Jefferson walked to the table and took the ticket, but instead of turning around, simply held the ticket so that the printing was facing Georgia Tom.

"V.S. stands for Victor Stuart. Perhaps you never heard of him, but it was your men who killed him."

One of the men raced forward and put Jefferson in a full-nelson, thrusting his head down so that his forehead was touching the cheap flimsy table that Georgia Tom was using as a desk.

Then Tom grabbed Jefferson's hair with his hand and tilted his head backwards so that he could look into the older man's face. "You know you don't have a way of ingratiating yourself, does you? I was going to let you go out of here free as the breeze and now you're forcing me to do something to you. You see, I had to tell just how smart you was before I dids anything, cause I knew that ticket, but I didn't want to say anything—don't think I'm dumb cause I ain't. I'll do anything that I want and no two-bit nigger from Bella County is going to tell me what to do, or disturbs me in any way, do you hear me?" Tom talked in a calm voice, emphasizing the last words as he also tightened his grip on Jefferson's hair and forced his head back even farther.

"Do you understand that?" he repeated, but Jefferson, unable to talk because of the position of his head, managed to gasp slightly to show Tom his situation, which in all truth, Tom had overlooked in his anger. Then Tom bounced Jefferson's head down onto the table so that it hit with a thud.

"What shall I do with him, boss, shoot him?"

Tom took out another cigarette even though there was one still burning in the ashtray, and lit it while sitting back. "No, as much as I'd like to, we'd better not, I've got to check with Sig first. That job in Bella was a sloppy one and it's too sensitive to take any chances. Better put him on number two; tie him to the bed and only let in one of the maids to bring him food.

"Billy, you check up on him in the mornings, and Poke you at night—not a lot, just to make sure that everything's all right, got it?"

Jefferson found himself stretched out with his hands feeling very cold and his ankles moist. The room was damp and full of some sort of mildew or other fungus. Jefferson alternatively fell to sleep and then woke up as the pain of his body made it impossible for him to relax at all, and the sheer exhaustion of the situation and all that had occurred made this tension even more intense on his aging corpus.

It seemed like an eternity that he lay there in that condition with the throbbing muscles in his back and the blood pounding in his ear (a consequence of his head having been bounced around). Jefferson didn't quite know what to do. He tried to focus his thoughts, but all that he could think about was his tremendous pain and how much longer he would have to endure it or when he might die.

The thought of death seemed almost like a fairy tale of peace and tranquility. Why couldn't he simply dance into its forests of delight and forget himself and all that he had come to know as suffering? His thoughts centered around this idyllic image as an echoing of Tom's voice would shatter the vision time and again: *we'd better not boys, Baltimore Baltimore, Baltimore*—And now he asked himself, who triumphs in the excess of derangement? Who gains when so much is twisted in society: both low life and high life? Had he made a formidable play for *nothing*? And what of John? Could he redeem Baltimore through his metaphorical son? *Out, out damned white spots. Winter is the season of snow and death.*

We'll talk to Sig first. I have to know what Wyse will say. *And the woman who he'd always loved lay motionless next to their dead child. This game is too tough for me—too hard—I'm not made for...* Jefferson gasped and slid into unconsciousness.

Chapter 4

"Concerning a Financial Crisis which Faces Several Families in Varner's Junction"

"It's a sad situation gentlemen, but you all know the current financial situation," said Johnston very solemnly.

"But the first time you assured us—"

"Who can assure anything?" replied Johnston. "As you gentlemen know, I've never pretended to deal in certainties, but only probabilities. At present the market is responding in a poorer fashion that had been expected. There are companies that are going bankrupt all over the country, but this is no reason to panic, all that it means is that we have to make a decision as to how sincere we are going to be with our company. 1930 can be one of the greatest years of prosperity in the history of our country but only if people don't take a dim view of things and start to panic. Why I don't know if any of you heard about the fire that they had in Charleston a few years ago in a theater? Well I was in the place when it happened, and we all started smelling smoke, and then someone spotted flames from the scenery up top, and after that, no one had a chance. People were rushing all over the place screaming and acting like animals—yes just like animals they were. I tell you I was ashamed to be alive when I got out. Of course the whole place burned down, but it didn't have to. That scenery wasn't a real danger to anybody (suspended as it was). But in the panic, no care was taken for any of it and what might have been avoided had cool heads prevailed. What turned into a disaster (because people went and panicked) could have been a mere second intermission in the drama."

"I can appreciate your story about the fire, Mr. Johnston," began Oscar Whren, "but what about us, what do you propose to do about our situation? And when will we be able to get some money?"

"Well, as you know, you've all continued to receive dividends despite the problems on Wall Street and the northern banks. There has never been any scrimping on those."

"No, they've been just as expected," said another.

"What I've always said, is that you can always tell something about a company that always makes its dividends," said Johnston.

"We're not trying to say that our company is in bad shape, sir," replied Whren, "but what we do want to know is why it is necessary to put added money into this venture when we've put all that we can spare into it already."

There were some murmurings that indicated that Oscar's sentiments expressed the feelings of the others.

"I know that you've all put up quite a burden as well as the non-committee members of the company. And I realize that it would be impossible for us to realistically raise the kind of bond that the bank now requires for collateral on all its loans; I have therefore negotiated a deal whereby we need not pay another cent, ever, on the loan until we're ready to sell. What this would entail would be for some of us to get together and underwrite the loan, using our properties as security for the loan,"

"You mean we'd risk losing our land?" asked Jackson, who had rarely talked at the committee meetings.

"There'd only be as much risk involved as you have faith, or lack of it, in our company."

"It's not a question of faith, Mr. Johnston," started another, "but my home is all I have. I don't have any land, except my yard. I don't see as my home would be much good to any bank."

"Well, I've also considered this question as well, and have decided that it would be somehow unfair to the stockholders who underwrite the loan and take the theoretical risk to be in an equal position as those who don't take any risk. I therefore propose that either there be a stock split and the underwriters get most of the extra stock, making the holdings of the non-riskers very small indeed, or we ask anyone not interested in underwriting to give up their stock all together."

"I don't think we can ask anyone to give up their stock," said Vanderkamp, who didn't like the idea of underwriting anything with his land, no matter how strong he believed in it. However, he also thought it would be disruptive to state that he was unilaterally opposed to the proposition.

Charles felt that the company had been a good idea. It was time that Varner's Junction stepped forward as a potential source of economic power. All over the country, during the past decade, people had been getting rich, except in rural areas like southern Georgia. Why shouldn't they share in the economic bonanza?

There didn't seem to be any reason to him. In a great part, the idea for the company had been fostered and supported by himself. If it hadn't been for himself and Whren, there might never have been a company. Originally, it had been simply a move to balance the economic initiative in the town as George Dodson had seemed to many people to be quite frightening in the way he appeared to be taking over. But now Dodson had been stopped, as a result of more years, less activity, and the Beauchay land deal, where he was made to look like a fool. This motivation no longer stood as a principal rationale for the company. Now it was primarily a legitimate company that had to survive on its own merit. It was certainly possible for the old staunch citizens of the community to change with the times and be the leaders of the new age as well. That sort of transition gave character and heritage to a region, as his neighbor and he used to agree. It was necessary for this company to work because it was supported by the old established people, with a few new ones, like Oscar Whren, who almost seemed like one of the old names the way he fit in. The established order could control the destiny of Varner's Junction and Bella County and didn't need any help from the young upstarts in the eastern part of the county who were so against everybody else that they didn't like to associate with anybody unless it was acknowledged how smart and smooth they were with their college or Northern ideas (even though they might have never crossed the Mason-Dixon line in their life, and veiled their notions as progressive economics or some such rubbish—all of which equated to buying when you didn't have money and selling what you didn't have and not giving a damn about anybody).

There were things about this company that didn't appeal to Charles, like the way that they had overextended themselves, but he was willing to make some concessions to the progressive economics so long as he wasn't being forced into anything, and it was his choice. This Mr. Johnston was a little pushy, but not excessively so, Charles and a few others made sure of that. They kept him in his place when he wanted to buy more land with money they didn't have in June. Just think of the situation they'd be in if they had done that? Sometimes, common sense couldn't be topped by slick theories. His family had lived and farmed their land for over a hundred and forty years and in that time they had learned the lessons that the land had to give and they weren't easy ones either, coming at the expense of hunger and near failure. But they were too sound to merely throw away at some new theory simply because it was new.

He felt strongly about the land and keeping to established ways, but he also felt that it was his destiny to help lead the town into new realms of prosperity which a successful company might engender. There were so many things that might be done with adequate resources: new designing, new building, better schools, a hospital, cultural activities—everything that the rest of the country already had. These could belong to the proud Georgians of Bella County.

Yes, some concessions must be made, but *how many* and *how far* were the questions Vanderkamp trusted to Oscar Whren. It greatly affected him when, after much discussion on the matter, Whren spoke, "I don't like the idea of taking stock away from anybody, but I do agree that it would be hardly fair to the persons who underwrite this project to not be rewarded for their efforts in some way, so I move that we vote a stock split to be given to the members who make certain risks in regard to underwriting, and I also offer at this time to put up my house and my hotel as security for my part."

The motion was carried and they went around the room asking the members whether they'd underwrite, and the extent that their property was already mortgaged. Jackson said he wouldn't mortgage and that he didn't like the idea, and wished that he had never gotten involved with the whole enterprise and said that they could vote down his stock to any little pittance they wanted to but that he didn't care because he was resigning from the committee and going home.

Aside from this demonstration, however, there was unanimous support in the committee, though the reaction in the general membership was closer to Jackson's position than the committee at a whole. However, with the considerable Vanderkamp estate and the holdings of Oscar Whren, the loan had ample backing despite the rebellious membership. The doubters, Charles Vanderkamp thought, were shortsighted and would regret this day that they didn't step forward and embrace the future.

Chapter 5

"An Unexpected Visitor"

Sigmund Wyse—*Sig. It was Sigmund Wyse* The name kept going through Jefferson's head as his pain subsided. Then he opened his eyes. The room was light and his muscles ached. He became aware that he was no longer bound and that the agony of the past night now seemed to be only relegated to the status of a forgotten dream— a horror that still seemed all too real to him. He was again in his right mind and relatively safe, at least for the time being, and someone had undone his bonds.

It's strange that I didn't awaken, he thought. His ankles were bandaged and through the gauze he could see blood stains. Someone's looked after me, all right, he thought. His ear was also cleaned as was every part of him that had been damaged. His body felt very heavy as he moved about, happy to be free again, but at the same time sorry that his age should become so apparent to him in the stiffness that he was experiencing. He tried to imagine how he might have reacted when he was younger to the same or similar experience, but somehow the thought never developed as he suddenly remembered the name of Sigmund Wyse. It had been dancing in his head, where had he heard it? Of course, it had been the man who had once, for a short while, run the gambling house in Varner's Junction just after the Lucius Smith murder. He had disappeared shortly after the drugstore had opened and Bill Marsh had taken over both concerns, but why would that name suddenly come to him?

The heavy perfume smell returned to him and he suddenly realized that he was probably in a brothel. Was it the same building that he had seen Georgia Tom in? What an ingenious idea, he thought, to work out of a brothel, especially in Savannah, where there was never any problem of the police interfering with such establishments as long as the payoffs came regularly. Jefferson looked out of the window to try and establish what part of town he was in, but a large brick wall that was almost within reach made such determination impossible. All that he could tell from the smell of the air was that he was still in the heart of the city and that they hadn't departed the basic area that he'd been combing for months off and on without any success. How did it happen that he was contacted? Could it have been the pool hall, or was it an accumulation of everything that had gone before and that was only the incident that touched it off? After all, Georgia Tom had said, "I heard you were looking for me," and that indicated that he knew about it. But that could mean anything, and Jefferson knew it. Perhaps there had been two, or the scout might have signaled that he was coming to someone—anything, but the question was still intriguing.

Then Jefferson went to the door and looked out through the keyhole, but unfortunately couldn't see anything. *I wonder if they have a guard on me*, he thought. His mind instantly ran through some possible escapes. He didn't know how much time he had before something else would happen. His death sentence? Uncertainty was not in his favor. He could see from the window that he was only a couple stories from the ground counting European style, but at the bottom was a lot of trash and metal that would make jumping impossible. Also, he couldn't try to brace himself between the buildings as the surface of the other was smooth and would make such a project too difficult.

No, the only way he could get out would be to get hold of a rope of some kind and climb down, but what if there was a guard at the bottom who waited for something like that? And even if he did make it, could he be quiet enough with all those trash cans at the bottom? The project seemed fraught with difficulties at best and foolhardy at worst. But uncertain death is better than certain death, he told himself when he heard a sound in the hall.

Quickly he got into his bed, lay down, and closed his eyes.

The door opened and in came a woman dressed as a maid. She wore a plain white dress. The woman was clearly of mixed blood, though her complexion was more light than dark and her features were angular rather than smooth, but the most attractive feature about her was her beautiful brown eyes, which seemed to calm and sooth. It was into those eyes that Jefferson first gazed when he felt her cold hand upon his forehead.

"I see you are awake. You've been out for quite a long time."

Jefferson smiled. Before him was a woman he thought was quite stunning, though her face indicated that she'd experienced her share of stress. Was this beauty his saving grace?

"I thought you might have been in for it after last night," she said. "I saw you early this morning and decided that you wouldn't escape if I—" then the girl jumped back as Jefferson sat up.

He thought that his sitting up must have upset her, as she dropped the pail she was carrying and gasped as if she'd seen a spirit.

"What's the matter?" he said getting out of bed and setting her pail right. Jefferson was afraid that the guard might come bursting in when he heard the sound of the pail drop. But no one came in. Perhaps the sound had been muffled by the rug?

The woman, meanwhile, kept stepping backwards. "It can't be, it isn't—are you Jefferson?"

This identification startled Jefferson. Those calm, familiar eyes now seemed filled with some anxiety which had been absent just moments before.

"Yes, but how do you—"

"I don't suppose that you remember me, as I was only seventeen when I last saw you, though you haven't changed in twenty years. My name is Myra Bakersfield, you knew me by Myra Dow."

Jefferson knitted his eyebrows. Could it be that he had finally located the mother of John, the same mother that John had always wanted to see, on the very mission, which was about saving her son? How was it that she was working in a brothel? And why and how could it have been possible that she should happen to turn up at that precise moment in time—the whole situation seemed unreal to him. Myra Dow, or Bakersfield, whatever, was standing before him: the girl who had left Bella County in shame and whose son was now on the run for a crime that he didn't commit. Now she could help him, somehow, if he could escape, but there were so many things that he had to tell her first, where could he begin? What did he want to say? Twenty years had passed and he wanted to tell her what a fine boy her John was and what he meant to him, but there were no words as there was no place to start.

"How is the old farm? Is it still operating?" she asked.

"Oh yes, very well. In fact we just finished a very good harvest of sufficient magnitude that may offset the current low prices."

"Things are bad everywhere, even here. I suppose you've guessed what this is?"

"With the perfume scent everywhere it has to be either a perfumery or a bordello, and this isn't Paris, France."

Myra laughed, "Right you are; this isn't Paris, but it is Savannah, Georgia and one thing that we have an abundance of in this town are first-rate cat houses."

There was a slight pause as Jefferson stammered, "You, ah, just a maid, or you clean up do you?" He was trying to find out whether she worked there in any other capacity without sounding accusatory or judgmental, but for Jefferson, this was a little difficult under the circumstances.

"You want to know if I'm a whore?" put Myra bluntly.

Jefferson didn't say anything and tried not to react in any way to this paraphrasing so as not to give offense. Myra laughed, "No, I'm just a maid, I'd never have the stomach for the likes of who comes in here. Besides, I'm too old, at thirty-seven I look like forty and nobody wants a woman over twenty-five around here."

"Well, how long have you, ah worked here?"

"Before I left Tennessee, about a year now. I worked in a department store in Nashville for ten years until I got married and then after being married for only eleven months, my husband goes and drops dead. Can you imagine the gall? I mean we saved for three years to get married and then when we finally did it, he goes and croaks."

Jefferson listened to her flip account, but the voice had a practiced quality about it and there wasn't a real abandon in her casualness that suggested to Jefferson that she really did feel that way about her husband, whose name she still used. Jefferson thought she used her delivery as a guard against any feeling or reoccurrence of sorrow, for Jefferson believed Dr. Samuel Johnson's words that we all try to put grief of the dead behind us as soon as possible, and that it is natural and right to do so.

"And after that I decided that I didn't really like Nashville and so I came back here. Funny, but I've been kind of driftin' for a while, and as jobs are pretty hard to come by these days, I got connected here. It isn't too bad. Nobody to bother you or tell you what to do. I just do my job, which was outlined to me when I came, and go about my business and no one interferes. That's the way I like it; just do my work and go home."

"And then?" asked Jefferson, hardly knowing why he asked such a stupid question, but feeling a slight bit of curiosity about Myra, and what had happened to her, and what was happening in her life.

"Nothing much really. I don't drink, so I don't want to go to the bootleggers who outnumber the ministers in this town. And I don't feel like being friendly, really. I guess I read magazines and listen to the radio, and sometimes go to the movies. It's not too bad—though I'll admit that it certainly sounds dull, it has its advantages, nobody bothers you and one's life is exactly as ya wants it."

Jefferson looked at this woman before him. How much she had changed from the bubbling, friendly girl who had worked in the store and delivered orders after hours—how time and circumstances had taken their toll, though he couldn't blame her for wanting to establish herself in the most secure position that she could, people can't abide being hurt especially when they don't really wish to allow themselves to be hurt—it wasn't natural. But yet, there must be times when some people want to be hurt, like Peabody, his old friend—*Blessed are you when men revile you and persecute you and utter all kinds of evil against you falsely on my account, rejoice and be glad for your reward is great in heaven*--they allowed themselves to be hurt for a reason, but what did this mean? Didn't it seem rather masochistic to allow oneself to be in pain when a single action can bring pleasure, or absolution of the pain? *Wasn't it Socrates who said that all men desire pleasure first, yet didn't he die for the sake of affirming the sovereignty of the state, or law in general: --You break-up your strike or else something ugly is going to happen—How could the paradox be reconciled? Wasn't it a simple fact that pain was bad and pleasure good? And yet there were surely different kinds of pleasure. For example, working in the fields for a day might not seem as pleasurable as lying in the shade, and yet when the day was over, Jefferson knew he would feel better, experience more pleasure after having worked in the fields as opposed to opting for what might have appeared from the outset to have been the more pleasurable alternative. The principle was complicated as Plato had outlined so many years before, but what seemed more difficult was the case for staying somewhere that continually causes one pain. In such a case, one should leave so that she might be somewhere in which her higher goals in life might be achieved.*

Peabody did not have a yearning for pain, as he did many little things to make his life more pleasurable. And he didn't have a longing for death as he had folded to pressure the first time it had been applied, before Jefferson had come. And then tried to protect his residence against attack. He wasn't reckless, so what then was the purpose of it all? Surely no one except Jefferson really understood his death, and his, Jefferson's, own understanding was that Peabody was an unassuming person who simply wanted to do something to make his city better. He would have eschewed the thought of dying in itself, as it would have meant surrender to the very forces that he was in combat with. But yet when he was in extreme danger he did not yield, trusting faith in God or something—but what did this mean?

Peabody lost. He was killed and no good came of it. So what about the God card? What did it mean to play it? For example, if God were transcendent, or actually anything except an anthropomorphized father figure, Zeus atop Olympius, then what good did it do to trust in something that would not alter the course of necessity? Kant truly said that the phenomenal world operates under the laws of necessity. If this is so, then how could such a trust be anything but a wild hope within the absurd? Or perhaps it was a hope in life, but at the same time a declaration that the subject was willing to accept whatever outcome happened to transpire. It was perhaps an embracing of a future that already was but could not be immediately felt, an acceptance that those actions of the future were real in the same way as those of the past, except that they aren't seen, but only vaguely felt as non-immediate--more or less depending on the disposition of the individual. Thus it would be that actions that had not yet happened would assume a character of their own as formless possibilities that when pondered about may be felt as in some sense non-immediate.

Indeed, as Henri Bergson points out, when future events are thought of as a series of alternatives, the decision has already been made. This shows the fallacy in Boethius' argument regarding free will that was so much respected by the Church over the ages. It is only when one remains in the immediate that one can be (in any sense) a free agent. For it is the realm of the immediate that one shapes in every conscious duration. Any attempts to link the immediate with the non-immediate will create a false paradigm and therefore misrepresent human experience. Choices are not made through time, but in a single duration, as the subject is slightly different in each experiential duration. Yet this difference must constitute a difference in degree and coloration and not in kind (i.e., creating a difference in the character or essential nature of the consciousness, namely that subject is the same in different durations, but that it may be painted in different colors and gyrating to different rhythms). Thus it is that moral responsibility isn't merely a fiction or illusion. In fact, it is to this very realm of duty within the ethical that the Peabodies of the world dedicate their lives to uphold it by endeavoring in every way to strengthen and improve it. By striving to purify the structure, they leave themselves vulnerable to that which they are trying to eradicate. It is a daring gamble, and sometimes it works and other times it doesn't. Perhaps it is an object that many men undertake in their lives in various ways, but how can the effect be judged? What of the failure? What of the mistaken man? What of the man who dies for higher realms?

None of these questions seemed in any way answerable to him as he sat looking at lovely Myra, for so she seemed to him. Though her face was a little older than her years, it still was well formed. The lines on her skin were not those of anger and malice, but those that gave dignity to her. Jefferson felt, though he didn't consciously think it, that such lines befit a woman more than natural beauty as she forms these lines out of her own behavior whereas her first beauty was given to her by chance and might tell nothing about her character.

"Things have changed a lot since you left, Myra," said Jefferson, mentioning her name almost shyly, as the other noticed this as well. "For example, some of the farms in the eastern half of the county have changed hands, and we have a new section of houses in town near the cemetery, very nice too. There's a place you can buy gasoline for your car if you have one. Old Mr. Beauchay is still holding out against them, says that they pollute the air and foul up the place and that he won't have any part of them. But if I know his son, Jason, he'll have a car before he finishes up at Yale."

They both smiled as Jefferson felt that the mentioning of Jason obliged him to tell her about her own boy, which he wanted to do, if he could find a place to begin, but before he could start she asked him, "If you'll excuse my question, how come you're here in Savannah lying in a bed tied up, or so you was last night? Are you in some kind of trouble?"

"It's a long story. You see there was a murder in the town. Victor Stuart, not the old man, but his son. And they accused one person of the crime and he high tailed it out of town and now I'm trying to find out who really did it. By mere chance, my inquiries landed me here last night after I tangled with Georgia Tom."

"So it was Tom, eh? I thought it probably was. He's no good, that man. I've only been here a year, but a person can learn plenty in that time, believe you me." Myra leaned back in the chair that she was sitting in as if she was thinking about something.

"It must be quite a friend for you to risk so much to try and clear him," she said.

"He is," replied Jefferson. "He's your son, John."

At these words, Myra's head jutted forward in surprise. "My what?" she started to say, but even as she uttered these words, she realized what Jefferson was talking about and began to laugh.

"What's the matter?" said Jefferson thoroughly perplexed by her behavior—was she getting hysterical? He wondered.

"Are you talking about the boy who was left at the Beauchay's? The boy who was the reason that I left Bella County?"

Jefferson didn't reply, but involuntarily nodded his head.

"That wasn't my child."

Chapter 6

"An Interesting Answer to an Old Mystery"

Jefferson couldn't quite grasp exactly what she was saying. What did she mean he wasn't her child? The entire county knew the parentage of the notorious birth of John. How could she pretend that she wasn't the mother?

"I see you don't believe me," replied Myra, "well I don't blame you. It was made to appear that way. You see, someone had quite a vested interest that the real truth not come out, and I, as you might say, accepted a little money to take the rap, and I quietly vanished according to the script."

Jefferson felt shocked that she should talk of Mr. Beauchay that way, the man he, Jefferson, had always considered to be so honest, but perhaps it wasn't him at all, but really the shopkeeper as some have suggested all along.

"You see, Dorthay Beauchay was still unmarried. . ." she began hesitantly. Then she proceeded to tell Jefferson the story of how she had been taken aside by Dorthay when they had first been called to the house and offered some money which she had at first refused, but after a very sorrowful story and a realistic account of her own prospects in the county, which no matter what she did, were bad, Myra finally accepted her proposition. However, Myra stipulated that she would never actually make public consent to the deed, but wouldn't deny it either. She would go along with any punishment that was meted out, which Dorthay assured her would be no more than banishment.

When she had finished, Jefferson was amazed. "So John was a *Beauchay* after all." As he thought back on it he did remember a traveling salesman about that time. But was he colored? It certainly seemed so to Jefferson. He decided to ask Myra. "Who was the father? Was he colored?"

"He was a salesman who came to the store a few times. He was only around for a couple of weeks. I don't know for sure. I always assumed he was. But you know in the sales business you make more money by *passin'* than by setting your cards on the table. I guess no one knows except for Dorthay, herself."

Jefferson remembered that Jessy, the cook, had made a big fuss about how many times the salesman had come to the house. Jessy thought that the salesman was trying to get orders from Dorthay. Jessy didn't like it. It was true, in one way, that the man was selling something.

"You know that boy has led his whole life believing that you were his mother," said Jefferson.

"He wouldn't have known who his mother was in any case, if I hadn't allowed my name to be used, but you're right, perhaps it wasn't the best thing to have done—"

"I'm not accusing you or judging you, but I wonder how it will affect him knowing who his parents really are. He's always assumed that it was Beauchay and you. That would make him colored in the eyes of the South."

"But it will be the same thing if you switch the father and the mother. He's still mixed. And as you know in the South: mixed means *colored*."

Then there was a knocking on the door.

Jefferson crawled back into bed, while Myra yelled, "What do you want?"

"You've had enough time in there to clean the whole goddamn room twice, hurry up."

"Keep your pants on buster, I'll take all the time I need. It's my job if I don't."

"And it's my ass if you take too much time, so hurry up."

Jefferson looked up to Myra. "Then there is a guard outside?"

"Sure, and every so often one of the big thugs will come in to look after you, that's how I saw you last night, I had to come in with him, because he was afraid that you might slip out of the bed or something."

Jefferson forced a small laugh.

"Look, how long are they holding you for?"

"I don't know, but I seem to remember something about consulting someone or something like that—It's all too vague for me to remember."

"Was it Eddy?" she asked.

"No, I don't think so," replied Jefferson. "But you know it could have been, I just can't say for certain; my head was too jumbled at the time."

Then Myra paused a moment, "It wasn't Sig, the Link, was it?"

Then Jefferson remembered Sig Wyse, of course Sigmund Wyse! "That's it, Sig. It was Sig. I know him, he's called Sigmund Wyse. I remember now, he said Sig and then Wyse. He ran the gambling place in Varner's Junction for a short time."

"A gambling house in Varner's Junction?"

"Oh, yes, but of course, that was after you left, another new feature of our thriving village is that it supports two gambling establishments, the flimsier one was run by this Sig fellow."

"He's dangerous and big, too."

"Well maybe he is now, but then he was just a punk for some syndicate, some people think that he also had associations with George Dodson."

"Well, I don't know anything about that, but now he's known as the Link and he's very powerful and always goes around with a body guard."

"I must be pretty important or (more likely) maybe I've stumbled onto something bigger than I thought."

"I don't like it. You may be heading for an early grave."

"I was thinking the same thing myself."

There was another knocking at the door.

"All right, I'm coming," yelled Myra. "Listen, Jefferson, if I can call you that?" Jefferson smiled, showing that he didn't mind.

"This Sig always comes on Friday and as it's only Monday now, we have some time to figure out a way to get you out of here, but just in case he comes earlier, or I hear something different about anything that means that it might become dangerous for you, I'll try to get you out earlier, the only thing is that you have to do what I say quickly, because I'm only allowed to clean in here every week, so it will have to be an exceptional circumstance."

There was another knock.

"I've got to go."

"Thank you," said Jefferson as she hurried out of the room.

Chapter 7

"About an Interesting Conversation Involving John"

"What's it feel like to be a nigger?" asked Martin.

"Do you want to know what it feels like to get a fat lip?" responded John.

"What's the matter, are you sensitive about it? You shouldn't be. Look, I'm not sensitive about being *what I am*, why should you be touchy about *what you are*? It isn't that much worse."

"Have you got eyes, boy? If you have, you'll see that mine are blue. Black people don't have blue eyes."

"You're wrong there, Johnny boy. Some *do*. Why I knew one who was coal black and he had blue eyes: blue as the ocean. You see it's all a matter of degrees and percentages. Blacks dominate over white biologically, and that's why you always see the offspring of the mixed couples to look like the nigger and not like the white mother. They say it takes a long time to get the nigger out of the blood of some stock; a long time—and by the way, my name's Martin."

"Well, Martin, it just so happens that I know my parents very well, and neither of them are black, so there goes your theory."

The little man chuckled as if, John thought, he knew that John was telling him a lie and that he knew that John had no idea who his parents were or whether they were purple. But, John told himself, he shouldn't be bothered by such a little runt as that, and asked him, "When are you going to let me out of this little prison that you've devised for me?"

"There's no prison, you are free to go at any time," replied Martin.

"All right, show me the door; I'm going."

"Fine, but I'd think that one over first, remember you don't have a place to go back to, your friends have made sure of that, and no one in town will put you up, you may be sure of that. You're a hunted man, you know."

John wasn't sure in what sense that the dwarf meant that. Did he know that he was wanted for murder? Could he take that chance that he might tell everything if he left?

John pursed his lips.

True, he now had some money, but it would be no good to him unless he could get out. In the village he was a despised man. The scab who didn't follow the strike. The dirty scab who went to work for Fred Hansen. No, the town was out of the question, but he had to get away.

"Well, you just show me the door and I'll make any decision in regards to that," replied John.

"As you want," replied Martin, "I've been instructed to be very good to you."

"Instructed, by whom?"

Martin didn't answer, but only exploded into his high disconcerting laugh again. John got up (he was dressed in his old clothes, refusing to put on the clothes that were laid out for him) and felt that he was a little dizzy, but he was determined to leave, at least for a little while.

The dwarf led him back out of his room down the small hall and out into the dusty room again.

"You see, this house was built in the time of the Indians, and the original owner thought it prudent to have a few secret rooms in case they were ever required. Now you and I habitate there instead, just as secret as the original intent, but completely safe from the Indians, of course."

He showed John how to operate the handle and how to close it from the inside so that everything shut up securely.

Then John went outside.

The air was thin and easy to breathe, which made John take several large breaths so that he could feel the light *ruah*, breath of life, within his body. For the first two days he had felt so queer inside the room, with no real light and the feeling that everything was dream-like. It was almost as if he had been drugged, which he wouldn't have put below the little man, who he imagined capable of anything. All the while, he could vaguely remember the dwarf's devilish laugh as John would often try to express himself, but begin talking about something that he had no intention of talking about. But John felt enslaved because of the laugh of the little demon to follow *his* direction. He remembered the urge to strike the little man, and then falling out of bed as he vainly lunged and hit the floor.

When he got to his feet, he remembered the old woman. At first she was merely an image in the mirror. Normally when you look into a mirror you see a reflection of yourself. But in this case he saw an old woman whose image soon dissolved into John's own image.

Who was this old woman? Was she real? John thought he remembered that once he woke up briefly and saw the old woman in his bed. She was not asleep, but propped up on her elbow, staring at him. She wore no clothing. She had a smooth face with fierce white hair and several teeth missing. Her nails were very long and they were painted black. She reached out and scratched John on the neck. She drew blood and licked it off her finger. Then John dropped his jaw as she transformed into a young woman.

That was the last thing John remembered.

***

John was now outside by himself. He had assumed all along that it had been the next morning, but now that he remembered these weird dreams that seemed to go on forever, it didn't seem possible that it could really have transpired in a single day or night. He checked his pockets. He had the fifty dollars. He checked his neck. It so was badly scratched that the closed wound was raised. What had happened to him? Was this real or illusory? What could he believe when all was so strange to him?

The old house looked to him as if it were going to fall down at any minute. A full one-half of it had been gutted by fire, probably a long time ago, thought John, by the way much of it had been smoothed by the elements. What an elegant place it must have been to have stood in this field, a regular fortress, he thought. The grass would have been shorter and the grounds probably decorated in some sort of fashion of the day. Had this place stood the War? Was it destroyed by the War? How much had been destroyed by the War?

But from where did the dwarf come in? He was shown the secret levers, but how had the dwarf discovered these? And what of the old woman who transformed? Who was she? A ghost of a former era? So much seemed not to make any sense. But then, John's life seemed not to make any sense.

Where was Julia now, and what was she thinking and doing? He wanted to know whether she still cared for him as much as he did for her. It only took an absence such as he had for him to realize how much Julia was the kind of woman that might make a very good companion for him. She possessed all of the basic qualities that he felt a person should have, and most of all, he felt comfortable when he was with her. Certainly, he felt a passion of sorts, but most of all he felt an easiness that he had never experienced with another. He could talk to her and he saw her not as something to be desired like Balzac's violin that Mr. Russel liked to talk about, but rather like a very good friend. She wasn't like Cindy or Maria in any way, she didn't excite an impatient uncontrollability, but rather a quiet yearning. He desired to talk with her for the longest time and discuss with her what he thought concerning all the new ideas that had come into his head of late. Somehow, he was sure that she'd understand. She was that way. Whenever he left her company, he knew that he stood a little lower now. She elevated him with her knowledge and character. This is why he longed to be with her.

Along with Jefferson, she was the only person he felt that he could really trust, and somehow that feeling of trust made all of the difference. He knew that he had to get back to her as soon as he could—safety or no safety. They must make some kind of plan about a rendezvous, but how and where? He must get to another town and wire her from there and arrange something in either Atlanta or Savanna (as they were the most accessible big cities from Varner's Junction via rail).

Having made his resolution, he decided to go back to the house and inquire how he could get to another town. John remembered the mechanism of how to operate the wall, but when he got there he could not find the lever. It wasn't where it was supposed to be. Then John heard the sound of bees. This wasn't the season for bees! He turned around and made his hasty exit.

"You can never escape, no matter where you go!" the voice rang in his head. Whose voice was it? The old woman's? Was he going crazy?

John ran through the tall grass in the field. He knew the woods well enough to survive until he found a road or something. He could then spend the money that he had been given. As he ran, his body seemed to sing a dirge. He wanted to cry, but he felt the impulse to be completely inappropriate—*I don't want your old book; I don't want it. I have my own that I have to read.* No that wasn't right, he had to change it, --*thank you very much, he said knowing that he would never even open* it.

John was running as hard as he could, the weakness of the past month now seemed departed from his body completely as he felt as if he were almost carried by the wind as the grass brushed against his clothing.

He didn't have far to go until he found an old dirt road that led to a paved road. He waited for a car or something, and in a few hours he was riding toward a town. Everything was etched in his mind, the house, the dwarf, and the woman—it seemed as if he hadn't left, but he vowed to himself that he would never go back there. He was afraid of the house.

When he got to town, he went into a cafe and had lunch. When he reached into his pocket to pay the bill, he took out the fifty-dollar bill. "Sorry, this is a rather large bill, can you give me change?"

"I've heard that one before. You give me the bill; I'm sure we can cash it. What is it a ten note?" said the man with a smile.

"Here, then, cash it if you can," said John handing the man the fifty-dollar bill.

"What is this, some kind of joke?" said the man at first seeing the bill, but then for some reason, he looked at John in a funny way as if there was something wrong about John, and said, "Sure buddy, right away."

John couldn't understand what was the matter, as the man made for the door. "I've got to go to the bank, sir, I don't keep money like that around here, you know," said the man rapidly in an altogether different tone.

When the man returned he shakily handed John his $49.50 change and then bid him good-bye. As John stepped outside he felt two hands on his shoulders and two guns pushed into his side, "All right buster, freeze."

It was the police. "Thought you could spend the money right away, eh?" said the man who put handcuffs on him and led him to the jail. John's mind was confused, how could they have known that it was him who was the recipient of the dwarf's money? Maybe it had something to do with the money, was it counterfeit? He had never considered that possibility, but it certainly seemed possible to him. What could it have been—the look on the waiter's face had changed immediately when John had handed him the fifty-dollar bill, so it had to have something to do with that. Perhaps they had no idea who they had, and he could free himself before they found out.

"Do you mind, officers, telling me what I'm under arrest for?"

"Why you—" began one of the men, hitting John on the top of the back, forcing him to the ground. John fell with great force onto his knees, which felt as if they cracked at impact.

"Leave him alone, Lou."

"But did you hear what he said?"

"I heard."

"Well, I'm not going to allow any two-bit bank robber to get away with saying that garbage around me. He killed a cop, you know."

"I know, I read the reports, same as you."

"But—"

"But nothin', we check out his story to see if we have the right man. Then we bust him, get me?"

"Right," said the other smiling at the expectation.

They put John into a jail cell with a drunk who was asleep on the only bed in the cell.

"We'll get him out of there for you tonight. He's usually sober by two or three," said the mild guard.

"Say, would you mind telling me what I'm here for?"

"Robbing a bank, as if you didn't know."

"But I didn't do it, and I can prove it."

"Yeah? how?"

"My name's John Brown, and you can telegraph Girard and ask for Charles Dumont. He'll tell you that I've been working at the mill, so that I couldn't have busted the bank."

"Charles Dumont, eh?"

"That's right," said John.

Chapter 8

"More About our Hero in Jail"

John waited for what seemed to be an interminably long time in the cell. The hours, if they were hours, as John had no way of measuring time, seemed to pass ever so slowly. John wondered whether they had found out about his real identity in Girard. He almost reconciled himself to being taken back to Varner's Junction in the next few hours. At least he would have a better chance at a fair trial now than he would have had before. It had been worthwhile running, he told himself. But what if they went harder on him for having fled the first time? He knew something about Georgia law; if he pleaded guilty, they couldn't execute him and he'd get a life sentence that would mean about twenty years, which was awful, but wasn't his entire life. He might still have something left, he thought. But just think where that twenty years would be; it would be the best part of his life. But if it had to be, he might as well accept it. It seemed better to John that he expect the worst and then be surprised if something better should come his way than if he expected too much; for he couldn't abide being disappointed. At least if he were returned, he could get to see his Julia again. And there would be Jefferson there to support him. To have friends like that, John thought, was one of the greatest treasures in the world. John became very emotional and almost began to cry, when he suddenly wondered if he was going crazy. He had all the symptoms:

changeable disposition, nervousness, obsessions, and compulsive drives. The thought scared him, and immediately he became very depressed. How awful it would be to be crazy, but of course he wasn't going crazy or anything like it. The entire idea was utterly absurd, singularly ridiculous—but oh, how possible. How could he defend himself if he went off the deep end and lost his ability to communicate to others? He might be committed to one of those institutions where people were chained to the walls like animals: far worse punishment than he'd ever face in prison for murder. John put his hands together and tried to pray. He hadn't thought about God for a long time, but now at this intense point of fear it was the only thing that he could think about. He thought about his life and how sinful it had been.

"What an evil creature I am," thought John. "If I get out of this, I will never do anything bad again, I promise, I will try to always be upright. Please give me another chance. I'll do better this time, believe me, I won't forget—don't let me go insane, please don't let me go insane."

But at the same time that he was praying he questioned why he was doing it. Hadn't Jefferson always told him that God doesn't break the natural laws but is the embodiment of them? To ask for something that may not be is to ask for a contradiction, and certainly that is ridiculous, then that prayer was also stupid and a waste of time—*but then what else have I left to do, but pray*? "Oh God, I haven't thought a lot about you in the past, but I promise that in the future, I will, really I will."

John was beside himself with fear that any moment he would become hopelessly insane as his mind raced madly about seeing things in several perspectives whereas he had only been used to seeing problems in one light previously. It had only been in the last half-year that he'd really begun to see that so many simple things weren't really simple at all. He couldn't only look at them as they appeared immediately to him, but he should also strive to see *into* them. He should have thought about what would have been the result of handing the waiter the fifty- dollar bill. No normal person walks around with a twenty-dollar bill, much less a fifty. Such an act—especially from a young man dressed as if he were a bum—looked mighty suspicious. If he had only *thought* before he acted, he might have saved his life. "Premeditation." That was a word that Jefferson used to drill into him. One had to *think* first *act* second. Now that is not always possible—as in an emergency. But getting a cup of coffee and some food was no emergency.

But John was making some progress on this front. He had proven it at the Martinez's farm. He had respected Maria, protected the family, and left when it looked probable that he would bring trouble on them and on himself. This represented some progress in his life as he hadn't always practiced pre-meditation.

It *was* a nice approach to life, but one that wouldn't come naturally, at least not right away, he had always thought. It would take time, but was that something that he had a lot of? Soon, he might be out of society and not have anywhere to practice it. These thoughts calmed his mind for a moment, when suddenly he wondered whether his new plan was really good or whether the adoption of it might have disastrous consequences. Perhaps those who meditate and pre-meditate are among the insane? If the first was about the present and the second about the future, then all this mental activity might alter things as they really are. He instantly remembered the transformation of the lady in the mirror who sometimes changed to a beautiful young girl, and then to someone seductive like Cindy or alluring like Maria, but never Julia. Where was his Julia? If he could only get out, he would arrange a rendezvous.

What an impossible comfort that would be to see and talk with his beloved lady again. There was no doubt in his mind that she must still love him as much as he loved her.

Then the jailer came. *It's finally three*, thought John, *and I can have that bed all to myself.* He would be happy to get the smelly old codger out of the cell with him, as the smell turned John's stomach along with his slovenliness. Yet at the same time, John felt sorry for the man. *He probably doesn't really want to be that way*, thought John to himself, *I wonder what made him that way?* Then a sense of compassion replaced the revulsion that he had experienced earlier, though it was hard not to be sensibly repulsed by the man, still he was a man and had the dignity of a man. The see-saw of compassion and repulsion weighed back and forth as the jailer opened the door and announced, "All night, Brown, you're free to go."

"You called Mr. Dumont."

"Yes, he said that you had been in an accident several days ago and that you might be suffering from dizziness or something, but that you were definitely working a week ago when the bank was robbed; so you're free."

"Thank you," said John, and he got up unsteadily to walk out. "Oh, one more thing," began the jailer. John stopped.

"He said thank you for joining the strike. He thinks the man will crack soon."

John tensed his lips and shuffled out of the jail. He immediately went over to the telegraph office and sent a message to Julia, signing it simply "J." He waited around for a few hours until he got a reply and then bought a one-way bus ticket for Atlanta.

Chapter 9

"The Telegram"

It wasn't that Charles Vanderkamp disliked John particularly, it was just that he didn't want his only daughter connected with a criminal, and secondly to someone who didn't have any money or family. He had always thought that Julia would be right for Victor Stuart, but now that he had been murdered, it would be highly inappropriate for her to marry the very man accused of killing him. The atmosphere around Bella County assumed that John was the culprit. Why else would he have run away? It was partially for this reason that he tried to persuade Julia to visit her aunt.

"But I don't want to 'come out,'" said Julia.

"No one will force you if you don't want to, but it is always good to broaden one's horizons. You know your mother had been to four states in the South when I married her, and I'm convinced that it made a better woman out of her. I've never enjoyed traveling much, so I suppose I've neglected you and Rodney in this area, but I do heartily believe in it for young people. Often it gives them entirely different outlooks on things."

"I'm satisfied with my outlook on things."

"I know that you can't tell an eighteen year old girl much. She thinks that just because she's of age that she can sashay about as she pleases, but just let me tell you there are a few things that you haven't learned yet in the world, young lady, that I can teach you."

"I don't doubt it father, and I've always respected your opinions on every matter. But why should I have to go to Atlanta if I don't want to go? I'd just as soon stay here with you."

"Well, I'd like you to stay with me, dumpling, but you see, I think that it would be healthier for you if you were to go to Atlanta for a while like your father suggests. You'd get a chance to go to the theater, something that we don't have in Varner's Junction. Atlanta has orchestras and concerts. These broaden the mind. A young lady must learn the cultivation that goes with art, though I must confess that I've never really enjoyed it myself, I still think it's something that one should experience. It's good for you. I've sat through many plays with your mother, often just to please her. Now can't you do the same for your papa?"

All these arguments were very persuasive. Julia felt extremely guilty to refuse her father when he put the question in that form. She had to go or be an undutiful daughter, an ungrateful wretch, and yet at the same time she felt that she should be able to have some say in what she did; after all she was eighteen years old.

Her own mother was married at that age! But still, Julia loved her father and would endeavor to please him in any way that she felt could be accommodated. Of course she didn't want to sacrifice some more important ideal to which she held. What she feared was that by going to Atlanta she might miss John's communication. This might prove to be important. She loved John. How was one to weigh the devotion owed to one's parents against the loyalty owed to a lover? The one bond was older, but the latter bond was one which she hoped would last forever. It was the natural way of life for a woman to leave her family and be with her man, but the question was, when did her balance of loyalty shift from her parents to her lover? Was it only after the marriage? But that seemed absurd, for how could she feel any more devotion for him after a simple ceremony, when the real elements of a marriage, love and trust and devotion must be evident before—and in ample quantities. If she felt such a strong devotion to Dow, should she not give *him* her loyalty first? But again this seemed not clear, for she could not love him completely unless he loved her in the same way, and this she could not know as they had only known such brief moments together, and those moments might have not been enough to completely win his heart. Maybe he had turned to someone else?

She thought about Cindy Pancroft. The thought of John in another's arms was a painful one. She understood the general theory that a man was to have several amours in his life and a good woman only one. Still, it seemed hard to reconcile this with the way she felt. She wanted John all to herself. Perhaps that was selfish, but then she'd be selfish. She hoped there was no one else.

"I'll go to Atlanta, father, but will you allow me to pick the day when I'll go?"

This unexpected victory caught Charles Vanderkamp by surprise. "Of course, my dumpling, you go when it suits you, but don't take too long about it, aunty will want a reply soon."

These last words he added least she try and choose sometime in the distant future and thus circumvent the invitation. He left his daughter, confident that he was doing the proper thing for her as a father and was all together fully satisfied with himself.

Mr. Vanderkamp had hardly left the house when the front bell rang and, as Julia was quite near, she answered it.

"Telegram, m'am," said a boy in a voice that cracked slightly as he was at that particular age. Julia took the telegram. It was addressed to her. She opened it and read:

I want to see you stop meet me at the Atlanta rail station in five days stop I'll wait near the train from Varner's Junction.

J.

Julia went to find a pencil and paper to write a reply. Then she got her purse and gave the boy the money and a tip for his services.

That settled it, she'd go to Atlanta now, and on the way to her aunt's she would meet John. It would all be very convenient. Meanwhile the telegraph operator in Varner's Junction began to wonder at this strange correspondence. True, he did have a lot of work each day, but a small town operator doesn't have that much work that he can't spend a little time trying to figure out a little riddle like the one he had. Not many people signed just one initial, sometimes their first initial and last name, or first name, middle initial and surname, or even the first two initials and surname, and even rarely all three initials, but then usually only in the case of husbands and wives, or someone quite familiar or intimate with the person. However, it was quite well known that Julia Vanderkamp was not married or engaged. Also, there had been quite a lot of attention paid to the fact that immediately before Victor's death she had been playing court, or so the county believed, to the two boys: Victor Stuart and John Dow, who was now quite well known as an outlaw.

All these factors made the telegraph operator a little more than curious so that he decided finally to re-read the message that he had taken earlier in the day concerning a "J." to Miss. Julia Vanderkamp. Might this J. have been none other than John Dow? The prospect excited the operator, who in all honesty never got a lot of excitement in his line of work and often jumped at the chance of finding out anything salacious about any one of his customers.

After inspecting the note a few times, he decided that it was his patriotic duty to inform the sheriff.

"But it has to be," said the operator. "J. must stand for John Dow. It all fits, don't you see—the lovers meet for secret rendezvous? Pretty good, eh?"

"I don't know, I've heard your theories before, and most of them are a bunch of hogwash."

"Not this one sheriff, listen, it all makes sense, you gotta believe me."

"But I've believed you before, and usually to my regret," replied the sheriff, taking a chaw of tobacco.

"I've been right before, what about the time at the state convention?" said the operator, referring to the time when he correctly surmised by the wording of an invitation to the state law enforcers convention in Savannah, that a contribution would be expected towards the new pension scheme that they were devising.

And that in the follow-up messages that the operator sent out to confirm his idea he found that he had been right down to the last detail, thus saving the sheriff a considerable amount of money that he should have had to fork out for an idea that was since abandoned.

"I admit that you've been right on some occasions, I don't deny it." Then pausing as his tobacco was getting juicy, he finally added, "Let me take a look at that myself." The sheriff looked at the letter and concluded that just possibly it was worth sticking his neck out for, and so he instructed the operator to send a message to the Atlanta police alerting them of the possibility, and explaining the circumstances, and to take all precaution that the Vanderkamp girl would not be injured.

After so much exhausting labor, the sheriff decided that he owed it to himself and the town to go back to his office for a long nap before dinner.

Chapter 10

"The Dustbin"

It was the early part of the evening when Jefferson's door was opened by a hand holding a machine gun saying, "All right, but be quick about it. The spook's to have no visitors."

"I ain't a visitor, do you think I like working around the likes of these scum? Why did you know that once I—"

"Yeah, that's fine, I don't really want to hear about what you used to do, just get on with it and collect your garbage."

Myra came in rolling a large round bin full of paper and waste that she was collecting.

"Hello," said Jefferson.

Myra put her finger to her lip indicating that he should be very quiet.

"He's a suspicious one; I think he's listening," she whispered.

"I didn't expect you again so soon," replied Jefferson.

"I got a hold of some bad news. The Link's coming *tonight*. I don't understand it, he's usually so regular, it isn't like him to break routine like this. I think something *big* is in the works," she said.

"Well, that doesn't look too good for me, does it?"

"Shh," she said and went over to his bed and took one of the blankets and the pillow and rolled the blanket and shaped the pillow under the covers to appear as if a man was sleeping in the bed.

Then she brought a chair over to the dustbin and motioned for him to get inside.

"What?" replied Jefferson.

"Hurry, the longer we take, the less chance we have of succeeding," she said impatiently. Jefferson got into the container and arranged the debris so that it was covering him. Myra helped him and put the finishing touch on by placing a cardboard box over his head and covering that too. Then she knocked on the door and the guard opened the door, but before she could get out he looked in the room to try and locate the prisoner.

Myra was silent. She was afraid that something might go wrong. What if he saw something amiss, or wanted to see the fellow's face for himself, what would she do then? She wouldn't have a chance trying to run. She'd be dead before she got to the landing. Besides, the guards at the front door would grab her and that would be the end.

The guard, who was blowing bubbles with his gum and cracking it loudly, stepped inside the room. *What was he looking for*, she thought. *Did he suspect something?*

Jefferson didn't know what was happening, but felt a sneeze coming on from all the dust around him. This would be fatal, he knew. He tried to *will* himself to stop, but the more he thought about it, the harder it was to hold, then he made an audible gasp, as he held the sneeze.

The guard turned around, hearing something, but not being able to distinguish what it was as his gum chewing was too loud.

"What was that?"

"Nothing, just about to sneeze that's all," said Myra, who couldn't tell whether the guard knew that she was lying or not. Should she have said that something had slipped inside the bin? What if he could detect that the noise had come from inside the bin and not from her own throat?

The guard walked over to the bin and put his hand inside. Jefferson heard the rustle of papers over his head and felt that at any second a cold barrel of a rifle would be sticking into his neck. There was nothing that he could do. He resigned himself completely to what would happen, but somehow he felt terrified to think that he *might* be, probably *would* be dead in just moments. It didn't seem right to him that his life should end this way: inside a garbage bin. Then Jefferson heard a ripping of paper. The guard pulled his hand out of the bin and took a small piece of paper and spit his gum into it.

"You know this gum loses its flavor in only about an hour, and then it gets bitter," he said, tossing the gum into the bin. Then the guard walked over and closed the door. "Well, get on with you, blackie's sleeping away; we wouldn't want to disturb him," said the guard, smiling, as he had suddenly become aware that despite being a little past her prime, Myra had a very good figure, and that he wouldn't mind seeing a little more of her after he was relieved of his watch.

"What time do you get off?" asked the guard.

"Eleven," replied Myra, winking at the guard, as she could detect exactly what was on his mind as she rolled the dust bin into the dumb waiter that they used for transporting heavy objects between floors. Myra pressed the next floor below, and then turned and walked downstairs. At this level she pressed the basement, and quickly hurried down to try and beat the elevator, but not wanting to seem in any unusual hurry that might seem odd or out of place. In the basement, she took out the dustbin and unloaded the garbage around Jefferson who was tucked into a ball at the bottom.

Jefferson, not knowing what was happening still, looked up in fright as Myra took out the things atop him. Myra gave a little laugh when she saw the fright in his eyes. "Don't worry, it's only me," she said. "We've gotten through the hardest part, but now we've got to get out of the basement. I suggest the door above the coalscuttle. You'll get a little dirty, but I think it's the safest way."

Jefferson, who accepted Myra's hand to help himself out of the bin, was in no mood to argue, as he tried to quickly loosen his muscles which had become very stiff in the uncomfortable position. These vehicles weren't constructed for interlopers over sixty, he told himself.

He scrambled up the coalscuttle and Myra went around outside to open the window, whose lock was broken. There was no trouble, as no one was about at this time of night, which was between the hours when Tom's boys would be coming in and the time when the night clients would be showing up.

"Come on," said Myra, taking Jefferson's hand and leading him down a back alley through a maze of streets, which he couldn't follow. At times they would run and at others they would walk, especially when there were people around. Finally, they stopped at an old hotel, and Myra told him to go up to the fourth floor via the fire escape and wait for her. When Myra got to her place she'd open the backdoor to the fire escape for Jefferson.

"This is the first place that I ever came to when Mama and I came to Savannah after leaving the Estate. It isn't much, but at least it isn't a very likely place to be found." The room was small, but had a mirror, which was brown around the edges, and a sink. There were two single beds that were made and one window that looked out onto the street.

"They'll figure out that you've gone soon, and that I helped you. For a short while, I don't think this place is too risky for us," she said.

Jefferson walked over to the window and looked outside. "You don't think they'll find this place?"

"Hope, the girl at the desk, didn't think I was in too much of a hurry. She has no idea that you're here, so she couldn't tip anyone off. But I don't think we should stay around very long. Those guys have a way of finding people sooner or later."

"You're right," said Jefferson as he slowly turned around and walked over to one of the beds and sat down (there were no chairs in the room). "Why did you put yourself out for me like this? I mean you told me about your secure existence that was so quiet and happy, and now I've gone and destroyed it for you."

"You didn't destroy it. I allowed it to be destroyed."

"But why? You know I don't know how to thank you for what you've done. I mean, we're not out of it yet; but you've risked a lot for no reason."

"I couldn't very well let you get killed." Myra turned and walked away from Jefferson.

There was a silence in which Jefferson wished to tell her how he owed her his life, and how he would be ever in her debt, but somehow when he thought of words to say, they seemed inadequate to what he really wanted to express.

"I just want to tell you that I still intend to pursue the man who killed Victor, but that I won't do anything more until I know that you are safe somewhere."

"But I have nowhere to go," said Myra.

"Why don't you return to the Estate? You'll be safe there, and I know that I can get you some easy work to do; maybe something around the house."

"Thank you, but remember I was banished from there, and I can't go back. Besides, people don't forget other's misfortunes easily. There'll be a lot of gossipy people and I couldn't abide that."

"The county has changed quite a bit. News doesn't pass like it used to. Now it stays in certain little groups. Besides, there is a greater difference between the town and the farms than there was when you left. It's like two separate communities now; neither knows the other. There are so many new people that probably three quarters have never even heard of you, and the other quarter doesn't care. As for the banishment, I'm sure Mr. Beauchay will rescind. He's a fair man; he won't be stubborn."

"But to get him to rescind, he'll have to know the truth."

"Yes, I'll have to do that, but that's something that's best I think for all concerned. I tell you what, I'll leave tomorrow, and you lie low here for a few days until I make all the arrangements and then I'll come back and everything will be fine."

Myra was silent. She looked at Jefferson's face as he expounded his idea. His face became animated like a young man. There was, she thought, nothing old about Jefferson. His face was like that of a much younger man, but he moved stiffly at times. But then who wouldn't be moving stiffly having been through what he had in the last days? Why had she helped? How could she have done anything else?

"I don't have any of my work bags," she said. "If I'm to lay low, I should go back and get my real clothes and my money."

"Too dangerous," said Jefferson. "I'll go if you draw me a map of how to get there, I'll get it for you. But I'll need a map because to confess to you plainly, I'm lost."

"I'll draw you a map, but you cannot get my bag because too many people there know you. Besides, the maid closet is not for men."

"But I don't want you taking needless risks."

"Now don't talk foolish," replied Myra

Jefferson seemed to agree as he stopped the debate, dropped backwards, and bounced on the bed like a little boy. "Imagine, what a stroke of luck finding *you* after all these years; my little helper," he laughed. "My lucky star must be shining brightly."

Chapter 11

"Containing Matter Accommodated to Every Taste"

Myra improvised a map for Jefferson on the dust that lay thickly on the small table that was at the end of the bed. It wasn't too difficult. Jefferson wasn't going to retrieve her work bag, but he did have unfinished business. Jefferson went around the neighborhood to get oriented. Then he tried to create a cautious route to where Myra worked. Once he had this in his head, Jefferson made his way to the train station where he retrieved his suitcase from one of the pay lockers. Then, Jefferson decided to return to Myra's now vacant apartment. He had to be careful, for though Myra didn't think they knew where she lived, it was probable that they had found out somehow, and might be lying in ambush for him. Better to go up the fire escape again.

Jefferson climbed the steps deliberately, trying to discern any unusual noises. Suddenly he stopped. He heard a sound. Freezing in tense anticipation, he waited for his foe to attack him, but instead he saw the form of a cat walking across the metal grating two floors up.

Jefferson was so relieved that he felt like going to the cat and petting its black fur. When he got to the fourth floor, he slid over onto a large ledge and looked through the window into the room and thought about where he would hide his suitcase. Myra was not there, so he pushed at the window. By wiggling the window some he succeeded in unfastening the catch and entering the apartment, but he had made a little noise in the process. *Let's hope someone doesn't call the police*, thought Jefferson. He went through all the areas that Myra had told him to and was in the midst of packing the suitcase when he heard a board creak. Jefferson knew that someone was outside the apartment.

There was a hand on the door knob. Quickly Jefferson snuck over to the door as he could hear a card being pushed between the door jam and the lock bolt. It wasn't the police, or they would have a key. The only problem was if there was more than one of them. The door moved open cautiously as a figure suddenly burst in and swung his gun around, but not seeing anyone put his arm holding the gun down. This was what Jefferson had been waiting for as he sprung out at the arm, twisting it violently backwards so that the gun dropped. Then Jefferson delivered a blow to the back of the neck, followed by bringing his foe down to the ground in a wrestling hold. The man was so startled as he had been sure that the room was vacant that he was little match for the quicker Jefferson.

"All right," said Jefferson, taking the other's gun, "you have ten seconds to tell me who you are, and what you're here for before I blow your brains out." Jefferson had no intention of doing anything to the man but somehow the situation made him very charged up and he was acting according to what the situation dictated.

"Hey man, lay off. I'm clean."

Jefferson stuck the gun into his back with greater force.

"Okay, my name's Coody. The Link sent me to knock off a nigger and a girl who might be here." The man on the bottom was black, but the way he said 'nigger' seemed to Jefferson to imply that he, Jefferson, was somehow not seen to be the same or equal to the "virile" specimen who was now lying on the floor.

"Well, here's your nigger ordering you to get up and go over to that chair and sit down and do what I say because to tell you the truth, I don't care if I blow your brains all over these apartment walls."

The man quickly obeyed and Jefferson shut the door, which was still ajar. Jefferson motioned the man to walk toward the window.

"Are you crazy?" said Coody.

"Move," said Jefferson, thinking that perhaps this man had a friend waiting for him down the hall or outside. Jefferson had the man lay on his stomach by the window until Myra came home.

***

"What did you do?" asked Myra.

"I got a willing assistant here who's going to help us any way that he can, isn't that right, Coody?" asked Jefferson, pushing the gun into the man's back

Coody grunted.

"You see he has a rather limited vocabulary, but I think that with a little help he can be straightened out, eh?" Again the barrel was pushed into his back, followed by a, "Yeah."

"That's better already, from a grunt to a word in the first lesson." The man was still lying on his stomach. Jefferson tossed Myra some cord that he had found in her place to tie his hands and feet with.

"Do a good job, because it'll have to hold him until I get back."

"You're not leaving him with me, are you?" asked Myra.

"It'll only be for a day: a few hours to Varner's Junction and then a few hours back. That's all."

"Well, I hope that's all. Any amount of time with this gorilla is too much, if you ask me." Jefferson laughed as they secured their man, tying his wrists to his ankles behind his back.

They slept, somewhat lightly as the man lay on the floor between the two beds and made quite a bit of noise as he tossed about in the night. Jefferson slept with the gun (after putting on the safety) in case there would be any trouble, but there wasn't.

The next morning Jefferson asked Coody a few questions, but the man was reluctant to talk.

"Now, it could become hard with you, and you wouldn't want that, would you, I mean you fellows taught me a lot about making people want to talk, but I don't think you'll be difficult, will you?"

As Jefferson constructed his ruse, he felt that he wouldn't hurt this man, but he knew that he had to scare him. With threat plus time, the sum might be some valuable information.

"Look I told you, the Link sent me to kill you if you showed up at the girl's apartment."

"Why did he want me dead?" asked Jefferson.

"How should I know, I'm a busy man, you weren't anything special, just one of the many duties that I was to carry out."

"What were the others?"

"No," said the man, indicating that he wouldn't talk.

Then Myra came back with some food, and the two of them ate. "Are you hungry?" asked Jefferson.

Coody didn't answer.

"Look, I'm a good sort. You talk and I'll give you some food. Fair enough? I mean, what do you owe to those guys? Nothing, eh?"

But still Coody wouldn't talk. They ate and Jefferson told Myra that he would take the eleven o'clock train so that he would have to leave in an hour or so. "I guess if this guy won't talk, we'll have to turn him over to the police," said Jefferson.

"Hey, don't do that," said Coody.

"Well, you're a criminal, you tried to murder me. I'll testify to that, as well as to your associating with criminals, and I'll testify to that, too. I mean it's my duty to turn you over to the police, right?"

"But if you do that I'm a dead man for sure."

"I'm sure that you're exaggerating. Why would you be killed?"

"Look, when they want a man dead they do it very messily. Gives me a break, huh?"

Jefferson didn't respond but handed the gun over to Myra and explained to her how to operate it.

"Okay, I'll tell you what you wants to know, but you've gotta promise not to turn me in."

"I won't promise anything," said Jefferson. "Why did they want me killed?"

"Because of the deal, they didn't want anything to spoil the deal."

"What deal, what sort of deal?"

"I don't know, do you think they tell things like that to a punk like me? They just give me a list of things to do and that's it."

"What else were you supposed to do?"

"I had an errand, and then I was to knock you off, and finally I was to deliver a message."

"What kind of message, and to whom?"

"What is this, what does it have to do with you?"

Jefferson jumped down at the man on the floor and held him by the throat. "Listen I have a good friend that is probably going to hang unless I get some answers, now talk."

Coody thought that Jefferson was referring to him hanging, and so replied, "It was about the deal, a man's coming from Detroit, the Link told me to give him his contract."

"What are you talking about?"

"A gun, you know, a good gun, to kill a guy."

"Who's the guy?"

"What does it matter?"

"Who's the guy?"

"His name's Daniels."

Myra gasped, and walked over to Jefferson. "He's a big man around the city in gambling, they say that he's got lots of money from the outside."

"But why do you want to kill Daniels?"

"I don't know, who do you think I am anyway? Look I'm just a two-bit punk, I don't know anything, except that there's some kind of big deal and that I had to deliver a package, kill you, and deliver this message to this gun from Detroit."

"What's the gun's name?"

"I don't know, probably doesn't have a name."

Jefferson grabbed him by the throat again.

"Listen I'm telling you the truth," gasped Coody. "I don't know his name, I never know anyone's name."

Jefferson let go of Coody. He didn't want to hurt him, and he didn't want to physically abuse him, but it seemed the only thing that the fellow understood. Jefferson knew that he certainly couldn't seriously hurt or beat the man as he himself had been beaten, but he could bluff. The man probably had thought that his, Jefferson's, heart was full of revenge at the bad way they had treated him. It's what the man probably would have felt himself had the situations been reversed, and so expected the same treatment from Jefferson.

Yet, Jefferson had to admit to himself that he was being more violent than he wished to be under the circumstances. This violence within him (that he didn't know was there) frightened Jefferson. Once when he had put his hand to the other's throat, he had actually thought of how easy it would have been to snap the fellow's neck right there—how that man's life was within his hands and how something inside him almost wanted to take that final step and squeeze the life from that fragile windpipe. But even while he contemplated this, his sense of revulsion was tremendous. He was sickened by himself ever entertaining such thoughts. How wrong it would be to kill; how un-Christ-like.

"They never tell me any more than they have to. I was to meet him at The Three Stars tomorrow night, near the corner. I was supposed to be reading the newspaper. That's all I know. Really."

"What were you supposed to do between last night and then?"

"Nothing, honest, I got some money for the job, and I could do whatever I wanted. My time's my own when I'm not on a job. I've told you everything, buddy."

Strange how 'nigger' had changed to 'buddy,' thought Jefferson, but he let it pass as he got up and talked to Myra. Everything was spinning around and he had to have time to sort things out. He told Myra what to do until he returned and then paused, taking her hand and kissing it tenderly.

"Be careful," he warned.

"You too," she replied as Jefferson shut the door.

Chapter 12

"A Measure of Philosophical Reflection on Board the Train"

The train left five minutes late, though this fact was not even noticed by Jefferson, who was huddled in a corner trying to get his thoughts in order as he was preparing to return to his home, a place now so distant in his immediate sensations that it could have been the other side of the world. The events of the past days had passed so quickly that he could scarcely recollect what had happened in the tangle of actions and reactions. On the whole, Jefferson was satisfied and thankful at what had happened. He hadn't acted completely out of character, yet he had not been exactly as he might have predicted.

The thought struck Jefferson that there might be some sort of discontinuity between the many thoughts that he had on various subjects and his actions when he was in situations where careful consideration of the ramifications of what he was doing was impossible. Hopefully, careful consideration in an equilibrium could aid one when he was confronted with a less than tranquil situation where quick action was required. *The individual, who had considered many types of alternatives, might be in a better position to make a decision, or act in a way that he later would assess to be consistent with his general life outlook. It would result* in an action he could be proud to have executed. And yet how much was this true? Could it be that there were factors that might so alter the particular situation? From its scenario counterpart, Jefferson needed to consider how the particular case might relate to more general principles that might give this present situation a proper context. This is what philosophers do, and Jefferson considered himself to be a philosopher—both by training and by disposition.

Of course when one enters the realm of the general, he leaves the particular behind. In this new arena there are only general thoughts interacting with other general thoughts. These are what Plato called the world of Forms—also called the world of Ideas. When Forms interact with each other, the result will be another Form. Is this enough? Some certainly thought so. Immanuel Kant's first depiction of the categorical imperative showed which general imperatives were impermissible. For example, if 'lying' is a general type of behavior and is defined as: (a) saying that which is known by the agent to be untrue, and (b) the agent uses this untruth in order to deceive another, then lying (a general concept) can be processed via the categorical imperative (Act only on that maxim through which you can at the same time will that it should become a universal law). This processing amounts to trying to imagine a society in which everyone lies to everyone else. But this is logically impossible since if everyone in a society is a liar, then whenever agent X says to Y (both members of the liars' society) "It is raining" Y will believe that "It is not raining." Thus, the second condition of telling a lie (acting to deceive) cannot be executed. If X tries to be clever and states the proper weather condition: "It is not raining" then he has deceived Y but at the expense of not fulfilling the first condition (saying that which is known by the agent to be untrue). In short, to fulfill the first condition means that you cannot fulfill the second and vice versa. Because 'lying' is logically inconsistent under the rules of the general categorical imperative, it is also immoral and should not be undertaken. It is immoral because it is illogical. This *is an absolute law. It exists in the realm of the general. But unfortunately none of us lives in the realm of the general.*

When one returns to the realm of the particular, there may be a disconnect. For example, right now he, Jefferson, is trying to find the killer of Victor Stuart in order to free John. This particular quest is inherently good. If it requires Jefferson to bend various truths and rules in the process, then so be it: particularity trumps. It would be wrong in a deeper sense to obey some general rule and let an innocent man hang.

Now it was requisite for Jefferson to examine the particularity before him. Somehow he had to use the information that his prisoner had given him in order to shake-up the plans of the criminal community. They appear to be so strong, yet there has to be a crack in their façade. Jefferson believed this in the general sense, since immorality is built upon ignorance. Find the most glaring case of illogic, and Jefferson can destroy their sham empire.

It was a case of the philosopher against the world. People generally laugh at philosophers. They have their heads in the clouds and so tumble into wells. But Thales also correctly predicted the boom olive harvest and had rented most of the olive presses ahead of time. Made a killing, Thales did. Ridicule Thales all you want, but he had the last laugh.

The train was making up its lost time. It would probably pull into Varner's Junction according to schedule. The setback in Savanna was being overcome by the engineer. Jefferson smiled as he watched the scenery rush by.

He was returning to Varner's Junction, hopeful.

Preview of *Georgia*: Part Three

Part Three begins as Jefferson returns from Savannah. He wants to close a loop concerning John's heritage (which he had just discovered) with the folks back in Bella County. This was one important step in bringing John out of the shadows and allowing him to move on in his life. Of course, there is the minor detail of John being a runaway fugitive who is accused of first-degree murder. The intrigue behind his investigation is daunting. The organized crime units of George Dodson are well-constructed. Is there any way to confront such a powerful cartel? There is one man dedicated to the cause and his name is: Jefferson John Brown, philosopher.

Other Novels by Michael Boylan

Rainbow Curve (2014) Fans of baseball's history will appreciate this compelling tale about race, politics, and corrupting power and one's man's courage to stand-up. *De Anima #1*

The Extinction of Desire (2007) What would you do if you suddenly became rich? *De Anima #2*

To the Promised Land (2015) Are there limits to forgiveness: personal, corporate, and political? *De Anima #3*

Maya (forthcoming) Follow the fate of an Irish-American family through three generations in the U.S.A. It's the story of immigrants and a story of History. *De Anima #4*.

Naked Reverse (2016) There is a backdoor to the ivory tower. Find out what happens to one college professor who escapes. *Archē #1*

Georgia: Part One (2106) *and Part Three* (forthcoming) A novel told in three parts. Explore racial identity through a murder mystery set in the early 20th century. *Archē #2, 4*

T-Rx: The History of a Radical Leader (forthcoming) An epistolary novel about radicalization in the Vietnam-era. What are and what are *not* legitimate tactics for social/political change? *Archē #5*

The Long Fall of the Ball from the Wall (forthcoming) A novel set in the investigation of the JFK assassination that connects this event to larger social phenomena. *Archē #6*

www.ingramcontent.com/pod-product-compliance
Lightning Source LLC
Chambersburg PA
CBHW030850030726
47495CB00005B/1459